"Every now an   s the horror
genre. A book   become a
landmark. PS P   Basil Copper's
short stories is ju

—Tales from the Black Abyss

Collected together for the first time in three paperback volumes from PS Publishing are all the supernatural and macabre short stories and novellas of legendary British writer Basil Copper.

Drawn from numerous collections, anthologies and magazines as varied as the legendary *Pan Book of Horror Stories* series, rare and collectible compilations edited by Peter Haining and August Derleth, and the author's own highly-prized books from Arkham House, these three extensive volumes contain more than four decades' worth of weird fiction from one of the genre's most renowned practitioners.

In this initial volume you will find such classics of the macabre as the author's first professionally published short story, 'The Spider', along with memorable tales like "Camera Obscura' (adapted by Rod Serling for the TV series *Night Gallery*), 'The Janissaries of Emillion', 'The Academy of Pain', 'Amber Print' and 'The Recompensing of Albano Pizar', which was dramatised by BBC Radio 4.

With an historical Introduction by editor Stephen Jones, Volume One of *Darkness, Mist and Shadow: The Collected Macabre Tales of Basil Copper* also contains original illustrations by Les Edwards, Gary Gianni and Allen Koszowski, along with a stunning cover painting by Stephen E. Fabian.

— Volume One —

Darkness, Mist & Shadow

Volume One

The Collected Macabre Tales Of

Basil Copper

Edited by Stephen Jones

DIP

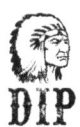

DARKNESS, MIST & SHADOW
(VOLUME I)
Copyright © The Estate of Basil Copper 2010, 2013

INTRODUCTION
Copyright © Stephen Jones 2010, 2013

COVER ART
Copyright © Stephen E. Fabian

INTERIOR ART
Copyright © 2010 & 2013 by Gary Gianni (page 10), Les Edwards (page 266), Allen Koszowski (page 336)

BACKCOVER PHOTOGRAPH
Copyright © Estate of Basil Copper

First published in hardcover in 2010. This paperback edition published in August 2013 by Drugstore Indian Press, an imprint of PS Publishing Ltd by arrangement with the Estate of the author and Stephen Jones. The book was reprinted in June 2014.

All rights reserved by the Estate of the author. The right of Basil Copper to be identified as Author of this Work has been asserted by him in accordance with the Copyright, Designs and Patents Act 1988.

This book is a work of fiction. Names, characters, places and incidents either are products of the author's imagination or are used fictitiously. Any resemblance to actual events or locales or persons, living or dead, is entirely coincidental.

FIRST EDITION

2 4 6 8 10 9 7 5 3

ISBN
978-1-848636-33-0 (Volume I)

Design & Layout by Michael Smith

Printed and Bound in England by T.J. International

Drugstore Indian Press
Grosvenor House
1 New Road
Hornsea, HU18 1PG, England

editor@pspublishing.co.uk
www.pspublishing.co.uk

Contents

xi	Introduction by Stephen Jones
3	The Spider
11	Camera Obscura
31	The Janissaries Of Emillion
52	The Cave
76	The Grey House
119	Old Mrs. Cartwright
126	Charon
140	The Great Vore
210	The Academy Of Pain
221	Doctor Porthos
228	Archives Of The Dead
265	Amber Print
283	Out Of The Fog
297	The House By The Tarn
311	The Knocker At The Portico
324	The Second Passenger
335	The Recompensing Of Albano Pizar
353	The Gossips
395	A Very Pleasant Fellow
417	A Message From The Stars
432	Cry Wolf
442	The Trodes
452	Dust To Dust

Acknowledgements

Special thanks to Basil & Annie Copper, Peter and Nicky Crowther, Val and Les Edwards, Stephen E. Fabian, Gary Gianni, Peter Coleborn, Michael Smith, Robert F. Wexler and all the guys at T. J. International.

THE SPIDER copyright © Basil Copper 1964. Originally published in *The Fifth Pan Book of Horror Stories* edited by Herbert van Thal.
CAMERA OBSCURA copyright © Basil Copper 1965. Originally published in *The Sixth Pan Book of Horror Stories* edited by Herbert van Thal.
THE JANISSARIES OF EMILION copyright © Basil Copper 1967. Originally published in *The Eighth Pan Book of Horror Stories* edited by Herbert van Thal.
THE CAVE copyright © Basil Copper 1967. Originally published in *Not After Nightfall: Stories of the Strange and the Terrible.*
THE GREY HOUSE copyright © Basil Copper 1967. Originally published in *Not After Nightfall: Stories of the Strange and the Terrible.*
OLD MRS. CARTWRIGHT copyright © Basil Copper 1967. Originally published in *Not After Nightfall: Stories of the Strange and the Terrible.*
CHARON copyright © Basil Copper 1967. Originally published in *Not After Nightfall: Stories of the Strange and the Terrible.*
THE GREAT VORE copyright © Basil Copper 1967. Originally published in *Not After Nightfall: Stories of the Strange and the Terrible.*

Darkness, Mist & Shadow

THE ACADEMY OF PAIN copyright © Basil Copper 1968. Originally published in *Legends for the Dark: Tales of Fantasy and Horror* edited by Peter Haining.

DOCTOR PORTHOS copyright © Basil Copper 1968. Originally published in *The Midnight People: Being Eighteen Terrifying and Bizarre Tales of Vampires* edited by Peter Haining.

ARCHIVES OF THE DEAD copyright © Basil Copper 1968. Originally published in *The Evil People: Being Thirteen Strange and Terrible Accounts of Witchcraft, Black Magic and Voodoo* edited by Peter Haining.

AMBER PRINT copyright © Basil Copper 1969. Originally published in *Dr. Caligari's Black Book* edited by Peter Haining.

OUT OF THE FOG copyright © Basil Copper 1970. Originally published in *Argosy* Vol.XXXI, No.9, September 1970.

THE HOUSE BY THE TARN copyright © Basil Copper 1971. Originally published in *Dark Things* edited by August Derleth.

THE KNOCKER AT THE PORTICO copyright © Basil Copper 1971. Originally published in *Dark Things* edited by August Derleth.

THE SECOND PASSENGER copyright © Basil Copper 1973. Originally published in *The Dark Brotherhood Journal 3*, Vol.2, No.1, July 1973.

THE RECOMPENSING OF ALBANO PIZAR copyright © Basil Copper 1973. Originally published in *The Year's Best Horror Stories No.3* edited by Richard Davis.

THE GOSSIPS copyright © Basil Copper 1973. Originally published in *From Evil's Pillow*.

A VERY PLEASANT FELLOW copyright © Basil Copper 1973. Originally published in *From Evil's Pillow*.

A MESSAGE FROM THE STARS copyright © Basil Copper 1974. Originally published in *Space 2: A Collection of Science Fiction Stories* edited by Richard Davis.

CRY WOLF copyright © Basil Copper 1974. Originally published in *Vampires, Werewolves and Other Monsters* edited by Roger Elwood.

THE TRODES copyright © Basil Copper 1975. Originally published in *Armada Sci-Fi* edited by Richard Davis.

Acknowledgements

DUST TO DUST copyright © Basil Copper 1976. Originally published in *Midnight Sun*, Number 4, August 1976 edited by Gary Hoppenstand.

All stories reprinted by permission of the author.

⚜ Introduction

Basil Copper's first macabre story, 'The Curse', appeared in the March 1938 issue of *S-X-R: The Magazine of the Tonbridge Senior Boys School* when the author was just fourteen years old.

Two years later he wrote 'The Grass' while working as an apprentice journalist. The story would not appear in print for almost another sixty years.

However, his "official" debut as a horror writer is generally considered to have occurred in 1964, when editor Herbert van Thal accepted 'The Spider' for the princely sum of £10.00 for the fifth volume in the notorious *Pan Book of Horror Stories* series. As with many of the author's works, the idea grew from a relatively mundane event when he and his wife discovered an enormous arachnid in their bedroom during a holiday in France.

Prior to that first professional sale, Basil had already experienced a busy life. He had been put in charge of a county newspaper office at the age of seventeen; served in the Royal Navy's Light Coastal Forces for four years during World War II, taking part in the D-Day landings; edited a Kent county newspaper while also contributing to several national titles and—perhaps most importantly of all—had married Annie Renée Guerin in 1960. Almost fifty years later he is still happily married to the French student he met while she was learning English in Kent.

A voracious reader, Basil had been a fan of the works of M.R. James and Edgar Allan Poe from an early age, and his stories for *The Pan*

Book of Horror Stories (which also included the classics 'Camera Obscura' and 'The Janissaries of Emilion') grew out of his interest in Gothic and supernatural fiction.

Despite his fascination with the macabre, the author's first novel was a hard-boiled thriller in the tradition of Raymond Chandler and Dashiell Hammett. Published in hardcover by Robert Hale in 1966, *The Dark Mirror* was the first of an astonishing fifty-two volumes featuring Los Angeles private investigator "Mike Faraday". It is an impressive total for a single series, but what is even more remarkable is that Basil has never been to California. He constructed Faraday's mean streets of LA from map books and old movies!

The following year, New English Library published Basil's first collection of supernatural fiction as a paperback original. *Not After Nightful* contained eight stories and novellas, all but the three from the *Pan* series original to the volume.

Over the next decade or so three further collections of mostly original tales—*When Footsteps Echo: Tales of Terror and the Unknown* (1975), *Here Be Daemons: Tales of Horror and the Uneasy* (1978) and *Voices of Doom: Tales of Terror and the Uncanny* (1980)—were published in hardcover on both sides of the Atlantic.

More significantly during this period, Basil began corresponding with the legendary Arkham House editor August Derleth. Both men were keen admirers of the work of H.P. Lovecraft, and Derleth was so enthusiastic about the British writer's fiction that he included two of Basil's stories, 'The House by the Tarn' and 'The Knocker at the Portico', in his 1971 anthology *Dark Things*.

As he had done for other British authors such as Ramsey Campbell and Brian Lumley, Derleth used his anthologies to introduce unfamiliar writers to Arkham House readers before issuing their own volumes under the imprint.

This happened two years later when, despite August Derleth's untimely death in 1971, Arkham House finally published *From Evil's Pillow*. It collected five of Basil's stories, two original to the volume. A second volume of the author's work, *And Afterward the Dark*, appeared from Arkham in 1977.

Meanwhile, Basil's stories were starting to appear more regularly in

INTRODUCTION

anthologies and magazines. Britain's premier anthologist, Peter Haining, who while working at NEL was probably responsible for publishing *Not After Nightfall* back in 1967, began including Basil's work in his own compilations. During this period Haining published such memorable tales by Basil as 'The Academy of Pain', 'Doctor Porthos' and the marvellous 'Amber Print', the latter tale inspired by the author's life-long interest in motion pictures, as both an avid collector and historian.

In fact, the 1970s were a busy time for Basil. Not only was he churning out short stories and novellas, and continuing his Mike Faraday series at two or more novels a year, but he ghosted two novels about masked hero "The Phantom" under creator Lee Falk's by-line. He also produced two popular non-fiction studies, *The Vampire: In Legend, Fact and Art* (1973) and *The Werewolf: In Legend, Fact and Art* (1977), and contributed the sleeve notes to a 1974 LP of *Hammer Presents Dracula* narrated by Christopher Lee.

Basil's story 'Camera Obscura' was adapted for NBC-TV's *Night Gallery* in 1971 by the show's creator, Rod Serling, although proposed script for 'Doctor Porthos' never made it before the cameras, and the author himself wrote an unproduced television treatment of M.R. James' classic story 'Count Magnus'.

It was inevitable that Basil would want to deal with the supernatural in longer form, and in 1974 Robert Hale published his Lovecraftian novel *The Great White Space*, about an expedition to the centre of the Earth and the horrors they discovered there. It was followed two years later by the historical Gothic *The Curse of the Fleers* which, unfortunately, was butchered by its hardcover publisher.

In 1980 Basil contributed a major novella, 'Shaft Number 247', to Ramsey Campbell's Arkham House anthology *New Tales of the Cthulhu Mythos*. So it seems especially odd that Arkham was not the publisher of *The Great White Space*—especially given the novel's connection to H.P. Lovecraft's fictional mythology (the book is dedicated to both Lovecraft and Derleth). However, Derleth's successor at the imprint, James Turner, rectified this oversight with the publication of the Victorian mystery *Necropolis* in 1980.

Darkness, Mist & Shadow

The volume quickly sold out of its 4,000-copy print-run and became the first non-Lovecraft title from Arkham House to be reprinted.

It was followed by Basil's favourite of his own novels, the werewolf thriller *The House of the Wolf*, in 1983. Arkham House approached Stephen E. Fabian to contribute more than forty chapter-headings, along with the atmospheric dust-jacket painting.

James Turner had also commissioned Basil to revise August Derleth's entire canon of seventy short stories and a novel about 1920s Sherlockian detective "Solar Pons" for the 1982 two-volume set *The Solar Pons Omnibus*. Because Derleth had never visited Britain, much of the terminology and many of the descriptions that he used were wrong, and it took Basil around eighteen months to correct more than 2,000 textual errors.

Although some fans of Derleth's Pontine stories were outraged by this "tampering", Turner was delighted with Basil's work and offered the author the opportunity to continue the adventures of Solar Pons and his assistant Dr. Lyndon Parker is a new series of stories and a novel.

Initially intended to be published by Arkham House—probably under its companion Mycroft & Moran imprint—some of the stories eventually appeared in four paperback collections from Pinnacle Books. Unfortunately, as had happened with *Curse of the Fleers*, these volumes were poorly "revised" by the American in-house editors. The "definitive" versions of Basil's Solar Pons stories have eventually appeared from a variety of imprints, including Academy Chicago, Fedogan & Bremer and Sarob Press.

Following the publication of his novel *Into the Silence* (1983), another "journey beneath the Earth" adventure only published in Britain, Basil's stories continued to appear in anthologies edited by the redoubtable Peter Haining, Richard Dalby, Edward E. Kramer, Maxim Jakubowski, and myself (notably the Lovecraftian novella 'Beyond the Reef' in *Shadows Over Innsmouth*).

But it was not until the early 1990s that Fedogan & Bremer published his next novel, *The Black Death*, the longest and most ambitious Gothic Basil had written. The same publisher followed it up

✒ INTRODUCTION

at the end of the decade with a long-overdue new collection of macabre fiction by the author. *Whispers in the Night: Stories of the Mysterious and the Macabre* (1999) contained eleven tales, eight of them original to the volume (including that story he originally wrote in 1940 while still an apprentice journalist).

Cold Hand on My Shoulder: Tales of Terror & Suspense followed from Welsh imprint Sarob in 2002. Four of its nine stories were previously unpublished. Illustrated by Randy Broecker, it was limited to just 300 hardcovers and a further fifty-two signed and lettered deluxe copies.

Even rarer was the self-published *Knife in the Back: Tales of Twilight and Torment* (2005), which was issued in an edition of only 150 signed hardcover copies under the Cauchemar imprint. Of the eight stories included, six were original.

And that, except for a few uncollected tales, was that. Of course, Basil's earlier stories are still being reprinted in anthologies all over the world but, now in his mid-eighties and having problems with his eyesight, he himself has admitted that he is "all written out".

But what a body of work he created during that forty-year period! Along with such authors as R. Chetwynd-Hayes, Sydney J. Bounds and John Burke, amongst others, he created a backbone of British horror fiction that has sustained and carried the genre from the 1960s, through the boom years of the 1970s and '80s, right up to the present day.

Basil and I have known each other for more than twenty of those years (and I have been a fan of his work for even longer than that). We have been friends and colleagues throughout that time, and it has been my great honour and pleasure to publish much of his work in my anthologies, interview him in front of a live audience, and compile the 2008 biblio-biography *Basil Copper: A Life in Books*, from PS Publishing.

So when Basil mentioned that he had always wanted to see all his macabre and supernatural stories collected in one place, I approached those good people at PS again and between us we worked out a way of bringing Basil's substantial *oeuvre* of short fiction together. These three impressive volumes are the result.

Too often we honour our authors when they are no longer with us. That is something that has always bothered me about our genre. So I was delighted that we were able to compile this set while Basil was still around to participate in the creative process and reap the rewards.

Here are all his major short stories and novellas arranged in publication order, including the original version of his most recently published tale, 'Voices in the Water', which we adapted into a Mythos story for its appearance in my 2005 anthology *Weird Shadows Over Innsmouth*.

These two volumes are a fitting tribute to one of the giants of the British weird fiction tradition but—perhaps more importantly—they preserve between hardcovers not only all of Basil Copper's macabre short stories and novellas, but some of the best horror fiction published over the past four decades.

—Stephen Jones
London, England
August, 2009

Darkness, Mist & Shadow

Volume One

✑ The Spider

M. Pinet arrived at the small country hotel just as dusk was falling on a wet October day. All about him was the melancholy of autumn, and the headlights of his car stencilled a pallid path across the glaucous surface of the soaking, leaf-scattered road.

M. Pinet was feeling pleased with himself. A representative of a large firm of Paris textile manufacturers, he had previously travelled the flat, monotonous areas of Northern France and had felt his mind becoming as rigid and unyielding as the poplar-lined roads he had daily traversed.

But now, he had been given another district, from Lyons in the south to the Île de France, with an increase in salary as well, and he greatly appreciated the change. The beauty of his new surroundings, moreover, the different atmosphere of a novel routine, had released all his pent-up drive; his latest had been a very successful tour indeed and his wallet bulged with the notes and banker's orders of clients.

At present he was about fifty miles south of Paris and had decided that he was too tired to push on to his home in the suburb of Courbevoie. He had already driven all the way from Auxerre and hadn't started until the afternoon, but he had made good time nevertheless. His bags of samples and the long bolts of cloth in the back of his small estate wagon shifted from side to side as he turned on the bad surface of the second-class road through the forest.

He was feeling more than usually tired and the traffic in the Paris direction had been even heavier than normal for the time of year.

He had reached the outskirts of a small village that was unfamiliar to him and had then spotted the lights of a fair-sized auberge set back from the road, amid clean-smelling pine trees. The chairs and tables of summer were now stacked under canvas between the box hedges, but there came a welcome glow of light from the hallway and as he ran his car in under the heavy shadow of the trees he could see a zinc-covered bar and a thousand reflections from bottles that looked as though they contained most warming liquids. There were no other vehicles parked in front of the inn, but that did not worry M. Pinet. He had no particular desire for company; uppermost in his mind was the thought of a half bottle of wine to chase away the dank chill of autumn, a good dinner, and eight hours' refreshing sleep before pushing on to Paris in the morning.

He parked his car, securely locked it, and a few moments later found himself in a delightful looking hall, containing a bar, some leather stools, and a profusion of late summer flowers. A cat lay stretched on the polished tile floor. There was no other sign of life, apart from a man dressed in city clothes who was drinking cognac. He went out a moment after M. Pinet came in, muttering a *sotto voce* good-evening, and a short time later M. Pinet saw a big blue Mercedes, which had evidently been parked lower down the road, go by the window.

In response to the sharp, insistent bell on the zinc counter there presently came the shuffling of slippers and the patron appeared. He was all *bonhomie* and effusive welcome; yes, of course monsieur could have a room and dinner if he desired. It was the end of the season and he would not find it very gay—there was no one else dining in, but the chef could make him anything within reason. He would have his baggage fetched, if he wished.

All this was very gratifying and as M. Pinet signed the register he should have been pleased. He had brought his solitary valise in with him and after an aperitif he began to forget the dreariness of the autumn evening and the mile after mile of sodden woods outside. He was agreeably surprised, too, at the sumptuous furnishings of the dining-room, which could easily have seated over two hundred

The Spider

people; the patron explained that many visitors came out from Paris to dine during the season.

M. Pinet felt he was being unfair, but it was the character of the landlord which spoiled what otherwise would have been a delightful *sojourn*. He hadn't caught the man's name, but there was something about him which put M. Pinet off. He was an average-sized man with a triangular yellow face, a bald head, and unnaturally large ears. His little eyes sparkled meanly, redolent of greed and insincerity, and his wide slit mouth, which often parted to reveal gold teeth, was the crowning glory of an exceedingly ugly visage.

To M. Pinet's discomfort this individual set out to make himself ingratiatingly helpful, and personally waited on him at dinner. Of other staff M. Pinet saw none, though there must have been people in the kitchen beyond as he frequently heard the low murmur of voices and once a plump woman in a low-cut black frock, possibly the patron's wife, walked by in the distance, giving him a stiff nod.

But first M. Pinet wanted a wash and the landlord indicated the door of the toilet. It was down a short corridor off the dining-room; he had to fumble for the light switch and he then saw to his disgust that there was a large brown spider on the floor of the cracked stone corridor.

It seemed to watch him with little metallic eyes, and with a sense of bubbling horror M. Pinet felt it crack beneath his foot as he ground it with his heel. He had an innate fear of spiders, almost pathological in its intensity, and the violent physical nausea stayed with him until after dinner.

As he opened the door of the toilet and switched on the light there, M. Pinet could not repress a cry of panic. Faugh! There were two more of the monsters here, one on the wall near his head and the other on the floor near the toilet seat. M. Pinet fancied he could almost hear the low scratch of its legs, as it moved experimentally, its strange blue metallic eyes—the most curious he had ever seen in an insect—seeming to gaze at him with reproach. As it crunched beneath his almost hysterically wielded shoe, the eyes faded as the creature died. The other fled like lightning to a spot behind the lavatory cistern, wrenching another involuntary cry from M. Pinet's lips.

A moment later the landlord was at his side. He seemed amused and his small eyes were dancing.

"No, monsieur," he said. "Nothing to be alarmed about. The damp weather always brings them from the woods at this time of year. They will not harm you. They are my pets."

He made a sort of clucking noise with his mouth, which M. Pinet found hideously revolting, and the great brown horror behind the cistern stirred. Before M. Pinet's disbelieving eyes it scuttled onto the landlord's open palm, where he stroked it and crooned to it in a thoroughly disgusting manner.

M. Pinet, pale and disconcerted, excused himself and made shift by washing his hands and face at the washbasin in the corridor. Back in the dining-room he felt better and was relieved to see the patron first put the spider somewhere outside the back door. He was pleased too, to see this strange character wash his own hands before disappearing into the kitchen.

The dinner was an excellent one and as M. Pinet tipped his croutons into the soup, he felt his spirits revive; the landlord was undoubtedly a somewhat peculiar man but he certainly knew how to produce a fine meal. M. Pinet was by this time so far soothed by his surroundings that he invited the landlord to join him at the table for a drink after his dinner was over. Contrary to his expectations the landlord seemed to draw more out of him than the information he gained in return. In answer to M. Pinet's point-blank question, as to whether he had been at the inn long, the patron replied, "No, not long. We move around quite a bit, my wife and I."

M. Pinet did not pursue the subject. He had decided to pay for his meal before going to bed and settle for his accommodation in the morning. He was a methodically minded man and though it all came to the same thing in the end, he preferred to do it this way. He had stepped up to the desk in a corner of the dining-room and the landlord's eyes glistened and narrowed in an unpleasant manner as he spotted the huge bundle of notes in M. Pinet's wallet. The latter realized this was a mistake and somewhat awkwardly tried to cover them over with a batch of letters he carried, but this only served to draw more attention by its obvious clumsiness.

The Spider

The landlord stared at him unblinkingly, as he said, quite without emphasis, "You have had a successful season, monsieur." It was a statement, not a question, and M. Pinet managed to turn the conversation quickly to the subject of his room. A few moments later he said goodnight and carried his own bag up to the chamber indicated on the first floor.

The well-carpeted corridor had bowls of flowers on tables at intervals and bright lights were 'burning; there was an uneasy moment, however, as M. Pinet put his key in the lock of room Number 12. All the lights in the corridor suddenly went out, evidently controlled from downstairs, and for a long minute M. Pinet was in total darkness. A faint scratching noise away to his left brought sweat to his forehead, but a moment later he was inside his room and light flooded from the ceiling fixture. He locked the door and stood against it for a few seconds, taking in the contents of the room.

It was a prettily conceived chamber and any other time M. Pinet would have been taken with its heavily contrived charm; but tonight, with his nerves curiously shaken, he was in no mood for atmosphere. He merely undressed as quickly as he could, turned up his bed, got a novel from his valise, and noisily cleaned his teeth in the basin in the corner. The mirror reflected back an image that was noticeably pale. Before getting into bed he heard the faint noise of footsteps outside and looking through the window was disconcerted to see the figure of the landlord, silhouetted against the light from an open door, furtively studying his car. A moment later he moved off and M. Pinet heard a door slam somewhere below him. He got into bed.

The novel was a bad one and M. Pinet was greatly tired but somehow he did not want to sleep. He kept his bedside lamp burning but despite this eventually drifted off into a doze. Some time later he was awakened by the noise of a car driving away from the inn. Even as he became fully conscious he heard the faint sound of its engine die with a hum in the distance as the trees enveloped it.

For some reason M. Pinet's mind became agitated at this and he felt a great desire to look out the window to see if his car was still in front of the hotel. Before he could move, however, he heard a faint scratching noise; his nerves strained as they were, he turned his head

◈ Darkness, Mist & Shadow

with infinite slowness in an effort to locate the sound. Eventually—a quick glance at his watch showed him that it was after 2:00 A.M.—he narrowed down the source of the sound as coming from the triangular area formed by the corner of the ceiling farthest from him.

It was in the gloomiest part of the chamber, for the light from the reading lamp extended only a yard or two; to switch on the main light M. Pinet would have to cross over to the door and he was loath to do this, particularly in his bare feet. He compromised by turning up the bedside lamp so that the light shone towards the far corner of the room. There was something there, but it was still so wrapped in shadow that he could not make out what it was.

He groped for his glasses on the table by the bed; to do this he had to lower the lamp to its usual position, and while he was fumbling with this he heard his spectacle case fall with a soft thump onto the carpet at his bedside. He looked down; the spectacles were only about two feet from him but again, he had great reserve about stretching out his hand to the carpet. Dry-mouthed he turned, as the scratching noise came again and a cry was strangled in his throat as he saw the shadowy thing scuttle a little closer towards him across the ceiling; even without his glasses he did not need to be told what it was, but his senses still refused to believe.

Something furry, like a tarantula, bigger than a soup-plate, round and with legs as thick as telephone cables. Its legs rustled together as it came across the ceiling with old-maidish deliberation and a thin purring noise came from it. As it edged forward into the brightness of the lamp M. Pinet saw with sick fear that it was covered with brown fur and had an obscene parody of a mouth.

He looked round desperately for a stick or any other weapon, but there was nothing; his tongue stuck to the roof of his mouth, denying him the shriek which would have saved him; his pyjamas streamed with perspiration and moisture dabbled his forehead. He closed his eyes once and opened them with an effort, hoping against hope that he was in the grip of nightmare. But the obscene, sliding thing was nearer still and M. Pinet gave up hope. He saw now that the creature had metallic blue eyes, like the eyes of the insects he had crushed in the washroom, and as they glared into his own with implacable

⚘ The Spider

hatred he noticed with a last shock of surprise that they were very like the landlord's.

The insect paused and then launched itself on a thick silken thread; a nauseous stench was in his nostrils, the great spider gave a sibilant rattle and then it was on his mouth, covering his face and eyes with its bloated, sticky carcase. M. Pinet gave shriek after shriek as consciousness mercifully expired.

"A most curious case," said the doctor, washing his hands in the washbasin of M. Pinet's room. "Heart sound as a bell, yet he must have died instantaneously from some great shock. Never come across anything like it. There'll have to be an inquiry, of course."

And the doctor, who was a matter-of-fact human being, gave a heavy sigh. The landlord's wife, who stood just inside the door of the death chamber, timidly assented.

Down below in the bar the landlord, who lived by the secret fears of his customers, smiled a curious smile. He fondled a thick bundle of notes under the counter.

In the room above, a tiny brown spider, not more than an eighth of an inch across, scuttled nervously across the dead man's forehead. The doctor brushed it impatiently away and it fell out of sight by the side of the bed.

✤ Camera Obscura

As Mr. Sharsted pushed his way up the narrow, fussily conceived lanes that led to the older part of the town, he was increasingly aware that there was something about Mr. Gingold he didn't like. It was not only the old-fashioned, outdated air of courtesy that irritated the moneylender but the gentle, absent-minded way in which he continually put off settlement. Almost as if money were of no importance.

The moneylender hesitated even to say this to himself; the thought was a blasphemy that rocked the very foundations of his world. He pursed his lips grimly and set himself to mount the ill-paved and flinty roadway that bisected the hilly terrain of this remote part of the town.

The moneylender's narrow, lopsided face was perspiring under his hard hat; lank hair started from beneath the brim, which lent him a curious aspect. This, combined with the green-tinted spectacles he wore, gave him a sinister, decayed look, like someone long dead. The thought may have occurred to the few, scattered passers-by he met in the course of his ascent, for almost to a person they gave one cautious glance and then hurried on as though eager to be rid of his presence.

He turned in at a small courtyard and stood in the shelter of a great old ruined church to catch his breath; his heart was thumping uncomfortably in the confines of his narrow chest and his breath rasped in his throat. Assuredly, he was out of condition, he told himself. Long hours of sedentary work huddled over his accounts were taking their toll; he really must get out more and take some exercise.

◢ Darkness, Mist & Shadow

The moneylender's sallow face brightened momentarily as he thought of his increasing prosperity, but then he frowned again as he remembered the purpose of his errand. Gingold must be made to toe the line, he told himself, as he set out over the last half-mile of his journey.

If he couldn't raise the necessary cash, there must be many valuables in that rambling old house of his which he could sell and realize on. As Mr. Sharsted forged his way deeper into this forgotten corner of the town, the sun, which was already low in the sky, seemed to have already set, the light was so constricted by the maze of small courts and alleys into which he had plunged. He was panting again when he came at last, abruptly, to a large green door, set crookedly at the top of a flight of time-worn steps.

He stood arrested for a moment or two, one hand grasping the old balustrade, even his mean soul uplifted momentarily by the sight of the smoky haze of the town below, tilted beneath the yellow sky. Everything seemed to be set awry upon this hill, so that the very horizon rushed slanting across the far distance, giving the spectator a feeling of vertigo. A bell pealed faintly as he seized an iron scrollwork pull set into a metal rose alongside the front door. The moneylender's thoughts were turned to irritation again; everything about Mr. Gingold was peculiar, he felt. Even the fittings of his household were things one never saw elsewhere.

Though this might be an advantage if he ever gained control of Mr. Gingold's assets and had need to sell the property; there must be a lot of valuable stuff in this old house he had never seen, he mused. Which was another reason he felt it strange that the old man was unable to pay his dues; he must have a great deal of money, if not in cash, in property, one way or another.

He found it difficult to realize why Mr. Gingold kept hedging over a matter of three hundred pounds; he could easily sell the old place and go to live in a more attractive part of town in a modern, well-appointed villa and still keep his antiquarian interests. Mr. Sharsted sighed. Still, it was none of his business.

All he was concerned with was the matter of the money; he had been kept waiting long enough, and he wouldn't be fobbed off any longer. Gingold had got to settle by Monday, or he'd make things unpleasant for him.

Mr. Sharsted's thin lips tightened in an ugly manner as he mused on, oblivious of the sunset staining the upper storeys of the old houses and dyeing the mean streets below the hill a rich carmine. He pulled the bell again impatiently, and this time the door was opened almost immediately.

Mr. Gingold was a very tall, white-haired man with a gentle, almost apologetic manner. He stood slightly stooping in the doorway, blinking as though astonished at the sunlight, half afraid it would fade him if he allowed too much of it to absorb him.

His clothes, which were of good quality and cut, were untidy and sagged loosely on his big frame; they seemed washed out in the bright light of the sun and appeared to Mr. Sharsted to be all of a part with the man himself; indeed, Mr. Gingold was rinsed to a pale, insipid shade by the sunshine, so that his white hair and face and clothing ran into one another and, somehow, the different aspects of the picture became blurred and indeterminate.

To Mr. Sharsted he bore the aspect of an old photograph which had never been properly fixed and had turned brown and faded with time. Mr. Sharsted thought he might blow away with the breeze that had started up, but Mr. Gingold merely smiled shyly and said, "Oh, there you are, Sharsted. Come on in," as though he had been expecting him all the time.

Surprisingly, Mr. Gingold's eyes were of a marvellous shade of blue and they made his whole face come vividly alive, fighting and challenging the overall neutral tints of his clothing and features. He led the way into a cavernous hall. Mr. Sharsted followed cautiously, his eyes adjusting with difficulty to the cool gloom of the ulterior. With courteous, old-world motions Mr. Gingold beckoned him forward.

The two men ascended a finely carved staircase, whose balustrades, convoluted and serpentine, seemed to writhe sinuously upwards into the darkness.

"My business will only take a moment," protested Sharsted, anxious to present his ultimatum and depart. But Mr. Gingold merely continued to ascend the staircase.

"Come along, come along," he said gently, as though he hadn't heard Mr. Sharsted's expostulation. "You must take a glass of wine with me. I have so few visitors..."

Mr. Sharsted looked about him curiously; he had never been in this part of the house. Usually, Mr. Gingold received occasional callers in a big, cluttered room on the ground floor. This afternoon, for some reason known only to himself, he had chosen to show Mr. Sharsted another part of his domain. Mr. Sharsted thought that perhaps Mr. Gingold intended to settle the matter of his repayments. This might be where he transacted business, perhaps kept his money. His thin fingers twitched with nervous excitement.

They continued to ascend what seemed to the moneylender to be enormous distances. The staircase still unwound in front of their measured progress. From the little light which filtered in through rounded windows, Sharsted caught occasional glimpses of objects that aroused his professional curiosity and acquisitive sense. Here a large oil painting swung into view round the bend of the stair; in the necessarily brief glance that Mr. Sharsted caught, he could have sworn it was a Poussin.

A moment later, a large sideboard laden with porcelain slid by the corner of his eye. He stumbled on the stair as he glanced back over his shoulder and in so doing, almost missed a rare suit of Genoese armour which stood concealed in a niche set back from the staircase. The moneylender had reached a state of confused bewilderment when at length Mr. Gingold flung aside a large mahogany door, high up in the house and motioned him forward.

Mr. Gingold must be a wealthy man and could easily realize enormous amounts on any one of the *objets d'art* Sharsted had seen; why then, thought the latter, did he find it necessary to borrow so frequently, and why was it so difficult to obtain repayment? With interest, the sum owed Sharsted had now risen to a considerable figure; Mr. Gingold must be a compulsive buyer of rare items. Allied to the general shabbiness of the house as seen by the casual visitor, it must mean that his collector's instinct would refuse to allow him to part with anything once bought, which had made him run himself

A Camera Obscura

into debt. The moneylender's lips tightened again; well, he must be made to settle his debts, like anyone else.

If not, perhaps Sharsted could force him to part with something—porcelain, a picture—that could be made to realize a handsome profit on the deal. Business was business, and Gingold could not expect him to wait for ever. His musings were interrupted by a query from his host and Sharsted muttered an apology as he saw that Mr. Gingold was waiting, one hand on the neck of a heavy silver and crystal decanter.

"Yes, yes, a sherry, thank you," he murmured in confusion, moving awkwardly. The light was so bad in this place that he felt it difficult to focus his eyes, and objects had a habit of shifting and billowing as though seen under water. Mr. Sharsted was forced to wear tinted spectacles, as his eyes had been weak from childhood. They made these apartments seem twice as dark as they might be. But though Mr. Sharsted squinted over the top of his lenses as Mr. Gingold poured the sherry, he still could not make out objects clearly. He really would have to consult his oculist soon, if this trouble continued.

His voice sounded hollow to his own ears as he ventured a commonplace when Mr. Gingold handed him the glass. He sat down gingerly on a ladderback chair indicated to him by Mr. Gingold, and sipped at the amber liquid in a hesitant fashion. It tasted uncommonly good, but this unexpected hospitality was putting him on a wrong footing with Gingold. He must assert himself and broach the subject of his business. But he felt a curious reluctance and merely sat on in embarrassed silence, one hand round the stem of his goblet, listening to the soothing tick of an old clock, which was the only thing which broke the silence.

He saw now that he was in a large apartment, expensively furnished, which must be high up in the house, under the eaves. Hardly a sound from outside penetrated the windows, which were hung with thick blue-velvet curtains; the parquet floor was covered with exquisitely worked Chinese rugs and the room was apparently divided in half by heavy velvet curtaining to match those which masked the windows.

⨕ Darkness, Mist & Shadow

Mr. Gingold said little, but sat at a large mahogany table, tapping his sherry glass with his long fingers; his bright blue eyes looked with mild interest at Mr. Sharsted as they spoke of everyday matters. At last Mr. Sharsted was moved to broach the object of his visit. He spoke of the long-outstanding sum which he had advanced to Mr. Gingold, of the continued applications for settlement and of the necessity of securing early payment. Strangely, as Mr. Sharsted progressed, his voice began to stammer and eventually he was at a loss for words; normally, as working-class people in the town had reason to know, he was brusque, businesslike, and ruthless. He never hesitated to distrain on debtors' goods, or to evict if necessary and that he was the object of universal hatred in the outside world, bothered him not in the slightest.

In fact, he felt it to be an asset; his reputation in business affairs preceded him, as it were, and acted as an incentive to prompt repayment. If people were fool enough to be poor or to run into debt and couldn't meet their dues, well then, let them; it was all grist to his mill and he could not be expected to run his business on a lot of sentimental nonsense. He felt more irritated with Mr. Gingold than he need have been, for his money was obviously safe; but what continued to baffle him was the man's gentle docility, his obvious wealth, and his reluctance to settle his debts.

Something of this must have eventually permeated his conversation, for Mr. Gingold shifted in his seat, made no comment whatever on Mr. Sharsted's pressing demands and only said, in another of his softly spoken sentences, "Do have another sherry, Mr. Sharsted."

The moneylender felt all the strength going out of him as he weakly assented. He leaned back on his comfortable chair with a swimming head and allowed the second glass to be pressed into his hand, the thread of his discourse completely lost. He mentally cursed himself for a dithering fool and tried to concentrate, but Mr. Gingold's benevolent smile, the curious way the objects in the room shifted and wavered in the heat haze; the general gloom and the discreet curtaining, came more and more to weigh on and oppress his spirits.

So it was with something like relief that Sharsted saw his host rise from the table. He had not changed the topic, but continued to speak

◈ Camera Obscura

as though Mr. Sharsted had never mentioned money to him at all; he merely ignored the whole situation and with an enthusiasm Sharsted found difficult to share, murmured soothingly on about Chinese wall paintings, a subject of which Mr. Sharsted knew nothing.

He found his eyes closing and with an effort opened them again. Mr. Gingold was saying, "I think this will interest you, Mr. Sharsted. Come along..."

His host had moved forward and the moneylender, following him down the room, saw that the large expanse of velvet curtaining was in motion. The two men walked through the parted curtains, which closed behind them, and Mr. Sharsted then saw that they were in a semicircular chamber.

This room was, if anything, even dimmer than the one they had just left. But the moneylender's interest began to revive; his head felt clearer and he took in a large circular table, some brass wheels and levers which winked in the gloom, and a long shaft which went up to the ceiling.

"This has almost become an obsession with me," murmured Mr. Gingold, as though apologizing to his guest. "You are aware of the principles of the camera obscura, Mr. Sharsted?"

The moneylender pondered slowly, reaching back into memory. "Some sort of Victorian toy, isn't it?" he said at length. Mr. Gingold looked pained but the expression of his voice did not change.

"Hardly that, Mr. Sharsted," he rejoined. "A most fascinating pursuit. Few people of my acquaintance have been here and seen what you are going to see."

He motioned to the shafting, which passed up through a louvre in the ceiling.

"These controls are coupled to the system of lenses and prisms on the roof. As you will see, the hidden camera, as the Victorian scientists came to call it, gathers a panorama of the town below and transmits it here on to the viewing table. An absorbing study, one's fellow man, don't you think? I spend many hours up here."

Mr. Sharsted had never heard Mr. Gingold in such a talkative mood and now that the wretchedness which had assailed him earlier had disappeared, he felt more suited to tackle him about his debts. First, he would humour him by feigning interest in his stupid toy. But Mr. Sharsted had to admit, almost with a gasp of surprise, that Mr. Gingold's obsession had a valid cause.

For suddenly, as Mr. Gingold moved his hand upon the lever, the room was flooded with light of blinding clarity and the moneylender saw why gloom was a necessity in this chamber. Presumably, a shutter over the camera obscura slid away upon the rooftop and almost at the same moment, a panel in the ceiling opened to admit a shaft of light directed upon the table before them.

In a second of God-like vision, Mr. Sharsted saw a panorama of part of the old town spread out before him in superbly natural colour. Here were the quaint, cobbled streets dropping to the valley, with the blue hills beyond; factory chimneys smoked in the early evening air; people went about their business in half a hundred roads; distant traffic went noiselessly on its way; once, even, a great white bird soared across the field of vision, so apparently close that Mr. Sharsted started back from the table.

Mr. Gingold gave a dry chuckle and moved a brass wheel at his elbow. The viewpoint abruptly shifted and Mr. Sharsted saw with another gasp, a sparkling vista of the estuary with a big coaling ship moving slowly out to sea. Gulls soared in the foreground and the sullen wash of the tide ringed the shore. Mr. Sharsted his errand quite forgotten, was fascinated. Half an hour must have passed, each view more enchanting than the last; from this height, the squalor of the town was quite transformed.

He was abruptly recalled to the present, however, by the latest of the views; Mr. Gingold spun the control for the last time and a huddle of crumbling tenements wheeled into view. "The former home of Mrs. Thwaites, I believe," said Mr. Gingold mildly.

Mr. Sharsted flushed and bit his lip in anger. The Thwaites business had aroused more notoriety than he had intended; the woman had borrowed a greater sum than she could afford, the interest mounted, she borrowed again; could he help it if she had a tubercular husband and three children? He had to make an example of her in order to keep his other clients in line; now there was a distraint on the furniture and the Thwaiteses were being turned on to the street. Could he

A CAMERA OBSCURA

help this? If only people would repay their debts all would be well; he wasn't a philanthropic institution, he told himself angrily.

And at this reference to what was rapidly becoming a scandal in the town, all his smouldering resentment against Mr. Gingold broke out afresh; enough of all these views and childish playthings. Camera Obscura, indeed; if Mr. Gingold did not meet his obligations like a gentleman he could sell this pretty toy to meet his debt.

He controlled himself with an effort as he turned to meet Mr. Gingold's gently ironic gaze.

"Ah, yes," said Mr. Sharsted. "The Thwaites business is my affair, Mr. Gingold. Will you please confine yourself to the matter in hand. I have had to come here again at great inconvenience; I must tell you that if the £300, representing the current instalment on our loan is not forthcoming by Monday, I shall be obliged to take legal action."

Mr. Sharsted's cheeks were burning and his voice trembled as he pronounced these words; if he expected a violent reaction from Mr. Gingold, he was disappointed. The latter merely gazed at him in mute reproach.

"This is your last word?" he said regretfully. "You will not reconsider?"

"Certainly not," snapped Mr. Sharsted. "I must have the money by Monday."

"You misunderstand me, Mr. Sharsted," said Mr. Gingold, still in that irritatingly mild voice. "I was referring to Mrs. Thwaites. Must you carry on with this unnecessary and somewhat inhuman action? I would..."

"Please mind your own business!" retorted Mr. Sharsted, exasperated beyond measure. "Mind what I say..."

He looked wildly round for the door through which he had entered.

"That is your last word?" said Mr. Gingold again. One look at the moneylender's set, white face was his mute answer.

"Very well, then," said Mr. Gingold, with a heavy sigh. "So be it. I will see you on your way."

He moved forward again, pulling a heavy velvet cloth over the table of the camera obscura. The louvre in the ceiling closed with a barely audible rumble. To Mr. Sharsted's surprise, he found himself following his host up yet another flight of stairs; these were of stone, fringed with an iron balustrade which was cold to the touch.

His anger was now subsiding as quickly as it had come; he was already regretting losing his temper over the Thwaites business and he hadn't intended to sound so crude and cold blooded. What must Mr. Gingold think of him? Strange how the story could have got to his ears; surprising how much information about the outside world a recluse could obtain just by sitting still.

Though, on this hill, he supposed Mr. Gingold could be said to be at the centre of things. He shuddered suddenly, for the air seemed to have grown cold. Through a slit in the stone wall he could see the evening sky was already darkening. He really must be on his way; how did the old fool expect him to find his way out when they were still mounting to the very top of the house?

Mr. Sharsted regretted, too, that in antagonizing Mr. Gingold, he might have made it even more difficult to obtain his money; it was almost as though, in mentioning Mrs. Thwaites and trying to take her part, he had been trying a form of subtle blackmail.

He would not have expected it of Gingold; it was not like him to meddle in other people's affairs. If he was so fond of the poor and needy he could well afford to advance the family some money himself to tide them over their difficulties.

His brain seething with these confused and angry thoughts, Mr. Sharsted, panting and dishevelled, now found himself on a worn stone platform where Mr. Gingold was putting the key into an ancient wooden lock.

"My workshop," he explained, with a shy smile to Mr. Sharsted, who felt his tension eased away by this drop in the emotional atmosphere. Looking through an old, nearly triangular window in front of him, Mr. Sharsted could see that they were in a small, turreted superstructure which towered a good twenty feet over the main roof of the house. There was a sprawl of unfamiliar alleys at the foot of the steep overhang of the building, as far as he could make out through the grimy panes.

"There is a staircase down the outside," explained Mr. Gingold, opening the door. "It will lead you down the other side of the hill and cut over half a mile off your journey."

The moneylender felt a sudden rush of relief at this. He had come almost to fear this deceptively mild and quiet old man who, though he said little and threatened not at all, had begun to exude a faint air of menace to Mr. Sharsted's now overheated imagination.

"But first," said Mr. Gingold, taking the other man's arm in a surprisingly powerful grip, "I want to show you something else—and this really has been seen by very few people indeed."

Mr. Sharsted looked at the other quickly, but could read nothing in Mr. Gingold's enigmatic blue eyes.

He was surprised to find a similar, though smaller, chamber to the one they had just left. There was another table, another shaft ascending to a domed cupola in the ceiling, and a further arrangement of wheels and tubes.

"This camera obscura," said Mr. Gingold, "is a very rare model, to be sure. In fact, I believe there are only three in existence today, and one of those is in Northern Italy."

Mr. Sharsted cleared his throat and made a non-committal reply.

"I felt sure you would like to see this before you leave," said Mr. Gingold softly. "You are quite sure you won't change your mind?" he added, almost inaudibly, as he bent to the levers. "About Mrs. Thwaites, I mean."

Sharsted felt another sudden spurt of anger, but kept his feelings under control.

"I'm sorry . . . " he began.

"No matter," said Mr. Gingold, regretfully. "I only wanted to make sure, before we had a look at this."

He laid his hand with infinite tenderness on Mr. Sharsted's shoulder as he drew him forward.

He pressed the lever and Mr. Sharsted almost cried out with the suddenness of the vision. He was God; the world was spread out before him in a crazy pattern, or at least the segment of it representing the part of the town surrounding the house in which he stood.

He viewed it from a great height, as a man might from an aeroplane; though nothing was quite in perspective.

⌐ Darkness, Mist & Shadow

The picture was of enormous clarity; it was like looking into an old cheval glass which had a faint distorting quality. There was something oblique and elliptical about the sprawl of alleys and roads that spread about the foot of the hill.

The shadows were mauve and violet, and the extremes of the picture were still tinged with the blood red of the dying sun.

It was an appalling, cataclysmic vision, and Mr. Sharsted was shattered; he felt suspended in space, and almost cried out at the dizziness of the height.

When Mr. Gingold twirled the wheel and the picture slowly began to revolve, Mr. Sharsted did cry out and had to clutch at the back of a chair to prevent himself from falling.

He was perturbed, too, as he caught a glimpse of a big, white building in the foreground of the picture.

"I thought that was the old Corn Exchange," he said in bewilderment. "Surely that burned down before the last war?"

"Eigh," said Mr. Gingold, as though he hadn't heard.

"It doesn't matter," said Mr. Sharsted, who now felt quite confused and ill. It must be the combination of the sherry and the enormous height at which he was viewing the vision in the camera obscura.

It was a demoniacal toy and he shrank away from the figure of Mr. Gingold, which looked somewhat sinister in the blood-red and mauve light reflected from the image in the polished table surface.

"I thought you'd like to see this one," said Mr. Gingold, in that same maddening, insipid voice. "It's really special, isn't it? Quite the best of the two ... you can see all sorts of things that are normally hidden."

As he spoke there appeared on the screen two old buildings which Mr. Sharsted was sure had been destroyed during the war; in fact, he was certain that a public garden and car park had now been erected on the site. His mouth suddenly became dry; he was not sure whether he had drunk too much sherry or the heat of the day had been too much for him.

He had been about to make a sharp remark that the sale of the camera obscura would liquidate Mr. Gingold's current debt, but he felt this would not be a wise comment to make at this juncture. He felt faint, his brow went hot and cold and Mr. Gingold was at his side in an instant.

Mr. Sharsted became aware that the picture had faded from the table and that the day was rapidly turning to dusk outside the dusty windows.

"I really must be going," he said with feeble desperation, trying to free himself from Mr. Gingold's quietly persistent grip.

"Certainly, Mr. Sharsted," said his host. "This way." He led him without ceremony over to a small oval doorway in a corner of the far wall.

"Just go down the stairs. It will bring you on to the street. Please slam the bottom door—it will lock itself." As he spoke, he opened the door and Mr. Sharsted saw a flight of clean, dry stone steps leading downwards. Light still flooded in from windows set in the circular walls.

Mr. Gingold did not offer his hand and Mr. Sharsted stood rather awkwardly, holding the door ajar.

"Until Monday, then," he said.

Mr. Gingold flatly ignored this.

"Goodnight, Mr. Gingold," said the moneylender with nervous haste, anxious to be gone.

"Goodbye, Mr. Sharsted," said Mr. Gingold with kind finality.

Mr. Sharsted almost thrust himself through the door and nervously fled down the staircase, mentally cursing himself for all sorts of a fool. His feet beat a rapid tattoo that echoed eerily up and down the old tower. Fortunately, there was still plenty of light; this would be a nasty place in the dark. He slowed his pace after a few moments and thought bitterly of the way he had allowed old Gingold to gain the ascendancy over him; and what an impertinence of the man to interfere in the matter of the Thwaites woman.

He would see what sort of man Mr. Sharsted was when Monday came and the eviction went according to plan. Monday would also be a day of reckoning for Mr. Gingold—it was a day they would both remember and Mr. Sharsted felt himself quite looking forward to it.

He quickened his pace again, and presently found himself confronted by a thick oak door.

It gave beneath his hand as he lifted the big, well-oiled catch and the next moment he was in a high-walled alley leading to the street. The door slammed hollowly behind him and he breathed in the cool evening air with a sigh of relief. He jammed his hard hat back on to his head and strode out over the cobbles, as though to affirm the solidity of the outside world.

Once in the street, which seemed somewhat unfamiliar to him, he hesitated which way to go and then set off to the right.

He remembered that Mr. Gingold had told him that this way took him over the other side of the hill; he had never been in this part of the town and the walk would do him good.

The sun had quite gone and a thin sliver of moon was showing in the early evening sky. There seemed few people about and when, ten minutes later, Mr. Sharsted came out into a large square which had five or six roads leading off it, he determined to ask the correct way back down to his part of the town. With luck he could catch a tram, for he had now had enough of walking for one day.

There was a large, smoke-grimed chapel on a corner of this square and as Mr. Sharsted passed it, he caught a glimpse of a board with gold-painted letters.

NINIAN'S REVIVALIST BROTHERHOOD, it said. The date, in flaked gold paint, was 1925.

Mr. Sharsted walked on and selected the most important of the roads which faced him. It was getting quite dark and the lamps had not yet been lit on this part of the hill. As he went farther down, the buildings closed in about his head, and the lights of the town below disappeared. Mr. Sharsted felt lost and a little forlorn. Due, no doubt, to the faintly incredible atmosphere of Mr. Gingold's big house.

He determined to ask the next passer-by for the right direction, but for the moment he couldn't see anyone about; the absence of street lights also bothered him. The municipal authorities must have overlooked this section when they switched on at dusk, unless it came under the jurisdiction of another body.

Mr. Sharsted was musing in this manner when he turned the corner of a narrow street and came out opposite a large, white building that looked familiar. For years Mr. Sharsted had a picture of it

◈ Camera Obscura

on the yearly calendar sent by a local tradesman, which used to hang in his office. He gazed at its façade with mounting bewilderment as he approached. The title, CORN EXCHANGE, winked back dully in the moonlight as he got near enough to make out the lettering.

Mr. Sharsted's bewilderment changed to distinct unease as he thought frantically that he had already seen this building once before this evening, in the image captured by the lens of Mr. Gingold's second camera obscura. And he knew with numbing certainty that the old Corn Exchange had burned down in the late thirties.

He swallowed heavily, and hurried on; there was something devilishly wrong, unless he were the victim of an optical illusion engendered by the violence of his thoughts, the unaccustomed walking he had done that day, and the two glasses of sherry.

He had the uncomfortable feeling that Mr. Gingold might be watching him at that very moment, on the table of his camera obscura, and at the thought a cold sweat burst out on his forehead.

He sent himself forward at a smart trot and had soon left the Corn Exchange far behind. In the distance he heard the sharp clopping and the grating rattle of a horse and cart, but as he gained the entrance of an alley he was disappointed to see its shadow disappear round the corner into the next road. He still could not see any people about and again had difficulty in fixing his position in relation to the town.

He set off once more, with a show of determination he was far from feeling, and five minutes later arrived in the middle of a square which was already familiar to him.

There was a chapel on the corner and Mr. Sharsted read for the second time that evening the legend: NINIAN'S REVIVALIST BROTHERHOOD.

He stamped his foot in anger. He had walked quite three miles and had been fool enough to describe a complete circle; here he was, not five minutes from Gingold's house, where he had set out, nearly an hour before.

He pulled out his watch at this and was surprised to find it was only a quarter past six, though he could have sworn this was the time he had left Gingold.

Though it could have been a quarter past five; he hardly knew what he was doing this afternoon. He shook it to make sure it was still going and then replaced it in his pocket.

His feet beat the pavement in his fury as he ran down the length of the square. This time he wouldn't make the same silly mistake. He unhesitatingly chose a large, well-kept metalled road that ran fair and square in the direction he knew must take him back to the centre of the town. He found himself humming a little tune under his breath. As he turned the next corner, his confidence increased.

Lights burned brightly on every hand; the authorities must have realized their mistake and finally switched on. But again he was mistaken; there was a little cart parked at the side of the road, with a horse in the shafts. An old man mounted a ladder set against a lamp-post and Mr. Sharsted saw the thin blue flame in the gloom and then the mellow blossoming of the gas lamp.

Now he felt irritated again; what an incredibly archaic part of the town old Gingold lived in. It would just suit him. Gas lamps! And what a system for lighting them; Sharsted thought this method had gone out with the Ark.

Nevertheless, he was most polite.

"Good evening," he said, and the figure at the top of the lamp-post stirred uneasily. The face was in deep shadow.

"Good evening, sir," the lamplighter said in a muffled voice. He started climbing down.

"Could you direct me to the town centre?" said Mr. Sharsted with simulated confidence. He took a couple of paces forward and was then arrested with a shock.

There was a strange, sickly stench which reminded him of something he was unable to place. Really, the drains in this place were terrible; he certainly would have to write to the town hall about this backward part of the locality.

The lamplighter had descended to the ground now and he put something down in the back of his cart; the horse shifted uneasily and again Mr. Sharsted caught the charnel stench, sickly sweet on the summer air.

"This is the town centre as far as I know, sir," said the lamplighter.

A Camera Obscura

As he spoke he stepped forward and the pale lamplight fell on to his face, which had been in shadow before.

Mr. Sharsted no longer waited to ask for any more directions but set off down the road at breakneck speed, not sure whether the green pallor of the man's face was due to a terrible suspicion or to the green-tinted glasses he wore.

What he was certain of was that something like a mass of writhing worms projected below the man's cap, where his hair would normally have been. Mr. Sharsted hadn't waited to find out if this Medusa-like supposition were correct; beneath his hideous fear burned a savage anger at Gingold, whom somehow he suspected to be at the back of all these troubles.

Mr. Sharsted fervently hoped that he might soon wake to find himself at home in bed, ready to begin the day that had ended so ignominiously at Gingold's, but even as he formulated the thought, he knew this was reality. This cold moonlight, the hard pavement, his frantic flight, and the breath rasping and sobbing in his throat.

As the mist cleared from in front of his eyes, he slowed to a walk and then found himself in the middle of a square; he knew where he was and he had to force his nerves into a terrible, unnatural calm, just this side of despair. He walked with controlled casualness past the legend, NINIAN'S REVIVALIST BROTHERHOOD, and this time chose the most unlikely road of all, little more than a narrow alley that appeared to lead in the wrong direction.

Mr. Sharsted was willing to try anything which would lead him off this terrifying, accursed hill. There were no lights here and his feet stumbled on the rough stones and flints of the unmade roadway, but at least he was going downhill and the track gradually spiralled until he was in the right direction.

For some little while Mr. Sharsted had heard faint, elusive stirrings in the darkness about him and once he was startled to hear, some way ahead of him, a muffled cough. At least there were other people about, at last, he thought and he was comforted, too, to see, far ahead of him, the dim lights of the town.

As he grew nearer, Mr. Sharsted recovered his spirits and was relieved to see that they did not recede from him, as he had half suspected they might. The shapes about him, too, were solid enough. Their feet rang hollow on the roadway; evidently they were on their way to a meeting.

As Mr. Sharsted came under the light of the first lamp, his earlier panic fear had abated. He still couldn't recognize exactly where he was, but the trim villas they were passing were more reminiscent of the town proper.

Mr. Sharsted stepped up on to the pavement when they reached the well-lit area and in so doing, cannoned into a large well-built man who had just emerged from a gateway to join the throng in the roadway.

Mr. Sharsted staggered under the impact and once again his nostrils caught the sickly sweet perfume of decay. The man caught him by the front of the coat to prevent him from falling.

"Evening, Mordecai," he said in a thick voice. "I thought you'd be coming, sooner or later."

Mr. Sharsted could not resist a cry of bubbling terror. It was not just the greenish pallor of the man's face or the rotted, leathery lips drawn back from the decayed teeth. He fell back against the fence as Abel Joyce passed on—Abel Joyce, a fellow moneylender and usurer who had died in the nineteen-twenties and whose funeral Mr. Sharsted had attended.

Blackness was about him as he rushed away, a sobbing whistle in his throat. He was beginning to understand Mr. Gingold and that devilish camera obscura; the lost and the damned. He began to babble to himself under his breath.

Now and again he cast a sidelong glimpse at his companions as he ran; there was old Mrs. Sanderson who used to lay out corpses and rob her charges; there Grayson, the estate agent and undertaker; Amos, the war profiteer; Drucker, a swindler, all green of pallor and bearing with them the charnel stench.

All people Mr. Sharsted had business with at one time or another and all of whom had one thing in common. Without exception all had been dead for quite a number of years. Mr. Sharsted stuffed his handkerchief over his mouth to blot out that unbearable odour and heard the mocking laughter as his racing feet carried him past.

A Camera Obscura

"Evening, Mordecai," they said. "We thought you'd be joining us."

Mr. Gingold equated him with these ghouls, he sobbed, as he ran on at headlong speed; if only he could make him understand. Sharsted didn't deserve such treatment. He was a businessman, not like these bloodsuckers on society; the lost and the damned. Now he knew why the Corn Exchange still stood and why the town was unfamiliar. It existed only in the eye of the camera obscura. Now he knew that Mr. Gingold had been trying to give him a last chance and why he had said goodbye, instead of goodnight.

There was just one hope; if he could find the door back to Mr. Gingold's perhaps he could make him change his mind. Mr. Sharsted's feet flew over the cobbles as he thought this, his hat fell down and he scraped his hands against the wall. He left the walking corpses far behind, but though he was now looking for the familiar square he seemed to be finding his way back to the Corn Exchange.

He stopped for a moment to regain his breath. He must work this out logically. How had it happened before? Why, of course, by walking away from the desired destination. Mr. Sharsted turned back and set himself to walk steadily towards the lights. Though terrified, he did not despair, now that he knew what he was up against. He felt himself a match for Mr. Gingold. If only he could find the door!

As he reached the warm circle cast by the glow of the street lamps, Mr. Sharsted breathed a sigh of relief. For as he turned a corner there was the big square, with the soot-grimed chapel on the corner. He hurried on. He must remember exactly the turnings he had taken; he couldn't afford to make a mistake.

Mr. Sharsted groaned as he remembered the face of one old woman he had seen earlier that evening—or what was left of that face, after years of wind and weather. He suddenly recalled that she had died before the 1914 war. The sweat burst out on his forehead and he tried not to think of it.

Once off the square, he plunged into the alley he remembered. Ah! there it was. Now all he had to do was to go to the left and there was the door. His heart beat higher and he began to hope, with a sick longing, for the security of his well-appointed house and his rows of friendly ledgers. Only one more corner. He ran on and turned up the road towards Mr. Gingold's door. Another thirty yards to the peace of the ordinary world.

The moonlight winked on a wide, well-paved square. Shone, too, on a legend painted in gold leaf on a large board: NINIAN'S REVIVALIST BROTHERHOOD. The date was 1925.

Mr. Sharsted gave a hideous yell of fear and despair and fell to the pavement.

Mr. Gingold sighed heavily and yawned. He glanced at the clock. It was time for bed. He went over once again and stared into the camera obscura. It had been a not altogether unsuccessful day. He put a black velvet cloth over the image in the lens and went off slowly to bed.

Under the cloth, in pitiless detail, was reflected the narrow tangle of streets round Mr. Gingold's house, seen as through the eye of God; there went Mr. Sharsted and his colleagues, the lost and the damned, trapped for eternity, stumbling, weeping, swearing, as they slipped and scrabbled along the alleys and squares of their own private hell, under the pale light of the stars.

The Janissaries Of Emilion

1

He awoke, for the third consecutive occasion at dawn, sweating and terrified, with the details of the dream vivid in his mind. His hands were clutching the simple iron frame of the bedstead above his head and the dews of his night terror had soaked the linen of the bedding so profusely that he could not believe it was simply the result of the heat of the summer air.

He lay quietly, taking in the soothing details of the plainly furnished room, with its restful cream walls. It was just turned five and the solitary calls of newly-awakened birds were beginning to penetrate from the green wall of the garden but his ears still seemed lapped in the soft susurrance of the surf.

The dream had begun in a very casual and haphazard manner but its details had tended to clarify and repeat themselves on subsequent occasions, so that each repetition added a strata to his consciousness, as an artist adds pigment at the successive stages of a painting.

It was not until much later that Farlow had been admitted to Greenmansion which was, not to put too fine a point on it, a luxuriously appointed mental home. The Superintendent had kept copious notes on the case, which interested him very much indeed, but for obvious reasons the denouement of the affair had been kept from the attention of the larger world.

Farlow was an old friend of mine and I have pieced the story together as it was told me over a longish space of time, both from his own lips and from those of the Superintendent,

Dr. Sondquist, a psychiatrist of great sympathy and brilliance, who had been responsible for some spectacular cures. Farlow was an extraordinary man in many ways; hypersensitive perhaps, but a genius in his line—that of higher physics—and it was at his own request that he had been admitted as a private patient to Greenmansion, for 'rest and observation'. I visited him there on many occasions, as often as my own duties permitted, but I had heard the beginning of his story long before he took what his friends considered this last drastic step. It was as strange a tale in its way as I had ever heard and, considering its bizarre and horrible end, a remarkable one.

It had begun, he told me, in the most prosaic and ordinary manner. It had been just six months before and he had perhaps, as he put it, been rather overdoing things; long hours in the laboratory, hurried lunches and evenings devoted to calculus had developed both nerves and mind to a high pitch of strain and sensitivity. He had come home tired out one evening and after several hours of fruitless calculation on his current abstruse problem, he had put down the elaborate figures for the night.

By now it was past one o'clock in the morning and not the best time for a heavy meal, followed by almost a pint of black coffee. Be that as it may Farlow had eaten little since midday and he was the last man to bother about what he put in his insides. The demands of science had left him little time for seeking the company of the gentler sex, and so he had never married; his simple needs were looked after by a housekeeper of dour aspect but efficient habits and she went off duty at nine o'clock.

So Farlow made this heavy and ill-advised meal, swallowed the coffee and made his way slowly to bed, his head throbbing with exhaustion, his mind chagrined at the inconclusive results of his long labours over the elusive problem. Not unnaturally he slept badly, and it must have been at least 3:00 A.M. before sleep finally found him. But suddenly, it seemed to him, he was wide awake. I should imagine we have all had that sort of experience at one time or another. It is simply that we are dreaming that we are awake. We believe ourselves to be awake but subconsciously know ourselves to be still within the dream. I put this to Farlow the first time he started to unburden himself to me on the subject. That was not so, he said. Though he was within the dream he knew himself to be awake.

Everything was so vividly real; every touch and sensation of this often-repeated dream was so actually realized that it was his own room and everyday life that afterwards seemed so dim and faded. It was as if he had at night escaped to another life which was more immediate and more exciting than the world of reality. That his dream-world was a place of terror and fear for him, was neither here nor there. Farlow also believed in the physical reality of this world, though he had subsequently studied maps and atlases of obscure parts of the world in vain.

And despite the fact that the aspects of what I will continue to call his dream-world bore this terrible air of menace, Farlow was convinced that if he could but overcome the sinister shadows of the dream he could be happier than any man could hope to be in the everyday world of ordinary life. Now, I must emphasize, at this point, that Farlow was as sane as you or I; possibly saner, for his work as a scientist compelled him to weigh every grain of truth and to proceed to his results by empirical methods. At no time, even during his sojourn in Greenmansion, did he exceed the normal, according to Dr. Sondquist, save in this one matter of the dream.

And that was something no one was in a position to disprove save Farlow himself; for he was the one who was experiencing the reality of his vision. Judging by the end of it all, Farlow was possibly the sanest man among us. And if that were so, what terrors lie in wait just behind the curtain of what we call consciousness may well give pause to the boldest of us, when criticizing a man like Farlow. It was my own belief that in his refined and hypersensitive way he had merely gone beyond the stage arrived at by the norm of coarser mortals, and a veil had been torn aside or breached in some unusual manner.

To put it more simply, what happened was this. It was just ten-past three when Farlow was last awake, for he switched on the light and looked at his bedside clock. At the conclusion of his dream, for reasons which will be apparent later, he again switched on his light and the time was only twenty-past three. Yet Farlow, with all the gravity of which a scientist is capable assured me solemnly that he had been away for more than three hours. It was a ridiculous assertion, on the surface that is, for we all know that a second or two in a dream may be stretched to eternity for the sleeper; and in the split second before awakening at a heavy noise, the brain may substitute a whole chain of events in a minute space of time, to account for the sound.

Be that as it may and bearing in mind Farlow's own remarks on the aftermath of the dream, which I would not for one moment doubt, I am inclined to believe him. He slept and yet he awoke a short while afterwards and this is what he experienced. He was cold; he was in water and he was, or had been a little before, in deadly danger of his life. His mouth was soaked with moisture and salt and he coughed heavily as he thrashed feebly about in shallow water. He felt the rough kiss of sand between his bare toes and when he opened his eyes he found himself in the shallows of a wild, bleak shore. Exhaustedly, he started to drag himself on to a long beach of sloping white sand. He lay on his side coughing as the water receded and watched a rosy dawn fingering the sky.

That was all on this occasion. He awoke, or rather he then returned to the normal twentieth century world and the nightmare of his own position. Farlow had become aware of the difficulties of his 'dream', from the very first moment he had, as he continued to say, pierced the curtain. For in his terror, as he fumbled to switch on the light and look at the clock, he found sand between his toes and his pyjamas were soaked with cold, salt water.

2

The reaction of Farlow to the bizarre and terrible situation in which he found himself may easily be imagined; certainly no one but Farlow himself could comprehend the shock to mind and system. It was months before he could bring himself to speak to me of this first 'expedition beyond the veil', as he termed it. For two nights following this extraordinary awakening he did not dare to sleep. And on the third night his exhaustion was too great for dreaming.

For over a week his sleep was normal and then he had the second experience. He had retired soon after midnight and went straight from a sleeping to an 'awake' state. Once again he was struggling in a shallow sea, once again he dragged himself painfully ashore, but this time the vision, call it what you will, went on a little longer. Farlow lay on the beach, coughing out salt water and intermittently opening his eyes; he saw dawn creep slowly up that wild and beautiful shore and knew himself to be somewhere in the East. But it was not the East as known today, but at a time of great antiquity.

And then, as the sun came up through the mist, the scene changed like the opening of a door and Farlow awoke in his own bed, once again soaked to the skin with salt water. It was about that time that he consulted a doctor friend who was, of course, unable to help. Farlow somewhat naturally did not tell him the whole story, not wishing to be thought insane, and without the terrible awakenings, the matter seemed no more to the doctor than a dream which repeated itself, as sometimes happens to many people.

It was difficult for an outsider to conceive the torment of Farlow's mind at this time; it would have been bad enough for a normal person but Farlow was a scientist and his mind rejected such things automatically. It was against all the known laws of nature, and yet it was happening. The third dream was a repetition of the others but to Farlow's relief it began with him already lying on the beach. The sun was a little higher in the sky and the mist was beginning to disperse. Strangely, he retained his fear of drowning in the dream state, but he noticed vividly that he appeared to have recovered from the experience of being in the sea. With this so-called evidence and the heat of the sun on the beach, he estimated that he had been lying on the sand for about three hours.

Thus it appeared to him that the dreams were progressive in time and that if they continued, the incidents would overlap in the manner of a cinema film projected over and over again, with the difference that a little more of the action would be revealed each time. It took him quite a long while to work this out, of course, for his waking self at first rejected the implications. In the fourth dream the sun was higher in the sky, the mist was thinning out a little and when he awoke to his own room in the twentieth century he had been able to see that he was dressed in some sort of open-necked blouse made of linen of an antique cut.

The lower half of his body was clad in baggy pantaloons of some dark material of a type quite beyond his experience, and as he had noticed on the first occasion, his feet were bare. The most extraordinary thing about this fourth dream was that though he had awakened on the three previous occasions drenched in what appeared to be sea-water, he woke this last time with his skin barely damp. Farlow then argued that his experience in the dream state had a physical or rational basis, and from this he deduced that the sun beating on his other self was drying him out.

At this stage he was still trying to rationalize his terrors and one thing which greatly exercised his mind was the minor curiosity of how the physical situation of his dream self could be carried over into real life in one case and not the other. He was referring, naturally, to the water on his skin which was physically evident on awakening and the fact that he was still dressed in his pyjamas. If the same rules applied in transferring one substance from the dream to another dimension then in theory he should have still been dressed in the shirt and trousers. At least so he argued.

His analytical powers were beginning to be affected at this stage, and there was the additional problem of what happened to his pyjamas while 'he' was on the beach. Or were there two selves existing in different planes? But however he argued it, Farlow met with a breakdown of all logical rules, whenever he applied them to one set of circumstances or the other—the dream-world or the real. The line between the two was becoming very blurred.

This sort of thing had been going on for several months when Farlow began to take me into his confidence. He was always a thin, finely-strung sort of man and his experiences of the past weeks had put deep shadows under his eyes and his physical frame looked frailer than at any time I remembered. It took several evenings of half-coherent, hedging talk before he really broached the subject, but once he had got fairly started his thoughts came tumbling out like water released from a floodgate.

His greatest fear was that I should suppose his sanity to be in question, but after I had listened to him for several evenings and questioned him keenly about certain points, I was able to reassure him on this. If ever a man was sane in the true sense of the word, it was Farlow. He had told me about the first half dozen or so dreams, which had taken him to a point higher up the beach. It was warm and comfortable there, in the hot sand, and as the dreams or visions or whatever you like to call them, now began with him already ashore and dry, there were no unpleasant physical effects on awakening, for which he was thankful.

So far as he could make out, for he did not always check by the clock, the duration of each dream was firmly stamped in his mind as being about three hours, but the actual time in this world amounted to ten minutes. He saw no particular significance in this, but he made the curious remark that if the dream had commenced with him far at sea, and several miles from land, and he could not have swum to shore in the three hours allowed, he would have drowned. I did not see how he could possibly argue that and I felt it was time to turn his thoughts away from such morbid directions. But though I spoke warmly and, as I thought, sensibly on the point, he brushed my valid objections aside with a sigh. He just felt convinced that it would be so, he said, and nothing I could say would turn him aside from this.

I asked him then if he thought that there would have been a drowned corpse in the bed when he came back to this world, and he answered quite simply in the affirmative. This impelled me to question him further; it was implicit in his argument that his physical self was absent from his bed during the course of the dreams, and I offered to keep watch in his room if that would help. This he would not have at any price; he gave no reason, but looked at me curiously and it was my own personal view that he feared that any intervention by another person, however well meant, might endanger him and prevent him from 'getting back'.

I did not press the matter, for I saw how serious the situation had become. The next evening I visited Farlow he seemed calmer and

◈ Darkness, Mist & Shadow

more rational. He had had a quiet night and he proceeded to bring me up to date on his reasoning. The dreams now began with him lying, fully conscious, far up the beach, well rested and quite dry in the heat of the sun. The sand stretched for mile after mile and he seemed to know in his heart that he was in the East and in an ancient time. The mist was clearing as the sun rose, the waves moved languidly in the sunlight, and far off to the east the spires of some city at the edge of the shore were revealing themselves.

All through his series of visions Farlow, even in his dream state, had no notion of who he was, how he had come to be in the sea, or what he was doing on the shore. He was invariably dressed in the blouse and dark pantaloons and always woke with a dry skin and dressed in pyjamas. The fear of the dream had not yet begun, and so far as he could estimate the pattern of three hours dream and ten minutes real time continued.

The dreams averaged about one a week—though there were occasions when there were two—and were always progressive. They usually occurred when Farlow was more than ordinarily tired, which gave him the notion that the barriers of everyday were broken down at those times. His doctor friend had been unable to help. It was in these circumstances that he resolved to bring something back with him from the dream world of the shore, if it were physically possible. I was sitting in Farlow's study after dinner late one evening when he told me this. I could see that it had cost him a great effort to speak of it.

"And were you successful?" I asked, forcing the words out.

Farlow's eyes were dark caverns of somber knowledge as he nodded slowly. Abruptly he got up and went over to his desk. He unlocked one of the drawers, drew out something wrapped in white cloth and put it down on the table in front of me.

"Have a look at this," he said. "You need not be alarmed. It isn't anything unpleasant."

I must confess my hand was a little unsteady as I unwrapped the cloth. Perhaps I was disappointed or it may have been a curious look on my face, but Farlow relaxed and smiled grimly. What I had before me was a piece of reddish coloured rock, about six inches long and three wide, weighing perhaps a couple of pounds. I looked at it stupefied.

"You don't mean to say that you actually brought this back from your dream?" I said. Nothing could have been more banal than my sentence but I was even more surprised when Farlow agreed.

"Yes," he said simply. "That is exactly what I do mean."

I couldn't think of anything to say that was neither idiotic nor a reflection on Farlow's sanity, so I turned the piece of rock over in my hand and added, "Have you had someone look at this?"

Farlow nodded again. "Smithers. One of the best geologists we've got. He was quite excited. He was damned puzzled too. He places it at the time of Christ. What upset him was the fact that there had been no weathering since."

Farlow and I exchanged a long glance. Then I held up my whisky glass for the stiff peg he started to pour me. There was nothing to say.

3

I was unavoidably called away on business soon after Farlow's incredible revelation and though I kept in touch by letter, it was more than three weeks before I saw him again. Brief as the interval had been here was as indefinable difference in his face; a subtle fear lurking at the back of his eyes which I did not like. It took a day or two to regain the old intimacy and it was not until several nights later that he started to bring me up to date. There had been more dreams, of course; that much he had already hinted on my return.

They had been progressive, I knew, though he had not gone into detail, but now they had taken a more sinister turn. He had been sitting halfway up the beach, fully recovered from his ordeal in the sea. His memory in the dream recalled this fact, but nothing beyond it. He still did not know his identity or the location of the shore. It was lighter now and the mist was almost gone. The turrets and spires of the distant city winked and shimmered through the grey wisps of morning haze and he felt a lightening of the heart.

Over several sittings Farlow took me through a whole series of dreams, in which the pattern gradually became darker until eventually horror tinged the atmosphere. How he first heard, Farlow did not remember, but over a period which lasted about ten days, he absorbed the fact that the city was called Emilion. He was dreaming almost every night now and each time the dream began with him sitting on the beach, with the sky brighter, the mists thinning away, the fair face of the city more clearly revealed.

The brightness and beauty of Emilion was something beyond this world, said Farlow; it gladdened the heart and filled his whole being with joy. And as he daily gained in strength in the dream, he started to run on the beach and splash in and out of the warm water, as he gazed at the distant city, which rose spire on golden spire out of a sea of rosy mist.

The only thing to compare with it in this world, said Farlow, was Mont St Michel on a bright spring morning with the sun gilding the tops of the wavelets; but lovely as that was by earthly standards, it was a poor thing compared with the unearthly beauty of the dream.

"Multiply Mont St Michel a hundredfold and there you have Emilion," Farlow told me simply, the firelight coming and going on his dark, tired face.

Even during the daytime waking hours, the name of Emilion had filled his soul with quiet contentment and he had spent much of his spare time brooding over old maps and atlases, particularly those of mediaeval times, but without success. Emilion as a city seemed to belong to the land of make-believe. Then, one night, about a week before my return the dream had begun to change. The banners and turrets and spires of Emilion were seen across a vast stretch of foaming strand, more than a mile wide, which was stained all pink and gold with the light of the rising sun, as the shallow waves broke across it. There was a woman in the city, whom Farlow loved, I gathered.

He himself was only vaguely aware of this, but gradually through the whole astonishing series of dreams, the fact had permeated his heart. He did not know her name; only that he loved; that the girl was there; and that to Emilion he must find his way. And yet, as is the way with dreams, even of the vivid kind which Farlow was experiencing, the thing could not be rushed. He could not simply proceed to the city as one would in normal life. In timeless, slow-motion sequences, the dream proceeded from night to night. Each time Farlow would be but a few feet nearer the edge of the vast foaming foreshore which separated him from the city. And then one night there came a subtle change in the picture.

For as he gazed across at the turrets of Emilion, he became aware of a faint white swathe, like a hazy touch of gauze along the base of the picture. It swirled across the sand, beneath the city walls, more than a mile and a half away. It was stationary, yet seemed to move with incredible speed and Farlow was conscious of a faint unease. A breath of cold wind seemed to disperse the last folds of mist still hanging over the surface of the sea, and a strange fear gnawed at his heart. He stopped walking towards the city and gazed at the faint patch of white that blurred the far distance. And then he awoke to nameless dread and an icy dew on his forehead.

He feared sleep the following night but it overtook him just the same; he was on the shore looking across the far strand and there, in the distance, was the strange misty cloud that moved with such tremendous speed. And it seemed to him that it had come a little nearer. The cold wind blew on Farlow and he felt the deep-rooted fear there is no allaying. And once again he awoke. Several times more he dreamed and each time it was the same; every night the city of Emilion shone across the foaming water but the patch of white had spread and begun to reveal itself in detail.

And the wind blew with a cold breath and it seemed to Farlow that it made a whispering murmur in the sky. And what it said with such insidious clamour in his ear was; 'THE JANISSARIES OF EMILION!' And Farlow woke with a shrieking cry.

4

"What do you make of it?" Farlow asked me for the fourth time. I lit a cigarette with a hand which was none too steady.

"The Janissaries were a sort of mameluke, weren't they?" I said at last.

Farlow nodded. He reached down a thick tome from one of his shelves.

"I wasted no time in looking them up," he said. He read from the reference work in front of him. According to this the Janissaries were a body of Turkish infantry in olden times, forming the personal bodyguard of the Sultan of Turkey. They had been abolished in 1826. The reference book also gave them as; Personal instrument of tyranny. Turkish soldier.

I tried to look wiser than I felt as Farlow finished reading.

"How does this tie in with the period being 2,000 years ago? Or the East ?" I asked quickly, before Farlow could speak.

"The Janissaries were a terribly ancient force which existed under many names," Farlow replied quietly. "They were mounted at an earlier period. And they operated outside Turkey. In the East particularly. And you must remember that Turkey was an Oriental Empire. It was only since Ataturk..."

"Very well," I interrupted him. "You surely can't take this latest phase seriously."

Farlow held up his hand to stop me from saying anything further. One look at his face was enough for me to see that he was deadly serious.

"You have not heard me out," he said patiently. There have been more dreams since those of which I have just told you.'

Put briefly, Farlow's dream self had stood upon the shore and as the vision progressed from day to day had seen the white cloud grow, until it had blossomed into something which resembled a dark mass of many points, topped with a hazy, billowing mist. On the last occasion on which he had dreamed, he had seen little spurts of foam as the mass entered the surf on the far side of the gulf which separated it from him. And the great fear which had paralysed him seemed to fix on his heart like a stone and the freezing wind which followed had again whispered; 'THE JANISSARIES OF EMILION!'

And like a man who escapes from a nightmare to find himself still within it, the wretched Farlow had screamed awake to find his day but the prelude to the fears of the following night. I tried to comfort my friend as best I could, though it was scant encouragement my presence was able to give. I was of the opinion that a priest or psychiatrist might do more good; but who could accompany him within this dark dream and stand at his side in strong support against the nightmare which menaced him? It was an insidious, sombre battle being waged nightly within the man's mind and I feared the end as I heard his next words.

He sat quietly at the table and said to me in even tones, "I have thought it out carefully. In the last dream, only two nights ago, I was able to distinguish clearly for the first time the nature of the threat. I shall never reach the city. Crossing the water to reach me are a body of horsemen, clad in white robes, moving at a tremendous speed. Even at the slow rate at which the dream progresses the end cannot be long delayed. A few weeks at most."

I sought to reassure him with some platitude but the words died in my throat.

'They are the Janissaries of Emilion!' Farlow called out in a strangled voice. "I can begin to distinguish the cruel Oriental faces. I have become a man on whom they had revenge in the ancient times."

"But what can a dream do to harm you?" I burst out impatiently, in spite of myself.

"Fool!" Farlow almost shrieked. "They will kill me! When they catch me I shall die."

I was silent before this outburst. Farlow had turned away and stood looking unseeingly at the bookcase.

I reached for my hat. "In my opinion, you need good medical advice, my friend, and at once," I said. "If I might recommend..."

"Good evening," said Farlow in dead, measured tones.

I went out and quietly closed the door behind me. That night even I doubted Farlow's sanity.

5

In this extreme crisis, and with Farlow's sanity and even life at stake I sought out Dr. Sondquist. In as subtle a manner as I could I laid something of the case before him. To my relief Dr. Sondquist treated the matter as being within the normal bounds of psychiatric practice. He had an impressive-sounding line of Jungian and Alderian quotations and his crisp, incisive manner convinced me that here was a man who could recall Farlow from the dark shore-line to which his mind had wandered, if anyone could.

To my relief, my next interview with Farlow passed off much better than I had expected. My friend seemed to have forgotten his outburst of the previous day. Though he was pale and distraught he had lost something of the terrible atmosphere of nerves at cracking point which had previously surrounded him. We spoke quietly and calmly. I gathered that his sleep had been dreamless for once. The upshot of our conversation was that Farlow agreed to go and see Dr. Sondquist. A week later, after much careful heart-searching, he entered Greenmansion for the rest and observation to which I have already referred.

I thus necessarily lost something of the close contact which we had formerly enjoyed, though I was able to visit Farlow twice a week in the earlier stages and Dr. Sondquist kept me fully informed of his patient's progress. The end of the story I had to piece together for myself from Farlow's own conversation, from a diary he left which the Superintendent allowed me to examine and from my last terrible conversation with Sondquist.

When I first saw Farlow after his entry into Greenmansion I was disturbed to note that he appeared even more fine-drawn and gaunt than before. But the white-painted walls of the sanatorium and the air of quiet efficiency and bustle which radiated from the nursing and medical staff had had a beneficial effect, I should have said.

Without preamble he plunged at once into the details of his latest visions, as though they were more than he could bear to contemplate alone, which was, after all, no more than the truth. He had dreamed twice more, he said; it was the same and yet not the same. The Janissaries, for so he had identified them, were much nearer. He was still rooted to the shore, but the white-cloaked riders were now splashing through the shallows about halfway across the foaming stretch of water which barred his way to the city of Emilion.

He could see that they carried some sort of banner which bore the green crescent, and the short, heavy-bladed swords they waved, glinted in the bright sunshine of mid-morning. Their turbanned heads bobbed rhythmically as they rode and their black horses, bunched closely together, clove the white, frothing water with their steel-shod hooves. But what gave Farlow such a terrible sense of impending doom was the cruelty of the faces beneath the turbans of the Janissaries of Emilion. Their bearded jaws, the narrow, blazing eyes and the red, thin lips which parted to reveal the shining, sharp-pointed white teeth looked so rapacious and sadistic that his dream self was near to fainting with fear.

In the last dream of the previous night they were so close that he could hear the guttural cries they uttered and see the details of the elaborate bits on the bridles of the horses. The riders wore boots of soft leather and the metal spurs they used, dug deeply into the flanks of the plunging horses. And again the cold wind blew across the blue sky, bringing with it the great chilling despair and for the twentieth or thirtieth time Farlow awoke to nightmare.

I gave my unfortunate friend what comfort I could and took my leave. Unfortunately, Sondquist was away that day so I could not have the conversation with him which might have made some difference to the outcome of the business, though I was rapidly coming to the same conclusion that had plunged Farlow into such profound melancholy; namely, that the outcome of the dream could not be halted, but what that outcome was, none of us, least of all Farlow, fortunately, could have foreseen.

My next information came from the diary Farlow had kept over the last few months. The extract which I have summarized is from the period immediately following my last visit. Farlow was by this time having shock treatment of a particularly violent type, and his days had thus begun to assume the detached, unworldly aspect as that of his nights.

Sondquist was worried about him, beneath the urbane professional surface, and the object of the special treatment was to break up the dream patterns and so disperse them. At least, this is how the diary of Farlow read to the mind of a layman. There was much abstruse speculation of a supra-metaphysical type, which was a bit too heavy going for me, and I skipped those pages in which Farlow gave himself up to such musings on the physical laws of nature and of the construction of the universe.

But the effect of the treatment had been merely to delay the progress of the dreams; so that where Farlow had, for example, been experiencing three sequences of the dream-state in a week, he now had one. So the object realized had been only that of a slowing-up process; the treatment had no power to disrupt, destroy or dispel the pattern which had assumed a cloud of such alarming proportion on Farlow's mental horizon. He spent such part of his day not occupied in treatment, lying on the small iron bed, fully clothed, looking up at the ceiling and listening to the soothing noises of the birds from the garden beyond. He lay listening to the roaring of the blood in his ears; he could hear the fluids of his body bubbling beneath the surface of his skin. He was enormously conscious of being alive; he could almost feel his toenails growing underneath his socks. And with this tremendous feeling, this consciousness of the vital force within himself, Farlow, at forty-nine, realized that he had much to live for, much yet to give the world in the way of knowledge and research; with this realization came a tremendous effort to shake off the dark sense of doom which now not only filled the horizon of his dream but the entire horizon of his waking life.

One of his last entries in the diary said with tragic foreknowledge, "Those faces, those ghastly, cruel faces! And those eyes! If Sondquist is not successful, they will reach me soon. And that will be the end..."

6

The end came sooner than expected. To me it was a profound shock. I had been unable to visit Farlow for nearly a week. When I telephoned Greenmansion to inquire about my friend, the matron had been evasive and had put me on to the doctor in charge. He in turn had not been helpful and had referred me to Sondquist. But as Sondquist himself was too busy to come to the phone it did not get me much farther forward. I was not at all satisfied and decided to visit the sanatorium in person.

It was a day of early summer in which the shimmering haze, the contented songs of birds and the heavy warmth which rose from the ground, spoke of even greater heat to come. As I drove out to Greenmansion, the beauty of the afternoon made a vivid contrast in my mind to the dark situation in which the unfortunate Farlow found himself. As soon as I arrived I saw that there was something wrong. The main gates of the sanatorium were shut and locked and I had to ring at the porter's lodge.

He in turn had to phone the main building to get permission for me to proceed. While he was doing this I left my car and quietly opened the small gate at the side of the lodge, which was unlocked. As I slipped past I heard the porter's cry of protest, but he was too late. I was in the grounds and rapidly walking towards the house. As soon as I came up to the front steps I could see by the unusual activity that I was too late to help my friend. An ambulance from the State Department concerned was parked against the side of the lawn and next to it two big blue police cars with State license plates. I was met by a white-faced matron who tried to dissuade me from seeing Dr. Sondquist.

"Ring the Superintendent tonight, please," she said. "It will be best."

I shook my head. "I wish to see Dr. Sondquist at once," I said firmly. She hesitated and then reluctantly went into her office. I had waited in the hall for nearly ten minutes before the measured tread of the doctor sounded along the corridor. He looked harassed and worn.

"I wish to see Farlow," I said without further preamble. Sondquist shook his head and a curious look came and went in his eyes.

"I have bad news for you, I am afraid," he said. "Farlow died last night."

The information took some moments to sink in and I then became aware that Sondquist had led me to a chair; the matron hovered in the background. The Superintendent handed me a glass of brandy and I mechanically swallowed it.

"What happened?" I stammered, as soon as I had recovered my senses somewhat.

Again the curious look passed over Sondquist's face. "He had a heart attack in the night," he said. "There was nothing we could do."

I just did not believe him and my disbelief must have shown in my next words.

"Then why are the police here?" I asked in stumbling tones.

Sondquist shook his head impatiently. 'That is about another matter altogether,' he said hurriedly. Spots of red stood out high on his cheekbones. He put his hand on my shoulder in a kindly manner.

"I have much to do at the moment. Why not ring me this evening and we will arrange an appointment for tomorrow, when I have more time. Then I will answer all your questions."

I agreed dully and a few minutes later drove back to town. But the interview with the doctor next day did not seem at all satisfactory to me and there were many of my questions left unanswered. The funeral took place quietly and the weeks passed by and poor Farlow and his problems seemed forgotten by the world at large. But I had not forgotten. I kept up my acquaintance with Sondquist and after many visits, when he had come to trust me and had seen that there was more than morbid curiosity in my questioning, he satisfied my queries. Sometimes I wish he hadn't. For then I should sleep better at nights.

It was more than a year afterwards before he could bring himself to confide in me. It was almost September and a thin fire of twigs crackled in his study at Greenmansion, for though the days continued in blazing heat, there was an underlying chill in the evenings. He had got out some of the record books on Farlow's treatment and had allowed me to look at the patient's own diary.

After we had been talking for some time, I asked him, "Do you think Farlow was mad?"

Sondquist hesitated and then shook his head emphatically. "I sometimes feel that I may be," he said enigmatically and a look of strain showed in his eyes.

"What does that mean?" I asked.

The doctor drummed nervously with his long thin fingers on the desk, then picked up his glass of wine and drained it.

"Would you really like to know how Farlow died?" he said. I

nodded. The doctor turned and stared sombrely into the fire, as though the answer to the problem of Farlow lay somewhere amid the flickering flames.

"I can rely on your complete discretion in this matter?" he said after a long silence.

"Absolutely," I said.

Sondquist turned to face me and looked me straight in the eyes as he told me the end of the story.

"You are completely aware of all the progressive stages of Farlow's dreams or visions, I take it?" he asked.

"He gave me his confidence," I said.

Sondquist told me that Farlow had been quiet and cooperative, as he always was, during the last day or two of his treatment. But on the afternoon before his death he had become more than usually agitated and in a long interview with Dr. Sondquist had gone deeply into his fears. The import of his story was that the Janissaries of Emilion were so close to him in his last dream that he could almost touch them. If he slept that night he felt they would destroy him somehow, that he would die.

Sondquist, who had, of course, a different interpretation of the dream, held that the final vision would have been the catalyst; that it held the kernel of the problem. He told Farlow that in the crisis of his last dream he would finally overcome his fear and be able to live a normal life. After that night, if it came, he said, Farlow would be cured. My friend's reaction to this was the expected. He became violent, said that Sondquist had no notion of the real problem, and that the Superintendent's life was not at stake. In the end he became so agitated that he had to be physically restrained by the attendants. He shrieked a good deal about the Janissaries of Emilion and begged Sondquist to have a guard placed over him that night.

The Superintendent put him under sedatives and the night staff were instructed to look at him from time to time during the dark hours. Farlow had been taken to a padded room, though a straitjacket had not been thought necessary, and he was sleeping a normal sleep in his bed, when one of the male nurses last looked in through the peephole at about 2:00 A.M.

Darkness, Mist & Shadow

The sanatorium was roused by the most appalling screams around four in the morning. The uproar had come from Farlow's room, and it was like nothing else in the Superintendent's experience. The first male nurse to look through the peephole in Farlow's door had a violent fit of vomiting and the matron fainted. It was with some difficulty that Sondquist was able to take charge; after a careful examination of the contents of the room the police were sent for, photographs were taken, and the subsequent investigation, undertaken at County level, had lasted more than a week.

For the sake of public opinion as well as that of Greenmansion and the reputation of Dr. Sondquist, the highest authorities, among them the County Coroner, had agreed that no public examination of the matter should take place and the affair was hushed over. The truth was so fantastic that the only written record of it remained in the private files of Dr. Sondquist and these were kept perpetually locked in a private safe-deposit, to be opened only on his death.

It was at this point that I put my final questions, Dr. Sondquist made his answers and permitted me to see some photographs which I felt would have been better destroyed. I can never forget what they depicted. Sick at heart, I at length took my leave and drove like a drunken man back to my house. When I had recovered my senses somewhat, I wrapped the piece of rock Farlow had given me in a piece of sacking, and weighted it with stones secured by a wire.

Then I drove out to the Point and hurled it into the deepest part of the sea. That done some of the shadow seemed lifted from my mind. But the thing haunts my brain and latterly my sleep too has become more and more broken. Pray God that I do not dream the same dream as Farlow.

What Sondquist had told me and what the photographs depicted had been like something from an obscene slaughterhouse. For in Farlow's room, which was padded and contained no sharp edges of any kind, much less a weapon, the gutted, disembowelled and eviscerated monstrosity which had once been my friend was spread about in carmine horror; there an eyeball, here a leg or an arm like some demoniac scene in a canvas by Bosch. Save that this was gory reality. No wonder the staff had fainted or that the ambulance attendants had used masks and tongs when clearing up.

Said Sondquist in a trembling voice as I took my leave, "Make no mistake about it, though the thing is scientifically impossible, Farlow had been hacked to pieces as surely as if a dozen men had attacked him with sharpened swords or knives!"

.

✑ THE CAVE

"FEAR IS A STRANGE THING, AND YET A COMPARATIVE THING," said Wilson. "It means something different to you, something again to me. Temperament has so much to do with it; one man is afraid of heights, another of the dark, a third of the illogical in life."

The small group in the dining club stirred and gazed expectantly. Nobody answered. Encouraged, Wilson went on.

"In fiction anything to do with the illogical, the mysterious, or the macabre has to be stage-managed. The *misé-en-scene* is set about with darkness, storms, scudding clouds, and all the apparatus of the Victorian Gothic novella. Life isn't like that and fear often comes, as the Bible says, at noonday. And this is the most frightful type of fear of all."

I put down my newspaper and Fender followed suit. The half dozen or so of us in the room gathered about the big central mahogany dining-table, facing Wilson in his comfortable chair by the fire.

"I remember a particular instance which fitted no pattern imposed by logic," said Wilson, "and yet it was a perfect example of the terror by noonday. I had it at first-hand from an unimpeachable witness. It was simply that Gilles Sanroche, a middle-aged farmer, went stark-raving mad in the middle of a wheatfield, at noonday, in perfect August weather, on a hillside above Epoisses in Central France. It was not sunstroke, there was nothing in the field, and in fact the affair would have been an absolute mystery but for one thing.

The Cave

"The man was able to babble about 'something in the wheat' and there were three witnesses who came forward to say that they had seen great waves of wind following a fixed pattern in the corn surrounding the unfortunate man. And there was no wind at all on the day in question."

Wilson paused again to see that his words were taking effect. No one ventured an opinion, so he resumed his apparently disconnected musings.

"There's a mystery for you, if you like. And what drove Sanroche insane in broad daylight on a beautiful day in a French cornfield has never been discovered. But the local people spoke of 'the Devil snarling and prowling in the wind' up and down the valleys, and in fact a mediaeval inscription speaks to that effect in one of the local churches.

"There is a germ of truth in the superstitions of these country folk and they talked, in a picturesque phrase, of the 'fence of the priesthood being thin' in that part of France. I was much taken with this simile, I must say; it was as though the physical presence of the clergy were spread in a living chain through the mountains and valleys of the country, literally fencing out the Devil.

"Whether the Devil actually appeared to Gilles Sanroche I have no idea; he may have thought he did. But there is no doubt in my mind that fear took away his sanity that hot August afternoon. In one of his stories somewhere, de Maupassant strikingly illustrates the effect of fear on the human mind. He describes a night in a mountain hut—a night of appalling fear for the occupant—but dawn finds a logical explanation. The hideous face at the window was merely the narrator's dog and the remainder of the story was supplied by the atmosphere of the lonely hut and the man's own terror.

"I was greatly impressed with this story when I first read it as a young man," Wilson continued, "and I have often returned to it since, as it strikingly parallels an experience of my own—also in the mountains—which again, though unexplainable, communicated to me the most fearful sensations of my life. The difference in my case being that though I myself saw or experienced very little in the way of concrete happenings, the facts underlying the experience were very terrible indeed, as subsequent events made clear."

Darkness, Mist & Shadow

There was by now a deep and expectant silence in the room, broken only by the hardly discernible crackling of the fire. Fender hastily passed the whisky decanter to me, refilled his own glass, and we then gave our undivided attention to Wilson who sat, one hand supporting his head, gazing fixedly into the fire.

"I had gone on the second of a series of long walking tours in the Austrian Tyrol," he said. "All this was many years ago. I was then a young man of about twenty-nine years, I should say; strong, well built, untiring after eight hours' walking over rough country. Sound in wind and limb in every way and not at all imaginative or given to morbid fancies or anything of that kind.

"I enjoyed long holidays in those days and I expected to spend at least two months in the exhilarating atmosphere of those great mountains. I was in good spirits, in first-class condition after three weeks' hard tramping, and in addition I was in the early stages of love.

"I had met the girl who was later to become my wife in Innsbruck the first day of my holiday, and when our ways parted a week later, I had arranged to meet her again some weeks after. In the meantime I intended to explore some of the more remote valleys and photograph the carvings in a number of the older churches.

"I had spent the greater part of one day slogging my way up an immense shoulder of foothill, stumbling on scree and awkwardly threading up through dense forests of pine and fir. By late afternoon I became painfully aware that I had little idea of my whereabouts. The village I had been making for that morning should have been, according to my map, down the next valley but I could see nothing but the green tops of the pines marching to the horizon. It seemed obvious that I had passed the valley entrance in making my long circuit of the shoulder; I had little alternative than to press on farther up the hill or camp where I remained. I was ill-equipped for the latter; I had few provisions and not much more than a ground sheet and a couple of blankets strapped to my back.

"It did not take me long to make up my mind. There were quite a few more hours of daylight left and once I had quit the shadows of the forest and regained open country I should be walking in the sunshine. I decided to see what awaited me at the summit of the foothill; in the

The Cave

meantime I spent ten minutes resting, smoking, and admiring the view. I found half a packet of chocolate in my pocket and fortified by this went forward up the last half mile, if not with *élan*, at least with more cheerfulness.

"I was pleased to find with the thinning out of the trees at the top, that I had chanced on a small road which evidently led from one valley to another. It was little more than a cart track but nevertheless a heartening sign of civilization, and with the help of my map I was able to orientate myself. I soon saw where I had gone wrong and assumed, correctly, that the road I had found would take me over to the next village to the west of the one I had originally intended making for.

"I was glad to be out of the sombre gloom of the forest, and the upland road with its air of height and spaciousness, together with the sun which danced on the ground ahead of me, completely restored my spirits. I had walked for over an hour, and the road again began to descend into a valley, when I eventually saw the wooden spire of a tall church piercing the roof of the pines below me. A minute or two more and a sizeable community of thirty or forty houses spread itself out in the evening light.

"But as I descended to the village I caught sight of a large sign at the roadside: Gasthof. Set back from the road were heavy wooden gates, which were flung open. A drive corkscrewed its way upwards and a few paces round the corner I could see a large hotel of the chalet type, its pine construction gleaming cheerfully in the fading sunlight. The trim grass in front was kept in bounds by a blaze of flowers. The whole place had a magnificent view of the valley below and it was this, as much as the prospect of saving myself a walk, that decided me to put up here for the night.

"Though the accommodation would probably be expensive, it would be worth it for the view alone. Alas, for my hopes. A stout, Brunnhilde type of woman, her blonde hair scraped back in a large bun, who appeared in the hotel foyer in response to my repeated ringing at the outer door, shook her head. Nein, she said, the guesthouse was closed for the season.

"Here was a blow. Worse was to come. The woman, who I seemed to be some sort of caretaker, explained in bad English, prompted by my halting German, that the hotels in the village were closed also—it was the end of the season. I could try but she very much doubted if I would be successful. There were only two hotels and she herself knew that the proprietor of one had closed and taken himself and his family off for their own holiday in Switzerland.

"By this time the woman had been joined in front of the hotel by a brace of savage wolfhounds, who kept up menacing growls. I was glad I had not encountered them in the grounds and said as much to the woman, who gave me a wintry smile. What was I to do, I asked. She shrugged. My best hope was to try one or two houses where families took in occasional boarders. I could obtain advice from the police station.

"I thanked her and was already retracing my footsteps along the drive when she recalled me with a word. She apologized; she didn't know what she had been thinking of. If I didn't mind another short walk in the forest she was sure Herr Steiner could offer me accommodation. It would be of a simple sort... She shrugged again.

"She pointed out a path which twisted between the hotel flower beds and descended steeply through the inevitable pine trees. I gathered the place was half inn, half private residence, run by a middle-aged German couple. In the season it acted as a sort of over flow annexe to the hotel, as it was only a quarter of a mile away, though quite secluded. Herr Steiner had an arrangement with the hotel over sending him guests; there was a monetary aspect and he was no doubt pleased of the extra custom for his own remote establishment. The woman apologized once again; she came from another district and was deputizing for her sister, otherwise she would have remembered the guesthouse earlier. I thanked her once more. She told me then that the road I had found earlier looped just before it reached the village and met Herr Steiner's establishment. I could either take the path from the hotel grounds or go along the road.

"I made my farewell and decided to take the road. The dark path looked uninviting, the sun was sinking, and the thin tinkling of water from far distances lent a melancholy aspect to the evening. Besides, I had no wish to meet the wolfhounds in some lonely clearing, so I waved the woman good-bye.

The Cave

"In another five minutes I had descended the road, found the fork she spoke of, and then, a couple of hundred yards farther on, was rewarded by lights shining through the trees. It was now dusk and the noise of water was louder. I threaded a moss-grown path and saw a substantially built gasthof, of the traditional chalet pattern, with carved porch and vast, overhanging eaves.

"Herr Steiner and his wife Martha, the couple who owned the gasthof, were an amiable pair and made me welcome, late in the season though it was. The husband, a man of late middle age, tall, stoop-shouldered, with a drooping ginger moustache, was much given to sitting by the kitchen fire by the hour, reading all the news in the ill-printed local newspaper, holding up the sheet close to the eyes and studying the small print with the aid of a pocket magnifier.

"He seemed to go through every scrap of information it contained, including the small advertisements, and it was always with regret that he at last closed the lens with a snap, disappointed that there was nothing further to read. His wife was quite elderly, at least fifteen years older, I should have said, reserved and quiet. She flitted like a shadow in the background but nevertheless it was flitting to some purpose for her establishment was impeccably clean, the meals punctual and of excellent quality.

"I was only with the Steiners three days, but it did seem to me as though some trouble lurked at the back of Steiner's eyes, and once or twice I caught him, when he thought himself unobserved, in a curious posture, his newspaper dropped unnoticed to his knees, his head on one side, as though he were listening for someone or something.

"For in truth, though their establishment was within such a short distance of both the village and the more imposing establishment higher up the hill, it appeared both lonely and isolated, mainly due to the overhanging hillside which cut it off from the main hotel, and to the thickly overgrown woodland with which it was surrounded.

"This made the place seem damp and melancholy, and on my first evening, pushing open the shutters of my bedroom window, the impression given by the falling of water from somewhere below, in the silence of the night, affected my heart with a profound sadness. In all other matters, however, I saw nothing untoward. The Steiners were reasonably cheerful landlords, the terms moderate, the food of the best, as I have said, and all in all I counted myself fortunate to have such a headquarters while I continued on my walks and explorations of the neighbourhood.

"I had proposed staying for a week, but events conspired to make this impossible, as you will see. On my first morning at the Steiners I set out soon after breakfast to reconnoitre the neighbourhood. I decided to leave the village until later and concentrated on the thick shelf of woodland on which the lower guesthouse was built.

"This ran slanting across the mountainside and eventually came out onto a cliff-like plateau. Below was a superb panorama of the village and the forests beyond; above, more forest and the uplands on which the large hotel stood. It was a day of bright sunshine and it was with considerable contentment that I left the last of the trees behind and was able to walk freely on mossy undersoil, split here and there by outcrops of rock. I wandered in this way for an hour or more until I at length came out on a precipitous bluff and was rewarded by a magnificent view of the entire valley.

"It was as I was coming away, half drugged by the beauties of the scene, that my eye was arrested by a patch of bold colour in the landscape. This was unusual in this region of dark greens of pines and fir, and the russet hue irritated my mind, so that I turned aside my steps and went to see what it was. An unpleasant shock then, in that time and place, my thoughts quite unprepared for such a thing, to find that what had attracted my eye was the scarlet of blood.

"Great splashes and gouts were spread over the rocks and it was with considerable alarm that I followed a short trail. A few yards away, on the other side of a large boulder, lay the corpse of a young goat, evidently not long dead. I must say I looked about me with considerable unease, for I had at first thought the creature might have fallen from the rocks. I then plainly saw I had been mistaken and that the animal's throat had been torn out, and its breast viciously savaged.

"This was evidently the work of some large and dangerous animal, and I make no apology for stating that I broke off a heavy tree branch and armed in this fashion set back on my walk to the guesthouse. On the way I met a man, who from his dress seemed like a shepherd, and told him of my discovery. He went pale and swore at some length.

"'We have been troubled with this beast for some time,' he said, so far as I could make out from his heavy German accent. He told me too that even cattle had been dragged off from herds in the vicinity over the past few months. He thanked me and said he would warn the municipal authorities.

"I was glad to arrive back to find the usual peaceful atmosphere in the guesthouse. My lunch was just coming up to the table, Herr Steiner as usual, reading by a fire which simmered in the great kitchen range.

"There being no other guests in the hotel, I chose to have my meals in the great beamed kitchen with the Steiners, and they were cheerful company in the evenings. My landlord had quite a good command of English, so conversation was not the strain it might have been for me.

"I set to with eagerness, for the walk had sharpened my appetite. The main course over, I sipped my beer contentedly, and fell into conversation with Herr Steiner. But when I mentioned the matter of the dead goat it had an unlooked-for effect. Steiner turned quite white and sat with his mouth open, staring at me. I was rescued from this somewhat embarrassing moment by a loud crash in the background. Frau Steiner had gone to fetch the dessert and there was the bowl shattered on the floor of the kitchen.

"What with apologies, moppings up, and the preparation of a fresh dessert, the incident passed over. When we again returned to it at the end of the meal, Steiner remarked, with an obviously simulated ease, that there had been some ravages among livestock by a beast which local hunters had so far failed to kill. He had been taken aback, he said, by the fact that the goat may have been from their own herd, but this could not be so as they were completely enclosed in the meadow below the house.

"I accepted this explanation, not wanting to appear over-curious, but I remained convinced in my own mind that Steiner was lying. The old couple's alarm was too great for such an incident as they had suggested, but the matter was their concern, not mine, and there I was prepared to leave it. But the business continued to fret my mind and after lunch, somewhat ashamed of my over precipitate retreat from the area where I had found the goat, I set out to explore once again. On the way through the outbuildings surrounding the Steiners' establishment, I caught sight of the block where the old man had been chopping up firewood, and, almost without thinking, seized the small hand axe which stood on the block, and thrust it into my belt.

"It would make a useful weapon if need be and it boosted my morale no end. I eventually found my way back to the scene of my unnerving experience; the patch of blood was still there, dried and black in the sun, but the goat had disappeared, removed no doubt by the foresters. Or had the beast which killed it, disturbed by my appearance, hidden and retrieved its prey after I had returned to the inn? That was an even more disturbing thought and it was with a valour that surprised myself, that I took out my axe and started a circular search to see if the dead beast had been dragged off.

"I was not at first successful. The bleeding had stopped and there was only an occasional splash. But then I was rewarded by a wavering line in the dust, apparently made by the goat's hind legs. It had been dragged back in the direction it had already traversed in its dying struggles. I felt a slight tickling of the hair at the base of my neck when I saw these faint scratch marks, and I must confess I looked round me sharply in every direction and tightened my grip on the axe.

"Though I am no expert tracker, the marks seemed to prove that the beast concerned could not be a very big one, as it would otherwise have carried the goat clear of the ground. My experiences in India proved my point, for I have seen a tiger carry a full-grown bullock clear of the ground, its enormous strength capable of tremendous leverage, once its jaws were firmly fixed in the centre of the bullock's back.

"But nothing stirred in all the wide expanse of foothill, apart from the soft movement of the branches of the trees, and the sun continued to pour down onto a beneficent world. The scratching on the earth gradually ceased and eventually, when thick grass was reached, the trail petered out. But I had already noted the general direction in which the goat was being dragged and I continued to

The Cave

push on towards a region of cliffs and rocky outcrops in the distance as I felt the end of my search might well lie there.

"I had by now gone about two miles and when I eventually reached my destination the sun had sunk a considerable distance in the sky, though not enough to give me any anxiety, as there were several hours of daylight left. I felt I could remain on this spot about an hour and a half, for under the circumstances and not knowing with what type of beast I might be dealing, I judged it prudent to gain the inn over the long forest road while daylight lasted.

"And yet the end of my journey was almost an anticlimax. There was no sign of a trail, which had long disappeared, neither could I see any trace of the goat, as I studied the terrain from the pinnacle of a rocky hillock. I walked a little closer to the frowning cliffs facing me and after a while found myself in a small gorge. I gripped the axe tightly as I rounded the last corner and discovered it was a cul-de-sac. There was no trace of anything having passed, which was not surprising, as the valley floor was almost entirely composed of solid rock.

"I was about to retrace my steps when I spotted the dark entrance of a cave, half seen beyond the lip of a mountainous pile of boulders and rubble. As I approached I saw that it was of vast size. The gloomy entrance went up perhaps forty feet into the solid cliff above, which ended in an overhang. In front of the cave was a belt of sand and I stood for a moment, shading my eyes, attempting to penetrate the deep shadow beyond. I could see nothing from where I stood.

"I hesitated a moment longer. There was no sound anywhere; not even a bird's cry broke the stillness, and the paternal sun shone blandly down, gilding everything in a limpid golden light. I grasped the axe again and then went forward in a rush, rather more hysterically than I had intended. This brought me almost to the cave entrance; the shadow lay not more than six feet away and with this proximity came a layer of dank air.

"It was a strange feeling, almost like stepping into a bath of cold water. The sun warmed my back but on my face and all the front of my body fell the dampness and mouldiness of decay. My last steps had also taken me to one side and I could now see the carcase of the goat lying half-in, half-out of the shadow. The head had been eaten, but the rest of the body was intact. I saw something else too; scattered in the gloom of the cave mouth were a few bones of small animals, morsels of flesh. I recognized a thigh bone of something and farther back a rib cage.

"Still militant, I went forward again and then my axe fell to my side. Once within the shadow, the clamminess and coldness completely enveloped me. I saw nothing more, nothing moved, but I sensed, rather than saw, that the cave went back to vast depths into the earth. And I knew then that I could not, to save my life, venture into it and retain my sanity. With this knowledge came relief. I was able to take four paces backwards—I dare not turn my back on the place—and once again stood in the freshness of the sunshine.

"It was then that I heard the faintest scratching noise from the interior of the cave and I realized with a certainty that something was watching me. My nerve almost snapped, but if I gave way to panic, it would be fatal. I had the strength and fortitude to retain my hold on the axe, my one frail defence against the terror that was threatening to master me, and step by step, walking backwards I progressed from that sinister place into sanity.

"I had got almost to the area where the grass met the first rocky outcrops some hundreds of yards away, and a ludicrous sight I must have been to any observer, when there came the final incident which broke my nerve. It was nothing by itself, but it seemed to paralyze my will and send a scalding thrill of terror down into my entrails.

"From somewhere within the area of the cave came a low, dry, rasping cough—it wasn't repeated and there was nothing exceptional about it—but the terrible thing to me was, that it was like the furtive, half-stifled throat clearance of a human being. Something went then; I could not face that sound again and I whirled on my toes and flailing with the axe before me I ran for my life, with stark fear at my heels, until the blood drumming in my head and the wild thumping of my heart at last forced me to collapse onto a rock half a mile from the area I had just quitted.

"The sun was by now a good way down the sky. Nothing had followed me, but I still had a longish walk through the forest, so after a

THE CAVE

short breather I set out again, albeit more sedately, until I at last came to the inn and the safety of my own room.

"I was late down to supper that evening. I had debated long with myself over the wisdom of revealing what I had discovered to the Steiners. Their reactions of the morning had been so extreme that I feared what might be the outcome. In the event I waited until Frau Steiner had retired, then I tackled her husband. He sat smoking his pipe in the kitchen as usual, politely waiting until I had finished my after-dinner brandy, so that he could clear away.

"Though his face turned an ashen colour, he was surprisingly calm and we discussed for some time the implications of my discovery. He told me that he would let the civil authorities know the following morning; no doubt they would arrange for a shoot to take place if the depredations among goats and cattle continued. I had naturally made nothing of the more sombre side of the matter. I merely told him I had found the cave and that it did seem to me that it might be the lair of the beast responsible for cattle killing.

"But there still remained the problem of Herr Steiner's manner. Both he and his wife had given me the impression that they were well aware of the strange and sinister creature that was taking such a toll of the livestock; that they were secretly afraid and they themselves had no intention of initiating any action against it. It may have been, I felt, turning it over in my mind yet again in my bedroom later that evening, that they had a similar experience to myself. Remembering the incident of the cave and the whole atmosphere of these dark and stifling woods, I could not say that I particularly blamed them.

"Anyway, it was no business of mine; I was merely a passing stranger and expected to be on my way shortly. Though I was extremely comfortable at their inn, I had had my fill of walking recently and was inclined to linger. It was pleasant to know, as one trudged back in the twilight of these great woods, that a pleasant meal was awaiting one, with friendly faces and a good bed assured. Fortified by these and similar thoughts I soon slept.

"Next morning I decided to take a stroll down into Grafstein; it was similar to a thousand other small villages of its type scattered about Central Europe—a huddle of timbered homes, a small central platz, the whole thing pivoting on the large, splendidly carved fourteenth-century church, the town hall, the two hotels, and an arcade or two of shops, some unfortunately modernized to take advantage of the tourist trade.

"While I was in the village I enjoyed a really excellent coffee and pastries at the only coffee shop and then called in at the small police station. Here I reported the matter of the goat and the cave to the local sergeant. He thanked me for my cooperation, and I showed him the location on his large-scale map, but I did not gather from his manner that the matter was regarded as of any great importance, or that anything would be done about it in the immediate future. This sort of thing was a commonplace in the forests thereabouts, he told me.

"I looked in at the church before going back to my own guesthouse for lunch. I had brought my camera and busied myself by taking some close-ups of the really magnificent carvings; the pastor was away, I was told, but I had readily obtained permission from his housekeeper, for the small intrusion my photo-making would incur. The skill of these old carvers, most of them anonymous, was really incredible, and once more I was thrilled and uplifted by the beauty and elaboration of their work.

"I finished the spool in my camera with half a dozen shots of the finely carved details of the front row pews, immediately facing the altar. They represented, so far as I could make out, scenes from the Book of Job, but one of them gave me something of a shock. It was a most unpleasant carving, of most exquisite workmanship, but the result was malevolent and forbidding in the extreme. I expect you all remember the gargoyles on Notre Dame and the way these old stone-masons had given vent to their expression of the powers of darkness that surrounded them.

"Well, this was something of the same kind, but intensified for me a hundredfold. It may have been the darkness and quiet of the old church, but I found my hands trembling as I went to set up my camera for a time exposure. The carving represented some disgusting creature with a misshapen head; incredibly emaciated, it stood erect, most of its body mercifully hidden in what I took to be reeds or grasses.

✣ The Cave

"Its long neck was disfigured by large nodules of immense size, the teeth were curved and sharp, like a boar, the eyes like a serpent. In its two, claw-like hands it held the body of a human being. It had just bitten off the head, much as one would eat a stick of celery, and the carver had cleverly managed to suggest that the creature was in the process of spitting out the head before making a start on the meal proper.

"I cannot tell you what nausea this loathsome creature inspired in me; it seemed almost to move in its frame of dark wood, so brilliantly had the carver, an artist of some genius, depicted his subject. In the flat terms which I have just used, it is impossible to convey my impressions of that moment. But loathsome or not, I knew that I had to have the carving on film and that when I returned to England I should want to find out more about it.

"So I hastily completed my preparations for the picture, pressed the catch, and waited for the clicking of the time-exposure mechanism to cease before dismantling my tripod and equipment. As the mechanism died and the exposure was made, there was a loud noise somewhere at the back of the church. This startled me for some reason, but I thought that perhaps the verger, or whatever his German equivalent might be, had come in to see that all was well.

"However, the interruption caused me considerable unease and I hastily packed up my gear and made my way back up the aisle of the church and into the open air. To my surprise, there appeared to be nobody else in the building, neither could I see any reason for the noise. Nothing appeared to have fallen down in the church; but I was late for lunch and hurried out of Grafstein and back to my hotel.

"During the afternoon I wrote some letters and apart from a short excursion down to the village to post them in the early evening, did nothing else of note that day. I lay down in my room for an hour or two before supper; when I got up again it was quite dark and I felt I had overslept. But a glance at the luminous dial of my wristwatch was enough to reassure me that the time was only half-past eight. We did not eat usually until nine or half-past, so I had plenty of time.

"I had not switched on the light and I stood at the window for a moment, looking down into the valley. It was a beautiful moonlit night and the pine forests spread out below me, with the spire of the church sticking up far beneath, looked like an old cut by Dürer.

"I was about to turn away when I heard the big sheepdog of the Steiners start barking down at the side of the hotel; I opened the window and looked out, but could see nothing. The dog was still growling, and then I heard the faintest crackling rustle in the undergrowth surrounding the hotel. The dog did not follow the noise but suddenly began to make a high, howling whine and then I heard Steiner come out with curses and cuff the dog, shouting to it to go back indoors.

"The noise continued for a few moments, farther away now, a faint abrasive, sinister rustling like someone or something making its way with definite aim and purpose. It slowly passed away over the ridge and the night was silent again. Considerably troubled about this, though I could not really say why, I eventually made my way down to supper.

"The meal, as usual, was excellent, and sitting in the warm, high-beamed kitchen with the firelight dancing on gleaming brass and pewter, I once again counted myself fortunate in my accommodation and we passed a jolly evening. Tonight, for some reason or other, I had spread out on another part of the huge central table my route maps, notes, and other material for my research, and after supper it was my wish to continue work on this.

"It was now about half-past ten and I busied myself in clearing up the material, preparatory to taking it up to my room. Frau Steiner had gone to bed, but my host, who as usual remained with me to smoke and read his paper, would have none of this.

"Work there," he said jovially, motioning me to leave my things where they were. I protested that my notes and route-preparations might take me until midnight. He merely said that he was going to bed anyway and that if I would see that I switched off the lights before I came up, I could stay there as long as I liked.

"This suited me nicely. The autumn nights were chilly and the warm atmosphere of the kitchen was preferable to that of my own room; apart from this, Herr Steiner pushed a plate of cakes and sandwiches, together with half a bottle of beer towards me, giving me a

THE CAVE

broad wink as he left. Thus it was that I came to be working in the kitchen of the Gasthof on that night, the only person on the ground floor.

"The dog was locked up somewhere in the outbuildings at the rear and to all intents I was alone in the world. One curious feature of the establishment was the fact that the kitchen door was never locked, winter or summer, as long as the Steiners were in residence. The main entrance and a door on the other side of the guesthouse were scrupulously locked every night, but for some reason, the kitchen door was excluded from this.

"It was true, it faced the main road and the village rather more conveniently than did the hotel entrance proper, though I could not quite see the point of this. The real explanation that offered itself to me was that the only means of securing the kitchen door was by a massive baulk of timber which fitted into two metal clips set either side of the door frame. Possibly because of the trouble involved in lifting this into place every night and removing it each morning, the Steiners had let the custom lapse. And for some other reason they had omitted to have the door fitted with an ordinary lock.

"Anyway, there I was, working away quietly, enjoying the warmth of the fire and the simple excellence of the food and the beer. I completed my notes and had got well on with the details of my route for the next part of my holiday. By this time it was approaching midnight and I had begun to feel a certain tiredness coming on.

"I stretched myself and went to poke up the kitchen range fire into a blaze again, when I became aware of a faint noise. I listened intently. The sound did not emanate from inside the inn but from the outside. It was too subtle to make out at first. It was not the tinkle of running water nor the footsteps of a passing villager. I looked at my watch again and realized it was far too late in any case for these simple folk, who sought their beds early, to be about.

"Walking on tip-toe, so that I could still hear perfectly—though why I did this was somewhat obscure to me—I crossed the kitchen and stood near the window. The noise came again, a moment or two later, unpleasantly like the rustling I had heard in the wood earlier, when looking from the upstairs window.

"I do not know if you can picture my situation, and it is a difficult scene to recapture, sitting as we are in the middle of London this evening. The rustling, or scratching, call it what you will, was agonizingly slow and deliberate, and it came to my mind that it would be similar to that made by a badly crippled person walking with the aid of two sticks. There was a moment of silence, followed shortly by the scratching noise, like two sticks being dragged painfully across the ground. At that moment, the dog gave an agonizing howl from the back of the hotel somewhere.

"That just about finished me, I can tell you, tensed up as I was. Far from being a reassurance, it meant that the dog knew there was something foul and unnatural outside which wanted to get in. As this thought came to me, I looked wildly at the door, with the obvious intention of locking it. I am not normally a nervous or timid sort of man, but something had got hold of me that evening and I was not my usual self.

"The baulk of timber was obviously too big and heavy to manoeuvre into place without a lot of noise, and besides, something kept me rooted to the spot, so that I seemed incapable of action.

"The electric light still burned on, comfortingly modern, etching everything in bright relief. I had stood to one side of the window, so that my shadow could not be seen, but I felt that whoever—whatever—was outside, very well knew who was there. And I would not, for any money you can name, have turned out the light, for reasons too obvious to go into.

"As the scratching noise was repeated, and, as it seemed to my hypersensitive nerves, even nearer, I looked around again for a weapon of some sort, but without success. There was a long moment of silence and then, from outside the house, came the foul, low sort of snuffling cough I had heard in the cave. The dog gave another whine that set my jagged nerves aflame and there was a creak as the big old wooden latch of the door commenced to lift.

"I was galvanized into action then. I did not know what might be outside but I only knew that I should become insane if I met it face to face. I threw myself at the door and put all my weight on the latch, forcing it downwards. The pressure was not resisted, but a moment or two later I found it rising, with irresistible force. For a horrifying second or so the door actually opened an inch, perhaps two, then with the strength of fear I hurled it closed and clung to the latch with all the weight of my body.

"Once more I felt it being raised, despite all I could do to stop it. But now I had got my feet jammed against a brick in the irregular stone floor and I exerted all my strength to prevent what was outside from coming in. I was still terribly afraid but something of that first appalling fear, which saps all will power from the brain, had left me, and as I was forced fractionally back, I cast looks about me for aid.

"Then I saw the beam lying in the angle of the wall, not more than four feet from me. I crashed the door back into its framework, and jamming my foot against the bottom, I seized the huge piece of wood and with the strength of terror man-handled it towards me. My foot slipped on the floor as the door pressed in on me, and the end of the beam, rasping across the kitchen wall, upset a large brass warming pan which fell down to the stone floor with a tremendous crash. I think this is what saved the situation, for hitherto this insidious struggle in which I had been engaged, had been fought implacably, in silence.

"The door gaped wide for a moment, but then the dog, aroused by the crash commenced barking angrily; and at the same instant Herr Steiner, woken by the noise, shouted down the stairs. Light sprang on in the upper-storey, and as the pressure on the door melted away I fell against it and slammed the beam home in the metal stanchions with almost hysterical strength. Then I fell onto the kitchen floor, all the purpose gone from my legs.

"I will not weary you with the scene that followed; the amazed and terrified appearance of the Steiners; the temporary insanity of the dog; the pouring of brandy down my throat; my disconnected story to the innkeeper and his wife. Needless to say none of us slept for the remainder of the night; we piled the heaviest furniture we could find against all three doors—even this took considerable resolve under the circumstances—and it was as much as I could do to carry out my part of the undertaking.

"Never have I felt such fear as I encountered that night; it turned my limbs to water, sapped all my will power; it took all the strength of character I possessed to double-rivet my soul back into my body, if you can understand such a term. After I had recovered myself a little—a false recovery, as it turned out, engendered largely by the brandy—Steiner and I secured all the doors and windows, as I have said. Then we retired to the top-most room of the house, leaving every light in the building burning. Steiner had the excellent idea of scattering the staircase with copper pans and utensils, so that we should have prior warning of anything moving towards us up the stairs.

"He then took three enormous sporting rifles—one more like a blunderbuss—with him, and we all three locked ourselves in the bedroom with the stoutest door. We had more than four hours to wait until dawn—it was by now about half-past one—but since the commotion in the kitchen when I fell to the ground there had mercifully been no further sound from out of doors.

"We passed a wretched time, talking in half-whispers and starting at the slightest sound outside—from the night wind to the faint tapping of a branch upon a topmost windowpane. After my explanation, we did not refer directly to the situation, but approached it by oblique routes, and I was more than ever convinced that the Steiners knew more than they were willing to tell.

"Once I heard his wife mumble, 'But they have never come this far before,' and then her husband clamped his hand over her arm and she lapsed into silence. For my part, I was alone with the terrible truth of the situation; for which among God's creatures has the wit and intelligence to lift a door latch in the manner of a human being? An ape or monkey perhaps? Perhaps. But ridiculous to think of such a thing in these forests.

"Another type of animal such as a deer might lift a door latch by accident, when its horn caught underneath, but the thing which had been on the other side of the door had lifted the catch easily, much as a human being would; and there had been a terrible force and purpose in the pressure which had accompanied that silent and sinister incursion into my reason. And I had been convinced from the beginning that no human being was responsible.

The Cave

"I gave it up at last and slept brokenly, sitting in a corner of the room, my back against the wall, my head on my upraised knees, clutching one of Steiner's antiquated rifles. Dawn came at about six o'clock, and though I was not awake to see it, when I did become aware of it I have never been so thankful, not even during the war years. The sounds of everyday came up to us with increasing clarity; the chant of a rooster, the grunting of pigs, the little, fussy noises of hens, and then, eventually, the reawakened bark of the old sheepdog, his fears of the night dispersed.

"But it was not until past seven o'clock, that we dared stir downstairs. We first opened windows on every side of the house but could see nothing alarming. Then a creaking farm cart passed, with a man riding on top and another walking by the shafts, and this shamed us so much, particularly as the Steiners were usually abroad looking after their livestock before six, that we all three went downstairs at once, albeit we were talking and making rather too much noise.

"The lights still burned, the copper pans were undisturbed; all was as it had been, even down to the unquestioned fact of the warming pan which I had knocked down in my superhuman efforts to get the door barred. While the Steiners set the kitchen to rights and prepared the breakfast, I mustered my courage to unbar the door and set foot outside. I must say that I waited until I heard the approach of another cart, and then with a sort of tottering bravado hefted the massive beam to the ground and stepped out into the sunlight.

"My nightmare of the evening before might never have been. I breathed in the fresh morning air, said good-day to the two fine fellows on the cart, and then received my second shock of the last twelve hours. There had been no fantasy in the strength which had resisted mine an inch-door panel away from me, and neither was there in the curious prints of the thing which had stood without the door. I stumbled and almost fell.

"Picture if you can, the prints which met my eye that autumn morning in the foothills of those Alps. I am certain that little similar has been seen since the dawn of time. There was nothing more than two holes which stood before the door. The impressions, which were quite small, were about six inches apart. They looked more like the imprints of the ferrules of a walking stick, except that they were both slightly elongated and oval in shape. I stared at these two slots in the ground until I thought I should go mad.

"No God-created beast could have made such imprints, and as I fell back from the door I saw that there were further sets; advancing to and retreating from the inn back along the forest path I had taken on my walks to the area of the cave. Faint scratch marks linked the sets of prints."

There was a long silence in the room, as Wilson broke off his narrative and sat looking into the depths of the fire.

"The prints of a deer, perhaps?" Fender eventually suggested nervously, as Wilson showed no sign of resuming his story.

He shook his head impatiently. "Impossible. I know the slots of a deer, man, as well as I know my own face in the glass. I said the prints were complete sets of two; in other words the thing, or whatever it was, was standing on its hind legs—or its only legs for all I know—while attempting to open the door.

"I followed the tracks back for a short way—a very short way, for they gradually faded out. And then perhaps I did a rather foolish thing, in the light of what happened afterwards. For in a fit of angry panic I went down the path and deliberately erased the last trace of those devilish tracks with my heavy walking boots.

"However, I felt I owed a very real duty to the Steiners and I spent most of the morning trying to dissuade them from stopping at the inn; I even tried to give them hints about the tracks I had seen, but the words wouldn't come properly. Naturally, the old couple wouldn't dream of giving up their home of a lifetime to move away at their age.

"'But, Herr Wilson,' said the old man, 'be reasonable. It is our living.' He had quite a point there, but it didn't dissuade me from asking them to go, for I was mortally afraid for the couple. They had been extraordinarily kind to me in the short time I had known them. But I saw it was no use in the end, though I did suggest that they buy a couple of wolfhounds like those at the hotel above and—before all—have a good set of bolts fitted to the kitchen door.

"Steiner almost gave himself away at the last for he looked at me

✐ The Cave

almost as though he would burst into tears, and said, 'Bolts are no good, in the end, against such things.' Then he saw the look on his wife's face and became silent; it was his last word on the topic and he never referred to it again. Naturally, I had no desire to remain any longer at the Gasthof where I had passed such a night; I had packed in the morning. The Steiners quite understood, but it was with a heavy heart that I said good-bye to them in the early afternoon, shouldered my rucksack, and set off through the forest once again.

"I made one last attempt before I left and said, 'At least see that the village mounts a hunt and cleans out that cave.' He looked at me in a sorrowful manner and waved good-bye. His last words to me were, 'Thank you, mein Herr. We know you are only trying to be helpful.' I had rerouted my trail, to pass at least eight miles to the west of the cave, so I set off down into the village and resumed my walking tour, the remainder of which was uneventful—insofar as it touches the core of this story, that is."

Wilson paused again and silently drained his glass. "You need not worry that I shall leave the story unfinished," he said. "There is a sequel and a terrible one, though by rights I should have left the thing where it was. But all the rest of my holiday I kept thinking about the old couple, the loneliness of the guesthouse, that cursed cave and the nature of the events which had given me such a dreadful night.

"I made the mistake of going back and thereby added guilt to my remembered fear. I made a slight detour on my way home to England and stopped off for a day on the way through. I was accompanied by three other people who don't concern the story, though one, as I have indicated already, was to concern me for the remainder of my life. I left them at the cafe and walked up the well-remembered hill to the hotel. On the way I met the sergeant of police and a lot of activity; cars and so forth coming down.

"I asked him what was the matter and he said, quite quietly and simply, that the old couple had been murdered; in the most brutal and sadistic fashion imaginable. They had been literally torn to pieces after barricading themselves in a bedroom, and—most foul detail of all—had been decapitated; the heads were never found. I thought of the carving in the church and felt sick.

◈ Darkness, Mist & Shadow

This terrible event had happened only two days before; the forests had been combed, but to no avail. We had by this time walked back down to the small police station, for I now had no wish to continue up the hill. I thought of the events of three weeks earlier and began in my mind the first of a hundred thousand regrets.

"And yet I was angry with the police, and the Steiners too, if I analyzed my own feelings; I asked the sergeant, rather roughly in the circumstances, whether he had taken my advice about the cave. Had they, in fact, organized a shooting party to kill the beast that I supposed lurked within it? The beast that might, in fact, be responsible for the Steiners' death?

"He looked at me stammering, his face quite pale. Nothing had been done, of course; the matter had been entirely overlooked—the village and the police particularly, had the murders to think of. But with typical German efficiency he immediately set about organizing a hunting party and two hours later a heavily armed posse of about forty expert shots streamed out of the village.

"I should have gone with them, but somehow I could not face it; the death of the Steiners had quite knocked me out; but we—that is, myself and my three friends—were put up for the night by one of the village families. The party, who, of course, knew the cave area well, returned long before nightfall. The sergeant, when I saw him again, was curiously reticent. It was, he said, a bad place.

"The men had not ventured far beyond the entrance; the labyrinth stretched for miles, they had been told; they were fetching dynamite in the morning, and an Army expert over from the garrison town, to block the entrance. He looked at me apologetically, as though I were about to accuse him and his colleagues of cowardice. But I could not say I blamed him. Had I not done exactly the same? And that is what they did. Brought down the entire mountainside and bottled in the thing or whatever it was; I kept in touch by letter and so far as I can learn the countryside has remained untroubled."

Wilson broke off once more to recharge his glass. "Which brings the wheel full circle," he said. "The problem of fear. Fear such as I have never experienced in my life, and which I could not possibly face again. To this day I could not tell you why. Yet I saw nothing,

✒ The Cave

unless you count two slots in the ground. And I felt little, except that tremendous pressure on a door; I heard little, except a muffled cough and some faint scratchings in the night. Little enough for a student of the macabre. Yet something devilish killed the Steiners."

"And you know nothing beyond that?" queried someone else, who sat in shadow beyond me.

"Only theories," said Wilson, lifting his head in the brindled firelight. "I developed my rolls of film when I got back home. All were perfect except one, inside the church, which was a complete blank, with never a trace of a picture. And I am sure you will know the picture I mean. But if my theory is correct it would explain their attitude."

There was a long silence again.

Then, "Pass the brandy, Fender," I said, rather more sharply than I had intended.

The Grey House

1

To Angele, standing in the sunlight of a late summer afternoon, The Grey House, as they came to call it, had an air of chill desolation that was at variance with the brightness and warmth of the day. It was uninhabited and had evidently been so for many years. But Philip was delighted with the place; he clapped his hands like a child of five and then strolled around, his arms folded, lost in silent admiration. He needs and must have it and wouldn't rest until he had rooted out the local agent and made an offer for the house.

Philip, her husband, was a writer; apart from a series of successful detective stories which brought him the larger part of his income, he was the author of a number of striking tales of mystery and the macabre. The Grey House would give him inspiration, he chuckled: Angele, stifling her doubts, didn't like to dampen her husband's enthusiasm and trailed round behind him and the estate agent with growing dislike.

They had spotted the place after a long day's drive in the older parts of Burgundy. Then in early afternoon, they had stopped for a late lunch in the small mediaeval city which nestled among the blue haze of the surrounding mountains. The view was enchanting and after lunch they spent a pleasant hour on the ramparts, tracing out the path of a small river which wound its way foaming between great boulders and woods of dark pines.

The Grey House

It was Philip who first sighted The Grey House. It was down a narrow lane and the path to it was long choked with nettles. It was the last house, separated from its neighbours by several hundreds of yards of rough cartway and trees, overgrown shrubbery and bushes. It was unquestionably a ruin. The place looked something like a barn or stable.

It was largely constructed of great blocks of grey stone, which decided them on its name, with one round-capped turret hanging at an insane angle over the big front door, large as a church. There was a round tower at one side, immensely old and covered in lichen. The roof, of red crab tiles, sagged ominously and would obviously need a lot of repairs.

The big old wooden door was locked but Philip led the way with enthusiasm, cutting a swathe through breast-high nettles for his wife. They followed the great frowning wall down the lane until the property obviously came to an end. The rest of the lane was an impenetrable mass of brambles. But Philip had seen enough. Through the trees below the bluff he could see the rusted iron railings of a balcony and there were even some outbuildings and what looked like an old water mill.

"We could get this place for a song," he told his wife gleefully. "It would want a lot of doing up of course, but the terrace would be ideal for my writing and what a view!"

Against such enthusism Angele could find no valid argument; so half an hour later found them back in the city square, at the office of M. Gasion, the principal of the main firm of estate agents in the area.

M. Gasion, a short broad-shouldered man of cheerful aspect and obviously addicted to the grape was shattered at the prospect of such a sale. The property had been on his books for more than forty years, over twenty years before he acquired the firm. Therefore, he was a little hazy about the antecedents of the estate. Yes, it would need a lot of doing up, he agreed; he did not think monsieur need worry about the price.

It would not be heavy and as they would see, though it needed a great deal of renovation, it had possibilities, distinct possibilities. He positively purred with enthusiasm and Angele could not help smiling to herself. A purchaser like Philip would hardly happen more than once in a life-time; no wonder M. Gasion was pleased.

It was absurdly cheap, she had to agree. The asking price was £300, which included the main building and tower, the terrace, outbuildings and mill house, together with a short strip of orchard below the bluff on which the terrace was set. Nothing would do but that Philip must conclude the deal then and there. This called for a great deal of bustle and the notaire was sent for, while Angele, Philip and the agent went on a tour of the building. There was further delay while the key was hunted up but at last the small procession set off.

The big door gave back with a creak after M. Gasion's repeated applications and the first ray of sunshine for something like forty years found difficulty in penetrating the interior. The unusual activity round the old building had not passed notice among the local people who lived higher up the lane and Angele had seen the curious glances they cast towards her, though Philip, as usual, was too absorbed in talk with the agent to notice anything.

Angele glanced over her shoulder as they went in the main door and was not surprised to see a small knot of gawping householders standing at the last bend in the lane in front of the house. Surprisingly, the house was wired for electricity but the main switchboard inside the door, fixed by great bolts directly into the ancient stone, was bare except for fragments of rusted wire and fittings covered with verdigris. The electricity had been cut off in the twenties, when the last tenants left, explained M. Gasion.

He carried a powerful electric lantern, despite the brightness of the afternoon. The house had formerly belonged to the de Menevals, the great landed proprietors who had now died out. They had owned a chateau which formerly stood in a vast park on the mountain opposite. The building had burned down in a great fire and explosion over a hundred years earlier and now only the stones remained. The last de Meneval, Gaston, had died a violent death, said M. Gasion with relish. He was apparently a great one for the ladies and had kept The Grey House for entertaining his girl friends.

"Une maison d'assignation," he explained to Philip with a smile, man to man. Philip returned the smile with a grin and the trio went

The Grey House

into the house. Angele could not repress a shudder at the interior and wondered what deeds the old house had seen. She and Philip had visited the ruins of the old chateau earlier the same afternoon; it was one of the sights of the district. The park was now kept as a public pleasance, and the guide had told the stories of blood and violence with distinct enthusiasm.

But one did not need even that to picture dark scenes of lust centuries before, as they gazed at the ruined and distorted remains of the house, which even now bore traces of charring on ancient beams and on the undersides of blackened stones. She was disquieted to hear that The Grey House had belonged to the de Menevals too, and her own French ancestry—her mother had come from these very parts—with its heightened sensibilities, rang a little bell somewhere back in her brain.

When the door swung open even the agent was not prepared for the long undisturbed foetor which met them; it was so strong that it seemed almost to darken the sunlight and they were forced to open the main door and remain outside for a few minutes before they could enter.

"Faugh!" said M. Gasion, with unrestrained disgust but even this did not seem to dampen Philip's ardour.

"Loads of atmosphere, eh?" he said, turning to Angele with a smile. After a minute they descended some broad stone steps. The smell was still strong but not so offensive and Angele had to admit that it was probably due to vegetable decay. To her surprise, the light of the agent's torch, supplemented by small windows high up, disclosed a vast stone hall. There was a fireplace to one side in which an ox could have been roasted and the remains of an old gallery which had collapsed with age and woodworm.

But the floor was covered with an indescribable medley of old rubbish. It was impossible to do more than look hurriedly around and be careful where one trod. Many of the massive roof beams would need replacing and Philip's face became more thoughtful as the tour continued. The house would evidently need a great deal more renovation than he had bargained for. However, he brightened as they went through into the other rooms. The stones of the house were sound and would merely need replastering and painting. There were two more large reception rooms, though nothing on the scale of the old hall, which was partly subterranean; another room was used as a kitchen.

On the top floor, under vast, sagging roof beams, through which the sky could be seen, was another huge room over the Great Hall below. This could be partitioned and would make a corridor with bathroom, and three large bedrooms, said Philip. Or he could make a study and leave one spare bedroom for guests. The open mass of the tower spread out from one end room of this large upper storey and Philip could find no place for that at the moment, in his ready-made scheme of things.

They had saved the best for last; off the kitchen, whose door was finally forced with screaming protest, they came upon the glory of The Grey House. It was nothing more or less than a large tiled terrace, but it gave the place a cachet that finally clinched the deal in Philip's mind, weighing the cost, as he was, against the utility and suitability of the house for his writing purposes.

The rusty iron railings which enclosed the terrace, had evidently been of great elegance, and would no doubt be so again; Philip was already confiding to M. Gasion that he would have them painted pale blue. He could have his writing table *comme ça* and they could eat dinner under electric light at night *sur le balcon*. Even the agent was momentarily impressed by his enthusiasm.

For the view was magnificent; that could not be gainsaid. Below the balcony, the terrain dropped sheer for forty feet or so over a stone outcrop, to the small strip of orchard which was part of the purchase. A thick belt of leafy trees blotted out the immediate view, but above them were wooded hills and valleys, with the stream trickling between until the eye was arrested by the mountain opposite surmounted by the ruins of the old chateau. Angele was surprised to see how the white of the stones stood out against the dark blue haze, even at that distance. Just below and to the left was the small stone building of the old water mill, through which the stream meandered beyond the orchard.

When they tore themselves away from the unearthly beauties of

⚜ THE GREY HOUSE

that sylvan view, dusk was already falling and the tinkle of the water in the mill house had assumed a melancholy that it had lacked in the sunlight of the earlier afternoon. A thin mist was already rising above the belt of dark trees which abutted the orchard. Angele pointed this out to Philip as perhaps being undesirable, unhealthy.

"Oh, no," said Philip with a short laugh. "Bound to get a mist with water at this time of the year, especially after the heat of the day. We're too high up for it to affect us in any case." But nevertheless, even as he spoke, the mist, white and clammy, almost like thick smoke, drifted up over the trees and already the farthest trees were wavering in its tendrils.

No more was said; the party went back indoors, led by M. Gasion's enormous torch and once outside, the door was firmly locked and secured by double padlocks. The trio were silent on the way back to the town and, after a little reflection, M. Gasion spoke to Angele. Philip had gone to get something from the car and they were alone for a moment in the office.

"You do not like the house, madame?"

Angele was non-committal. She did not want to spoil Philip's evident delight in the property, but at the same time she had many reservations of her own about the dark, silent grey pile above the water mill, which sounded so eerily in the dusk. Instead, she stammered some words about the property being so derelict and the enormous expense she was afraid her husband would be put to.

The agent's face cleared as though it had been sponged. If that was all that was worrying madame, he was prepared to lower the price.

Quite frankly, he had been rather taken aback by the degree of decay; he would be quite happy to take the equivalent of £250 to effect a quick sale. Philip had just returned from the car at this moment and was delighted with the news; so Angele had unwittingly been the means of sealing the bargain.

The notaire also, a lean, vulpine man named Morceau, had just arrived, cross at being disturbed at his favourite cafe. Introductions were made, M. Gasion produced a bottle and some glasses and over much agreeable smacking of lips and handing round of delectable little biscuits, the details of the sale were worked out.

An hour later Philip and Angele left the office, potential owners of The Grey House. They were to stay at a hotel in the city for a few days until the legal niceties had been gone into; that would take time, but there was nothing to stop monsieur from having the property surveyed or putting work in hand, for the remainder of the proceedings were a formality. So Philip signed a paper, handed over a cheque, wired his literary agent in London that he was staying on and would write, and worked himself into an agreeable enthusiasm over the possibilities of The Grey House.

It was decided between him and Angele that they would return to London for a couple of weeks, to wind up their immediate affairs and then return to Burgundy for the autumn. They would occupy themselves during that time by working on the house, assisted by local labour and then decide, with the assistance of a local architect, just what major repairs and alterations would be necessary. They would go back to London in November and keep in touch with the work through the architect. Then they intended to return to The Grey House in the spring to supervise the final stages and arrange for a housewarming.

By next summer Philip hoped they would be fully installed for a six-month season of prolific and profitable writing for him and a period of pleasure and entertaining for her. He was determined that they would make the old house a show place, a necessary pilgrimage for their London friends; and all that night, long after the rest of the hotel was asleep, he kept Angele awake with plans and possibilities. Angele had her reservations but kept her own counsel. She felt that she might be mistaken in her intuitions and after all, carpenters and builders could make a magnificent job of the old house. She would wait and see what transpired.

2

A month later The Grey House was already under siege. Philip had engaged a local builder and he, two assistants and Philip and Angele in their oldest clothes, were in a frenzy of demolition and renovation. Philip had decided that they would tackle the Great Hall first. It was mainly of stone and once they had got rid of the loathsome accumulation which littered the floor, they would rid the house of that putrescent smell. But first there was one setback.

Pierre, the builder they had engaged, was a stolid, good-looking man, broad as a barrel, in his early fifties; as was the custom he worked with his hands with his assistants, taking his share of the heavy work as well as directing operations. He was surprised, as were all the local people, that The Grey House was to be re-opened and lived in after all this time, but he was quite glad of the job.

But the first afternoon, there was a short consultation among his two workmen and they drew the builder to one side. Philip, who had been down the lane, returned at that moment and Pierre asked to speak to him. He seemed embarrassed and eventually said that nothing could be done until the electric light was in operation; his point was that the loathsome conditions underfoot in the Great Hall made good lighting essential.

This was understandable enough but Angele thought she could discern odd expressions in the eyes of the two workmen. Despite herself, she was convinced that they had other reasons for their request. Fortunately, a modern supply was already laid on to the house, and Philip had merely to request the local electricity company to restore the current. Like many English people he was naive about local conditions and Angele had laughingly assured him that it would take a month or more before anything would be done about it.

Philip told the assembled workmen that the current would be turned on that afternoon. There was a general air of disbelief but Philip said he had an appointment with the electricity people at two o'clock and sat down upon an upturned box in front of the house to wait. Pierre and his workmen chatted among themselves. Philip was the only person present to believe the statement.

When half-past three came with not a stroke of work done it became obvious even to Philip that the electricity would not be connected. He jumped up angrily and drove off in his car. He was unable to achieve any satisfaction and found the company office locked; no doubt the official in charge was in one of the local cafes.

Incensed at this lack of efficiency Philip phoned M. Gasion, who presently came down to the house himself. He assured Philip that he had sorted out the misunderstandings and that the workmen would be at The Grey House without fail the following day. Mollified, Philip announced that they could still get some work done while daylight lasted. It was not half past four, so, lighting a couple of lanterns, the party of five—M. Gasion having returned to his office—set off through the gloomy reception rooms to the terrace. Here, restored by the bright sunlight and the atmosphere of open countryside, the workmen unloaded their tools and set about clearing the area, amid jokes and laughter.

The whole terrace seemed to be covered with lichen and here and there fungoid growths; two of the workmen started scraping this off to reveal the intricately patterned tiles beneath, while Pierre, Philip and Angele busied themselves with clearing the area of brushwood, fallen branches and other debris which had accumulated over the years. This they threw off the balcony into the orchard below; it made loud crashing noises in the brittle branches of dead trees and for some reason gave Angele considerable uneasiness.

She looked sharply down to the water mill and the dark trees at the orchard end, but nothing moved and she attributed her feelings to nerves and the thin tinkle of falling water. In an hour, good progress had been made and when repeated applications with buckets of water had been carried out to the considerable area of tiling cleared by the workmen, it was seen that the whole terrace was one of considerable elegance and beauty.

Philip had recovered his good humour when he saw what an excellent start it was and how pleasantly and efficiently the workmen had carried out their task.

It was evident that with this team the house would be in good hands and Philip was obviously in a great hurry to complete the preliminaries and get to grips with the major problems. He spoke with Pierre of the work to be done to the main roof and the sagging turret; this would have to be a priority and needed to be started well before the winter. Pierre told him that work on this would commence within a fortnight, once working arrangements had been achieved inside.

⌘ THE GREY HOUSE

It was in this atmosphere of mutual satisfaction that the day's work ended. Dusk was falling and the lanterns had been carried on to the terrace to complete the clearing of the tiles. Another of the workmen was already chipping rust from the great sweep of the balcony. It made an ugly sound in the dusk and was re-echoed from the dark woods below. As they finished and carried the tools back into the house for the night, there was a faint rustling in the underbrush at the back of the house down by the water mill. Angele was the only one to hear it; she strained her eyes down to the orchard below and thought she could see the faintest shadow slip into the darker shade of the old trees at the end of the orchard.

Probably a cat. There were lots of them haunting the lanes down near The Grey House. Big, grey brutes they were, and sometimes she heard them howling sadly in the dusk when she and Philip went out. The big door of the house shrieked, as though annoyed at the intrusion into the long silence of forty years, when they left. Outside, on the small terrace in front of The Grey House, where Philip intended to lay tiles and build a small garage later, the employer and the employed congratulated one another and there was much shaking of hands.

Then Philip insisted on buying everyone a drink at the first cafe they came across. All parted with mutual expressions of goodwill and it was quite dark when Philip and Angele had got back to their hotel. He was resolved to make a good start the next day and had asked the electricity people to come in at nine o'clock. The workmen would arrive at twelve and with luck and sufficient illumination they could make a good start on clearing the Great Hall.

The following morning the electricity employees surprisingly arrived almost at the specified hour; The Grey House was opened again and around midday a jubilant Philip was allowed to pull the master switch and the Great Hall was flooded with light. Much of the house would need re-wiring and Philip had many special schemes for heating and outdoor floodlighting, but that would come later.

For the moment, naked bulbs and trailing lengths of flex were draped all over the house in order to give the workmen good light to work by. Philip hoped also to have two great picture windows opened

Darkness, Mist & Shadow

up in the stone work of the Great Hall to let light into the building during daytime.

This, and a number of other anomalies puzzled him and he resolved to look up the history of the de Menevals in the great historical library in the City Museum, when time would afford. That opportunity did not arise until the next year; in the meantime Philip and his wife, with their team of workmen, followed by the interest of M. Gasion, M. Morceau and later, the architect, went at the work of restoration with enthusiasm.

But strangely, the progress of the first day wasn't repeated. One of the workmen went sick the second afternoon and, assuredly, the stench from the floor of the Great Hall was such as to turn a strong stomach; Philip got round that with buckets of hot water and disinfectant and after a while they cleared some of the miasma which seemed to hang around the old foundations.

Lorry load after lorry load of malodorous rubbish left for the city tip and even the sick workman, who returned to duty the next day, had to admit there had been a great improvement. But there was something which made Angele vaguely uneasy, though Philip seemed as blind to the atmosphere of the place as ever. He was puzzled at the inordinate number of lights and flex positions the workmen were obliged to insist on, especially when working among the noisesome rafters and complained that the cost of electricity and bulbs would soon gross the total cost of the house if things went on that way.

Yet Angele understood perfectly the feelings of the workmen and marvelled again at the insensitivity of her husband to the atmosphere; especially as his name as an author had been largely made through the description of just such situations. About a week after the renovation of the house had begun the workmen were still clearing the upper storey and Pierre expected an early start to the roof repairs; Philip had been delighted with some unusual finds among the debris of centuries. A curiously marked ring, evidently belonging to a man of rank; a sword hilt, a tankard with a strange inscription in the Latin tongue and some porcelain jars and containers for which none of them could assign any known use.

Philip took them back to his hotel for cleaning and said he would use them for decorating the house when restoration was complete. One afternoon one of the workmen came to Philip with a bizarre object he had found in one of the upper rooms. It was a long instrument with a spike of very old metal on one end of it; the other end was a sort of whip or switch. The thongs were made of wire, stained with the rust of centuries.

A learned Abbe from the City University, with whom Philip had become great friends, was visiting The Grey House on the afternoon in question. Monsignor Joffroy turned quite pale, Angele noticed.

"May I see?" he asked, taking the whip from Philip with unseemly haste. He drew him on to one side. The good Abbe looked worried.

"I do not wish to alarm you, my friend, but this is an unclean thing," he said, almost fiercely.

"See." He pointed out an inscribed tablet on the shaft of the instrument. "These are the arms of the de Menevals. We have a locked room of the Musee d'Antiquities at the University, devoted to such relics of the sadistic de Menevals. If you would permit me, I will see it is deposited for safe keeping. It is not fit that such mementoes should be allowed in the outside world."

He crossed himself and Angele could not repress a shudder. Though inclined to be amused, Philip could not but be impressed by the earnestness and deadly seriousness of Monsignor Joffroy's manner and he readily assented to his friend's request.

"I should like to hear something of the history of the de Menevals from you, some time," he said. "It would make good material for some of my books."

The Abbe laid his hand on Philip's arm and looked steadily into his eyes.

"Believe me, my friend, such things are not for books—or rather for books of your sort. Your essays in the macabre, admirable and successful as they are, are children's nursery tales compared with the things that went on in the chateau above—now no more, praise be to God."

A few minutes later the Monsignor excused himself, made his farewells to Angele and returned to the university; he left behind him a somewhat thoughtful Philip and a thoroughly disturbed Angele.

Sensibly, Philip said nothing to Pierre and the workmen; and to M. Gasion, whom he met for an occasional glass of cassis at the latter's home, he was guarded; he made no comment on the curious whip, but discussed some of the other finds which the workmen had made. He did learn one thing about the de Menevals from the inscription on the tankard, but of this he said nothing, even to Angele.

She herself had one more unusual experience on the afternoon of the same day as Monsignor Jeffrey's visit. She was alone on the terrace at dusk; she was no longer afraid of the low tinkling of water, to which she had become accustomed and even the mist did not affect her with uneasiness. She was trimming branches of an old tree which overhung the balcony.

This was now almost complete, wanting only a few final touches and, with an electric light above the glazed double doors, was taking on an unaccustomed elegance. She had gone down to Philip to ask him about something and when she came back the last glow of the fading sun was sinking behind the mountain. She was overcome by the melancholy of the scene and had remained seated while her gaze played over the terrain spread out so enticingly before her. It was while she was so occupied that she felt rather than saw a faint, dark shadow steal out from one orchard tree and disappear behind another.

Why she did the next thing she was not quite sure; but on some obscure impulse she suddenly stooped, picked up a large bundle of chopped branches from the tree, stepped noiselessly to the edge of the balcony and hurled the mass of wood and foliage through the air into the orchard below. The bundle fell where she had aimed, quite by chance, and with a sharp, almost frightening crash into the tree beneath which the shape had melted.

More branches fell to the ground and from the midst of the splintered wood something dark and long launched itself like a streak through the orchard; the creature poised and jumped up on to the edge of an outbuilding of the water mill. As far as she could judge, Angele saw a huge, grey cat. It had enormous yellow eyes that flickered with anger in the dusk. It looked back over its shoulder at her reproachfully and then disappeared into the bushes.

The Grey House

A moment later she heard a stealthy swish as it vanished and was evidently making its way through the dark trees at the back of the orchard. More startled than alarmed she left the terrace rather hurriedly for the welcome shelter of the house, which now blazed with lights from every room.

The next day Monsignor Joffroy was dining with them on the terrace of their hotel and Angele mentioned the cat. It was the first time she had spoken of it. Philip seemed only mildly interested but the effect on the Abbe was electric. His hand twitched and his glass of cognac soaked the table cloth. There was a flurry of apologies and in the midst of mopping up, Angele felt the Abbe's eyes fixed on her.

"There is no such animal, madame," he said with terrible emphasis.

"Oh, come now, Monsignor," Philip laughed good-naturedly. "There's nothing so remarkable about that. There are dozens of cats around the lanes leading to The Grey House. I've seen 'em myself."

The Abbe continued to look at the girl. "Nevertheless, I must insist, there is no such animal. A trick of the light . . . "

Angele did not press the point and a moment or two later the conversation passed on to other topics. But she felt the Abbe's eyes on her from time to time during the evening, and she read concern in their friend's eyes.

The house was making excellent progress. As the autumn colours deepened and the melancholy around The Grey House gradually gave way to orderliness and a more modern atmosphere, Angele's unease subsided. The couple had arranged to leave for England in November as planned and would return in April, when the main architectural changes would be made and Philip would be on hand to supervise and give advice. They were due to depart on the following Tuesday, and in the meantime wandered about the house, idly watching the workmen and planning even more grandiose effects for the spring.

The architect they had finally engaged, Roget Frey, was thoroughly in accord with Philip's ideas and he had been enthusiastic about the designs the gifted young man had produced. Philip knew he could trust him to realise the effect he wanted. The house was to be a blend of ancient and modern, with every comfort, yet the mediaeval atmosphere was to be retained, particularly in the Great Hall and in the rooms above it.

The roof was more than half finished and two great picture windows had been punched into the ancient stonework high up in the eastern wall of the Great Hall, more than thirty feet above the fireplace.

Philip had ideas about these windows and he didn't want to reveal his special plans to Angele or the workmen until their return; Roget had worked out a fine design for his *piéce de resistance* and he was convinced his house would be a show place for his friends if the final result was only half as spectacular as his designs.

The work to be done in the winter would be long and arduous and Philip was glad they would be in the comfort of their London flat; there was no heating in The Grey House as yet and the wind and rain on that exposed ledge would find them totally unprepared. Pierre had promised that all would be up to schedule by spring, and in the warmer weather he and Angele could work out the elegant details, the central heating and style of radiators, the furnishing, the curtains and the hundred and one other things that would make The Grey House a masterful blend of old and new.

In the meantime Pierre and his men were to finish the roof; prepare and glaze new windows; install the central heating plant; build a garage and terrace in front of the house; scrape and plaster the interior walls and line the Great Hall with oak panelling. Philip could imagine the stupendous effect the whole thing would have when it was finished; he strolled around the house in a delighted daze, noting the fine new staircases, the cedar handrails in the modern parts of the house and the start already made in creating a streamlined kitchen for Angele.

The whole of the upper storey had yet to be converted into several rooms; there was much to be done. But he was glad he had given his confidence to Pierre and Roget. They would see that the work had a quality seldom seen nowadays. The men had already made a start on the interior of the Great Hall and their scaffolding and lights lined the walls at a dizzy height from the flagged floor; another gang was at work on the roof outside and the place resembled a great, humming factory.

In striking contrast to the mist-haunted ambience of their first sight of the place, Philip was pacing about on the terrace, smoking a pipe, and picturing himself writing a new series of novels of the macabre in this evocative atmosphere. He had two novels coming out shortly, but he would have to get down to some hard work in England in the coming winter. Then he would return to The Grey House and by late summer would be well back in his stride.

His publisher was pleased with the consistency of his output and he had no doubt that the quiet surroundings here would contribute a great deal to his writing. If only Angele liked the place a little better... Still, she had seemed more pleased with the house lately and he felt that, when she saw the new kitchen and all the latest gadgets he proposed to install for her, she would be as delighted with The Grey House as he.

His musings were suddenly interrupted by a startled cry.

It came from the direction of the Great Hall and in a few moments more he heard the sharp noise of running footsteps on the stone floor. It was Pierre.

"Monsieur!" There was a hard excitement in the voice, but no alarm. He quickened his own steps towards the builder. The couple met at the entrance of the Great Hall and an instant later Philip was sharing Pierre's excitement.

The workmen had been scraping down the wall of the Great Hall over the fireplace, preparatory to re-plastering; Philip had long pondered a centrepiece which would provide a striking point for the eye in this chamber and now he had the answer. Beneath the layers of old plaster on the surface of the ancient wall, a painting had begun to reveal itself.

When Philip arrived, two workmen were engrossed in clearing away an area which appeared to depict a man's blue waistcoat with gold gilt buttons. Philip joined them on the scaffolding and studied the painting, as it began to appear, with mounting excitement. Pierre seized a paint brush and a can of water and started clearing another area; the four men worked on.

✒ Darkness, Mist & Shadow

The rest of the house was silent, Angele and Monsignor Joffroy having gone for a walk and the men on the roof having a temporary break from their labours.

After an hour, a painting of unique and demoniac nature had emerged; viewing it from the floor of the Great Hall by the brilliant electric light which the workman held to illuminate it, Philip was jubilantly aware of having found his centrepiece—remarkably appropriate in view of his profession as a novelist of the macabre—and yet at the same time he could not help having serious doubts as to the effect it might have on his visitors.

The radiant colours were unblurred by their long sojourn under the whitewash of an earlier age and the painting really stood out remarkably. It depicted a singularly sinister old man, in a grey tricorn hat and blue coat with gold buttons. His knee breeches were caught in with gold cords and his black shoes had silver gilt buckles. He was pushing his way through some sort of dark, wet undergrowth with concentrated ferocity. In his arms and hanging head downwards as he dragged her into the darkling bushes was a young girl.

She was stark naked, her pink body, depicted with pitiless detail by the unknown painter of obvious genius, streaked with gouts of blood where the brambles had gashed her. Her eyes were closed, either in death or a faint, it was impossible to tell, and her long gold hair dragged through the wet grass. It was difficult to convey the hideous effect this painting of diabolical brilliance had upon the viewer.

In the old man's left hand, held towards the observer, was the curious spiked whip which Philip had seen in this very house not so many weeks before. The workmen were still busy washing away the covering whitewash from the bottom righthand corner of the picture and their backs obscured the details from Philip's view. He strode about the floor of the hall, trying to get a better perspective.

At the very bottom of the painting was an enamelled coat of arms with a Latin inscription underneath, which he would have translated later. He was no scholar and would ask Monsignor Joffroy what he made of it. As the workmen again began their interminable hammering upon the roof above his head, the footsteps of the Abbe himself were heard upon the entrance stair.

His face was pale in the light of the electric lamps and he seemed to stagger and made a warding off gesture with his hand, as he caught sight of the painting, which the workmen had now finished uncovering.

"For the love of God, Monsieur," he cried harshly. "Not this horror..."

Amazed, Philip ran to meet him but a startled shriek from the stairhead above interrupted the projected dialogue. Monsignor Joffroy, remarkably agile for his late middle-age, was even before Philip on the stair. The two men were just in time to save Angele as she fell fainting to the stone floor.

"Let us get her out of this hall," the priest whispered, his head close to Philip's, as they began to lift her. He waved off the alarmed-workmen who were swarming down the scaffolding. "Nothing, nothing at all. Just a fainting fit—madame was merely startled by the painting..."

Half an hour later, Philip re-entered the hall. Angele, pale and distraught, had returned to the hotel, driven by Roget Frey, who had called to see the work in progress. Finally calm, she had refused to say what was the cause of her alarm and had attributed it to the shock of seeing the painting in such vivid detail.

Viewed from the top of the stairs, it did strike one with terrific effect, Philip had to admit, pausing at the spot where Angele had stood. But even his stolid materialism had begun to crack with what he had learned in the past few minutes. Monsignor Joffroy, before leaving to comfort Angele, had advised him to have the painting effaced, or bricked over.

"No good can come of it," he insisted, but he would not, or could not, explain anything further. He had, however, confirmed what Philip had already guessed. The arms beneath the strange picture were those of the de Menevals. The motto beneath the escutcheon was the old and terrible one by which the de Menevals had lived; "Do as thou wilt."

But the thing which disturbed Philip most of all was the painting's final detail, which the workmen had uncovered last of all. Upon this point Monsignor Joffroy had persisted in a stubborn silence.

⚜ Darkness, Mist & Shadow

Philip looked at the picture again and certain words of the Abbe's came to his mind. Following behind the dreadful couple and gazing with sardonic expression at the viewer was a terrible cat, three times larger than any ever seen in this mortal life. A great, grey cat, with blazing yellow eyes.

⚜ 3

In London, Angele and Philip resumed the interrupted round of their life. The events of the previous autumn seemed blurred and far away and their strangeness something of the imagining, rather than reality. Their friends constantly chaffed them about their old grey house and their preferring to live in such a remote place, rather than to enjoy London life and all the privileges of a successful novelist there.

Philip, however, never tired of telling his friends what a fascinating gem he had unearthed and in truth he had a most interesting way of relating his stories so that his listeners were more than half convinced, even the most hidebound and deskbound of their acquaintances. A good dozen or more couples accepted invitations to visit them the following summer, seduced by the lift of Philip's voice, for his narration of the tale of The Grey House was almost as fascinating as his printed work.

Angele was, perhaps, pleased at this success and now that she was back in her own familiar atmosphere, the events at The Grey House seemed trivial and commonplace. She supposed it was something that could have happened to anybody. And environment could do many things. The Grey House had an undeniable ambience that spoke of matters best forgotten, but electric light and modern fittings would dispel them.

She should have been the novelist; Philip often teased her and said she was the one with all the imagination. It was true in a way, too; as she thought this, she looked over at him in a corner of the lounge, pipe in mouth and a pint tankard in one hand. He looked young and supple at forty-five, not a grey hair in his glossy black head; she was proud of him and the success they had made of life and their marriage.

It was silly to worry so about The Grey House and a ridiculous atmosphere; it was all the same in old houses. Come to that she had exactly the same sensation in the Paris Conciergerie with all its terrible associations with the Comite de Salut Public and Marie Antoinette. She dismissed the thoughts from her mind and listened with an interest that was not feigned when Philip read her the latest progress reports from Roget Frey or M. Gasion.

Sometimes, too, the Abbe would write them little notes in his scholarly handwriting, but he never referred to The Grey House, save in the most general way, or the painting. Particularly not the painting. Angele herself had seen it again since her stupid fainting fit on the staircase; she had to admit that in the daylight and with her husband and friends around her, it no longer frightened her.

It was a diabolical subject and he was a disgusting old man—the painter had caught a most sinister expression on his face, which left the viewer feeling uneasy—but that was all. Even the cat wasn't the same as the one she had fancied in the orchard; the one in the picture was at least the size of a bloodhound, but the eyes and face were different.

They even laughed at it, she and Philip and Roget; Philip had said it might have had nine lives but even a cat as big as that could hardly have lived for two hundred years into the late twentieth century. No, that no longer worried her. But what did worry her then, if the cause of the worry—the sight of a cat in an orchard; the atmosphere of an old house; the discovery of a painting—had no fear for her?

She was hard put to it to define a reason and eventually forgot all about it as her normal London life went on. Philip's two books were published, one in December, one in early spring, and achieved an even greater success than before. They had money in abundance and life seemed to hold great promise.

The progress reports on the house were satisfactory and as late spring advanced, Philip began to tear his thoughts away from his life in England and his mind flew to The Grey House, waiting for him to give it the final touches. A flurry of invitations went out from him and

Angele and then the couple found themselves with only two weeks to go before they were off again.

The regular letters told Philip that the roof had been completed; all the domestic arrangements were in the final stages; the panelling of the Great Hall and its picture windows had gone smoothly; the electric lighting was functioning satisfactorily. Roget Frey said that the surprise he and Philip had planned was also going to schedule; he had the work carried out in sections and the structure would be erected whenever Philip chose. The garage and the front terrace too, were nearly complete; the remainder of the work, including the reconstruction of the upper storey would await Philip's supervision in the spring.

The author was more than pleased; indeed, judging by the excellent photographs Roget had sent him, the house seemed even more impressive than he had envisaged when he started out on his elaborate scheme of renovation. The terrace overlooking the water mill also looked superb and he hoped to erect a glass marquee on one side so that they could eat in the open in summer even when it rained.

Much against the Abbe's advice, he had decided to keep the painting as the centrepiece of the Great Hall; from his researches he had considered that it represented the old Vicomte Hector de Meneval, one of the most debauched and sadistic of the line. It was no doubt how the old boy liked to see himself, in an obscene and allegorical situation, representing the black arts.

So he had instructed Frey to have the painting framed in oak and preserved under glass. In deference to Angele, the Abbe and other friends of more tender nerves, he had decided to have a plain sliding panel in the modern Swedish style erected over the work. In that way he could have his cake and eat it, he reflected. And at the press of a button the old rogue would be revealed, to shock his friends on a cold winter's night.

The two weeks drew to an end at last; Philip attended a dinner given in his honour by his publisher, extended the last of his invitations, drank through his last farewell party and in the first week in May—rather later than he had intended—he and Angele with the car

⁂ The Grey House

set off on the cross-channel ferry. They stopped at Fountainebleau for the night and next day made an uneventful journey south.

They had decided to camp out in the house temporarily, as the greater part was habitable; from what Roget had said, the bathroom was partly in order, the working parts of the kitchen completely so. They could extemporise and superintend the final arrangements themselves. But even so, both liked comfort and rather than arrive late in the afternoon with inadequate provision for food, they had booked in at their old hotel for two nights before deciding to launch themselves completely on to the facilities of The Grey House.

Their telegrams had preceded them and their old friends M. Gasion, Roget and the Abbe presented themselves punctually for dinner. It was a time of laughter and jokes shared, which Philip always remembered; and, when the builder Pierre put in an appearance just as they had given him up, the evening seemed complete. Afterwards, they sat out on the balcony, smoking, drinking their cognac and looking over the lights of the quiet city.

All was well at the house, the couple learned; things had gone even better than expected and Pierre and Roget Frey were obviously bubbling with enthusiasm. If they could decently have done so, they would have dragged Philip and Angele into the car that night and over to the house, late as it was.

Roget Frey and Philip chaffed the Abbe over what they called the "boxing in" of the painting, but though he good-humouredly smiled at their sallies, it was obvious that his eyes had a serious and thoughtful look. The party broke up late and Philip never had a chance to speak to any of his friends alone. The pair rose late the next morning.

It was after midday before Frey, the builder Pierre and M. Gasion arrived at the hotel to escort their friends in triumph to their new home. There had certainly been an extraordinary change in The Grey House. In front of the house was a terrace of pink tiles, the great entrance door sparkled with pale yellow paint and boxes of flowers garlanded the façade, with more flowers hanging in baskets on hooks suspended from the walls.

On the roof, new red tiles caught the sunshine and the straightened turret must have looked as it did in the eighteenth century. On one side, a new garage was nearing completion, needing but a final coat of paint, while white balustrades edging the terrace gave the last touch in a notable and inspired piece of restoration.

The ancient and the modern blended in perfect harmony and even Angele could not resist a gasp of pleasure. With congratulations on all sides, architect, builder and agent passed inside the great door to show the couple the wonders of the interior. It a happy afternoon and Philip was well pleased, not only with his choice of restorers but in his own ability to choose good men.

When the mutual congratulations were over, the party stayed on for a convivial dinner; and while the majority remained in the dining room, chatting over coffee and cognac, served by a local domestic, Philip and Roget Frey retired to the Great Hall to discuss the next stages of the work. Even the Abbe, when he put in an appearance around nine o'clock in the evening, had to admit that the house now had great charm and style; if he had any reservations he, at any rate, was wise enough to keep them to himself.

He glanced up at the space over the fireplace when he entered the Great Hall and appeared relieved to see nothing but a smooth wooden panel where the painting was formerly visible. During the next few days Philip and Angele settled down into a more or less stable routine. They had two small portable beds installed in one of the half-completed rooms on the first floor and ate in the kitchen or on the terrace.

This was in order to avoid inconvenience and extra trouble for the workmen, who were now proceeding with the later stages of the work under Pierre and Roget's direction. Philip was already writing and the steady clack of his typewriter could be heard from the terrace several hours each day. Roget was in and out several times a day, the work went well; all in all, it was a busy time for the young couple. Some evenings they would drive into the city for a meal or a drink with their friends; and, several afternoons a week, Angele would go shopping, either alone or with Philip.

She was busy ordering furniture, domestic utensils, hangings and the many hundreds of individual items which the house would need. Surprisingly, the renovation of The Grey House was not costing as

⚘ The Grey House

much as they had budgeted for, despite the extensive nature of the work; this was mainly due to Roget's goodness in the matter of fees and to the builder's reasonable rates and friendly attitude.

This meant that Angele had more to spend on furnishings and she wanted to make sure that her side of the decorating measured up to the high standards set by her husband. Angele was not troubled by any more disturbing thoughts and she had grown used to the tinkling of the water mill. The mist was now rising thickly from the area of trees at the bottom of the orchard, due to the extremely hot weather, but she paid no more attention to that either.

About the third week in July, the first of their friends from London arrived to inspect the progress of the house. Doreen and Charles Hendry were a jolly couple and they were delighted with The Grey House as they first saw it from their sports car one afternoon. But for some reason their enthusiasm evaporated after their first raptures. One of the guest rooms was now ready for occupation, though still unpainted. It overlooked, from a higher point, the orchard and the grove of trees at the foot of the terrace and it was this room which Doreen and Charles occupied their first night at The Grey House.

The next morning, at breakfast on the terrace, Angele could not help noticing that Doreen looked drawn and tired. Even Philip sensed this, for he asked, "Sleep well?"

Charles looked embarrassed. He glanced round the breakfast table and said with a short laugh, "Well, as a matter of fact we didn't sleep a wink. There was such a howling of cats all night, that we were awake most of the time. Never heard anything like it. One great brute was in the orchard. I got up to sling some water at it. It had burning yellow eyes—gave me quite a turn."

"Sorry about that," said Philip. "Yes, there are a lot of cats round here, now that you come to mention it, but I can't say they've bothered us to that extent. Have you heard them, dear?" he said, turning to Angele.

His wife had turned quite white. She stammered some casual remark and quickly excused herself. There was nothing else of moment during the Hendrys' short stay. And short it was. They had originally intended to remain for two weeks but after a few days

Charles pleaded urgent business which necessitated his return to England. As their sports car headed up the lane and Angele and Philip waved them off, Angele could have sworn there was relief in Doreen's eyes as they drove away from The Grey House.

Imagined or not, there was no doubt that Charles' business was a pretext, for Philip ran into him in one of the main squares of the city a couple of afternoons later, to their mutual embarrassment. On the Friday of the same week Philip made a startling discovery which did something to disturb the peace of his mind, while the effect on Angele was deeply felt. Philip returned from a walk with Roget and asked Pierre, "I say, did you know there was an old graveyard at the end of the lane?"

Pierre shrugged and answered that he believed that was so; but it was a good way from the house, well screened by trees. He could not see that it was of any importance. In face of this indifference Philip had to agree that the affair seemed of little moment. But the way of its discovery had been a shock to him, though he was loath to admit it.

He and Roget had been out surveying the extent of the property; Philip had wanted to have a closer look at the orchard and the water mill building and there was also the question of repair of walls and fences. When they had gone some way towards their boundary, forcing their way through breast-high nettles in places, Philip was surprised to see a large area of rusted iron railings and the white gleam of marble through the trees.

Roget was almost as surprised as he. The two men, impelled by some curiosity, the source of which was obscure, were soon confronted by an elaborate ironwork gate with a rusted metal scroll, whose hieroglyphs seemed familiar; the stone pillars on either side were covered with lichens and moss and the stone ball on one column had long fallen into the grass.

The gate was ajar and after some hesitation, the two men pushed it open and went on into the cemetery. Its extent was quite small but there was a frightful mouldering stench emanating from the ancient tombs with which they were surrounded, and the long, echoing screech the gate made as it went back on its age-old hinges, set the young men's teeth on edge.

✍ The Grey House

There seemed to be about thirty tombs in the cemetery and it was evident that a hundred years or more had passed since the latest occupant was laid to rest. As they gazed round, Roget said with a nervous catch in his breath, "This must be the old de Medieval graveyard. They were brought here from the chateau above. They had to be laid in this place, far from the town, because of the public outcry. I seem to remember in the old histories that the townspeople said they were an accursed strain and there was a great ecclesiastical debate over their being interred in the municipal cemetery. So the Bishop of the province had this private cimetiere set aside for the use of the family."

Philip could not hold back a shiver at these words, reinforced by the melancholy scene around him. He saw now that the dark grove of trees below the orchard had screened the graveyard from view, as no doubt it was meant to do. There was no doubt however, as to the reasons for the dank mist which rose over the orchard and surroundings at night. The place was unhealthy and Philip would have to seek the advice of the health authorities.

The pair had been traversing the small avenues which bisected the old graveyard and now found themselves in front of an imposing monument which stood in the most secluded part; overgrown hedges of laurel surrounded it and the lower part of the tomb was effaced by the encroachment of brambles and tangled grasses. Philip noticed with interest that the mausoleum was in the form of a great marble portico, in the style of a Greek temple, which evidently covered a vault of considerable proportions below.

On the face of the portico was repeated the escutcheon which appeared below the painting in the Great Hall of The Grey House; he saw the name of Hector de Meneval and others of his house, the dates of birth and death obliterated with time. But as he looked closer, he saw that he had been mistaken; the dates of birth were clearly given, but the remainder of the legend was left blank after each name— there was not even the customary dash. This was decidedly curious.

Roget had left his side for a moment and was puzzling out a massive Latin inscription which extended along the side of the mausoleum. Roughly translated it ran, "Mighty are they, great joy is theirs; they shall taste of Life Everlasting." Somehow, this inscription left a vaguely unpleasant impression on Philip's mind and he could not help remembering, for the first time, the sly and cunning expression of the old man in the painting.

He was about to retrace his steps towards the gate when there was a sharp exclamation from Roget. He joined his friend and saw, following the line of Roget's somewhat unsteady finger, that one side of the tomb had collapsed, after long years of erosion by wind and rain. The earth had fallen in, carrying with it fragments of marble and through the gaping hole in the side of the mausoleum could be seen part of the interior of the vault.

There were dark steps and even what looked like part of a catafalque some distance below. A faint miasma exuded from this charnel place and seemed to poison the air around the tomb. A little farther off, Philip noted another curious feature. The grass around the hole in the marble seemed crushed and torn, as though something heavy had been dragged along; the trail continued for some distance into the dark and sombre bushes which bordered the cemetery gate.

Neither man liked the idea of following that trail and after a few moments, by mutual, unspoken consent they hurried away to the healthy sanity of the upper lanes which led to the house. The gate shrieked mockingly behind them. Philip did not mention their visit to the old cemetery in any detail and after her first shock of alarm, Angele gave the matter no more thought. And the following week there was a minor celebration, culminating in the unveiling of Philip's surprise.

The principal of Philip's publishing firm was to be in Burgundy for a few days and had promised to spend a day with them and inspect their new quarters. Philip had laid on a party in his honour and the climax was to be the architectural coup he had planned for the Great Hall. This chamber had been barred to all members of the household and friends for three days beforehand and the noise of hammering and sawing echoed throughout the house all day long; Roget and Philip were in conference behind the locked doors and workmen carrying heavy baulks of timber and elaborately carved beams in and out, smilingly disclaimed all knowledge of the nature of the affair.

✥ The Grey House

The party was a big success and the unlocking of the Great Hall set the seal on a momentous occasion; tables laden with wine and food were set down the middle, an epic fire blazed in the hearth, for the stone hall was a cold place even in summer, despite the wooden panelling; and lights blazed from half a hundred metal wall fittings. But what enchanted the guests was the architectural feature on which Philip and Roget had worked for such a long time.

Completely surrounding the upper part of the hall, like a minstrel gallery, ran an airy balcony which continued over the fireplace round to a point above the huge door. Each side of the entrance, beautifully carved oak balustrades ran up to the balcony, encasing polished oak staircases. The whole length of the balconies themselves, except where the two great picture windows pierced the wall, were a blaze of colour; thousands of books, the cream of Philip's collection, lined the walls in finely fitted mahogany bookcases. The whole thing was a triumph and the guests could not resist audible murmurs of admiration.

A few minutes later, ascending the first staircase, hand in hand with Philip, Angele had to admit that the idea was the crown of the Great Hall. Thirty feet above the flagged pavement she looked down on the shimmering dazzle of faces and the babble of the guests' conversation rose like the noise of the sea above the clink of glasses. On the balconies themselves visitors could browse among the books set out row on row, spreading from wall to wall; the views from the picture windows were magnificent and with the stout railing at her back, Angele could see across mile after mile of hazy blue mountain.

The balcony ran across and dipped a little below the great central panel of the fireplace and this was the only unfortunate feature of the affair from her point of view; for whenever the panel was unrolled it must bring the viewer on the balcony in close proximity to the disturbing painting, even though it were still a good half dozen feet above.

It was this which caused the only disrupting element of the party for Angele. She and Philip were admiring the setting from this point when Roget or another friend in the hall below decided to demonstrate the ingenious panel for an intrigued guest. The button was pressed, the panel slid silently back and there, not two yards away,

Angele saw with a shock the same hideous scene. The sight was so unexpected that she gave a gasp and reeled back against the railing.

Philip was beside her in an instant, his face wrinkled with worry.

"What is it?" he asked, looking round him swiftly, in a manner she had never seen before.

"Nothing," she said. "I just feel faint, that's all. It must be the height."

As Philip led her below, a girl who had never had a qualm on even the loftiest mountain top, she looked again at the picture but she did not see repeated the optical illusion which had so unnerved her. That it must be an optical illusion, she did not doubt. But she could have sworn that the baleful eye of the old Vicomte had closed, for just the faintest fraction, in an obscene wink. The effect must be one of the texture of the paint, combined with the light on the glass above it. But she could not recapture the sensation, though she tried again as they went downstairs; and a few minutes later the panel closed again over it, to the wondering murmur of the assembled guests.

4

It was now again turning towards late summer. Philip was beginning to get in his stride with writing, Roget came seldom to the house, the remaining one or two workmen were pottering amiably on the sunny days, putting the finishing touches to the decor. Angele had been too busy to spare any thoughts for morbid imaginings, and she was well satisfied with the effect of the furniture and hangings she was arranging with such competent art.

But the Abbe came more often to the house than ever. Angele was glad of his company; and his benign eye, in which there shone such wisdom and benevolence, gave her a solid feeling of comfort and safety. Monsignor Joffroy spoke little of the matters which so deeply troubled him, but with humorous and interesting discourse kept the little dinner parties gay with laughter, as the night moths fluttered round the lamps as they took their evening ease on the balcony, whose magnificent views never ceased to delight them.

⚜ The Grey House

The couple had on two or three occasions been the guests of the Abbe at his quarters in the old university, and had duly marvelled at the extent and antiquity of the great library which was its proudest boast. It was on one of these occasions that Philip asked the old man if he could consult one of the rare and unexpurgated histories of the de Meneval family.

Monsignor Joffroy was reluctant to do this, but assented at last and eventually left Philip alone in his study with a great brass-bound book which had four locks. Translating the crabbed Latin was a long and tiresome task but Philip eventually unravelled a sickening story which explained much that was dark and horrifying about the de Menevals. He replaced the book on the shelf and sat pondering; for the first time he had some doubts about the wisdom of his purchase of The Grey House.

He ever afterwards refused to speak of what he had seen in the locked book, but he did hint to Roget Frey something of the practices of the old de Menevals which had led the people of the city a hundred years before to lay siege to the chateau and burn it about the ears of the atrocious occupants. The events which led the citizenry to this extreme measure had concerned the abduction of young girls from the neighbourhood, which the de Menevals were in the habit of procuring for their unspeakable rites.

Philip could not go on—the details were too blasphemous and appalling to contemplate, even in the Latin, but it did explain the curious content of the painting in the Great Hall. Philip was now convinced that the study depicted a literal subject and not an allegorical one and this caused him great disquiet. When he left the Abbe's library, the old man refused to discuss the subject with him. But Monsignor Joffroy looked him in the eye with great intensity and said with emphasis, "Take care of your wife, monsieur!"

For some days afterwards Philip was seen to wander about The Grey House with an odd and abstracted air, but he gradually recovered his spirits as the warm and sunny days went by. He had been to see the sanitary authorities regarding the old graveyard and had been promised that the thing would be looked into. But, as is the way in rural France, no action was immediately forthcoming, the weeks went by and Philip eventually forgot about it.

It was in early September, on a day of golden and benevolent splendour, that Angele had an odd experience. She had been standing on the balcony drinking in the beauty of the wild scene, against the backcloth of the far mountains. There was a hush, broken only by the faint tinkle of water. Philip had gone into town to see about some business with Roget and the only other thing which disturbed the silence was the occasional chink of china as Gisele, the hired girl, washed up the crockery from lunch.

She was thinking about nothing in particular, except possibly what they would be having for dinner. As she lowered her gaze from the distant mountain peaks and the white stones of the chateau on the heights above, her eye was arrested by the early leaves of autumn which fell like faint flakes of snow on to the golden foliage of the old orchard. She then heard a faint rustling sound and presently noticed the figure of a man.

He was standing in the far corner of the orchard, near the water mill, and she could not see him at all clearly. He wore a blue coat, like most French workmen wear, and he seemed to be shading his eyes against the sun. She was not at all alarmed, and as she cast her eyes on him, he gave her a long, piercing glance back over his shoulder, but owing to the intervening foliage she was not able to see his features with any detail. The gesture reminded her of something, though she could not for the moment place it, and when she looked again the man had gone.

She mentioned the matter to Philip when he arrived home and he only said with studied casualness, "Oh, I expect the sanitary people have got around to doing that work I asked them about."

This view was reinforced the following day when Pierre and Philip had occasion to go down the far lane on a matter connected with the outfall of the drainage. Philip pointed out to Pierre a long swathe which had been forced through the nettles.

The trail, which was in a different place from the route taken by Philip and Roget on the occasion of their visit, appeared to run from the old graveyard to a point by an ancient, broken-down fence, and

◢ The Grey House

then through the orchard below the house. Pierre said nothing but gave Philip a very curious look. The two men made no further reference to the matter.

It was when they were turning to go back that Philip asked Pierre whether they might not visit the orchard. He had never been there since his original inspection of the water mill, but his curiosity had been aroused by the tracks and he wanted to see if the municipal authorities had taken action. Pierre seemed strangely reluctant and mentioned the lateness of the hour; the setting sun was already casting long shadows and a faint swathe of mist could be seen faintly outlining the farthest trees.

Both men were by now rather disturbed by the atmosphere and Philip started when the long drawn-out yowl of a cat sounded from far away. They stood listening for a moment at the entrance of the orchard but the noise was not repeated. Then Philip went boldly crunching his way through a tangle of brush into the old place, more for his own peace of mind than to impress the builder with his English phlegm.

There was nothing out of the way in the orchard. The trail gave out in the centre. There were only a few rusted agricultural implements, half-hidden in the grass. But Philip was surprised to see that a long iron ladder, wreathed in a tangle of branches and mossy lichen, was stapled to the wall below The Grey House. It led up to a point just below the balcony. This was something he felt he ought to look into.

A few minutes later the two men were back in the sunlit uplands of the inhabited lanes leading to the town and were able to forget the strange, brooding atmosphere of the orchard area. Pierre shook his head when Philip mentioned the matter of the ladder. He imagined it would have been placed there in case of fire. For some reason this gave Philip an enormous peace of mind. He expanded in the glow of the sun and insisted that Pierre accompany him to a cafe for an aperitif.

When he arrived back at the house, he found Angele setting the table on the terrace, with Gisele prattling commonplaces as she bustled to and from the kitchen. On pretext of admiring the view, he looked eagerly for the ladder. Yes, there it was, in a rather different position from what he had imagined below. It must be the foreshortening. He did not know why, but he was disturbed to find that anyone coming from below could gain the balcony by this means, old and rusty as the ladder was. Though this in itself was illogical, for the ladder was surely designed to ensure that people from the house could gain the orchard in case of fire.

This again puzzled him, for the ladder ended about three feet from the balcony, in a tangle of brambles and bushes. He saw something else too, which disturbed him more than he cared to admit. The edges of the ladder were covered with lichen and moss. On all the rungs which he could see, the green of years had been torn away, as though by ascending feet.

Philip slept badly that night, but as day succeeded day and the calm of the Indian summer brought with it nothing but blue skies and contentment, he warmed again to The Grey House.

Angele was in good spirits and the couple made their usual visits. Though the work on the house was finished, their local friends were as before; Pierre, Roget, M. Gasion and the Abbe.

Philip was writing better than ever in the more peaceful atmosphere. A book of demoniac tales which he had finished shortly after arrival in Burgundy in May was having a sensational sale in England and the Continental and American rights were being negotiated. He had reason to feel satisfied. And though the Abbe had attempted to dissuade them from the idea, he had started on his most ambitious novel of the macabre to date, a history based loosely on that of the de Menevals. He had quite recovered his spirits and the odd events which earlier had set his mind on strange and sombre paths, now provided much the same material for his book.

His enthusiasm blazed up as day after day found him hunched over his typewriter and Angele could hear the machine clacking on into the long hours of the night. He preferred to work on the balcony even when the nights began to turn cold in early October. Angele remonstrated with him about this, but he laughed at her and her old wives' remedies for colds, and told her not to worry. He had a good sweater on and his pipe for company.

The days of October continued scorching hot, though the nights were cool and Philip was pleased with his progress on the book; he had five chapters finished and another three shaped out in the rough. He began to talk of finishing before the end of November so that he could get an early draft to the publishers before the new year.

Angele was pleased for his sake but troubled at his appearance. Philip had begun to get pale with overwork and his eyes had deep hollows under them which she had never seen before. She had hoped that they would be away to England before the winter set in, but to her alarm Philip had begun to talk of staying at The Grey House the whole winter round. It was all very well for him, with all his work to occupy him, but it would be a dull existence for her once the long, dark, wet days of the Burgundy winter set in.

They had left the matter open, without quarrelling over it, and Angele had Philip's promise that if the book was finished within the next month, as well it might be, then they would go back to London and he would deliver the manuscript to the publishers himself. He would not show her the material, for fear of spoiling the effect.

"It's the best thing I've ever done," he said, biting hard on his pipe in his enthusiasm. "I've never known a book come along so well. It's almost as though it's writing itself."

Angele shot him a sharp look, but said nothing.

"It's a curious thing," he went on, after a bit, his brows wrinkled over the mass of typed sheets before him. "There's some of this stuff I don't even remember writing. There's a bit here which gets the mediaeval atmosphere exactly... no, perhaps you'd better not read it now. Wait until the end. It spoils it to take it out of context."

Angele continued to watch her husband's progress on the novel with mounting alarm; she had never seen him like this, but consoled herself with the thought that it would do no good to interfere and at the rate he was going they would soon be away to England for the winter.

A few days later, Philip announced in triumph that the last chapter was in progress and that he would revise and reshape the book in England. Angele greeted the news with unconcealed relief. Philip looked at her in surprise. His face was white and his eyes looked wild with his long hours of composition. Then he put down his pipe and took her in his arms.

"I know it hasn't been much fun for you, darling," he said. "But it will only be a few days more now and then we're off home. I can promise you that the book will be the biggest thing I've ever done. I'm sure you will agree with me that it has all been worthwhile."

Husband and wife, both pleased at the turn of events, occupied themselves with planning their departure and in the evenings Philip pressed on at fever heat with the final pages of the book. They were to leave on the following Wednesday and some of their effects were already packed. The car was to go in for servicing the following day and Angele felt strangely content with her life, with her relationship with Philip and even with The Grey House. She supposed that by next year she would be quite used to its strange atmosphere.

On the Saturday evening Philip finished his work early. He had been at the book hard all afternoon but the climax he was shaping had finally eluded him. He had got up from the table on the terrace with an exclamation of disgust and carried the typewriter and the thick bundle of manuscript through into the dining room. She remembered him putting a fresh sheet of paper into the machine and then they went up to bed.

It was in the middle of the night when she awoke. At first she half drifted back into sleep but then came wide awake, her mind puzzled by a series of sharp, scratching noises. Then she turned, her mind at ease, as she realised Philip must be working again. He had evidently gone back to the novel he had discarded. But then a great fear came into her mind as her arm came into contact with her husband's body at her side and she heard his steady breathing. The scratching noise, loud in the still night, went on from the dining room, arousing a thousand fears in her confused brain.

By a great effort of willpower, for she was a brave woman, she steeled herself to get out of bed without waking her husband. Not bothering to put on a dressing gown, she tiptoed out of the room and down the short flight of stairs; she did not heed the chill of the night air on her skin or notice the coldness of the flagstones on her bare feet.

When she had closed the door of the bedroom behind her, she switched on the light. The blaze of yellow radiance on familiar things steadied her and left her with a core of hard anger; she went down the remaining stairs with a firm step. The scratching which had aroused her attention went on. As she advanced, she threw switch after switch and as light sprang up beneath her hand so her courage rose. When she was about ten yards away from the dining room a board suddenly creaked under her feet. The scratching immediately stopped and she heard an odd scrabbling noise on the floor.

As she pushed open the door with a furiously thudding heart and threw the switch, the sudden glare of light showed her that the room was empty. All was in its place, the whole house now silent, except for the faint tapping of the night wind against the balcony outside. As she thought of this, she set the great lights of the terrace aflame in the gloom but nothing moved in all the expanse of tile and wrought iron.

She forced herself to look at the table. Several sheets of new paper were laid on top of the typewriter ready for copying. The last sheet was in French, in painfully formed handwriting, covering half the page. She read, "And the flesh of virgins is desirable above all others and whosoever acquires this tenderest of all meat shall find the Everlasting Life. And the fairest of all the married women shall be taken to bride by the Whore-Master and the tomb shall flame forth brighter than the wedding-bower"... The words ended there, in midsentence, the ink still wet.

Angele, shaking and sick, as she backed away from the table, still had time to notice something on the cloth by the machine. It was a small piece of green lichen.

5

On the Tuesday, Philip and Angele had invited their friends to a farewell dinner and Philip was to read them portions of his novel. The remainder of the previous weekend was occupied in packing and on Monday afternoon Philip rushed in to Angele, jubilant. The book was finished and he waved the thick mass of manuscript over his head in triumph. Angele had not mentioned to him the events of Saturday evening; something dark hung over the

◈ Darkness, Mist & Shadow

house and she knew in her heart that whatever she could say would make no difference. She was only glad that she would soon be gone without the winter to face; in the meantime she shared Philip's joy in his completed work—on the surface at any event.

The pair spent the mid-afternoon talking over future plans and after an early tea, Philip left for Roget's house; he had arranged to have a drink with his friend and discuss some business. He had plans for the orchard and he proposed to have a big stone wall built to block off the old graveyard—a scheme with which Angele fervently agreed. Gisele was to stay with Angele and Philip intended to return about nine o'clock so that they could get in an early night.

They had to prepare for the party the following day and there would be much to do. It had been a hot day again and Gisele and her mistress sat chatting on the balcony; the steepening sun dyed the opposite mountains a deep carmine and as the rays dipped below the hills it left the valley in deep shadow. It began to be cold, the tinkle of water from the old mill house sounded oddly loud in the silence and thick swathes of mist billowed silently across the orchard.

The cats in the lane below the house seemed to be noisy tonight and Angele abruptly got up and went to fetch a woolly sweater. After a while, she and Gisele moved into the kitchen to continue their conversation but they kept the terrace lights on. Philip had left his thick bundle of manuscript to read; she had promised to give him her opinion on it when he returned, though she felt sure it would take her more than the three hours she had allowed herself.

From time to time, as the two girls were talking, Angele turned to look at the great pile of paper which stood on the typing table in the corner of the terrace where Philip usually worked. Presently she excused herself; Gisele had some cleaning to do and went to get out her vacuum cleaner. Angele took a cup of coffee on to the terrace and sat down at the table. She did not know why she did this, but she felt that Philip's novel had to be read on the terrace, where most of it had been written. The title page was headed; IN THE VALE OF CROTH.

She read on, fascinated. It was the most extraordinary thing Philip had ever written. She did not know how she could have

⚜ The Grey House

found the ideas in it revolting; perhaps she had started at the wrong page. Taken out of context such a book could give the wrong impression. An hour must have passed, an hour in which the silence was broken only by the measured rustle of turning pages or the faint noises of Gisele's cleaning operations. Her cup of coffee grew cold, untasted.

Presently she looked up, startled. Her eyes were shining and had an intense expression. Strangely, too, the terrace had suddenly grown oppressively hot. She knew she had to be properly prepared for the final part of the book. She had too many clothes on for this heat—she had to be prepared. When she emerged from her bedroom ten minutes later she had a strange, sly look on her face but her cheeks were burning and her eyes bright with longing. She was naked except for a flimsy nightgown which revealed every detail of her figure.

Her hair was freshly combed and she crept almost furtively past the room where Gisele was dusting. Once on the terrace she flung herself on the book and began to devour the pages with her eyes. Eight o'clock fled past and there were only a few dozen pages left. There was a lustful expression on her face and her whole body had begun to tremble. She paid no attention to the thin mist which had begun to envelope the balcony. She strained her eyes to learn the unmentionable secret revealed in the last page of the novel.

Her eyes glazed as she read what no woman was meant to read; something aeons old called through the pages to her. She thought of the whip with the spike and her flesh quivered with delicious terror. As she reached the last sentence of the book there was a rustling on the balcony, which did not distract her.

Her eyes took in the last words on the pages before her "Nude thou shalt be, naked thou shalt be, unashamed thou shalt be. Prepare thou then to do thy Master's will. Prepare thou BRIDE OF CROTH."

Angele was already on her feet; her eyes were closed, her tongue lolled out of her mouth, a bead of moisture rolled from under one eyelid.

"Take me, Master," she breathed. Something slit the thin silk of her nightgown, exposing her breasts to the chill air. An unutterable stench was in her nostrils, but she smiled happily as ancient arms lifted her from the balcony.

6

Philip returned happily from Roget's house a little after nine, but his casual homecoming soon changed into bewilderment, then terror. The maid, Gisele, sunk into an unnaturally deep sleep on a divan in the dining room, when aroused, expressed only astonishment; the last thing she remembered, she had been dusting the room. Philip went through the house calling his wife's name.

He found the floor of their bedroom littered with every last stitch of his wife's clothing. But it was on the balcony that stark fear leapt out at him for the first time. It was not the overturned coffee cup, the jumble of typed paper littered across the terrace or even the green, lichenous mould. But something had forced its way through the mass of brambles from the old ladder below the balcony; it was this, and the strands of his wife's blonde hair caught on the thorns which sent him almost out of his mind.

Seizing a powerful electric searchlight from the garage, he set off down the steep, nettle-grown lane, calling his wife's name, His voice echoed back eerily and once again he caught the loathsome stench of putrescence which seemed to emanate from the mist which swirled about these lower parts. His heart leaped in his throat as the beam of his lamp picked out something white in the gloom. It was then, he thinks, that he gave up hope of seeing Angele again; in the darkest moment of his life idiot fear babbled out at him as the probing beam caught Angele's pathetic, torn, blood-stained scrap of nightgown fast on a patch of nettles as the unnameable thing had carried her through the night.

Philip's knees gave under him and he trembled violently; for the path through the nettles led directly to the old graveyard and he knew that, much as he loved his wife, he dare not go there alone at night to face such forces. It was a nightmare journey as he stumbled back up the lane; falling, hacking his shins on outcrops of rock, cutting his face

⚜ THE GREY HOUSE

with brambles. He looked an appalling sight as he staggered into a cafe on the edge of the town and made his pathetic telephone plea to Roget Frey.

The young architect not only came in his car at once, but collected Monsignor Joffroy from the university on his way over. The couple were with the demented Philip in a quarter of an hour. His appearance shocked them both but a few words only told the old Abbe all he had suspected and feared from the first.

He had come fully prepared. Round his neck he had an ornate silver crucifix; he carried a prayer book in one hand and, curiously, a crowbar. Roget Frey had also armed himself with a revolver and in the back of his car were two enormous electric lamps, like car headlights.

"*Courage, mon pauvre ami,*" said Monsignor Joffroy, helping Philip into a seat beside him. "What must be done, must be done. I fear it is too late to save your dear wife, but we must do all we can to destroy this evil being in order to save her soul." Horrified, half dazed, understanding only a quarter of what he was told, Philip clutched the Monsignor's arm as Roget's sports car leapt like a demented thing down the narrow lane at suicidal speed.

At the bottom Frey drove straight at the wall of brambles and stinging nettles as far as he could. The headlights shone a brilliant radiance right down towards the cemetery gates. Frey left the lights on and the engine running.

"To remind us of normality," he said with great emphasis.

"This will do," said Monsignor Joffroy, making a great sign of the cross in the air before him. "The rest is in God's hands."

Roget handed a long crowbar to Philip, the prelate carried one searchlight and the other crowbar, and Roget had his revolver in one hand and the second searchlight in his left. The three men walked abreast through the wet grass, making no attempt at concealment. Philip put down his own flashlight at the cemetery entrance, which lit up a considerable part of the graveyard; he had recovered his courage now and led the way towards the de Meneval tomb.

Their feet echoed hollowly over the gravel and Philip dropped to one knee as a thing with great flaming eyes drove at them from the top of a gravestone. Frey's revolver roared twice, with deafening impact, and a broken-backed, yowling creature that had been the great cat went whimpering to die in the bushes. Consignor Joffroy had jumped up instantly and without swerving set off at a run towards the de Meneval tomb. The others followed, trembling from the sudden shock of the revolver shots.

Philip could never forget that charnel house scene. Like a tableau out of Goya, it ever haunted his life. The nude body of Angele, quite dead, splashed with gouts of blood, but with an expression of diabolical happiness on her face, was clutched fast in the arms of a thing which lay on its side at the entrance of the tomb, as though exhausted. It was dressed in a frayed and faded blue coat and the abomination had apparently broken one of its old and brittle legs as it dropped from the balcony. This had accounted for its slow progress to the malodorous lair beneath the old de Meneval mausoleum.

But the worst horror was to come. In one withered and grey, parchmentlike paw was clutched a whip-and-spike instrument dabbled with fresh young blood. The face, half eaten away and with the broken bones protruding from the split, rotted skin, was turned towards them. Something moved and the eyes, which were still alive, gazed balefully at the three men. Old de Meneval was malevolent to the last.

Monsignor Joffroy hesitated not an instant. Pronouncing the name of the Father, the Son and the Holy Ghost in a voice like thunder, he held aloft the cross. Then, handing it to Philip, he brought down the great crowbar again and again on the brittle ancient blasphemy that had once been a man. Teeth and hair flew in all directions, old bones cracked and split and dust and putrefaction rose in the still air. At length, all was quiet.

Panting, the Monsignor led the two men away. "This is all we can do for tonight," he said. "Much remains to be done in the morning, but this abomination will never walk again."

He sprinkled holy water from a bottle over the remains of Angele and covered it with a blanket from the car. To Philip's anguished protests over his wife, he remained adamant.

⚜ The Grey House

"We must not move her," he insisted. "She is no longer your wife, my poor friend. She belongs to them. For her own sake and for her immortal soul we must do what has to be done."

Little remains to be told, though the city will remember for many a long year the horrors which were found in the old de Meneval tomb. Monsignor Joffroy obtained a special dispensation from the Bishop that same night and the very next morning, at first light, a battalion of the Infanterie Coloniale were called in to work under the Abbe's directions.

These soldiers, hardened and toughened on the forge of war as they were, saw sights which made them act like frightened children when the vault below was opened. Monsignor Joffroy, calm and strong, prevented a panic and bore himself like a true man of the church that day. Indeed, many said that the sights he saw and the things he had to do hastened the good man's own end.

The body of Angele was taken to a hastily prepared pyre behind a canvas shelter in the old cemetery and burned while priests conducted a service. In the vault of the de Menevals a stupefying sight awaited the intruders, priest and soldier alike. Some say that there were more than thirty bodies, de Menevals and the naked corpses of fresh young girls, as undecayed as the day they were abducted from the neighbourhood upwards of two hundred years before.

The searchers also found vast passages and chambers under the earth, equipped as for the living, where the undead dead still held obscene and blasphemous rites. Be that as it may, and no one can now say for certain that all this is true, the Bishop himself with Monsignor Joffroy as his chaplain held a service of exorcism and afterwards the troops went in with flame guns and destroyed every last one of those horrors as they lay.

The underground chambers were blown up by Army engineers and the whole of the area cauterised and purified. Later, by order of the Bishop the field was concreted over and from that day to this the people of the city have remained unmolested, neither does mist appear in the orchard by the mill house.

The Grey House still stands, now fast falling to ruin and deserted. M. Gasion, greyer now, has retired and gone to live in a villa in

Normandy; Monsignor Joffroy is dead; and Roget Frey is a successful architect, practising in Paris.

7

Philip is still a successful novelist. He lives in London, with a very young wife, who is not serious at all, and is content with what she calls the simple things of life. He seldom goes abroad, very occasionally to France, and never to Burgundy. His stories now, while very popular in the English speaking world, are not what they were.

They are mainly comedies and light pieces, with an occasional political drama. Though he is still a year or so short of fifty, his hair is quite white and his face that of an old man. It is only when one looks closely into his eyes that one can see the fires of the pit.

Two small footnotes. Afterwards, in The Grey House, Roget Frey found a great pile of grey ash in a circular stone jar on the terrace.

In the Great Hall, the painting of the old man and the girl had disappeared; the whole wall had been gouged out from the balcony and the solid stone pitted as though with a pickaxe.

He did not make any inquiries and he had no theories, so the mysteries remain.

✑ Old Mrs. Cartwright

✑ 1

OLD MRS. CARTWRIGHT HOBBLED DOWN THE PATH OF THE Zoological Gardens in the gathering dusk in a state of apprehension verging on panic. Her figure was grotesque, even pathetic in the twilight; her black, flapping clothing hanging round her body awkwardly, her shadow stencilled on to the dust of the white concrete path like one of those Gilray-style passe-partout silhouette pictures of her youth.

She regretted, even as she panted past the antelope enclosure, that she had ever promised her sister she would look after the boy for the day. Lionel didn't like her; that was the truth; there was always trouble when he was about. And the Zoological Gardens idea had been a mistake from the start. Mrs. Cartwright had to admit to herself that she disliked the child even as much as he appeared to dislike her.

It was a terrible thing to say, even in the privacy of one's own thoughts, but there was the truth of it. Lionel was an odd child. His heavylidded, yellow eyes were more like an animal's than a human being and he had a disconcerting way of standing quite still and staring at her that she found unnerving; there was something of the animal too in this attitude, which he could keep up for minutes on end without seeming to tire. To be fair to the boy, most thirteen-year-olds had queer ways, old Mrs. Cartwright had to admit, though her experience of children was limited.

◈ Darkness, Mist & Shadow

Her own husband had been killed in the First World War and she had been left a young widow, like so many thousands of others. She had never married again. Her sister Sylvia was much younger than she; in fact something like eighteen years separated them, and her only child, Lionel, had been born late in life. Though Mrs. Cartwright hadn't liked to mention this to her sister, Lionel's attitude to his own mother seemed little better to her than the one he adopted to his aunt. But Sylvia didn't seem to notice; she doted on the boy, even though he was big for his age and quite grown-up in his attitude to adults.

There was something else old Mrs. Cartwright felt to be peculiar to Lionel, but for the moment it eluded her. It was something she could never quite pinpoint, but it stemmed from the uncanny way Lionel had of appearing and disappearing suddenly, usually at the most awkward moments. He seemed to walk so lightly on the balls of his feet, that he could appear right beside a person with no audible indication of his presence. That too was unnatural, the old woman thought, as she slackened her pace for a moment and peered about her in the dusk.

Sometimes the boy would sit in a curious, hunched-up posture as though listening for something, and then his yellow eyes would glow and his immobile figure and tense, catlike face would seem to contain such pent-up fury that old Mrs. Cartwright felt almost afraid. It was ridiculous, she would tell herself, but even though she repeated this a hundred times, she was always left with the same conclusion. There was something queer about the child and all Sylvia's praising of Lionel's virtues could not erase this impression from her mind.

Lionel had been more difficult than ever today. Sylvia had gone up to see relatives in Mitcham and the boy must go to the Zoo. He had already been up twice with school parties this year, so the request was a surprising one to old Mrs. Cartwright. But Sylvia had merely laughed with that maddeningly obtuse attitude she had to what her sister called 'situations' and had said it would do them both good. It had been a trying day. It had begun when Lionel had half-frightened to death another boy on the bus with something he had said or done. Whatever it was, the child had to be taken off by its parents, half-hysterical, and there was a nasty atmosphere for the rest of the journey.

Old Mrs. Cartwright

The conductor kept giving Lionel dark looks and had muttered something to Mrs. Cartwright about reporting the matter. And then when they got off there was a tremendous hullabaloo, with the conductor shouting that something had bit him. Everyone on the lower deck got up and hunted about for a dog and the conductor kept shouting and holding his leg. Old Mrs. Cartwright had to admit there was a tear in his trousers and what looked like a nasty gash beneath. The conductor looked around for Lionel but the boy was nowhere to be seen. He rang the bell with ill grace and as the bus went up the hill Mrs. Cartwright was left with the image of him binding up his leg with his handkerchief.

She retained a bad impression of the entire incident for the rest of the afternoon, an impression which was not improved by the spectacle of Lionel hiding in a gateway until the bus had passed out of sight. His deep yellow eyes glowed with pleasure and he was smiling quietly to himself as they walked the rest of the way to the Zoo.

Once in the Zoo it had been an enervating atmosphere for the old lady. The day was hot and the paddocks and enclosures were crowded; Mrs. Cartwright thought the monkeys with their red behinds were vulgar and disgusting and some of the manners of the visitors seemed little improvement on those of the animals. No, she said to herself, she was past enjoying these sort of places and in the company of such a boy the day was one in which enjoyment was hardly likely to figure.

She was getting old, she told herself; her heart was not what it was and the noise of the animals, the pressure of the crowds round the cages, and the heat had fatigued her greatly by early afternoon. But Lionel's interest in the animals was insatiable; it was his intention, no less, to see every single creature the Zoo contained, and he had mapped out an itinerary which would enable them to carry out this exhausting programme.

Old Mrs. Cartwright was more than glad when lunchtime came; though the restaurant was crowded the breeze from the fans, the pleasant view from the open window, the comfortable chair, the cheerfulness of the waitress and, above all, the scalding hot coffee with which they finished the salad and ice-cream meal, more than compensated for the tiresomeness of the morning and the presence of her nephew.

Lionel had been a little less trouble than usual. He ate his food with his usual unsmiling stolidity, answered his aunt's occasional comments in monosyllables and spent much time in consulting the elaborate chart of the Zoo enclosures he had drawn up. The only blot on the mealtime was the curious attitude of the waitress, who seemed to regard Lionel with considerable caution. Twice during the meal she asked if old Mrs. Cartwright had brought a dog in with her and though she was assured that this was not so, she continued to look under the table whenever she passed, with a worried expression on her pale, oval face.

It was when she had got up to pay the bill that Mrs. Cartwright heard the muffled clatter of dishes on the thick carpet; she found the waitress surrounded by a small crowd of diners. Her face was paler than ever and tears trembled on her eyelids.

"There was a dog under the table!" she said furiously.

She indicated her torn and laddered stocking; the skin of her leg was punctured and a thin trickle of blood ran down.

"It flew out when I was clearing away," she said, as someone helped her to a chair.

Mrs. Cartwright paid her bill and went out with a strange feeling of foreboding. Lionel was nowhere about. Fortunately, he had already left the restaurant before the affair with the dog. Mrs. Cartwright found him a moment or two later leaning up against the railings surrounding the bear-pit; she was glad that he had lost the sullen look. He was quite attractive when he smiled, though she did not much care for the way the edges of his mouth curled, which took away much of the attraction of the smile.

It was already getting late when old Mrs. Cartwright and Lionel entered by the Lion House. She hated big cats but the boy was fascinated by them and if there had been no regulation closing times in the Gardens, he might well have spent the night there. The house was half empty and the cats were quiet after having been fed. Old Mrs. Cartwright sank on to a bench with relief. With a little luck she could count on at least twenty minutes of freedom from anxiety and exertion. Lionel was already making a tour of the cages. A deep-throated

⚜ OLD MRS. CARTWRIGHT

roar throbbed through the Lion House and she heard with alarm a big body crash against the bars at the far end of the large Victorian structure. She was about to call out when the beast's roaring changed to deep purrs of contentment and she saw Lionel, his yellow eyes fixed on the lion's, as the two faced each other through the bars.

There were still several people in the Lion House and there was no further noise from the cages, so old Mrs. Cartwright dozed for a few minutes, mentally and physically exhausted by the exertions of the day. She slept longer than she intended and when she awoke saw with a start of alarm that it was already getting dark outside; the Lion House was quite deserted and the slanting red rays of the declining sun sent feeble beams through the oval windows. The yellow eyes of the cats blinked eerily at her from the dusk of the cages as she hurried past, and she thought once again uneasily of her nephew.

There was no sign of Lionel; and what was more the entire Gardens seemed to be deserted. Was it possible that they had already closed and her presence in the Lion House had somehow been overlooked? Mrs. Cartwright plodded grimly on down the never-ending paths; leaves rustled in the light wind which had sprung up and strange animal noises, like the sounds of the jungle, came across the park on the night air.

Old Mrs. Cartwright's heart was full of anger and irritation against the boy; it was just like Lionel to go off and leave her in this way. To tell the truth she hated most animals and the atmosphere of these nasty gardens at dusk was not at all to her taste. She had left her umbrella somewhere, her feet ached and on top of it all she could not seem to find her way out. She had been making for the northern entrance, but here she was once again back near the bear-pits. She moved on down the paths, a forlorn figure, her black, old-fashioned coat flapping in the breeze. A deep, belling vibration sounded from ahead; it made a mournful echo in the carmine dusk of the vast gardens. The cougar called again, twice more, each time a rasping weight on Mrs. Cartwright's heart, and then was silent.

She could feel her breath hissing in her throat as she came out at the junction of four concrete paths she had not noticed before. She stepped to the left along a paddock in which antlered forms moved mysteriously in the warm darkness. She walked away, out into the middle of the path, calling Lionel anxiously by name.

There was no reply, only a brittle echo, and the rustling of great wings from the aviary beyond. A bird called solemnly from one of the houses and the slow chorus was taken up by a dozen others. Old Mrs. Cartwright stood hesitant for a moment, wondering which path to take. The attenuated form of a crane was like a sinister pink question mark in the dusk.

Then she set off again, her pace slower now, tottering a little from the weight of the bag she carried, her heart thudding with frightening loudness.

She was passing along a narrow path fringed with bushes when she heard the rustling. At first she thought it came from the cages beyond and increased her pace a little. But it seemed to keep in step with her, just beyond the bushes to the left hand side. Old Mrs. Cartwright stopped and found that the noise had stopped also. She did not like this. The darkness had by now almost descended, there was no one at all in the Zoological Gardens, and she still seemed no nearer to finding her way out.

Her heart beat like a great bell in her throat. The rustling began again.

"Lionel, is that you?" she called in a tremulous voice. "Be a good boy and don't play games."

But there came no answer, only the vibrating echo of her own faltering tones. The lion roared again, from a long way across the park, and this was followed by myriad other noises. The animals seemed restless and uneasy. Mrs. Cartwright was glad they were in their cages; the cries were unnerving at this time of night.

The crackling in the bushes crept closer. She seemed unable to move. She could see the edges of the bushes quivering in the faint light that still came from the sky. She dropped the bag as something came at her throat out of the tunnel of boughs. Shriek after shriek left her and as life faded she was left only with the impression of the animal's burning yellow eyes.

⚜ OLD MRS. CARTWRIGHT

⚜ 2

The affair made a great scandal at the Zoo, whose authorities were, of course, aghast at any suggestion that one of their animals could have been responsible. A thorough check was made but every beast was accounted for and all the cages and enclosures were intact. The Medical Officer had a difficult passage explaining things to the Coroner when the time came.

Old Mrs. Cartwright had died of a heart attack, of course. But not before her tongue had been torn clean out of her mouth. Shock and loss of blood had been contributory factors. But some wild beast had been responsible and there was talk of rats or other nocturnal creatures from the park outside the Zoo walls. Another curious feature to the doctor's mind was the flesh found beneath the dead woman's fingernails. Although covered with thick black hairs, this was definitely human.

Old Mrs. Cartwright had been found only a hundred yards from one of the Zoo's main entrances where at least two of the keepers were still on duty. The boy Lionel had reported himself at the gate some while after. The doctor had felt it best not to distress the lad with his aunt's death and after taking Lionel's address had given him his bus fare home. Although Lionel's demeanour was normal and he told Doctor Swanson he had not been worried at being lock-ed in after dark, the doctor had his own misgivings.

His own private view was that the boy had been terrified. His face and forehead were covered with cuts and scratches, evidently caused by his hurried flight through the bushes. In fact the cuts were so bad that the doctor felt it necessary to give the boy treatment before sending him home.

Lionel's face was almost ecstatic and his yellow eyes glowed with pale fire as he let himself into the house with his own key.

"Did you have a nice time with Auntie, dear?" said his mother from her accustomed place in front of the television.

"Yes, mummy," said Lionel. "I had a lovely day at the Zoo."

✒ CHARON

✒ 1

MR. SOAMES GAVE A HEAVY SIGH, PUT DOWN HIS PEN ON the blotting pad in front of him, pushed back his chair from the battered desk and closed his aching eyes. The heat from the four bar gasfire in his little office was really stifling this evening though the cold was biting outside the window. Dusk was already falling over the town, the footsteps of passers-by sounded loud and brittle in the winter air, and the last rays of the red November sun stained the opposite rooftops with a final touch of gilt.

He was not at all well, had not been so for some weeks. He had been overdoing things of late; he supposed he really ought to see the doctor. The extra work in which he had been engaged and the lack of ventilation in the office were no doubt contributory factors. He passed his hand across a forehead on which beads of sweat had suddenly become apparent. He promised himself that he would seek medical advice if the trouble persisted.

It was not that there was anything badly wrong, Mr. Soames told himself; it was difficult to pin-point the cause of his concern. A slight dizziness, a tightness at the temples, pains in the chest; it was more likely to be indigestion than anything else. But one could not be too careful at his age. He led a sedentary life; too long hours and the constant sitting had led to an ungraceful thickening of the figure and he had read somewhere that the fifties were a dangerous period for men of his physique. Yet, as he was placed, he could not afford to

✒ CHARON

slacken off. Another career at his age was impossible to contemplate, yet there was no doubt in his own mind that a change of scenery and work in the open-air would have taken care of all his troubles and added a decade or two to his expectation of life.

Mr. Soames sighed again. The trouble was that there were too many accountants in business for a town of its size. And his own connection was too small and old-fashioned to compete with the bigger firms recently established and which were capturing all the industrial accounts of the area. He could not, for instance, afford the purchase of expensive electronic accounting equipment which would have taken much of the drudgery out of his day. So Mr. Soames, aided by his one typist, worked long hours in the two minute rooms which constituted his 'suite of offices' in the maze of alleys in the older and more unfashionable part of the town.

He was fortunate, he supposed, to still retain the brewery account; they had been good friends and one of his earliest clients when he had set up in business for himself over thirty years before. And he still did the work for most of the small traders and businessmen who had their premises about the Market Square in the same quarter in which his offices were situated. But these were only small accounts unfortunately, and the big money was with the rapidly expanding factory belt at the edge of the town.

So it was that Mr. Soames had to work long hours of overtime on the accounts, aided only by a neolithic typewriter. He always presented his figures neatly typed for the benefit of clients, but without modern equipment the columns of figures had to be added in the old way, so that he seemed to spend more and more time hunched over his desk, fountain pen in hand. But it was a living, Mr. Soames told himself for the hundredth time in the past six months.

Fortunately his eyes were as good as they had ever been; he wore glasses, of course, but his sight had never given him any trouble and for that he must be thankful. Unless one counted the recent headaches. But much of that might be laid to the smallness of the room and the excessive heat; he always meant to turn down the gasfire as the day progressed, but as always he forgot, so that around seven, if he were working on a difficult set of books, he would find the room beginning to spin around him and an intolerable headache like an iron band across his forehead.

Mr. Soames got up unsteadily and went over and turned off the gas. The brightness of the room faded as he did so and he had to clutch at the mantelpiece to prevent himself from falling. He fought for breath for a moment or two. Then, thoroughly frightened, he let himself out of the front door and stood gulping in the cold air of the night. He stood outside the office for perhaps ten minutes until the dizziness had receded and the constriction round his heart had subsided.

Then he made his way feebly into the bar of The Two Carters, which was almost opposite the office; it was a thing he never normally did and the landlord's surprise was evident on his face. Mr. Soames had a double whisky and then another. He sat in a corner by himself for almost half an hour, until he felt completely normal again. His breathing was easy and unhurried and his face had regained its customary pink complexion, he was glad to see, as he glanced in the mirror over the bar. He really must cut down on these late sessions; the lack of air and exercise must have brought on a giddy attack.

His fright quite forgotten, Mr. Soames found himself outside the public house. He hesitated on the pavement. The warm glow from his office shone across to him, but he didn't want to go back for the moment. He would take a short walk before locking up for the night. There were lights in many of the antique shops in the quaint little alleys of this part of the town, and Mr. Soames felt that a stroll through The Shades, as the area was picturesquely called, would be beneficial, placed as he was.

He had no family and lived with his widowed sister at the edge of the town. She rarely expected him before eight and they did not dine until nine so that he had plenty of time. So the accountant, his spirits quite restored, made his way through the stone-posted entrance of The Shades and set out across the cobbles to where lights shone invitingly from the shop windows. It was a long time since he had allowed himself such a luxury and Mr. Soames was enchanted with his promenade. It was clear that much in life was passing him by. He would have to cut down on his hours and get out and about more.

✐ Charon

Though he had left his hat and coat in the office, Mr. Soames had on a thick tweed suit and an equally thick waistcoat, so that he did not at all feel the cold, though there had been a piercing wind. But here in the small alleys which crowded together in riotous confusion, there was no wind; indeed, the atmosphere was almost warm and Mr. Soames wandered contentedly, stopping at window after window as the fancy took him. His interest revived as his gaze passed over some excellent china; he had once had a great interest in antiques in his earlier days, had begun collecting in a modest way, and now the contents of the more expensive antique shop windows began to have an enchanting effect on his mind.

There were few people about and the light from the occasional street lamps—Mr. Soames was glad to see that some of the town's remaining gas lamps had been allowed to exist here—cast a romantic, flickery light on the old buildings and the faded finery in the windows of the shops, two out of three of which seemed to be of the curiosity shop type. There was a sparkle in Mr. Soames' eye and a long absent vigour in his walk as he came at length into a very old square, of an antiquity greater than the rest. It was ill-lit—one lamp alone cast feeble rays across the worn cobbles—but a bright moon shone down and Mr. Soames could make out the details of the houses with extraordinary clarity.

None of the shop windows were illuminated and Mr. Soames was about to retrace his steps, when his attention was caught by a shop older even than those around it. There was nothing special about it but the wrought iron of its balconies and the old clapboard upper storeys of the premises had a certain period charm. He went over to the darkened windows and pressed his face against them. The shop appeared to be empty and all he could make out was moonlight, straggling down in misty swathes from the tall, narrow windows. Yet the atmosphere of the old shop seemed to give him a remarkable peace of mind and Mr. Soames was humming with pleasure as he came away. He made a mental note of the square so that he could come back and have a look in daylight.

As he turned to make his way back to his own part of the town he saw there was something stencilled on the windows of the great porch. He went back and gazed up at the faded gold lettering. It said: CHARON LTD. Exporters.

Mr. Soames smiled. There was nothing curious about that. Whoever the firm was, it must have gone out of business some while ago because the shop was quite empty. He would look them up in the street list the following day. He went back to his office, switched off the lights, locked up and putting on his hat and coat, walked home. The night seemed a lot colder but the dinner provided by his sister was excellent and before he went to bed Mr. Soames felt that both his business and his personal life might be a lot worse.

2

Next day Mr. Soames was rather busier than usual, but he took care not to work late and had the good sense not to have the gasfire too high and thus avoided a repetition of his unpleasant experience of the night before. It was not until he got home that night—he arrived at half-past six, an unheard-of occurrence to his sister's mind—that the shop in the old square came to recollection. He glanced round for the street directory and then remembered that his only copy was at the office. He felt a little put out about this, but then dismissed it with a smile. It was of no importance and he would ask his typist, Janet, to look it up in the morning. But as the evening went on he recalled again the quaint old square and experienced in memory the comforting feeling of peace he had felt when he had gazed through the windows of the shop.

On Wednesday Mr. Soames arrived earlier at his office than usual. It was pleasing to him that his health had been a little better in the last day or two; he put this down to his more sensible regime and the less rigorous office hours and resolved to adopt this course for the future, if he could possibly manage it. Once again he had a fairly busy morning, with far too many telephone calls necessitating his own attention and it was not until he was sipping the midday coffee that Janet had brought, that he again thought of the shop in the square.

Charon

He had Janet bring him the most up-to-date street directory she could find, but though the square was listed, to his annoyance he could find no reference to Charon Ltd. Then he looked at the cover of the book and found that the directory was more than two years old. Janet searched her own part of the office but no more recent issue was discoverable. Mr. Soames had to admit ruefully to himself that this was typical of his own firm.

However, he would ask the girl to ring up Directory Inquiries and no doubt they would be able to supply the correct information. Mr. Soames did not know really why he was bothering with this, but there was something about the shop in the square which intrigued him, so that he felt he had to know the answer. It was nearly one o'clock before Janet came to him to say that there was no listing from Directory Inquiries for the shop he wanted. He thanked Janet pleasantly enough, but there was a frown of annoyance on his brow. After the office shut for the lunch hour and the clacking of Janet's heels had died away down the street, Mr. Soames sat staring in front of him, but he did not see the blotter on his battered old desk nor the sets of figures on which he had been working.

Mr. Soames usually ate lunch at the Gaiety Cafe, a conservative old-fashioned type of restaurant on the High Street, where among the fumed-oak panelling he could greet his few acquaintances or clients, while being served at the soothing hands of the two maiden ladies who ran the establishment. But today he thought he would forsake his long cherished custom and have a stroll through The Shades. The walk would do him good, the excess weight avoided by missing the meal was on the credit side and the small expedition would put his mind at rest. If he could find the number of the shop he could then check again and discover why the premises had not been listed. Perhaps the proprietors of Charon Ltd. had left a very long time ago indeed, and the premises were now registered under another name altogether.

Mr. Soames once again told himself that the whole affair was too trivial to bother about; that he was a busy man and could more profitably occupy his time, but the shop in the square had been intriguing in the lamplight of the winter evening two nights ago and the area had all the novelty of a freshly discovered country to him. He told himself that he might be in for a disappointment; in the daylight the square would probably seem only tawdry and the disused shop dirty, even squalid.

Yet he hoped this would not be so. It was a cold but sunny afternoon and the wind of the last two days had died away. Mr. Soames felt positively robust as he strode along the small cobbled lanes of The Shades, glancing casually in the windows of the antique shops and taking in great gulps of clear, frosty air. He felt better in himself than he had for a long while and he squared his shoulders in his thick overcoat and stepped out in a way which would have caused surprise among his acquaintances. When Mr. Soames eventually arrived at his destination he was not disappointed; the little square was a positive gem from the past, its shops and premises bright with paint and glowing with brass fitments.

Mr. Soames had some difficulty in locating CHARON LTD. He had another slight pang of annoyance when he found that he had evidently been mistaken the other evening; it was several shops farther down than he had remembered and there was no wrought iron scrollwork that he could see. But the name, in gold leaf, was quite plain enough, and the legend underneath: Exporters.

Though he could have sworn that the premises were disused on the occasion of his first visit, Mr. Soames could now see well enough that not only was the shop occupied but quite plainly open for business, though there were no customers while he was in the vicinity. Mr. Soames looked in at the windows again; he could see long wooden counters, a pair of brass scales and large jars and bottles ranged round the walls. The light was difficult inside, but by dint of placing his hand over his eyes, Mr. Soames made out the tall figure of the proprietor or manager busying himself behind the counter.

He was dressed in a long shopman's smock of some dark material, belted at the waist, but Mr. Soames could not make out his face. He hesitated at the door for some minutes, but when the distant toll of a bell marked two o'clock, he realised that not only had he missed his lunch but that he would have to walk fast if he were to be at his premises in time for the reopening of the business.

◈ CHARON

Mr. Soames spent a puzzled afternoon. He found it difficult to concentrate on the columns of figures and they had a way of swimming in front of his eyes, so that Mr. Soames was afraid of a recurrence of his recent dizzy spell. He sent Janet out for tea, toast and cakes at four o'clock, to make up for his missed lunch and behind the locked door of his office he sipped the steaming amber liquid and wondered how he could have come to make such a mistake over the occupancy of the old shop in the square.

Janet came in to say goodnight at half-past five and to report that she had locked the front door. This was the usual routine but after she had left, Mr. Soames did something that he could not remember doing for more than two years. It was just twenty-five to six when he reached down his hat and coat from the peg, put out the lights and slammed the door behind him. A moment later he was striding out purposefully across the cobblestones and into The Shades.

He now felt that he knew the way by heart and in no time at all, it seemed, he was back in the little old square that was so strange and yet so familiar to him. To his relief the shop he sought was just as he remembered it but he was again surprised to see the clapboard staring white in the moonlight and the wrought iron of the scrollwork. The feeble light of the gas-lamp flickered uncertainly on the gold lettering of the sign but look as he would Mr. Soames could see no traces of the counters and shelves of the afternoon.

He prowled round the outside windows in a baffled manner, but his unease was giving way to the feeling of extraordinary calm and peace that he had felt on the previous occasion when he had visited the square by night. The interior of the shop appeared full of swirling moonlight and something that looked like ribbons of mist; the idea was absurd. It must have been some trick of the light combined with the shadows of the leaves of trees in front of the street lamp.

Mr. Soames was just about to leave the square when he was startled to see the tall figure of the shopman. He was half-turned towards Mr. Soames, but the latter could still not see his face. It was impossible to make out in the misty light, but the figure affected to wave in a jocular manner at the accountant. Mr. Soames should have been surprised but again he wasn't; it almost felt as though the shopman were an old friend. The encounter lasted only a matter of seconds and then the shopman had disappeared through a small door at the back of the premises, which Mr. Soames had not noticed before. There did not seem much point in hanging about in the empty square, and as a patrolling police-man was now regarding him somewhat suspiciously, Mr. Soames made haste to regain his own part of the town and the comfort of his sister's fireside.

3

During the days that passed, Mr. Soames sought to push the business of CHARON LTD. to the back of his mind, but the shop and latterly the figure of the shopman himself, had begun to occupy more and more the foreground of his thoughts. Mr. Soames was a practical man and though there was something a little peculiar about his experiences in the square, however easy to explain away they might be in the common light of reason, he somehow equated his visits with his recent improved state of health.

For there was no doubt about this; several of his acquaintances had remarked upon it and his sister had greeted with pleasure his earlier quittance of work and had rearranged the evening domestic schedule accordingly. There had been a greater increase of business at Mr. Soames' office recently and though he never stayed on in the evenings, he found his working time during the day fully taken up and had no occasion to turn his steps in the direction of the shop in the square.

But much of the evening time was spent dreaming of the curious old building and in speculation on its possible history, and Mr. Soames found the wildness of the winter nights entirely forgotten. He slept better also, the headaches and pressure round the heart had left him, and he enjoyed an occasional whisky at The Two Carters at six o'clock, on his way home. The image of the old shopman—Mr. Soames imagined him to be old, though he had never seen his face—constantly recurred and with it a tranquillity and all-consuming peace such as Mr. Soames had never known.

CHARON

It was nearly three weeks later before he found himself drawn again in the direction of the square. Here was the moonlight and the single lamp; the shop was in the recollected position—Mr. Soames had only visited it in daylight the once—and the combined light of the moon and the lamp shone on the white-boarded walls and the scrolls of ironwork.

To Mr. Soames' eyes the interior was just a shimmering chaos of misty light but the figure of the shopman, who seemed to work as late as Mr. Soames himself, was clearer and sharper in outline than he had ever seen it. He was now turned completely towards Mr. Soames and though his face should have been distinct, the light and the shadows made a blurred, shifting mask of it, so that the features ran together and changed with the patterns of the light. To Mr. Soames the shopman now assumed the appearance of an old friend and he was not at all surprised when the man gave him a definite signal. There was no mistaking the gesture of the upraised arm; the shopman wanted him to come in. Mr. Soames had actually stepped forward and was in the act of lifting the latch of the great door when he found the policeman almost at his elbow.

"Are you all right, sir?" said the officer in a kindly voice, putting a hand on his arm. "You look a little under the weather to me."

"Quite all right, thank you," said Mr. Soames in a confused and stammering voice. The officer saluted and passed on his round of shop doorways. He tested the door of CHARON LTD. which appeared to be locked. His footsteps passed across the square. When Mr. Soames himself tried the latch of the door he was disappointed to find the police officer's own assessment correct. And the figure of the shop owner was nowhere to be seen. Mr. Soames returned home in a more thoughtful frame of mind than ever.

4

Christmas passed away without incident. Mr. Soames' health continued to improve and business had held up surprisingly well during the past months. The end of the financial year in April should find Mr. Soames' affairs in better shape than they had been for years. The shop in the square was now only a vague blur in Mr. Soames' mind and there were whole weeks when he never thought about it at all. But in the kernel of his mind persisted the image of the little old man in the smock who owned the shop and he drew strange peace from this.

He knew also that his curiosity would never be satisfied until he had made the acquaintance of the shopman; it was now something he knew to be inevitable. With this firmly fixed in his consciousness he no longer found it necessary to hurry through the cobbled streets. What there would be between him and the old shopman was preordained; there was no need for haste. Mr. Soames was enjoying his days, he continued to keep his earlier hours, his health had improved beyond all measure, and all this he felt to be due to the peace which emanated from the little square in The Shades and in particular from the premises and personality of the owner of CHARON LTD.

And all this from a man whom he had never really met, though Mr. Soames felt he had known him all his life. It was the third week in January before he again felt the urge to visit the premises. It was daylight but this time Mr. Soames had been on one of his rare visits to a client in a neighbouring town. He had returned by train and after leaving the station was about to join a queue for a bus when he realised that if he walked along the main road, he would eventually enter the area of The Shades from the opposite side.

He had never been that way but after making inquiries of several people and being redirected as many times, he eventually entered the sprawl of alleys and at length found himself on the far side of the square. Once again the shop seemed to be in a different position, though this was no doubt due to his having approached from another direction. Mr. Soames felt almost exultant when he saw that the shop was open for business and his friend the shopman was again behind the counter.

As he hesitated in the doorway, the man turned towards him and Mr. Soames was impressed by the beauty of his eyes. A smile shifted and shimmered on his face, and his voice, as though from a great distance, said to Mr. Soames, "Do please enter, won't you?"

Charon

Mr. Soames had lifted up the latch and a great voice was singing in his ear, when he was suddenly buffeted. He came to himself to find a stout, coarse-looking stranger had collided with him right in the doorway of the shop.

"Do look where you are going!" the stout man said crossly, though it was he who was evidently to blame, and he went trotting off down the street. Mr. Soames tried the door but was not really surprised that it was locked, though he felt in his heart that it would have yielded easily enough had he not been interrupted by the stout man. When he looked around for the shopman he was nowhere to be seen.

Mr. Soames went away and it was not until several days later that he was able to put the matter entirely from his mind. But he knew that the urgent business he had with the shop proprietor could not be long delayed. His curiosity, it seemed to him, had been kept within bounds with admirable restraint on his part. He could not rest until he had discovered what it was, what great peace emanated from the curious little shop in the middle of this busy town.

In the meantime his business affairs flowed past like a dream and though his good health continued and he attended to the wants of clients efficiently enough, Janet in particular sensed that his mind was elsewhere these last few months. It was in mid-February that he paid his last visit to the shop. It had been a blustery day of icy rain, but towards evening the downpour stopped.

Janet locked up and said goodnight to her employer as usual. As soon as she had left the building Mr. Soames closed his desk, placed the cover over his typewriter and putting on his hat and coat left the office. The outer air struck chill and damp and the breath steamed from his mouth as he pushed on through the maze of alleys into The Shades. Here, the wind died away, and it was almost warm compared to the more exposed reaches of the town, but Mr. Soames had no thought for the weather, his business or anything else. He knew that tonight the face of his friend would be fully revealed.

He quickened his steps and on arriving at the square was astonished to see that the shop was a blaze of light. He hesitated t the entrance but was then reassured to see the shopman's friendly figure waving to him from inside. Mr. Soames hesitated but a moment longer. The shopman spoke and his voice was like the ringing of a thousand silver bells.

"What has kept you so long, my friend? I have been expecting you before."

Mr. Soames hesitated no longer. He pushed open the door, which gave easily to his touch. A wave of warm air rushed out and engulfed him. Music sounded in his ears. The interior of the shop was full of mist and moonbeams.

The little old shopman, in his long smock drawn in at the waist with its old black belt, stood smiling at him. His face, which seemed to shift and move in the strange light of the interior of the shop, yet seemed to Mr. Soames to be the most beautiful he had ever seen. And his eyes were the kindest in the world. He held out his hand to Mr. Soames and the touch was like fire.

"Come, be not afraid," he said.

Mr. Soames followed him through the shimmering moonlight and over the threshold of the little door. He felt no fear and his heart was filled with a tremendous peace. He followed the little old man down steps wreathed with warm mist. There, under ancient vaulted arches where torches burned and dark water lapped, the old man leapt aboard a great rocking barge.

To Mr. Soames it appeared to be full of mist and memories. There were people sitting on the benches of the ponderous craft. Their faces were happy, though they wore dark robes. Music sounded over the water and seemed to waft with it on heavy, sensuous waves, the laughter of women and happiness.

The little old man smiled at Mr. Soames and it was a smile of great certitude and great beauty. He held out his hand over the small gulf of rocking water that separated Mr. Soames from all that his heart desired. "Come, be not afraid," he said again, with the voice of a thousand bells. "We have just room for one more!"

Mr. Soames hesitated no longer. For the meaning of the words on the door had just become clear to him. His smile echoed the boatman's own and his heart was full of a great peace. He clasped the hand the dark man held out to him, and stepped aboard. The boat rocked as the shopman pushed it out from the shore.

Charon

5

The discovery of Mr. Soames' body huddled in an entry of Newport Square became quite a cause celebre in the town. It was something which Mr. Soames' friends and business acquaintances could never fathom and indeed the Coroner was at a loss to why one of the town's best-known businessmen should have been drawn to such a dilapidated, disused shop. For a police constable called to give evidence at the inquest had stated it he had seen the deceased man try the door of the shop late night on at least three occasions, and twice more had he seen Mr. Soames in the vicinity near midnight.

The Coroner had inquiries made into the history of the shop this produced no further evidence of interest. The Carron Engineering Company's Export Division had ceased trading at that address more than fifteen years earlier. One thing which struck all the witnesses, though, including Mr. Soames' sister had been the transfigured look on Mr. Soames' face.

One witness had described it as being twenty years younger. And indeed, all were agreed, that in Mr. Soames' visage, and in particular the eyes, there was a deep and lasting contentment.

✑ The Great Vore

✑ 1

THE MATTER FIRST CAME TO MY ATTENTION WHEN A CUTTING bureau whose services I used, sent me a sheaf of clippings. There was no covering letter, but a pencilled note which said: Think this may interest you. More to follow.

The first one I looked at, read: Followers of the Great Vore meet Gwyllim Chapel, Lantarch 12:00 P.M. Invocation of the Old Ones.

The cutting was dated a month earlier and extracted from a county series of newspapers.

The next was from the personal column of the *Daily Telegraph*, and said simply: Great Vore, High Tide Lantarch. Footsteps in the Mist.

And finally, another cutting from the *Evening News* a few nights later: Lantarch Chapel "Keels grate on the beach." The Great Vore. 12:00 P.M. Ask for Number One.

In my long career of investigating extraordinary occurrences in many parts of the world, a number of which had originated in apparently commonplace newspaper clippings, none promised so well on the surface as these announcements, and I looked forward with more than usual curiosity to the agency's next letter.

I half expected an anti-climax, as much of my work in this field often ends in disappointment or near-farce, but Wednesday's post brought a more sober note and a heightening of my interest.

All these cuttings were within a few days of one another, but

⚜ THE GREAT VORE

the next communication from the agency contained two, both more than a week after the first series.

One was from a national evening newspaper, and said: The Great Vore. Lantarch. Invocation of the Old Ones. Introduction of the Acolytes. Supreme Offering. 12:00 P.M.

This was decidedly curious, and though many cranks insert the most unadulterated drivel in the personal columns of newspapers, I knew that Carfax, the owner of the cuttings agency, must have got on to something of more than ordinary interest. Carfax had an unusual mind and he would not waste my time on trivia or foolery. The final cutting was from the front page of a national morning newspaper, just over a week old, and it made me unexpectedly crumble my toast, so that a large portion of it fell into my coffee cup, much to the amusement of my old friend Edwards, who was having breakfast with me.

The cutting was quite a long affair, and it absorbed me tremendously. It began, "Bristol police were this morning commencing an investigation into the murder of a man, whose body, bearing shocking wounds and mutilations, was picked up in the Bristol Channel by the freighter Nancy B, last night. When the ship docked this morning, Superintendent Neilson of Bristol Police, and other experts boarded the vessel to begin their preliminary inquiries.

"Later, Supt. Neilson announced that the man, who had not been identified, was aged about thirty-five and had been in the water more than a week, judging by the condition of the body. He was unclothed and though the immediate cause of death could not be ascertained, his throat had been cut, and there were curious wounds all over his body, which also bore deep knife marks of a ritualistic nature.

"The Superintendent said that it would take some time to complete inquiries. The possibility that the murder could have taken place aboard some ship could not be ruled out, which would considerably widen the scope of the investigations."

The rest of the article was of interest but not really germane to this story. When Edwards had departed, I carefully re-read the whole series of cuttings and then once again perused the note from Carfax. It ended with a series of statements.

Darkness, Mist & Shadow

Typical specimens were: Lantarch is on the south coast, is it not? Neilson is an old friend, I believe. The dates fit, don't they? Tide tables might help here.

Though this might seem the most obscure jumble to the layman, Carfax was thinking along the same lines as myself. As I worked through the last cutting concerning the murder, I had already bridged these gaps and was on the point of reaching down my gazetteer, when my friend Edwards, anticipating that I was about to become absorbed in some abtruse problem, with remarkable tact had made his excuses and left.

I went and looked out of the window in an absent-minded manner; a thin mist was coming up over the old London square in which I had my flat, and the outlines of the small park in the middle, were already becoming blurred. As I looked, the railings wavered and disappeared from sight. I returned to my table and put another bar of my gas-fire on. It already seemed like evening though it was only half-past nine in the morning.

After some slight hesitation I telephoned Carfax; he had already been at his office over an hour. His hearty tones boomed over the line, in striking contrast to the atmosphere in the flat, which the mist had already isolated in a veil which seemed to insulate all sound from outside.

"Ah, Professor Kane," he said. "I thought you'd enjoy this one. Any ideas?"

"It's a pretty long shot, linking these two sets of cuttings," I said drily. "But you may say, yes, I am interested. It was, I presume, the ritualistic nature of the killing and the remarkable coincidences in the two texts that first set you off?"

Carfax sounded enthusiastic. "I'll be pleased to hear what you make of it, Professor," he said. "The whole thing may be a frost, of course, but on the other hand there are strange similarities. It wasn't until the murder cutting landed on my desk yesterday, that the parallel pieces of information clicked. A bright young man in my office was collating some of the more bizarre news items, and he thought it might interest a specialist like yourself."

"Did he?" I said. "Full marks to him. You didn't remember, I suppose, to get me every possible news cutting from the nationals and locals on this Bristol Channel matter?"

Carfax chuckled. "As a matter of fact, we did," he said. "A large bundle of stuff should be with you by the midday post. And we are, of course, keeping a look-out for any more personal column announcements."

I mentally gave him a high rating, and rang off. The next two hours provided me with a most entertaining exercise. The cuttings, as Carfax had pointed out, could be linked in a number of ways. Apart from the obvious fact that there had been a murder, which the police had reported as being of a ritual nature, there were a series of other extraordinary coincidences between the two sets of cuttings.

I could, of course, make nothing of such phrases as The Great Vore. Invocation of the Old Ones was obviously an incantation connected with sacrifice, and was repeated twice in the series. Footsteps in the Mist and Keels Grate on the Beach, both reminiscent of the sea, could be passwords for the mysterious Number One—assuming that all this rigmarole was genuine.

The Introduction of the Acolytes smacked of some similar ceremony, and the Supreme Offering could refer to a human sacrifice; here, in the other cutting, we had a man who had been murdered in a most revolting manner and who bore ritual markings.

As Carfax had mentioned, Superintendent Neilson was an old friend; he had been a brilliant sergeant in the London flying squad some years earlier, and his path and mine had often crossed in those days. I should have to contact him, regarding the details of the markings. But my gazetteer and a nautical almanac supplied the most exciting series of possibilities.

Lantarch was a small town on the south coast of Wales, on a rugged and remote splinter of Pembrokeshire. My gazetteer gave no information other than that market day was Tuesday and that the population was just over 4,000. There was no mention of a Gwyllim Chapel, but I had hardly expected to come across that information.

Come to that, a chapel was the last place in which one would hope to find such a sect. The body had been picked up in the Bristol

Channel, it will be remembered. It had been in the water about a week, said the medical evidence. Cross-checking the dates of the newspaper cuttings I found that the Supreme Offering was to have taken place a week before.

Assuming that the body had been thrown into the sea off Lantarch a week earlier, give or take a day or two—here I did some calculations with my tide tables—the autumn tides in those parts could well have carried it up the Bristol Channel to the position where it was picked up by the freighter, at a point midway between Barry and Minehead.

The more I thought about it, the closer the facts seemed to fit. It was an absorbing theory, but I felt I should like to know a great deal about the dead man in the sea, before I offered a working thesis to the police, who would naturally laugh at any suggested connection between these bizarre personal clippings.

There was little I could do for the time being, so I occupied myself with other matters, though I awaited the midday post with undisguised impatience. It was rather later than anticipated, owing to the fog which had now become thicker; and it was nearer half-past twelve before I had the bundle of letters in my hand.

I recognised at once the bulky letter which contained the newspaper cuttings I was so eager to peruse, even without the stamp of the Carfax Agency; but I noticed also, a white, official looking envelope which bore a Bristol postmark. I had been thinking much of Superintendent Neilson today and it was indeed he.

The letter ran: "Dear Professor Kane, I hesitate to recall an old friendship when the recollection is likely to entail some work on your part, and I am loath to intrude on what must be an extremely busy life. However, you have no doubt read in the national press what a serious business we are engaged on here; the murder of an unknown man, whose body was taken from the sea by the crew of an incoming freighter. I take the liberty of appending official reports for your perusal. Where I think you will be able to help us considerably—and the Home Office agrees with me—is in the possible identification of some of the marks on the body, which, I am told by those who should know, are of a ritualistic nature.

"As you are one of the country's foremost living authorities on such

◄ THE GREAT VORE

subjects as the occult"—and here I stirred uncomfortably in my chair at the man's misuse of words—"we feel you may be able to assist by identifying the form and nature of the markings detailed in the enclosed photographs. These are of an official nature and are not intended for any other eyes than yours.

"I would appreciate the return of the pictures with your report, through official channels, as these are registered file copies. The pictures represent only areas of the body depicting the markings, which appear to have been inflicted with a sharp-bladed knife up to an hour before death, as they had bled considerably."

The remainder of the letter dealt with corresponding matters, and also mentioned that the police surgeon's report on the corpse was enclosed. A drawing of a reconstruction of the dead man's features was in circulation to press and television, the Superintendent concluded. To say that I was surprised at this turn of events would be to put it mildly; all the threads of the affair—that is, if they were connected—seemed to lead naturally to my hands, and it seemed that whether I would or not, the bizarre incident of the Bristol Channel murder was to be in the forefront of my attention.

I immediately dictated a letter on the transcript machine for my secretary to reply to the Superintendent that afternoon, and sat down to study the photographs and reports, and the sheaf of agency cuttings, which I had also opened.

All at once I began to sweat and the room seemed stuffy. Indeed, I got up to switch off the extra bar of the gas fire almost immediately.

The photographs of the markings on the dead man's chest, buttocks, back and legs represented black, blasphemous things that should have remained buried. There had been unnameable practices behind the carvings on this once-living flesh and I immediately thought I had better couch my report to the Superintendent in fairly guarded terms; I also realised I would have to type it myself and file the copy in my most secret dossier.

I almost retched as I traced some of the blasphemies indicated on the photographic prints, with a not-quite-steady forefinger; the Old Ones had indeed been invoked. The rites involved were so profane, obscene and of such an intricate ritual that only an immensely learned and an immensely depraved man would have been capable of carrying them out. Coupled with that was the thought that some of the implications were so awful, that I myself would not even like to invoke the names aloud.

I trembled as I forced myself to think along these lines; I was puzzled too, at some aspects of the pictures. For, mingled with the elaborate parallelograms, triangles and cabbalistic ciphers which had been traced on the victim's flesh were other, stranger markings; as near as I could make out, and I wished I had the police surgeon's colour originals, they were like oval wounds such as pincers might make, except that they were subtly different.

And one, at least, had a gaping mouth in the middle of the wound, which might have been sutured at one time or another. I put down the documents somewhat shakily, but the very nature of the death of this unknown man had given me some powerful inklings into how he might have come by his end. There were only four men in the whole of England who would have the knowledge and erudition to have been responsible for these markings—indeed, not a dozen in Europe.

And of these, I could rule out at least three. For depravity and debauchery were requirements which somewhat narrowed the field. One I knew as a man of blasphemous and decadent mind, but he was over eighty and I felt sure would not be physically capable of leading a coven such as the documents I had examined hinted at. That left, of the English savants, with whom it was logical to start; Sir Isidore Murdoch of Cumberland; Grantley Sattherwaite, the antiquarian; and two other probables whom I would have to examine.

I spent the rest of the afternoon looking up their records. My mind recoiled as I found myself delving into the proceedings of the Royal Society—I had not realised that I might have to accuse one or more such distinguished men. By the time the clock on my mantel shelf chimed five I had amassed four quite bulky dossiers. I ate a large tea with the feeling that the day represented something of an achievement.

Afterwards, I returned to my sitting-room and roughed out a long report to Superintendent Neilson. I indicated only the extent of the scholarship necessary to have inflicted the markings, and asked him to try and get the dead man identified; this might narrow the field. I had it in mind that this procedure would not only lessen the work but would greatly decrease the margin of possible error.

It could be a dangerous matter to accuse a member of the Royal Society of such a thing, and if he were our man it would obviously be dangerous in other ways also. My first letter had already been posted, so I sealed the latter report and slipped out to post it myself. I slept well that night, fortified by the knowledge that I had covered quite a lot of ground without moving from my chair.

2

The following morning I resumed my perusal of the clippings Carfax had sent me the previous midday; the mist had gone and feeble sunshine was attempting to gild the railings of the little square.

There was not a great deal new in the stories the newspapers had to tell. They were mainly variants of the original cutting and were evidently based on the same information. I turned to my copy of that morning's newspaper without any great hope of finding anything startling, but was electrified to discover that the identity of the body found floating in the Bristol Channel was known. It appeared that the police had kept back the information that the corpse bore on its left wrist a curious anchor and unicorn tattoo mark, as they were afraid publication of the news might give warning to any sea-faring friends who had knowledge of the murder.

However, the news was out now, and from the London end! This was a curious turn of the affair, and might make me review my theories, based as they were on events in the Wales-Bristol area. The man was named Esau Dobbs, an ex-seaman who had got a shore job and who had, at the time of his death, lived with his sister in Poplar. The sister had reported him missing from home almost three weeks before the discovery of the body and had stated that he had the strange tattoo-mark on the left wrist.

In the course of their investigations, the Bristol force had circulated a full description of the corpse and this had tallied with the London information already on file. The sister had travelled to Bristol the previous day and had identified the remains as being those of her brother, mainly basing this on the tattoo-mark, which would have been almost impossible to duplicate.

A fortuitous circumstance, which represented a remarkable short-cut in my investigations. I had still not formed any definite conclusions linking the murder with a possible sect of The Great Vore, but a visit to the sister's home might serve to connect the dead Dobbs with one of the four men on my shortlist, if such a link existed.

A few minutes later, I was speaking to a high ranking office at Scotland Yard, who had been of service to me on a number of occasions.

"Ah, Professor," said Commander Baron. "Many thanks for your help. Neilson has been in touch with us this morning, We may want to call on you again, now that the search seems to be moving to London."

"That's what I wanted to ask you," I replied. "If you have any officers going out to see the dead man's sister, I should be grateful if I could go along as an observer. I may be able to help and I should like to do so for my own interest."

Commander Baron was able to arrange this, and said that a patrol car would drop by to pick me up after lunch. I had just one other thing to do before then and that didn't take long. I put in a call to an old friend in Fleet Street. Mark Ingram was a sub-editor on the newspaper in which most of the personal notices relating to The Great Vore had been inserted. What I wanted to find out, if I could, was the name of the person who had placed the advertisements.

Ingram was silent for a moment after I had finished.

"It's a little out of my line, Professor," he said. "But I'll see what I can do. Our advertising boys usually regard these things as confidential. Can you give me any idea why you want the information?"

"Look, Mark," I said. "I can't promise anything, but if the line of inquiry I'm engaged in proves fruitful, I can guarantee you one of the most exclusive stories you've ever come across."

"Now you're talking," he said. "Right, just hold on a minute." In the event, it was ten minutes, but he had the information. This had me

⚘ The Great Vore

puzzled for a moment, but I realised the person who had inserted the series of advertisements could be an agent for someone else. I jotted the name and address down on my pad, thanked Ingram and rang off.

The name was Richard Abigail and the address was somewhere in Putney. All this might be leading nowhere, but the affair promised to be one of the most interesting in which I had been engaged. Then, prompted by an afterthought, I rang a second newspaper and made a similar inquiry of another acquaintance; after a while the reply came back—in both cases the name and address was the same. There was no possible doubt that the personal announcements relating to this curious sect emanated from the same source. I would have to get Carfax to check back in old files to see whether these announcements were annual or at long intervals.

It then occurred to me that the society, or whatever it was, might be a national organisation; the advertisements originated in London, a man found dead and murdered in ritual fashion, who might be connected with it, was in the Bristol Channel, and the meeting places were in Wales. The members would hardly travel all that way from as far afield as London if the meetings were frequent; or perhaps they met in different parts of the country at different times of the year? All sorts of intriguing questions were opened by this line of reasoning.

I had now done all I could that morning and, after an excellent lunch with Edwards, I returned to the flat half an hour before the police car was due to arrive. I spent the time in perusing the reports of the police surgeon who had made the original examination of Dobbs' body; the mutilation of the body had taken place before death, which was due to the cut throat; the markings would have taken upwards of an hour to inflict and the victim was conscious all the time. The throat was cut about fifteen minutes afterwards and the other strange marks on the body, which had the surgeon temporarily baffled, had been within minutes of death.

As I digested this extraordinary information, I made sure I had a complete tracing of the marks on the body and then sealed the original photographic prints in a plain envelope. A few minutes afterwards I handed them to Sergeant Mason, who called for me in a patrol car with other plain clothes officers, and asked him to return them to Neilson in Bristol in due course. He promised me his superiors would see this was done. The visit to Poplar was not entirely uneventful; Ethel Dobbs was a very ordinary woman who could say little to help the police. While Mason conducted the interview, I stood in the background making a few observations and afterwards, when Miss Dobbs led the way to the dead man's bedroom, I took the opportunity to speak to her quietly in the passage outside.

"Do you know if your brother belonged to any clubs or i societies of a confidential nature, Miss Dobbs?"

I had put the question in the most innocuous way I could, expecting perhaps some involuntary, sharp reaction, but the eyes beneath the thick glasses were quite blank.

"My brother never confided in me," she said. "He was a rough, roistering sort of man, even when he settled down on shore. He was out nearly every night in the pubs. He never told me anything. He could have belonged to a lot of things I never knew about."

She was quite palpably speaking the truth and it was obvious she knew nothing, so I thanked her and went into the bedroom. It was a small, squalid chamber with peeling brown, wallpaper; there looked to be little of interest, but the three detectives were hard at work. One had a phial of colourless liquids on a table; another was dusting for fingerprints. I do not know what they expected to find and my face must have shown it, for Mason gave me a smile and said, "Hard, extremely dull routine, Professor."

"It gets results, though," I said. What I was looking for was something in the nature of a letter or document relating to this sect of the Great Vore, for I was disinclined to abandon my cherished theory. The detectives were greatly interested in fragments of paper and charred ash which they had found j under the projecting frame of the gas fire in the grate.

They had them on a glass plate; they were fractional and were merely being examined as part of the routine, but I could see that the reconstruction of part of a letter, which it appeared to be, would probably take hours. That I could safely leave to the official force, who had far more facilities than I.

⚜ THE GREAT VORE

But as I leaned over the shoulder of a middle-aged man with the face of a scientist, who manipulated the fragments with a soft-haired brush and tweezers, I saw something that interested me very much indeed. It was the biggest single piece of paper, though it was barely a quarter of an inch across, and appeared to be part of a signature.

So far as I could make out, though the m was charred away almost beyond recognition, the letters stood for mur. I pressed my fingers together and could not deny myself the luxury of a thin smile; Sir Isidore Murdoch was one of the quartet of suspects whose names were on my file at home. The fragment proved nothing, but was interesting, distinctly interesting.

⚜ 3

"I really think we shall have to go to Wales, Watson," I said in a pompous voice, swivelling in my chair. Edwards was half asleep.

"High, what?" he said, struggling back to consciousness. Then he laughed. "Oh, I see what you mean. You're talking about this Bristol Channel business, I suppose?"

"Have you the time?" I asked him.

"I can spare a couple of days," he said, somewhat dubiously. "And providing we don't have to get up at some unearthly hour."

"You're not a bit like Watson," I said to him in a reproachful voice.

"Nor you like Holmes, either," he said. "He solved most of his cases."

We both burst out laughing at this, and I must say I deserved the reproof. However, we settled to leave next day and Edwards went off to see about tickets and so forth, while I made a few domestic arrangements before setting about packing.

I had allowed for being away about three days; Edwards was to telegraph for rooms at the Queensferry Arms, the most likely-seeming hostelry in Lantarch, and I had arranged to have any urgent messages sent on for me there.

I did not anticipate any further developments in the affair for the moment, but the day was to have yet two more surprises; three, if one counts a phone call from Carfax. His man had dug up one or two cuttings relating to The Great Vore. He was having them posted on. So far as they could make out at the agency, the sets were at six-monthly intervals and continued for several weeks. I asked him if he could dig back for the last three years to see what transpired. From what he said, I gathered the wording was much the same in every case, and they all referred to Lantarch and the Gwyllim Chapel.

Edwards called back to see me later and we made arrangements to meet at the station the following morning; he had managed to book the rooms without any trouble, and I could now complete my plans. My old friend still regarded the affair with some amusement; that is, the part which appertained to the newspaper cuttings. He refused to believe in the possibility of the murder in the Bristol Channel being linked with a sect, and had I been in his position I daresay I would have been much of the same mind. But he didn't have my knowledge of such dark affairs; even I had to admit that the chances of a coincidence were long ones, but it was possible and life occasionally throws up some extraordinary surprises.

Which made the case one of the most interesting and satisfying it has ever been my good fortune to investigate. I walked down with Edwards to the bus stop to see him on his way and on my return, my secretary, Miss Daniels, met me on the stairs with a worried expression on her face.

"A Mr. Henton called to see you, Professor," she said.

I thought for a moment. "I don't know anyone of that name," I said.

"He said you wouldn't know him," she replied. "He seemed very agitated and insisted he had to see you. But he couldn't say much about the nature of his business. I told him you wouldn't be long and at first he agreed to wait. Then he got very excited and came out into the passage about ten minutes later. He said he would get in touch with you again and that you seemed to be already engaged on the matter which interested him."

"What name did you say?" I asked.

"Philip Henton," Miss Daniels said. "I've got a note of his address."

We had been walking up the stairs as we talked, and on going into

◈ The Great Vore

my sitting-room, which I also used as a study and consulting room, I immediately noticed a crumpled newspaper lying on the floor by the chair in which my visitor had evidently been sitting. I picked it up idly and was about to place it in my waste basket, when my attention was arrested by some underscoring in ink on a paragraph on the front page, followed by two words inked alongside. I did not quite drop the newspaper, but my hand shook so much that I had to lay it down on the desk.

Miss Daniels had her back to me and noticed nothing. I read the cutting again. The paper was the London midday edition of that day's date. It referred to the Bristol murder. Halfway down the story, it said: "Professor Kane, who has been consulted by the Home Office as an authority in the field of sects and secret societies, said that the marks on the body of Dobbs were of a ritualistic nature. Whoever had performed what amounted to highly skilled surgery would have had considerable occult as well as medical knowledge. 'The man who carried out this disgusting operation has the knowledge of a savant,' said the Professor."

I clicked my tongue with annoyance; it was a pity that such information had been given out. It was evidently the work of the Bristol police who had no doubt wanted to give the press the impression that they were on the verge of an arrest. The lines of the story referring to my pronouncement had been underlined.

The two words which excited me most of all were written in block capitals alongside, across the face of another news item. They were thrice underlined and followed by two exclamation marks. Mr. Philip Henton had written simply: Great Vore!!

I turned to Miss Daniels. I had no time to go into this added complexity on the verge of our departure for Wales.

"Write to Mr. Henton straight away," I instructed her. "Ask him to let me know the nature of his business by letter, if he can; say that I would be most interested in his problem—that I have already guessed its subject and, if you can, arrange an appointment for him to come and see me the day after I get back from Wales."

Here, I consulted my pocket diary and gave her a date. I put the front page of the newspaper containing the item and the tantalising inscription in a locked bureau, which already contained the other material relating to the case. Then I had lunch.

The third surprise of the day occurred in the late afternoon. I had gone out to make one or two purchases and then dropped in to see my favourite bookseller. Crossing Bloomsbury, still in a mood of deep thought engendered by the possibilities of this strange business and partly by the autumnal melancholy of the day, I found myself opposite the fusty portals of the British Museum. Leaves rustled along the pavement in the wind and I stood idly for a moment, a package of books under my arm, looking at the thin knots of people who stringily ascended and descended the flights of steps under the massive portico.

As I went to move on again, a tall, lean man came suddenly through one of the gates in the railings and almost cannoned into me. We both drew back with mumbled apologies and I then recognised the pallid, vulpine features of Sir Isidore Murdoch. The situation was not without its piquancy and I felt rather grimly self-satisfied as I thought of my morrow's mission to Wales and the consequence it might have for him and his black affairs, if my suppositions proved correct.

He gave me a wry smile.

"Ah, it's you, Kane," he said. "I'm surprised to find a busy man like yourself loitering outside the gates of knowledge in such a fashion."

I was somewhat taken aback by his jocular tone and put him down instantly as a consummate actor. However, I was able to conceal my discomfiture and answered him in the same manner. It was no doubt foolish but I could not resist a thrust in order to see his reaction.

"To tell you the truth," I returned. "I was startled by your sudden appearance, Murdoch. I had supposed you to be in the Bristol area."

I had never been more disappointed in my life. If my words came as a shock to him, he was superbly in control of his emotions. A look of deep and ponderous puzzlement came over his long face with the black eyebrows that gave him the look of a satyr.

"And what led you to that supposition?" he asked.

"You have not seen the newspapers?" I asked, returning to safer ground.

His face cleared. "Oh, you mean this affair of the body? But I

⚜ THE GREAT VORE

thought you had been consulted over that. Didn't I see something only today in the late editions?"

He had me there; I had started off badly, with a leading question that must have tipped my hand if he were indeed my man, and I had gained nothing in return. I would not catch him off guard now.

After another moment or two of verbal fencing, he observed with an acid look, "An affair of the fourth power, I should suppose from the descriptions given, wouldn't you say?"

"I have not really made up my mind at the moment," I said, giving my remark as casual an air as I could muster. "It is a business which would greatly interest you, I should imagine."

He smiled sourly. "But they did not see fit to consult me, my dear Kane. Good afternoon."

He touched his hat and shrugged his thin shoulders, all in one movement, and adroitly silenced any questions I might have put by sidling swiftly away among the passersby.

I returned to my house in a more sober mood, but I had the feeling that I had made a dangerous enemy and that somehow he was aware of the knowledge I had gained over the last few days. I felt myself sweating in the Tube, a condition not entirely due to the atmosphere. Tomorrow we should be in Wales and with Murdoch in London, Edwards and I would be free to continue our inquiries without fear of being recognised.

⚜ 4

The prehistoric gloom of Paddington enveloped us and under the fusty Victorian roof, steam, soot and fire fought for mastery. I was glad to escape among the hordes of travellers, muffled to the eyes against the damp and thin mist. Edwards had already secured corner seats in a comfortable carriage and we were soon picking our way through the unlovely suburbs, as we sat in a brass and mahogany dining car and toyed with an early lunch.

It was a not unpleasant feeling that stayed with us for most of the journey; a feeling not entirely dispelled by the numerous changes we were compelled to make during the latter stages. I had read most of the newspapers within the first two hours and when we were fairly on our way, I lay back on my seat and gave myself up to speculation on the more obscure manifestations of this extraordinary business. I could not resist a smile when I reasoned that the whole affair might be two halves of sets of unconnected incidents. However, we should no doubt learn more at Lantarch. I was eager to get down to work and the following day should give a firm yes or no to this line of investigation.

By the time we got to the junction, the weather was deteriorating even further and a dank mist was swirling about the platforms. We made a smooth connection and were fortunate to find a buffet car had been included on the next train we joined. The green, wet hills of Wales slid by in the late dusk as we poured scalding hot tea from silver-plated teapots and sedulously avoided discussing the purpose of our visit.

Edwards was an ideal companion; not over-garrulous, sympathetic, a good listener, and with a fund of interesting stories. His nerve was commendably steady, too; in short, he was the obvious choice for the business I had somewhat rashly ventured on. The latter stages of our journey were not nearly so propitious, but we made the best of them. I had, perhaps, been over-optimistic in attempting the whole thing in one day, but to break our journey overnight in the wilds of Wales would have made a somewhat protracted saga of the expedition, which neither of us could really afford to do.

I was convinced that time was running out and the sooner we got down to our investigation the better. We made two changes on to little branch railways, the last a smoky, dirty, cold and unpunctual affair, which seemed to stop at every potty station on the line. The fog which had descended did not help matters and it was past nine in the evening before we were decanted on to a mouldering plank platform at a station at the world's end, and still a good dozen miles from our destination.

The little port of Lantarch was served by another railway which looped down from the north and so there was no direct connection by the way we had come. But the stationmaster-cum-ticket collector made himself useful and after a spate of singsong Welsh on his

✒ The Great Vore

neolithic telephone, eventually provided a taxi in which we made the last leg of the journey over steep, slippery roads.

The mist had rolled away a little when our vehicle turned over a great stone bridge, as a bell from a distant tower chimed a quarter after ten. We had arrived at Lantarch. The taxi left us outside the main steps of the Queensferry Arms and I found, to my agreeable surprise, that it was an enormous, prosperous looking affair of whitewashed stone, with modern cocktail lounges.

The interior was all soft carpeting, oak beams, bright firelight and highly burnished copper jugs. In one corner of a lounge we passed, the blue images of a television set flickered to an audience of dozing old men. In the main bar we had a whisky and soda, served by a good-looking blonde young woman with a musical voice, and as she went to get the book for us to sign in, I gazed reflectively at Edwards over the rim of my glass and thought that I had been to many a worse destination at the end of a long day's journey.

We signed and were then taken to two good single, adjoining rooms on the first floor. They were simply, but expensively furnished and, judged by the tariff, extremely good value for the money.

"I think I may like it here," said Edwards drily as the blonde girl informed us that, despite the lateness of the hour, we could still have a mixed grill and a cold sweet if we didn't mind using an improvised table in the corner of the dining room. Needless to say, we didn't mind, and it was not even a quarter to eleven when we sat down in the deserted room, a pint tankard at each other's elbow and inhaled the delightful aromas from the kitchen.

The meal tasted even better than the anticipation; we were both so hungry that we could have made shift with anything—as it was, I count it among the most memorable meals of my life.

"They didn't tell us about this on the travel posters," said Edwards at last, pensively studying the toe of his shoe, which was stretched out to catch the glow from the remains of a great fire on the open hearth.

"Good thing, too," I said. "We don't want everybody here, crowding the place out."

I picked up my tankard and pretended to examine some prints on the wall, as Edwards settled the bill; we had the run of the hotel, it seemed, as there were only three other people staying. It was my intention to have a quick reconnoitre of the harbour area, late as it was, and the receptionist, Ceinwen, had already told us we would find the main door open until midnight. After that, we would have to use the little side door in the courtyard reserved for patrons' cars.

Just in case we were late in, she handed us a key to the courtyard door, which I was begged to replace on the main board in the hallway.

"Though what you gentlemen will find to interest you in Lantarch, the Lord knows," she said with a smile, coyly fishing for information.

We didn't enlighten her, though nothing showed on her smooth, mobile face and a moment later we strolled out through the main doors into the empty street. I had asked the way down to the harbour and we immediately turned to our left and found ourselves, after a few yards, confronted by a second stone bridge, a companion to the one we had already crossed on our way up by taxi. It spanned a river which looped to join the sea lower down.

The mist was still thick, though not so impenetrable as it had been earlier, and I was glad to dig my chin into my warm trench coat and look down to the rough paving and the safe placing of my feet. As we traversed the silent street, I was astonished to see on what a large scale the buildings were constructed and I kept a sharp watch for the Gwyllim Chapel as building after building loomed by in the mist. A foolish fancy, perhaps, but at any rate my vigilance went unrewarded.

Edwards was wordless at my side and the only sound which broke the silence was the sharp clicking of our footsteps reechoing across the road as we gradually went downhill. As we did so, the small street got narrower and die houses began to close in on us. There were few lights in the cottages or in the back rooms of shops as we passed, and it was evident that many folk went to bed early at this time of year, out of season as it was.

We had walked, perhaps, for ten minutes and the long, dark lane we were following seemed about to peter out; I was just going to remark to Edwards that I must have mistaken the road, and that we ought to return to the hotel, when lights suddenly sprang up around a corner and the mournful note of a foghorn gave the lie to my timorousness.

THE GREAT VORE

A moment or two later we came out on to the cobbles of a large jetty which was also used as a fish market; lamps pricked the darkness about the square; talk and laughter was still coming from the interior of two brightly lit taverns flanking the quay, and as we emerged from the dimness of the lane into the first gleam of the gas lamps, the soft sussurance of the sea began to fall on the ear.

Skirting piles of netting and barrels, Edwards and I cautiously edged forward to the quayside; we were rewarded almost immediately by a puff or two of light wind, which cleared the fog, and there lay the sea, oily and sullen, about twenty feet below us. Lantarch was set in a precipitous notch of land, surrounded by hills, and the sea beat its way into the little harbour by means of a tortuous passage, through shoals and rocks, that owed as much to man's ingenuity as to nature.

Judging by the fiery eyes of the nearest buoys we could distinguish through the gloom, the place was a devilish one; tricky in even fair weather, I should judge, deadly and murderous on such a night as this. I could not repress a slight stirring of the flesh as I thought of our errand on this spot and of what we might discover during the next few days; it seemed fairly certain that one fiendish murder had been committed in the immediate neighbourhood of this sleepy port.

The perpetrator might even have brushed shoulders with us this very evening, in half a dozen of these quiet lanes leading down to the harbour. I had to smile quietly in the darkness at my fanciful suppositions; it was difficult to imagine Sir Isidore, urbane against the background of the British Museum, in a blue seaman's jersey and dufflecoat in this atmosphere.

The mournful cry of the foghorn again pierced the darkness;

I looked towards the end of the harbour and the open sea but the mist had closed down and I could distinguish only the faint phosphorescence of the nearest breakers, almost at our feet. They burst with a suave suggestiveness against the ancient piles fringing the pier.

For quite half an hour we stayed anchored to the spot; the little harbour of Lantarch, with the strange associations of our quest, had all the fascination a small seaport traditionally holds for the townsman.

But it began to be late, the last of the waterside pubs had long ceased its clamour, and a cold wind bearing salt spray from the harbour was chilling, so we turned our faces away and set out to climb the steep roads up from the sea.

It was nearer one than twelve when we regained the inn. I slept well that night, despite the problems that might face us in the immediate future. I awoke only once; faint and far away came the cry of the foghorn over the sleeping town. Reassured, I slept again.

5

The next morning, after a substantial breakfast, we set to work. We had arranged that Edwards would scout about town and earmark any likely buildings; he was to look particularly for the Gwyllim Chapel, of course, and, failing that, any deserted church buildings or halls which might be likely for our purpose—or rather, our man's purpose. I myself intended to start at the public library, and then tackle one of the local ministers, in a roundabout way and the quaint charm of the quarter, I almost wished our roles were reversed.

But I had already turned to the right, towards the High Street and, finding the wind biting, was glad to step into the Public Library, quite content with my self-imposed assignment. The Librarian, Mr. Price-Thomas, was most co-operative after he had learned my name and business. I did not, of course, apprise him of my real purpose and after ten minutes of unproductive conversation, he left me in a glumly painted annexe, where a young girl presently brought me two local directories and no less than half a dozen histories of the area.

But at least it was warm in the building, the high-backed chair I had been offered was comfortable, and I could smoke. I took off my trench coat and settled down with the miscellaneous volumes. The Curiosities of Lantarch, by someone called Septimus Griffiths M.A., I was glad to discard; it was full of material on the wrecking trade and smuggling, which had once apparently flourished in this quarter, but as it had been published in 1888 and seemed to favour events which

◊ The Great Vore

had occurred before the seventeenth century, its usefulness to me appeared to be strictly limited.

I then turned to the Directories and was gratified to find no less than half a dozen churches, chapels or mission halls listed. Lantarch appeared to be a bigger place than I had realised, and it was evident that reference books would be more help to us at this stage, than aimless walking about the streets looking for suitable buildings to house the sect of The Great Vore.

I must also not overlook the fact that the place where the rites were held, must necessarily be secret, and in that case it could be miles outside the town; perhaps at a lonely farm or in some disused building on a clifftop. It might be worth while investing in a large-scale ordnance survey map—one of those things where every edifice larger than a dog kennel was indicated.

As a start I took down the name and address of the Methodist minister, the Rev. Owen Thomas whose manse did not appear to be far from the spot where I now sat. He would obviously be a mine of information about the town, and it would also afford me the pretext of having a look at his own chapel. I skimmed through the remaining books the librarian had sent me; they were mainly the guide-book type of thing, most of them not more than five or ten years old. But they did have lists of historic buildings in the index, and I jotted down one or two likely names.

If Edwards felt energetic he might indulge in a country ramble this afternoon; I, of course, intended to be engaged in slightly less strenuous, but still important, pursuits.

I was in a somewhat more cheerful cast of mind when I knocked at the librarian's door with my bundle of books, half an hour later. We parted with many protestations of friendship, after he had pointed out to me, from a landing window, the general direction in which I should go to find the manse of Mr. Owen Thomas.

I soon found the manse, a gloomy, slate-roofed building set in an overgrown garden; fortunately Mr. Owen Thomas was at home and I was speedily shown into his presence by a shadowy housekeeper of the old-fashioned sort.

He was a youngish, moon-faced man with thick, horn-rimmed

spectacles, but his eyes were unexpectedly sharp and shrewd as he took my hand. The strong voice which invited me to sit down was overpowering for a small, cluttered study, and I imagined he would scourge his congregation in fine style.

He listened with a half smile, toying with a cheap plastic pen, as I spun him my yarn; I had evidently interrupted his addressing of circulars, and I saw at once that he was overburdened with work. I felt a momentary sense of shame at breaking up the busy course of his morning with my frivolous questions, but he didn't mind. I had kept to a prepared line about an illustrated book on certain aspects of Welsh Methodism—God forgive me—and his face was bright with interest, dying only when I mentioned his own chapel.

"Nothing for you there, Professor," he said, with an inclination of the head. "Victorian perpendicular, I can tell you. Built 1870; draughty and damp—roof needs re-doing. Not worth half a line in the local guide book. But you're welcome to have a look at it."

He rang and asked for coffee, and as we sipped the sweet mixture, dipping into a tin of biscuits on his littered desk, he stabbed the air with square, ink-stained fingers as he talked. I felt sure I would draw a blank here, but I had to drive on with my eliminating process. His face was impassive when I mentioned the Gwyllim Chapel.

"Not hereabouts," he said. "Only thing likely to produce a few pages in these parts is the Abbey, and that's a mile outside town."

After the coffee I thanked him, he fetched some keys, and we went along to the chapel. It did not take me more than a few seconds to see that I had come to the wrong place; the chapel was a big square building of the local flinty stone, set right in the middle of back-to-back houses. The activities I was investigating could not possibly take place without hundreds of people being aware of them.

We went up the big front steps, ludicrously out of scale and more suited to St. Paul's. I had to make a pretence of going over the place, now that I had gone this far.

"How often is the chapel in use?" I asked Thomas, as he fumbled at the main door.

"Almost every night," he said. "We have whist drives, socials, that sort of thing in the hall, and then of course, there are the special services."

The Great Vore

I said nothing but I had already mentally crossed the chapel off my list and was revolving the possibilities of the Abbey. It was a depressing place; the walls were green, with a brown dado, and hung with Victorian lithographs—Christ in the Garden, The Last Supper, and so forth. It may have been my imagination, but it seemed to me that Mr. Owen Thomas wore the lingering trace of a smile as we proceeded with our tour. My disappointment must have shown only too palpably as we paused on the front steps, while my companion relocked the door after us. His face creased into a wide smile and he laid his hand on my arm in the most friendly manner.

"What are you really looking for, Professor?" he asked. I hesitated for a moment, but only for a moment. By way of answer I produced one of the newspaper cuttings from my wallet; I had each mounted on a card, covered in cellophane for protection, as is my custom. He took the slip of pasteboard between thumb and forefinger, puckering his face in the strong wind which whipped across the porch.

"I presume this is genuine?" he asked at length, in that lilting voice.

"I'm treating it most seriously," I replied. "I'm afraid I am not at liberty to divulge the object of my inquiries, but I am anxious to trace the sect mentioned in this cutting."

I had not, of course, given him any material relating to the Bristol Channel murder. His expression was completely blank as he handed the card back.

"If there were any such organisation operating in Lantarch everyone here would know of it," he said. "Someone would have come to me eventually—these things get around in a small town."

"You think I'm on a fool's errand, then?" I asked.

"I wouldn't say that," he said, in his cautious way, as we descended the steps. "You might try outside the town. There's the old Abbey, as I said, and one or two biggish buildings in remote spots. But even in the countryside, there'd bound to be talk."

I could not but agree with him, and it was with a definite feeling of deflation that I parted from him at his front gate a few minutes later. Then I hurried back to the Queensferry Arms. Edwards had not yet returned and I whiled away a quarter of an hour in the bar before lunch. One look at him was enough, as he joined me, soon after one.

Darkness, Mist & Shadow

He ordered a drink in silence and then we sat down in the window alcove and awaited the meal.

I glanced moodily out of the window and thought that the weather looked twice as depressing as it had when we set out in the morning—such is the power of the mind over the evidence of the eyes. As we ate, we talked. Like myself, Edwards had drawn a blank; as far as he could see there wasn't a Gwyllim Chapel in Lantarch and never had been. He had talked in the waterfront pubs with some of the locals who would have been sure to know, but the answer was the same.

He had already covered, on foot, several of the buildings on the list. This left only the possibility of the Abbey and from what I could see, a last-ditch possibility at that. Edwards did his best to cheer me up; I was loath to abandon my cherished theory and though we discussed a number of ideas, we set out after lunch a somewhat crestfallen couple.

I had noticed a poster in a window advertising tours of the district for a bus company, and the Abbey had been mentioned. I thought we might take part in the next expedition, if times were convenient, leave the coach at the Abbey and walk back across the hills, investigating any other likely buildings on the way. This was really the only solution left to us; fortunately, another coach was leaving at 03:15 P.M., in just over twenty minutes' time and after joining a small queue at a ticket window, Edwards and I were glad to sink down on a comfortable seat in the warmth of the coach interior.

There were only half a dozen other people aboard, not surprising at this time of the year, though others would be picked up en route. At any other time it would have been a pleasant outing, but I purled my pipe furiously and wrinkled my brows in concentration, as the coach rumbled out across the stone bridge and set off over the hilly countryside.

The weather was cloudy, with a stiff wind, but the sunshine was bright and gave the illusion of warmth through the glass. I turned and twisted the problem in my mind, and then gave up and gazed benignly out of the window at rank upon rank of gently rolling hills.

The coach took a longish route and after calling at scattered villages was due to reach the Abbey as almost the last place of call. It

◦ʎ THE GREAT VORE

was on the way back to Lantarch and would leave us only a couple of miles to walk. We stopped first at a stone-cross memorial in a small, straggling village where another half dozen people joined us.

Edwards was silent as the coach threaded frowning lanes, hemmed in by tall, gaunt hedges, the vehicle seeming to race the great shadows swept along the floor of the valley by the sun penetrating the clouds. He only ventured one opinion in the hour's drive.

"It is," he said, clearing his throat with an effort, "rather difficult to leave a preconceived theory once it has been based on a particular set of circumstances. When the circumstances don't fit, then the theory must be changed."

I could not but agree with him, but I had no wish to hear this. We both preserved silence until the coach eventually put us down in the courtyard of the castle which was the principal glory of the tour. We obediently admired the surrounding countryside from the battlements, joined the throng to the dungeons and keep and sipped at the watery coffee dispensed at a refreshment stall entombed within a turreted portcullis arch, before rejoining the coach.

It was already nearly five before we stopped in view of the greygreen mass of the Abbey, set off the road, about half a mile across the fields. The coach party looked in amazement as we dismounted and wished the driver a good afternoon. It was wet, and colder than I had expected, and after ten minutes the Abbey looked no nearer; indeed it had completely disappeared, being hidden by a fold in the ground.

But eventually we gained its walls, brushing through a mass of sopping undergrowth which clothed the scree-strewn slope around it. Edwards and I exchanged glances, our last hopes gone, as we stood on the fragmented ruins of a once noble pavement. The walls of the old building had long since fallen in and it was open to the rain, wind and sky.

The moss underfoot had not been disturbed by man or beast for many a long day, and in any case the old ruin was completely unsuitable for the purposes of the sect of the Vore, as I supposed them to be. I had recently done some research on the point and had found that the name was an Anglicisation of an old Norse god, whose nature was voracious; but what such a sect would be doing reincarnating this being, and what form the worship would take, was problematical.

Without more ado, Edwards and I set back the long two miles across the soaking fields; we saw no other suitable buildings, apart from an obviously inhabited farmhouse, and when we arrived in Lantarch, damp and ill-tempered, it was mutually agreed that we would call off the search if nothing transpired during the course of the evening.

I went off to consult my timetables for a morning train back, while Edwards interrogated the receptionist about the possibilities of a hot bath. The evening passed pleasantly enough, with bar talk, and the dinner was excellent. We had exhausted our survey map and the guide book and both of us were regretting the keenness of the young man in the Carfax agency.

Next morning we secured the same taxi which had brought us two days earlier, in such a different atmosphere, and by midday were well on our way back to London. As the express rattled its way through the green countryside and the sunshine of another bitterly cold day beautified the faded fittings of our compartment, I gave myself up to much mind-searching.

Edwards was deep in a crossword, sensible man, and I believe his brain was as clear and untroubled as a child's. We had been on a fool's errand; never mind, it was two days well spent in a new atmosphere. The tea things had long been cleared and we were beginning the run in through the suburbs of London, when I saw the vision which made the whole visit well worthwhile.

We were, of course, travelling in the opposite direction to that in which we had made the outward journey and the setting sun was staining the mean streets and smoky rooftops to a fleeting glory.

By a fortunate chance I had sat on the right side of the dining car, facing in the same direction as the engine, and as I glanced up from my newspaper, my eyes were dazzled with letters of fire which writhed across the scene before me. I am afraid that I burst into somewhat wild laughter, seizing the bewildered Edwards by the sleeve and was attempting to execute a spirited dance, to the scandal of the other occupants of the compartment, when the great solution was cut off by the grimy segment of a passing building.

◈ The Great Vore

No matter; I would investigate as soon as we reached town. With Edwards spluttering questions behind me, I rushed for my compartment and waited impatiently for the train to enter the terminus. I had some telephoning to do.

◈ 6

Still fending off Edwards' hurried questions, I entered a phone box, glancing at my watch. It was almost 5:00 P.M., but there might just be time. To my surprise my call found my acquaintance at the British Museum still in his office; he was a man possessed of all sorts of odd knowledge and I was convinced he could help.

"Paddington Public Library," he said crisply. "You'll have to hurry. They close at six."

Of all places, this was the oddest. We bundled into a taxi and Edwards grew calmer as I began to explain. I had been afraid that his usual placidity would give way to violence at my failure to satisfy his questions.

"It was all a question of the seating," I said. "A fortunate coincidence."

It was more miraculous than coincidental, but it was all of a parcel with the whole of this extraordinary business; had we not gone to Wales in the first place I should never have clapped eyes on this particular stretch of railway track, which had placed us once more within the inner circle of the action.

For my great vision was simply this. The letters of fire which had burned themselves into my eyeballs were written in white along the rusty iron roof of a huge shed which seemed to hang suspended above the surrounding buildings in the great, rosy glow of the sunset. I only saw them for a few seconds. They said, quite plainly: GWYLLIM CHAPEL LANTARCH.

At the Paddington Library all was straightforward; we had half an hour before the building closed, but I knew the librarian and on my sending up my card we were received with great courtesy and affability. Mottershaw was a lean, lugubrious-looking individual but a

⚜ Darkness, Mist & Shadow

man of great efficiency and index-card memory. He had four large books on the desk within ten minutes and I found what I was looking for within five.

The first volume was a work on the curiosities of Victorian London; Edwards chuckled softly to himself as he read over my shoulder and I had to join with him. Supposition had placed me some hundreds of miles outside my range, when I might have found my answer here in London in the first place. Lantarch was the surname of an eccentric Welshman who had flourished in the London of the 1880's and over a period of twenty years had built a series of chapels in urban areas, devoted to the tenets of dissenting Methodism.

His name was Gwyllim—the Welsh variant for William, as any fool but myself might have supposed—so what we were looking for was the William Lantarch Chapel. The lettering on the roof I had glimpsed from the train was carried out in the old style, much as one still sees on the fascias of shops; Provision Merchant Jones Grocer. This was the form in which the newspaper announcements had carried the wording.

Two other books yielded no further information, but the fourth was a sort of directory of buildings devoted to religious purposes in the London area. To cut out a lot of tedious matter, we found that there were no less than twelve of the Lantarch chapels, any one or more of which might suit the purpose of my theory. I was now convinced that I was in the right direction and Edwards, obviously impressed by my sincerity, was rapidly covering pages of a notebook with the pencilled information he was copying down at my request.

I soon saw that we should have to follow up all of the buildings listed—they ranged from an address in Penge right up to North London and up and down the length of the Thames. I felt sure in my mind that the answer would lie somewhere with those buildings situated near the river, in view of the nautical wording of the newspaper cuttings, and so I underlined those areas which I felt might be close to the Thames. We would give those priority.

Of course the book from which we took the information— the volume was dated 1901—could only give facts appertaining to that period and many of the chapels referred to may long ago have been relegated to the developer's shovel or the ravages of two world wars.

⚜ The Great Vore

But I felt reasonably certain that at least one or two would have survived in a similar manner to the one I had so fortunately sighted from the train, and it was there, I was reasonably certain, that the next stage of this business would be set.

My face must have looked excited as we closed the last of the reference books, and even Edwards' usually sanguine features wore a look of suppressed alertness. But he said nothing, though I felt he was now convinced that I had got something, however wild my theory might appear. It was difficult to know what was in my mind; I myself felt half confused, half decided. The threads were all leading to my hands; an hour before all was blank and negative—now I had not one Gwyllim Chapel but twelve.

And it was at once evident to me that a visit to a letting or house agent might yield further information, such as the name and address of any persons who had bought or leased one of the old chapels. And it was reasonable to suppose also, that the name of Abigail would be met with once more. I rubbed my hands with barely concealed satisfaction as we returned the books to the librarian and Edwards had a job to keep up with me as I bounded down the steps. It was just five to six and the attendant had not yet bolted the door as we found our way out into the raw air of the Paddington streets.

We arranged to meet again at eight o'clock at my flat; in the meantime Edwards went off to his home while I sought the nearest Tube Station. He promised to bring back the notebook and type out the addresses for me later that evening. To my surprise Miss Daniels was at the flat, together with my housekeeper; normally she only came in every other day to attend to correspondence and so forth, while I was out of town, but in any case she would normally have gone by five o'clock.

Here it was, nearly seven, and the anxious look on her face told me that something important had happened, almost before I had finished opening the door. She is, I suppose, quite a good-looking sort of girl, if one likes that sort of thing, but her face was pale and there were dark stains under her eyes, which surprised me as she is normally a very healthy looking person.

"What on earth is the matter?" I asked as I drew her into the sitting room.

"You may well ask, Professor," she said. "You remember the Mr. Henton who called to see you before you left for Wales?"

I searched my mind for a moment, my thoughts still on the latest developments, and then I remembered the stranger who had quitted my rooms so precipitately and left the enigmatic pencillings on the newspaper behind him. Once again I had the feeling that things were pre-ordained.

"Go on," I said. She sank into a chair and lit a cigarette with a nervous, preoccupied air.

"Well, after he got the letter, he called round here twice, hoping you might have returned unexpectedly. He is in the most dreadful state; the matter concerns a girl he is—or was—very fond of, and is connected with this Bristol Channel murder. He won't go into details, but he seemed more upset than ever when I told him you had gone to Wales. I took the liberty of asking him to call round here this evening at about half-past nine, as you originally suggested he should come here as soon as you arrived back."

"You seem to have taken his trouble to heart yourself," I said drily, giving her a keen glance. To my surprise she flushed and bit her lip. But at that moment the telephone bell rang and she went to answer it.

I took the opportunity to remove my bags into the next room and had just finished washing my hands when Miss Daniels returned to say that Scotland Yard was on the phone. It was Neilson, and after the usual small talk, he asked me to come round to the Yard the following morning to discuss the business with him. He seemed out of sorts, not at all his usual ebullient self, but he evinced interest when I told him I had one or two theories.

By the time I had rung off, the housekeeper had appeared with two steaming cups of coffee and I gave her my orders for dinner while I ran through one or two letters which had arrived in my absence. There was a further note from Carfax, with a few cuttings relating to the investigations at Bristol, but nothing of any unusual interest.

I insisted that Miss Daniels join Edwards and myself for dinner and as we sipped our coffee, I made rough notes and questioned her further on Henton.

"You have seen him several times, then?" I asked.

The Great Vore

She hesitated and her eyes looked even more troubled.

"He was in such distress that I felt I had to help, Professor," she said. "He was vague about details, which he said were for your ears only, but his former fiancee, a girl called Shirley Smithson has apparently got mixed up with this awful sect of The Great Vore, or whatever they call it . . ."

I had to steady my hands on my coffee cup or it would have rattled perceptibly; the room seemed to recede away from me for a minute and I could not at first hear what Miss Daniels was saying.

I had a smug feeling of triumph and wondered what Edwards would say when he heard the latest development.

"You have done quite right, Miss Daniels," I said. "This is a most serious business. But how did Mr. Henton get on to this and how had his fiancee become involved?"

"It's a long story," she said. "I think you'd better hear it from his own lips. It's something to do with a letter he found. He kept a copy and when he saw the murder report in the newspaper and your name mentioned, he decided to come to you."

I nodded, my mind busily re-assessing this new information. We said nothing further before dinner and when Edwards arrived half an hour later, he listened with an intent expression on his face as I outlined the position. I had already told Miss Daniels, in strictest confidence, of our discoveries regarding the chapels, and she typed out two lists of addresses, in geographical areas, for the convenience of Edwards and myself.

We had now done as much as one could have expected in the space of the last three hours or so and we could only await the course of events; we all did justice to the excellent meal prepared for us and we were sitting around in the consulting room, smoking and talking as we toyed with our second glass of brandy, when Mr. Henton was announced.

He was over medium height, with regular features; good looking, in a dark manner. He had strong, square white teeth and was expensively, but unobtrusively dressed. I put his age at about thirty-two, but there was little time for further speculation on his appearance as we got up for Miss Daniels to introduce us.

◈ Darkness, Mist & Shadow

It was at once evident to me that my secretary and the young man had become firm friends, no doubt thrown together by the present trials through which he was passing; for his face was drawn and haggard and he ran his hands constantly through untidy hair.

As soon as the formalities were completed, he slumped into the easy chair indicated and relapsed into a moody silence in complete contrast to the simulated sparkle he had put into his greeting of Miss Daniels.

As much to put the company at ease, as to prompt him, I asked gently, "I understand you wish my help on a matter of some difficulty? If it will make things easier, I should tell you—or perhaps you know—that I am already engaged on the same business.

He remained silent so I pressed on. "What I am getting at, Mr. Henton, is the affair which is causing both of us a great deal of trouble. The murder of Esau Dobbs and this so-called sect of The Great Vore. That is why you marked the paper when you called on me earlier, wasn't it?"

He raised his head at that. "I knew I was right to come to you," he said. "I should be most grateful for your help."

He looked round him nervously. "I hardly know where to begin."

"If it would assist," I said. "I am sure my colleagues would not mind withdrawing, if you would prefer the discussion to be private."

He waved the suggestion away, with a faint air of protest. "Please... there is no necessity for that. I am sure your friends will be most helpful... Miss Daniels has already been so"—here his eyes sought hers in a silent appeal—"and I have the greatest confidence in you. I presume Miss Daniels has already mentioned the nature of my problem?"

"We have discussed it," I assured him. "It concerns your fiancee, does it not?"

"My former fiancee, yes," he corrected me quietly. "Even though we have parted, I can't bear to think of her in the hands of that—creature."

He almost vomited the last words out and I think we were all startled at the vehemence of his feelings. I felt the interview might proceed better if I conducted things on a question and answer basis.

◈ The Great Vore

"When did all this begin?" I asked, handing him a cigarette. He lit up, leaned back in his chair and spiralled smoke out through his nostrils before he replied.

"About a year ago," he said eventually; he was so long in answering that I thought he had forgotten the question and was about to repeat it.

"Shirley got a good job in an antique business in Kensington—she's always been mad on old things—and met this man in the shop one day. I believe he was a friend of the owner. Anyway, he invited her out, and from then on it was nothing else but this man; how much he knew; how outstanding he was and so on. This led to rows between us, naturally, but we kept on seeing each other—"

"Just a moment," I interrupted, "did she tell you this man's name? Did you ever meet him?"

He shook his head. "That was one of the most mysterious parts of the whole business. He had all sorts of queer people to his country house just outside London; they were occultists, table-turners, all that sort of mumbo-jumbo. Either he swore his intimates to close secrecy or they never knew him under his real name. It was all a lot of nonsense, or so I thought then. Shirley just referred to the fellow as 'him,' but when she started calling him 'The Master', I lost my temper and blew up. That was when we really started drifting apart. He seemed to take her over body and soul."

He was silent for a moment and there was an uneasy stirring of chairs.

"Do you have a photograph of her?" I asked. He produced a small cellophane case from his wallet and handed it to me. The photograph depicted a very striking-looking girl, in her late twenties, I should have said; she had long blonde hair, worn very fashionably. She was more sensuous than spiritual in nature, I felt; just the last type of person to become involved with Sir Isidore, if he were indeed the man I sought.

I handed back the photograph. "And you never saw this person called 'The Master'?" I prompted him.

"Just once," he said. "From a distance. I had gone out to Chelsea one evening to reason with her. Some instinct made me remain in my car; there was another car—it looked like a big Daimler—parked outside and after about ten minutes Shirley and this man came out. They were too far away for me to see clearly, and their faces were in shadow under a street lamp. I got the impression he was middle-aged, thickset and with a moustache. Then they drove off. That's all I know and I never saw him again."

"You didn't follow?" I asked.

He shook his head. "I felt too sick. I just stayed in my car and then drove home."

I thought for a moment; the description hardly fitted Sir Isidore. I handed him a glass of brandy and he took a sip before continuing.

"After that things got worse and worse. Shirley had joined this sect thing by then, and was going out to this man's house two or three nights a week. Her guardian—she's got no parents—didn't seem at all interested, and it got more and more difficult to get to see her. I wasn't giving up in a hurry though and I tried to make her see reason; to tell her that this man was wrong and evil and rotten, but it didn't do any good. I might just as well have saved my breath."

"You didn't think of calling in the police?" I asked.

He looked at me wearily. "What good would it have done?" he said. "No crime had been committed. Shirley's over twenty-one. They would have laughed. There are all sorts of crank sects about in London, most of them harmless enough.

"I couldn't prove anything bad was going on, and you need a warrant to search a private house. The police would have thought it was a case of a jealous boyfriend who'd had his girl stolen by an older man."

He sighed and paused again. Edwards made a sympathetic noise and reached for his box of matches. I thought Miss Daniels looked bright-eyed and flushed. I turned back to Henton. He had sat forward in his chair and was gazing fixedly into the fire.

"You didn't decide to call it a day?" I asked.

He looked me full in the face. "I couldn't at that time. I was very much in love, and I felt I had a duty to Shirley."

"You still feel the same way now?" I asked.

"Not that way, no," he said. "But it is very difficult to let a human being down when she is involved in such dark forces. You don't know

⚔ The Great Vore

what it is, Professor. This man—if he is a man—whom she calls Master has drained all her will. It's not only sex but drugs, flogging, every type of filthy perversion mixed up with black magic and witchcraft.

"When it began, she used to confide in me more; she was frightened at first and gave me some hints of what was going on. But afterwards, when I urged her to break with this sect, she only laughed and said her eyes had been opened and it was the only way to live. She talked of being on probation as an acolyte and said that later she would be admitted to the inner circle. There was a lot more nonsense about the Great Question and on at least two occasions I heard her speak of the thing they worshipped, The Great Vore."

"How did you come to connect the sect with the Bristol Channel murder?" I said.

"About a week before the body was found, there was a great upset," he replied. "Shirley came knocking on my door one night in extreme distress; she had no one else to turn to, she said. She was crying, wild in her looks and in a frightful state. She wouldn't tell me what had happened, but kept crying over and over again, 'Poor Mr. Dobbs, poor Mr. Dobbs'. It puzzled me at the time but a few days later I saw this front page murder and then the name 'Esau Dobbs'. It was an appalling moment, I can tell you, especially when I read about the ritual markings."

"By then I didn't want to go to the police, in case Shirley had been involved in some way, so when I saw your name in the paper, you seemed the logical person to turn to as an expert on the occult. What do you make of all this, Professor?"

"There are dark forces at work here," I replied. "It is easy to laugh at table-turning and all those innocent forms of parlour tricks which clairvoyants and others use. But there are obscure and terrible powers which some exceptional men master, not for their own good or that of others, but for the most vile and debased purposes. Their lives impinge on and blast the lives of lesser beings with whom they come into contact."

"I fear that your unfortunate friend may have gone too far along that path, from which it is so difficult to return. But I have a very good idea of who the man behind this revolting sect may be, and it may come about within the next two or three days we shall have located their meeting place."

Henton started up in his chair, his face alight with interest and enthusiasm.

"If I can be of any help, Professor, you can count on me," he said.

"We may need all the assistance we can get," I told him. "Before I speak of our future plans, I would like to get up to date on the situation. Have you seen Miss Smithson recently and have you any idea where she goes? Does she visit this man at his London home?"

He shook his head. "That I don't know. All my inquiries have produced nothing. I did see Shirley once again, about a week ago, but she seemed her normal self; she made no reference to the night Dobbs was murdered, if she had been talking about that, and she seems to be under this man's influence more, completely than ever. I did think of going to the police over the business of the murder, but I think I've made the right choice."

"It will be almost impossible to avoid involving Miss Smithson," I said. "This will not matter if she is innocent of any complicity in Dobbs' death. But I should make it clear that I am co-operating in every way I can with the official police force and that I shall lay most of the facts as I know them before the people at Scotland Yard tomorrow."

Henton nodded. "It is just as well," he said. "It has been like living with a nightmare during the past year. Anything that can clear it up is all to the good."

He put his hand in his pocket as though to rise and I started up, as I felt he wished to terminate the interview. But it was only to bring out a piece of typewritten paper, which he passed to me.

I sat down again as he said, "I almost forgot this. It is a copy of a note I found in Shirley's handbag about six months ago."

I looked at this remarkable document with considerable interest. It consisted of only about five lines and bore no date or address.

It said, "Dearest Acolyte, The time has come for your initiation into the secret practices. Do not be afraid; all will be well. I shall conduct your ritual myself. Remember my instructions and our tenet, 'Do as thou wilt'. Look for the personal column next week, as before. Your Master."

The Great Vore

I passed this on to Miss Daniels who copied it for filing, before handing it back to the unfortunate Henton. He still sat puffing at his cigarette and to relieve the atmosphere, I immediately plunged into a recital of some of our recent adventures.

I told him of the abortive trip Edwards and I had made to Wales, of my discovery of the chapels and the whole chain of extraordinary coincidences which had led up to the present interview. He was a changed man when I had finished and when we parted an hour later, it was agreed that he would come round to meet Edwards and myself soon after lunch the following day. I had my interview with Neilson in the morning, but I did not propose to bring in the sect of the Vore at this stage. I still felt he might laugh at us. I was also undecided about the problem of Miss Smithson.

I had asked Henton whether or not it would be prudent for me to call and see her, but he said she had now left home and so far as he could ascertain had taken a flat in another part of London. This address he had been unable to trace. It was a blow as Miss Smithson was our only tangible link with Murdoch. I was still assuming he was our man and I had so far seen no evidence to refute this assertion.

It might be a good idea, in as subtle a way as possible, to see if the police could keep a discreet eye on his movements for the next day or two. A lot depended on my interview of the morning; come what may, Edwards and I, with Miss Daniels and Henton as a reserve team, intended to set about tracking the chapels on our list the following afternoon.

If we were successful in finding the meeting place of this sect, then would be the time to put the full facts before Scotland Yard. Sir Isidore was the missing link in the chain, and until something came up to connect with him and in turn him with the body found in the Bristol Channel, we should be laughed out of court.

Even so, it was a big step forward and it was with considerable satisfaction that we said goodnight. Miss Daniels was to accompany Henton on his way and when the pair had gone, Edwards and I sat long into the night pondering the strange complexities of the human heart.

Darkness, Mist & Shadow

7

The following morning I was at Scotland Yard by half-past nine and was greeted cordially by Superintendent Neilson. He confessed that the Bristol Channel case was giving them a great deal of trouble and they had many hundreds of inquiries to make among sea-faring people. We had a long interview but I made some progress. I put out discreet feelers, made suggestions and was allowed to look at some of the items which the laboratory people were working on.

The charred fragment of letter found in Esau Dobbs' room had been assembled under a glass plate and this was of more than passing interest to me. I found I might have to revise some of my thinking. Neilson was surprised when I asked him if he could find out what persons had been reported missing from London riverside areas in the past two years, and called in the senior Scotland Yard official, whose office he was temporarily using.

This gentleman looked more puzzled than ever when I asked him to see what information could be traced on Shirley Smithson. He took down the name and address and went out; he did not say anything but the set of his neck and shoulders indicated his opinion of academics and amateur investigators in general. I told Neilson when we parted that I hoped to get in touch with him again within two days and left highly pleased with my visit.

I found Henton back at the flat with Miss Daniels and when Edwards arrived at one o'clock a surprisingly jocular little party sat down to lunch. Afterwards, we gathered in my consulting room for a council of war; as the only two people who knew what the score was, Edwards and I decided to proceed with our original plan. He would take six of the chapels and see how far he could get in the day; Henton would accompany me. Miss Daniels would remain, in case Scotland Yard got in touch regarding Miss Smithson.

She also had her own list of agents to contact regarding any possible lettings of the chapels. It was turned half-past two when Henton and I set out on our mission; he had a large-scale street map and a flashlight, while I had the list of addresses and my small 'emergency kit' in my pocket. This consisted of certain instruments and

⚘ The Great Vore

other implements mounted on felt and wrapped in a small waterproof container.

It occupied only the space taken up by the average tobacco pouch but had been of incalculable use to me in the past. Dusty sunshine picked out the grimy buildings as we took a taxi to our destination; I had decided to tackle the chapel I had spotted from the train first. We paid off the taxi about a mile from Euston, in a wilderness of crumbling side-streets.

I had pin-pointed the immediate area from my large-scale map and though I didn't expect much from this first contact with the object of our search, I hoped to learn something about the chapel, regarding its size and layout. The wind was piercingly cold and I was glad of the short walk; we were in an area of depressing commercial development. Factories, warehouses and high brick walls rose in monotonous succession and I had some difficulty in locating Fairmile Road.

It was with a most curious feeling that I saw the roof of the chapel rising up in the distance, surrounded by crane jibs and chimneys. As we approached it, I saw that our journey had been in vain, yet it was not entirely abortive. The entire area had been converted into a timber yard; one end of the chapel had been knocked out and countless tons of sawn timber was supported on steel racks within.

The building was of enormous size and I was impressed to note, as we made our way towards it across the muddy ground, that despite the interior being used for storage, there was still room at the front for offices and other facilities. If all the chapels were of the same size and pattern as this one—and there was no reason to believe they were not—then the sect of the Great Vore could have nourished unseen and unheard, especially if the chapel were situated on a secluded site; the roof spaces alone were tremendous, and might once have contained rooms, judging by the sawn-off beams we could see from below.

The owner of the yard, a broad, good-looking man in his mid-forties, was friendly and co-operative. The chapel had been derelict when he took it over ten years before, he said; other than that he knew nothing, but the place had been empty for many years. He willingly gave us the name of the agent from whom he had purchased the property.

As we came away, Henton, who had been silent for most of the day began to talk; most of it was private and almost entirely connected with the Smithson girl. I let him go on and walked by his side through the raw streets, content with a grunt or a nod from time to time to show that I was following his thought. Presently I asked him why, like me, he was convinced that the body of the man Dobbs had been connected with the sect led, as I thought, by the man Murdoch—though I did not tell him of my suspicions.

There was, of course, the link with the Smithson girl and her muttered remarks about Dobbs, but I was anxious to know how the man's body could have come to be picked up hundreds of miles from London, if he had been killed there. Henton might have had some ideas from what the girl had told him, but I was again destined to be disappointed. He seemed to think that the body might have been taken by car to some deserted spot, tipped into the sea and eventually washed up in the Bristol Channel. This explanation certainly did not satisfy me and I expected something at once more simple and more extraordinary of the affair.

However, we had little more time for further speculation; I had crossed off the first chapel and there were five more on the list in my pocket. We plunged into the mouth of the first Tube station we came to and set off to the next address; the day was a short one and all too soon it would be dark. I hoped Edwards might have located the object of our search by now, but at the same time I myself wanted the pleasure of the discovery, after all the time and trouble I had expended on what so far had proved an abortive search.

As we sat close together and the train rocked and howled its way through the darkness I recalled again the name of the man Abigail and the address in Putney; he might be, I had surmised originally, only an agent for Murdoch, but at least even this lead might help us in tracing Miss Smithson. And if all else failed there would be nothing for it but a direct confrontation with Murdoch; I sighed again as I reviewed these possibilities in my mind.

✒ The Great Vore

Even if we discovered the chapel today I was vague as to what our next move would be; Murdoch would have to be identified positively with the sect and the sect with the murder of Dobbs if we were to take action in the matter. But the main thing for the moment was the Lantarch chapel used as the headquarters of this devilish cult; all else would stem from any discoveries to be made there. I glanced again at address number two and followed Henton up the draughty escalator into the cold air of the street.

✒ 8

The air was blue with pipe and cigarette smoke. We sat looking gloomily at one another; Henton, Edwards, Miss Daniels and myself. Edwards had an abortive afternoon to match our own. Unlike us, however, he had managed to get round to see all the chapels on his list; the story was the same in each case, the buildings converted to other purposes or long ago knocked down.

There remained but the one chapel of those selected by me, but even I was now beginning to come round to Edwards' way of thinking. I had reached the low point of the case, but at the back of my mind still persisted the old, stubborn core of conviction—that the chapels and Murdoch and The Great Vore and the ritual crime were all part and parcel of the same whole—had to be.

Not just to fit my theory; my vanity was not great enough to support that. My reasoning was not based upon logic, but intuition. We decided after quite a long debate that Edwards and I would reconnoitre the last building the following day; if we failed here, then we would wait the next move by the police. Henton had departed, somewhat downcast, and Miss Daniels had accompanied him to the Tube station. The last evening newspapers had just come and the housekeeper had brought them in, after clearing the table.

Edwards had picked up one and was leisurely working his way down the columns when I heard him give a smothered exclamation. He handed me the folded newspaper without a word. I cast my eye over the column he had indicated and was conscious of an immediate feeling of deflation. It was a series of paragraphs devoted to the comings and goings of celebrities by air and sea.

The item which had riveted my friend's attention ran as follows: Queen Mary, via Le Havre, Sir Isidore Murdoch, for New York, on a lecture tour.

I am afraid that my first instinct was to crumple the newspaper and throw it into my waste basket, but I managed to control my ill-temper and stamped out of the room. Edwards looked up sympathetically as I went by. This was a facer, I had to admit.

For a few minutes I could not trust myself and letting myself out into the square, I commenced to walk slowly round in a great arc that eventually brought me back before my front door. The night air was cold but the quiet of the evening had somewhat dispelled the sourness of my temper when I turned in at my own porch.

As I gained the front of my house I had been half aware of a figure in a dark overcoat which hurried away into the gloom, and when I had let myself into the house I was surprised to see a white envelope staring at me from the floor. It was addressed to me too, I found on picking it up; so I tore it open.

It contained nothing but a slip of pasteboard. On this, written in boldly inked capitals, was the message: DO NOT MEDDLE IN MY AFFAIRS.

There was, of course, no signature and the envelope bore no address, stamp or post office date-mark. It may have been delivered by the dark-coated figure I had seen slipping away a minute or two before, as the envelope had certainly not been in the hall when I went out a quarter of an hour earlier.

I smiled thinly before putting the envelope in my pocket; if Sir Isidore were not my man—and his trip to America proved nothing one way or another—someone at least was worried about my activities. My spirits quite restored, I handed the card to Edwards when I gained the living room and asked him what he made of it; the envelope, when re-examined, bore the same inked capitals as the message itself and both had evidently been written by the identical hand.

Edwards handed it back to me with a non-committal smile but

ventured no comment. I appreciated his reserve as I had begun to have grave doubts of my cherished thesis, and it would have been awkward, to say the least, to have had to abandon the elaborate structure I had built up in my mind about this curious situation

However, what we might have discussed would have to wait as the telephone rang at that moment; as it happened I got to the instrument before my housekeeper. It was Henton and he sounded excited.

"Sorry to bother you again, Professor," he said. "I wouldn't have rung, but something important has happened. I've just seen Shirky and I know where she's being held by this man."

I motioned to Edwards, who had seen by my animated expression that something important was afoot, and was already hastening towards me. He passed over a pencil and paper and I jotted down the address Henton gave me. To my surprise it was in Bloomsbury, at a place called Cadogan Gardens; I vaguely recalled it as being somewhere at the back of the British Museum.

"Wait there," I told Henton. "We'll get a taxi and be over as soon as possible."

While I dashed upstairs to warn my housekeeper that we might be back late, Edwards rang for a taxi. By the time I got back downstairs, I could hear a cab pull up at the door. It was still only about a quarter past ten when we reached a street of tall, dark houses and paid off the cab. It was a raw, cheerless night and I drew my trench coat about me. I saw the white name-plate bearing the legend—Cadogan Gardens, and then Henton was at our elbow, gliding noiselessly up to us from his hiding place in the shadow of the trees fringing a small public park.

"Thank God, Professor," he said. "I was afraid they might leave and I wouldn't be able to follow."

"Where are they?" I said. He pointed across the road to one of the tall, silent houses opposite and as if in response to his motion, a yellow square of light sprang up in one of the rooms on the second floor.

"What's our next move?" asked Edwards. I was beginning to wonder myself at that, but this was no time for indecision.

"How on earth did you trace Miss Smithson?" I asked Henton.

"The greatest good fortune," he said. "I got out of the Tube station on my way home and I saw them in a nearby restaurant. It was one I used to take Shirley to quite frequently in the old days," he added in an apologetic tone. "I watched them through the window and saw them get ready to leave. She was with him, of course."

He didn't have to specify what he meant; I could tell by the tone of his voice and Edwards' face clearly indicated that he knew also.

"Fortunately, they didn't take a cab," Henton went on. "They walked home and I followed. They went in at No. 10. I waited until I was sure they weren't coming out again and phoned from the box on the corner of the square."

I patted his arm. "You've done well," I said, "and once again pure chance has aided us in an extraordinary manner. Follow me."

I hadn't quite decided on my course of action, but I knew we had to find out what was in that house; I half expected to discover that Sir Isidore had not taken his trip to America after all, so I strode rapidly across the road and knocked peremptorily with the brass knocker of the blue-painted door which faced us at the top of some imposing steps. There was silence for a short while and I was about to repeat my tattoo, when the door was softly opened. A youngish, clerical-looking man in a sober grey suit stood in the entrance. He looked apprehensively at our party, which was indeed rather crowding the doorway, now that I came to notice the fact.

"I wish to see the owner of the house," I said, putting as much authority as I could into my voice.

He hesitated, but only countered in a mild manner. "What name shall I say?"

"Professor Kane," I answered, but before he could make any further rejoinder there was a footfall on the staircase and a loud, high voice called down, "What's this? Who are you sir, and what is this disturbance at this time of night?"

I hesitated no longer but shouldered the man in the grey suit aside and followed by his protests and the bulky forms of Henton and Edwards went forward into an elegantly-furnished hall. Candelabra shed a soft glow over expensive silk wallpaper, but I was given no time to admire the decorations for the same high voice was again raised in admonition.

The Great Vore

"How dare you, sir! By what right do you force your way into my house?"

I turned to face the voice and saw that it belonged to a stockily-built man of medium height; he was almost bald, with long sideburns, and a more dark and dissipated-looking face I've seldom seen in all my travels. Irie was dressed in a wine-red quilted smoking jacket and I could see braided dress trousers underneath. His eyes smouldered angrily but he kept his temper within bounds. He stood clutching the wooden balustrade before him as he gazed down at us from the top of the stairs. For a moment he had us at a slight disadvantage, but cutting him short, I sought to hide my shock and disappointment by calling up to him.

"We are friends of Miss Smithson and we have reason to believe she is here. Will you please ask her to come down?"

In truth I had been taken aback for the man before me, whom I had felt certain to be Sir Isidore Murdoch, was a complete stranger to me; he was evidently the owner of the house but I had never set eyes on him in my life. I began to feel angry myself and irritated with Henton, whom I suspected of mistaking the house in the dark; what if there had been some appalling error and we had broken into some perfectly innocent person's dwelling?

But the feeling lasted only a moment; for the thickset man before us had a dark smudge of moustache under his nose, which I had not noticed before, owing to the heavy shadow across the lower part of his face, and which recalled Henton's description. At any event we would have to go carefully.

While I was debating what to do if the stranger refused our request, I was saved any further trouble by Henton, who freed himself from the restraining hand of the man in the grey suit and bounded halfway up the staircase. He started to mouth something which he never finished, but the burly man's reaction removed all doubt from my mind. I had begun to feel that Henton might even have mistaken the identities of two strangers in the gloomy street when he followed them but this possibility was immediately erased by our host's words.

He thrust his hands deep into the pockets of his smoking jacket and said with an ill-concealed sneer, "Ah, Miss Smithson's protector, once again. I can now see with whom I have to deal. Will you not take no for an answer?"

For the first time he seemed to catch a clear sight of me and stepped forward to the head of the stairs. "And Professor Kane, if I am not mistaken. I am afraid I have not had the pleasure of the acquaintance of my third uninvited guest. Meddlers all and I will thank you to leave my house immediately, or I shall be forced to call the police."

"That sounds like a very good idea," said Henton calmly.

The owner of the house shrugged slightly, "As you wish," he said.

"I must confess I relish police interference even less than your own. You may see Miss Smithson for a moment if you please. It can do no harm to me and will certainly mean no good to you. Miss Smithson is a free agent. When she tells you to leave I hope you will have the decency and good sense to do so."

He nodded to the man in the grey suit, who shot us a glance of dislike, and went quietly up the staircase. He disappeared and our host stood perfectly at ease, his hands in his pockets as he surveyed us. He made no attempt to move and stood blocking the entire staircase.

"May I ask whom I have the pleasure of addressing?" I asked with what I hoped was faint sarcasm in my voice.

"You may not," he said crisply, making no attempt to conceal the sarcasm in his. "I have already warned you and this gentleman and I will not tolerate any more interference from either of you."

"Thank you for your note," I told him. "My eyesight is not so good as it was and I'm afraid I didn't get the message."

He glowered at me and it was with some dislike that I saw he had crocodile-skin shoes with white insets, peeping from underneath the edges of his dress trousers. He was not only a thoroughly dangerous and decadent human being, but his sense of taste was abominable also.

We had but a moment or two to wait and then the man in grey returned, bringing with him a tall and attractive girl whom I immediately recognised from the photograph Henton had shown us. She turned white and made as though to descend the staircase but the stocky man restrained her.

⚜ The Great Vore

"Philip, what are you doing here?" she asked. "And who are these gentlemen?"

"We've come to take you away, Shirley," he replied. "Come with us—it may be your last chance."

He went to continue but she stopped him with an angry stamp of her foot.

"How many more times must I tell you?" she said hotly. "I have made my choice and this is what I want to do. I'm sorry, Philip, but you shouldn't have come here. The only way you can help me is to leave as soon as possible."

Henton backed down the stairs, an expression of mingled anger and chagrin on his face and my pity for him was immediately succeeded by stronger feelings, directed, I am afraid, against the man at the head of the staircase, who had put his arm familiarly round the young woman's waist and was regarding us with an oily smile.

"And now get out," he snapped, "and leave us in peace."

Henton turned back as though to mount the stairs but Edwards took his arm.

"He's quite right," I told my companions. "We have no legal grounds for being here and now, quite obviously, no moral ones either."

"You are a wise man, Professor," our host said levelly. "You alone of these people recognise demanded by a superior being."

"I recognise only one thing," I said coolly. "That I am in the presence of a dangerous and unnatural creature whose propensities for evil are equalled only by his personal vanity. Believe me, I shall make it my business to interfere in your affairs with good cause."

I spoke somewhat imprudently in my anger, but the look on Henton's face and the whole smug attitude of this man had worn my nerves thin. He said nothing but stood with small spots burning red on his cheeks, as we turned to the door.

"You may show these gentlemen out, Abigail," he said, motioning the man in the grey suit forward. I was startled at the name and repeated it mechanically.

"My secretary," he said civilly enough. "Goodnight, Professor."

A moment later we were back in the raw air of the Bloomsbury night, the big door slammed to behind us and we could hear the bolts being shot. Henton was muttering indignantly and Edwards was trying to soothe his anger. We strode out for the street corner, and stopped at the phone box from which Henton had called us earlier.

"I am sorry, my friend," I said to Henton, putting my hand on his arm. "We can do little to help your Miss Smithson in her present mood."

"What are you going to do?" Edwards asked me.

"Phone the police and let matters take their course," I said.

We all three crowded uncomfortably into the booth as I rang Scotland Yard. Neilson was not there, but fortunately Commander Baron was on duty. I put the matter to him, leaving out all the more fanciful supposition, and letting him know as much as I dared.

He seemed dubious. "Just what has this man supposed to have done?" he asked. "It's a pretty tall order. You don't even know his name."

"Trust me," I urged him. "Just get a squad round and then play it by ear. Say you had a report that three men had broken in. He could hardly deny that."

I gave him the address, he promised to see what he could do and I rang off, after arranging with him to let me know whenever he had any news. We looked up once again at 10, Cadogan Gardens, but the windows were now dark. There was nothing more to be gained by hanging about in the cold street; we could safely leave what had to be done to the official police, so we parted at the Tube station, Henton proceeding home and Edwards and I going several stations together before taking our own roads.

Henton promised to be round at my flat by nine the following morning. Come what might, Edwards and I intended to investigate the remaining chapel the next day; if we found anything there then would be the time to lay our theories before Neilson and Commander Baron. There was no message awaiting me on my return home; Miss Daniels had left an hour before and my housekeeper had been awaiting me with some anxiety.

I reassured her, swallowed a glass or two of wine by the dying fire

THE GREAT VORE

and went to bed. I was awakened some time during the night by the shrilling of the phone. I struggled awake to find it after 2:00 A.M.

It was Commander Baron's exultant voice. "Sorry to disturb you, Professor, but it looks like I owe you an apology."

"That's all right," I said. "How did you get on?"

"The birds had flown," he said. "The house was completely empty, and we can't trace the owner. But we found a number of curious things on the premises—things they didn't have time to hide. You must have scared them badly."

"Sometimes it pays to take an unofficial line," I said drily.

"Can you arrange to come and see me in the morning?" he said. "I'll have Neilson in and we'll discuss the whole matter. But I think this could be important."

"I'm convinced it is," I said. I arranged to go along to Scotland Yard at ten the next day—or rather this morning, I thought, looking wryly at my watch. Baron thanked me again and rang off. It sounded as though he was having a busy night. I turned over, put out the light and went almost immediately to sleep.

9

The following morning I conferred with Henton and Edwards when they arrived; I invited them to a late breakfast and when I left for Scotland Yard at about twenty past nine they were deep in conversation with Miss Daniels. We had arranged that they would try to check on the letting of the remaining chapel. If necessary Henton and Miss Daniels would visit the agent in the afternoon; during which time Edwards and I intended to pay it a visit in person. It was down the Thames, somewhere beyond Greenwich, and I had pinned my hopes on that being the meeting place of the sect of The Vore. If we failed there, then I was willing to give up and hand the whole thing over to Scotland Yard, for it would mean the complete collapse of my theories.

It was with some trepidation that I went into my interview with Commander Baron and Neilson; they were armed with sheaves of official reports, medical dossiers and the like. I had little to go on but a few newspaper clippings, some theories and an innate conviction that though I might have mistaken the perpetrator I was basically right in my assumptions. There were to be some shocks on both sides.

I spent an absorbing two hours with my police colleagues on the puzzle of Esau Dobbs; though much of my theorising must have seemed fantastic to them, my reputation and the information I had unearthed on the ritual markings on the body, outweighed the strangeness of my ideas.

"I may be in a position to let you know more by tonight," I added.

I had apprised them of my intentions of the afternoon, without revealing any details, and both Baron and Neilson, as the two men immediately responsible for the Dobbs operations, looked dubious.

"You realise, Professor, that what you are doing is completely outside the law?" said Baron. "If things misfire, we shall be unable to help you."

"Precisely," I said with a smile. "It is because we are amateurs and are prepared to take a risk in this matter that we may well be more successful than the official force."

Baron gave a throaty laugh at this and held out his hand. "Well, good luck, Professor," he said. "I'll warn the nearest station of your operations so that if anything does go wrong, the local Superintendent will know what to do. Beyond that, I cannot help you further."

"Don't worry," I said. "I'll ring in tonight and let you know what progress we've made."

Though I sounded confident, I was in truth rather nervous, and as I sped back to my flat I once again reviewed the situation in the light of the knowledge I had gained that morning. After a rapid and uncomfortable lunch, I packed some special equipment and we made our dispositions for the afternoon. After much telephoning, Miss Daniels had finally traced the agents responsible for the letting of this last Lantarch Chapel, and she and Henton had made an appointment with the principal of the firm that afternoon.

This time Edwards had brought along his own car, a powerful but unobtrusively coloured Daimler of uncertain vintage, whose long

⚜ The Great Vore

bonnet concealed a lot of horsepower. I sank back in the cushions and smoked comfortably as Edwards drove with quiet competence through the milling traffic. It was gone two when we left and already not yet three before he had threaded the hooting pandemonium of the City and by way of back streets had proceeded well into the long run through the seediness of the East End.

Surprisingly soon, factory chimneys and warehouses superseded the busy streets and across a loop of the brown and turgid Thames where barges butted aside the thrusting waters, I caught a glimpse of the rigging of the Cutty Sark. On again and in a wilderness of dingy alleys and turnings, where rusted fencing fretted in the mournful wind, he brought the Daimler to a halt alongside the black tarred doors of a deserted warehouse.

From here we went on foot. The mournful sound of a siren floated across the water and the breeze blew fresh and strong from off the river. With unerring accuracy Edwards had found the place and within five minutes we had come out against a large timber yard and wharf. Across the stacks of sawn deal and pine we once again saw the letters, this time printed in red: Gwyllim Chapel Lantarch.

It was a peculiar kind of thrill to me as I gazed at its mouldering frame and tightly shuttered windows; it stood almost on the river, with a jetty running in front, and a high board fence surrounding it. Better still, there was a large muddy space between it and the far wall of the timber yard, which had been torn and striated with the tyre marks of many cars. Edwards and I exchanged a long look; we were both wearing dark grey raincoats of an anonymous aspect and though we had met few people on our walk to the chapel, it was reasonable to suppose that we were as inconspicuous a pair as might be for these parts.

Nevertheless it was obvious that we would have to be careful in our movements. We stood in the shelter of a fence for a moment, and smoked while we thought out the next stage of the operation. I thought it best if I first reconnoitred alone, so I set off, leaving Edwards near the fence, walking into the wind, with my collar turned up and my face concealed. I went right round the chapel but found it surrounded on three sides by a stout board fence, over eight feet high.

It could be scaled, but not without attracting some attention from the people in the surrounding buildings, surely.

I tried the large double door let into the fence as I passed but it was securely padlocked. When I had walked all the way round, I found myself once again facing the Thames; on three sides was the fence while the fourth side ended in a board jetty giving directly on to the water. If we wanted to continue our search this afternoon it was pretty obvious that we would have to go by water, but it was no weather for swimming.

Beyond the chapel was a path which appeared to be little used and I followed it along for a couple of hundred yards; it gave on to the back of more houses and workshops and there were several ancient dinghies tied up at the stakes here. I glanced swiftly at the river and saw that the tide was setting upwards. This meant that if Edwards and I could abstract a dinghy unnoticed we could drop quietly along until we gained the jetty within the chapel grounds.

The only danger was that someone might notice the disappearance of the boat while we were within the chapel—for I was determined to break in if it were at all possible. If we wanted to return the same way we had come we would have to tie up the dinghy opposite the chapel and it would at once become obvious that the intruders could only be within the building. And if the dinghy belonged to our friend Abigail and his master, that could be very serious indeed. But it was a risk justified under the circumstances and when I had apprised Edwards of the scheme he at once agreed.

It was the work of only a few moments to put our plan into operation. We dropped into the nearest dinghy, apparently unnoticed, though my nerves were jarred by the hollow rattle made by one of the heavy oars which fell to the bottom of the boat as we boarded her. The oily water lapped mournfully at the slimy green piles of the jetty as we drifted, bumping occasionally as we strove to keep her out from the heavy baulks of timber. In a very few seconds we had come in under the chapel jetty and Edwards made the boat fast.

It was anxious work clawing up on to the boarding of the old wharf but I was relieved to see that even the windows of the chapel facing

⌘ The Great Vore

the river were boarded over. If there were anyone inside it was also certain that they would not see us. We wasted not a moment in crossing the weed-grown area between us and the mossy front steps, and I was pleased to see that there was abundant evidence of frequent comings and goings across the grass and up and down the steps.

A big iron-studded door faced us. It was, of course, locked when I tried the large handle, but the lock was well oiled and I felt my excitement mounting. We were making too conspicuous a sight from the river so we lost no time in getting round to the side of the building where we were protected both by the high board fence on two sides and by the thickly-set undergrowth at this point.

Strain our ears as we could, we heard not a sound from within but it was not likely that we should in any case, as the walls were solidly built and from what we had seen of the other chapels there were many chambers inside. Edwards swore as he stumbled into a half-hidden basement, and as he put out a hand to steady himself I saw that there was a six-feet drop down to a small area along the side of the building. We eased ourselves into this with as much caution as we could muster, and found ourselves in a narrow tunnel with the windows of the basement on our right hand. These were also boarded over but the battens had been heavily eroded by time and weather and the nails were loose and rusty. Exerting all our strength in the confined space, Edwards and I pulled at the shutter of the nearest window and felt it come away with a thin scream as the ancient nails tore through the damp wood.

Gently, we lowered the wooden cover to the ground and listened but there was no sound; we found ourselves staring into a shadowy, unlit basement. The window was a modern, metal-framed affair, whose outer glass was coated with cobwebs, but it was securely locked from the inside and I had no doubt we should find the same situation obtaining on all the others.

There was a risk of burglar alarms but we had come this far and there did not seem much point in backing out now; I was convinced that this had to be the headquarters of the mysterious sect linked with the murder of Esau Dobbs and there was only one way to find out.

The noise Edwards' half-brick made as he smashed in the glass round the handle of the window catch sounded tremendous to us, but I have no doubt it passed unnoticed from the river's edge.

Edwards reached in and turned the catch and in a few more moments the window was open and we had dropped on to a stone floor inside. We reached out and pulled the wooden shutter as far above the window as we could and then closed it behind us. Very little light was now admitted, but there was just enough to see that we were in a very spacious cellar and a glow from ahead showed where a modern, oil-fired central heating system was doing its work.

We listened again, but the noise of our entry had apparently not been noticed. Moving cautiously across the room Edwards found a light switch; we risked switching one ceiling light on and in the brief glimpse before switching off again, located a large wooden staircase which led within the chapel. In semi-darkness, we edged our way up, guiding ourselves by our finger-tips on the handrail and presently found a door leading out of the cellar.

The darkness was intense in here and I stood by the cellar entrance while Edwards crept out into a corridor to try to find a light switch. The place was silent and obviously empty, in that way one knows absolutely that a building is empty but the utmost care was paramount if we were not to be caught on the premises; indeed if such a thing happened, our whole enterprise was lost—we would have revealed our hand and have gained nothing. Edwards risked a match at this point and a moment later found a switch.

I have seen some elaborate Masonic temples in my time but this place was fantastically luxurious, almost sybaritic in taste. We were in the main body of what had evidently once been the chapel; the predominant theme was blue. There were finely appointed pews with luxurious leather armchairs instead of benches; the woods were mahogany, oak and exquisitely carved timber of a type unfamiliar to me.

Blue velvet curtainings covered the side of what appeared to be a staging of some sort. The floor was covered in thick grey carpeting and the heating was almost oppressive; I noticed there were thermostatic controls on the slim gold radiators which marched down the sides of the room.

⚜ The Great Vore

At the back of the hall rose sumptuously carpeted staircases leading to a gallery; there were benches and stools of leather in front of the ground floor seating, together with apparatus of which we could only guess the use. But I blanched to see the signs which had been emblazoned on the curtains, and Edwards drew back his lips from his teeth in a grimace which spoke more eloquently than words as he came across a rack of leather whips.

There was no doubt in my mind that we were within a temple devoted to the unholy arts and evidently used by the most decadent and perverted of frequenters. There were certain carved images set up in a niche which hinted at the seriousness of our discoveries and I was now convinced that Commander Baron would no longer remain sceptical when we delivered our report to him.

I took a quick glance through the thick curtains covering the proscenium arch in front of the seating and almost fell at the sight; I motioned Edwards away. There was an altar, a vast, blasphemous carving towering at the rostrum and other things which do not need to be mentioned here. I felt faint but was still sufficiently master of myself to make my way towards another large blue curtain at the side of the stage. It moved in a slight breeze and I could hear soft noises reminiscent of the splashing of water.

However, we were suddenly arrested by the noise of an automobile engine in front of the building.

"Quick!" Edwards whispered to me. "We must get the lights out. Someone is coming in."

I am not noted for my fleetness of foot but in an astonishingly short time Edwards and I were back under the gallery of that unholy temple, panting and dishevelled. I first shut the cellar door and then nodded to Edwards at the light switch. Before the faint click had died away I had my hand on his arm in the darkness and we crawled our way along a row of leather pews until I judged we would be safely out of sight of a casual observer. I was curious to see who the visitors might be.

No sooner had we settled ourselves than there came a rattling at the big outer door and a short while afterwards, the sound of it being softly closed. Light shone through the cracks of a side door leading to an entrance hall we had not noticed in our earlier exploration. Edwards and I were lying uncomfortably, squeezed in between two rows of pews and with a pile of leather cushions helping to conceal us, so that we were not well placed for observation.

There was an agonisingly long wait and then a beam of light reached a pallid finger across the floor as the entrance hall door was cautiously opened. The hall was flooded with light and Edwards and I flattened ourselves to the floor, though we need not have worried; our visitors were unaware of our presence and had no time for anyone but themselves. We heard the soft murmur of voices and opening my eyes, I could see two pairs of legs under the seating of the pews in front. One of them was the elegant legs of an attractive woman, clad in expensive silk stockings and high-heeled velvet shoes. But it was the other person I was interested in. I could not see the faces but the feet were enough; the man was wearing crocodile-skin shoes with white insets.

Edwards' grip on my arm was fiercely painful but I flashed him a look of triumph; we had now seen enough and it would be dangerous to linger, as there might be more visitors to come. The problem was how to leave without being seen. Fortunately, this was soon solved for us, when, with shattering abruptness, a great organ boomed out from the altar-end of the hall. It faded swiftly and as the volume rose and fell I realised that our friend was manipulating electronic loud-speaker apparatus.

Under cover of this cacophony we slid cautiously along the pew and seeing no one else in sight, rapidly gained the cellar door and safety.

We risked the light once we had gained the cellar and Edwards swiftly gathered up the last traces of glass we had left on the floor when we broke in. We could not do much about the broken pane of glass but found the remains of old hessian curtaining still mouldering on its hooks. We gently pulled the curtain about a foot farther along to cover the hole in the window.

Then we climbed out, re-locked the window through the hole in the glass and replaced the wooden shutter as best we could. It was already dark, the short winter dusk having descended, but lights from the timber yard pricked the darkness as we made our way across to

◈ The Great Vore

the jetty. A large Daimler stood silent and empty behind the locked gates of the entry. I took a note of the number plate for Commander Baron and then we found the dinghy and were rowing silently up against the tide. Not ten minutes later we began the long drive back to the West End.

Henton and Miss Daniels were anxiously awaiting us at my flat and while Edwards retailed our story I went hurriedly to my library shelves and did some quick research. Half an hour later Miss Daniels knocked at my door to say Carfax was on the telephone.

"Hullo, Professor. How are you making out?" his breezy voice asked.

"Well, it's an interesting case," I said cautiously. "I'll give you the details once we've sorted everything out. But I presume you rang me up with a specific purpose?"

He chuckled. "Just have a look at the Evening Standard," he said. "Have you seen tonight's edition?"

I hadn't of course, but Edwards kindly went out to procure one, while I noted Carfax's message. I thanked him and rang off. By the time Edwards returned, Henton, Miss Daniels and myself were gathered in my study with four sherry glasses shimmering in the firelight. I am afraid we all crowded round in a rather undignified manner as Edwards brought the paper in. Sandwiched in between the amusements guide and the tragic messages of estranged couples, we found what we were looking for.

The personal announcement read: The Great Vore. Gwyllim Chapel Lantarch. Invocation of the Old Ones. Supreme Offering. 12:00 P.M. Saturday.

We exchanged grim glances. The interesting point was that this was the first time I had seen in any of the announcements the mention of a day. The meeting was set for two days' time. Edwards had followed my line of reasoning in his silent fashion.

"An emergency evidently," he said.

"Prepared at short notice," I added. "You may say that what we saw tonight was the beginning of the dress rehearsal."

I got on the phone to Commander Baron. He might take some convincing but it would be essential to handle things my way.

Darkness, Mist & Shadow

10

Saturday dawned a raw, foggy day, but one well suited to our plans. We spent the afternoon running over the arrangements once again. Neilson and Baron, though dubious, had finally agreed to my suggestions. Edwards, myself and the two senior officers were to attempt to enter the chapel again soon after midnight and if possible observe the ceremonies taking place. Our actions after this would depend on the nature of the proceedings, but there was no doubt in my own mind that something devilish was afoot. We were all to be armed, though no one was to use a weapon without the direct order of Baron, who was in charge of the inside party.

Henton and Miss Daniels were to remain with the main body of the police well back from the chapel area; one man in plain clothes was to be stationed inconspicuously but near the chapel in order to hear the police whistle when the time came. Launches of the Thames River Police would also be in the vicinity to give assistance; indeed, they were providing a dinghy. The scheme was for we four to travel down-river in a police launch and then row for the chapel in the dinghy.

I was a little perturbed at this aspect; I am no sailor and if conditions on the river were foggy, it might be difficult to find the way. But there was no doubt that Baron's suggestion was the best. For if the sect were gathering in full strength tonight, there would be little chance of scaling the yard wall unobserved, especially as we could expect cars to be arriving at short intervals for the meeting.

This was then settled and after a high tea at six, Henton, Miss Daniels, Edwards and myself sat down in my sitting room to while away the hours as best we could. The clock hands crept round with infinite slowness but at last the hall chimes announced the hour of ten and a few minutes afterwards we heard the slamming of car doors as Baron and his group arrived.

Once outside I effected hasty introductions and then Henton and Miss Daniels got into the back of a police car and set off for their long drive down river. Edwards and I leaned back in the depths of a big Wolseley. Baron drove and Neilson was at his side. Most of the fog had

⚜ THE GREAT VORE

lifted, but thin wisps occasionally obscured the road ahead, as we sped towards Charing Cross. At the pier a sergeant of the river police was waiting to conduct us across the undulating pontoons to where the lights of a powerful police launch danced at anchor.

The fog had closed down on the river here, but we had plenty of time and as we nosed slowly out into the stream with the horn sounding at intervals, the four of us were glad to sit down in the cabin where a radio was spitting out tinny instructions. The launch was in short-wave contact with Superintendent Burrows and his men on shore and they were to signal us as soon as they were in position about a quarter of a mile from the chapel. The launch swayed alarmingly in the heavy swell, the fog curled in yellow ribbons at the open cabin door and the smell of the river came up heavy and dank, so that we clutched gratefully at the big mugs of hot coffee which Baron presently distributed.

We seemed to take an interminable time to get down and once a string of barges came dangerously close, their heavy wash causing the launch to buck and gyrate; Baron was anxious about the tow and one of the constables went back to the stern and paid out the dinghy painter. At last, the launch started to make better way over the foul tide, but I was startled to find on looking at my watch that it was already a quarter past eleven. I must have looked anxious for Neilson broke into my thoughts with a chuckle; "Not to worry, Professor, we're almost there."

Soon after he spoke, the engine of the launch throttled back and I heard the anchor go with a splash. We rocked in the tide and then the engine shut altogether and we felt completely cut off from the world, little visible around us but a wall of whiteness. But I could heard the slap of the tide against the shore not far away, and I judged that these men knew their business after all.

The sergeant in charge of the boat slipped off his earphones and handed them to Commander Baron; "For you, sir."

I heard Baron's muffled voice and then he came back with a thin smile. "Burrows' in position," he said. "Let's go."

The dinghy had been brought round from the stern, the sergeant got in and sat down at the tiller and all we had to do was row. It was a brisk pull against the stream running but in about ten minutes I saw the lights on our left hand and then walls and the shadowy outline of a pier came up. The sergeant, putting the tiller about, whispered to us to lay back on our oars and we drifted down beautifully to draw up at the landing stage almost without a bump. I felt the slimy rungs of a ladder under my hands and mounting, cautiously put my head a few inches above the board floor of the landing stage.

We were almost opposite the chapel but to my dismay I saw a light burning outside the big main door; there were two men inside the entrance and people were mounting the steps. This was a facer. I held a whispered consultation with the others in the boat. I felt the best move would be to pull up a short way until we reached a point just inside the board fence, make our way to the right of the chapel and go all the way round until we came to our original window of entry.

It was a great pity the fog was not so dense here but I have found the unforeseen continually upsetting the most carefully laid plans in life, ever to be surprised or regretful. I had enjoyed so many fortunate coincidences throughout this incredible case, that I continued to retain my confidence that we should now see this thing through triumphantly to the end—wherever that might lead.

So we pulled back and waited for the moment to disembark. I seized the slimy timbers of the jetty again; unfortunately there were only wooden cross-pieces here, highly dangerous to climb, and was then sprawling on the damp boarding of the pier. Baron quickly followed and then helped up Edwards and Neilson in quick succession. We huddled into the shadow of the board fence and then the mist came down again; we had our revolvers out by now and edged painfully along through the gloom. Now we could see the light glimmering in the porch but no one was visible and five minutes later we had passed on into the tangled undergrowth surrounding the chapel.

This was the worst part of the evening; we seemed to take an interminable time making our way through the soaking brambles of this long disused garden. But at last I could see the end of the building louring up through the whiteness of the misty background, and then we turned at right angles. It was easier going on the west side of the chapel, but it was already five to twelve when we four, plastered in

⚜ The Great Vore

mud and scratched by thorns, paused in the runnel by the shuttered window through which Edwards and I had made our entrance three days earlier.

The shutter lifted off easily and as we peered in we were encouraged to see that only the faint glow of the oil-heating plant pierced the darkness. Edwards reached in and unlocked the window and once more we found ourselves in the cellar. We closed the window behind us to hide traces of our entry; the two police officers had powerful electric torches with them and we used these in preference to switching on the light. It might be too dangerous if anyone came down to attend to the boiler and we did not yet know with how many people we might have to deal.

As we tiptoed up the staircase leading to the ground floor we could hear the pealing of organ-music, and the low, muffled chanting of voices and we knew that the ceremony of The Vore must have begun. I had kept in my mind clearly the layout of the hall; the door leading from the cellar was fortunately not squarely in the centre of the building, otherwise we should have come out in the middle of the aisle and it would have been impossible for us to have entered without being seen.

As things were, the high backs of the pews hid this and several other doors, and made a sort of corridor at the back of the chapel. It was my intention that we four should somehow conceal ourselves at the back of the pews in order to see what was going on. I opened the door an inch or two; the chanting was much louder, the room astonishingly warm and the smell of incense was in our nostrils.

I could see nothing from my position at the door and there appeared to be nobody in the space at the rear of the pews. But it immediately struck me that this would be a highly dangerous place in which to station ourselves. Firstly, people entering from the main entrance hall would be bound to surprise us, and secondly there was the added danger that others would discover us from three or four points merely by walking up one of the numerous gangways and along the back of the building.

I hesitated for a moment and then I had a better idea. As we had seen earlier, there was a finely-carved staircase leading up at the back of the chapel. We had no time to explore it, but there was no doubt in my mind that it led to a gallery, evidently used for an overflow at meetings. The side of the staircase was made of solid panelling and if we went on our hands and knees up the stairs we should not be seen from the altar position.

There was a risk that there might be people in the gallery but I did not think so. The chanting which now rose in front of us, though made by a considerable number of people, came from a long distance away and argued that only the first rows of pews were occupied. And so it proved to be when I crept out and looked slowly round the edge of the back row, though I was astonished to see that there must have been over a hundred people present.

But they took up only the first half dozen rows in this huge chapel, deeply engrossed in the ceremony taking place before them. I hesitated no longer, but whispering to the others to follow me, I slipped rapidly across the aisle, almost on my knees and found myself hidden by the outer wall of the staircase. I went softly upwards and then found myself in a spacious gallery filled with leather armchairs. I wriggled forward to the front and as the three others joined me without incident, I was adjusting my eyes to take in an astonishing scene.

The heat in the chapel was stifling and I then saw the reason for such elaborate arrangements. Most of the people present were nude and taking part in a series of disgusting rites. The curtains at the stage end were drawn back and a face of ancient and lewd aspect leered at us from the dawn of time. In between the huge statue's paws incense burned in a large dish sending out clouds of smoke that made the scene before us sway and undulate.

On the leather couches in front of the altar itself the naked forms of half a dozen men were being lashed by women wielding leather-thonged whips. Chanting filled the air and the reedy notes of the great organ, pealing from every corner of the building made our senses reel and tremble.

"Aie—ah, aie—ah," chanted the assembly as they followed the direction of a grotesque figure, who seemed to be master of ceremonies at this scene of mediaeval torture. He was a terrifying sight; a

⚔ The Great Vore

blue cloak completely concealed his body from head to foot, something like a gold mace glittered in his hands. The head was obscured by the bearded muzzle and horned head of a monstrous goat twice as large as life; the disguise of a high-priest of the Black Arts and one long familiar to me through years of study.

In front of him was the kneeling form of a young girl, whose long blonde hair formed a striking contrast to the blue cloak in which she was completely wrapped. In front of these two figures a long slab of black stone, carved in Runic form, was supported by massive iron brackets.

The goat figure held aloft the golden mace and shrieked, in a voice made more repellent by the muffling effect of his mask, "Who is the lord of all creation and the source of all power?"

"The Great Vore!" chanted the crowd, whom I now saw included young and old; there were ancient women with pendulous breasts, withered old men arm in arm with young girls; handsome young males partnered by middleaged women, all bound by some hideous spell, all wrapped in the darkness of the communal act in which they were indulging.

Baron turned to me and I saw sweat glisten on his forehead. When I looked back again, the goat-priest was shrieking, "Whom must we obey to the nethermost depths of the pit?"

"The Great Vore!" chanted the mob decisively. The whips rose and fell monotonously as this continued and I saw that at least two of the men on the divans had fainted.

"What is the will of The Vore?" asked the goat-figure.

"Do as thou wilt!" sang the crowd.

"Even unto death: "screamed the goat-priest.

"Even unto death for death is eternal life!" chanted the crowd.

The priest lifted his mace and the whips ceased to fall on the recumbent bodies of the men.

"There has been punishment enough," said the priest. "There are greater things afoot this night. The Vore demands a bride!"

"A bride!" the crowd chanted.

As the priest spoke the girl kneeling in front of him rose to her feet and with one harsh movement the goat-priest pulled the cloak from her shoulders. She stood in the light of the altar lamps stark naked and I heard Edwards gasp as he recognised Shirley Smithson.

"You are content to be the bride of The Vore?" asked the priest.

"I am so content," she said in a low voice, with hanging head.

"So be it," said the goat-priest. He led her to the altar and she lay upon it, face upwards, her neck in a circular notch set in its edge. I could now see, at this critical point in the proceedings, that a low ramp led from the end of the altar stone to a point just below the blue curtains at the right-hand side of the staging. Baron stirred at my side.

The goat-priest threw off his own robe. He was also naked except for a golden belt buckled round his waist. He sprinkled water on the recumbent body of the girl, chanting incantations in a language which I could not understand. He put down the mace and drew a long-bladed knife from the sheath at his belt.

"Thy bride, Oh Vore!" he shrieked. There was an unearthly silence and then the curtains at the side of the staging drew back; there was a splashing of water, something moved and a pale arm with red suckers groped in the air. Things became confused after this. In appalled wonder we four in the gallery rose; Commander Baron already had his revolver out—I believe it was his intention to fire in the air to bring these revolting proceedings to an end. I was close behind him, with the same intention; we blundered into one another, there was a sharp explosion and as we fell against the balcony one of the ceiling chandeliers, shattered by the Commander's bullet, burst loudly and showered splinters of glass over the naked bodies of the suddenly screaming worshippers. Neilson's police whistle shrilled.

The scene instantly dissolved into chaos. The worshippers rushed aimlessly in all directions and then there was another loud report as Edwards fired this time; one of the whip-wielding women went down with scarlet spreading on her shoulder. I fought my way down the narrow staircase, cursing, for I had seen the intention of the goat-priest, though I had not been so quick to react as my friend.

He stood before the altar and brought his knife down with delicate precision across the breasts and throat of Shirley Smithson; she shrieked then and my first bullet of the evening spun the goat-headed

THE GREAT VORE

madman round. I nailed my way through that loathsome naked congregation, my passage raising howls of agony; I lashed out at a pasty-faced youth and felt his bare toes crack under my heavy shoe. A fat woman with stinking breath fell against me and rebounded with a squeal.

I fired again as I leapt at the altar; the body of Shirley Smithson, streaming scarlet was already sliding down the inclined ramp. It fell with a heavy splash into a writhing mass of jelly-like legs and suckers which undulated primevally in a vast tank of water where steam rose from the heated surface.

The goat-priest was stretched in agony across the altar but as I came up he sprang at me, his good hand still holding the razor-edged knife. I had no time to feel fear and we were rolling on the floor, while I held his knife arm and tried to get my pistol to bear. He was screaming obscenities through the goat mask and red-rimmed eyes looked madness at me through the soulless sockets of the frightful goat-face.

I heard vast splashings and shudderings as we rolled over and then we were on our feet; something caught my ankle in a powerful grip and I went down.

The goat-priest lunged at me, hoarsely yelling, "The Vore triumphs!" but Neilson's bullet caught him in the chest and spun him round; he whirled and slid into the tank and the suckered arm, with lightning rapidity, released my ankle and closed about the naked body of the priest of blasphemy. The last coherent thing I remember is the goat-head in a feverish fury of suckered arms and two ghastly eyes, the whole turning into a sea of black as my three companions pumped shot after shot into that tank of infinite loathsomeness.

11

"Another sherry?" I said, pressing the glass upon Neilson. Considering the experiences we had been through a few days earlier, we were a moderately-gay dinner party gathered in my flat.

Darkness, Mist & Shadow

"What beats me, is though you were consistently wrong about Sir Isidore Murdoch from the beginning, you muddled your way through nevertheless," said Edwards maliciously.

"I wouldn't have put it quite like that, my dear fellow," I said, "but I must admit your remarks are more than justified. My original premise about Sir Isidore was wrongly based, I freely acknowledge. It arose in the first instance through my mis-reading of a signature on a scrap of paper found in Esau Dobbs' room. What I took to be 'mur' was in fact 'her'."

"Part of the name of Sattherwaite," said Neilson.

"Precisely," I agreed. "Grantley Sattherwaite, antiquarian, man of abominably perverted tastes and, I should have realised, had I pursued my inquiries in his direction, expert in marine biology. It was he who, in founding this obscene sect of The Vore, had the quite brilliant idea of introducing a non-existent god which he called The Great Vore. When the cult began to get out of hand, or anyone, sickened by excess, spoke of quitting or going to the police, Sattherwaite would eliminate him or her, by making a sacrifice. The victims were usually drugged or in a state of induced-hypnosis, quite believing that their introduction to The Great Vore was a form of promotion within the society."

Miss Daniels shuddered. "But what sort of people would indulge in such perverted practices?"

Commander Baron smiled thinly. "You'd be surprised, young lady," he said. "We have over 200 people we're working through who are mixed up with this sect. They range from old ladies, society people, to young men, criminal riff-raff, seamen and the scum of the earth. Age, class or sex make no difference to people with these sort of inclinations. And of course this form of blackmail and knowledge—he took lots of photographs—gave Sattherwaite a hold over them."

"But what was the thing which killed these people?" Henton burst out excitedly.

"Nothing less than a giant squid," I said calmly. "A monster bred up by Sattherwaite from a small specimen brought to him by one of the sect members who was a seaman off a cargo boat. He kept it in a specially heated tank of sea-water and fed the victims to it from time to time. This was the cause of the sucker marks on Dobbs' body which puzzled me so much on the post mortem photographs," I added, turning to Neilson.

"I shall scream in a minute if you don't make tilings a little clearer," said Edwards somewhat rudely. "All is not plain to us, I am afraid."

"Well," I continued, "Sattherwaite, having formed his sect and obtained his perverted satisfaction from sexual orgies and so forth, disposed of those who got out of line, as we have said. Dobbs was one of those who threatened to tell what he knew and was ritually killed, just as was the unfortunate Miss Smithson, though her death was mercifully quick."

I cast an embarrassed glance at Henton, but he was too busy looking at Miss Daniels, and hadn't caught my last remark.

"Dobbs was disposed of, with the aid of Sattherwaite's accomplices," I went on. "As you may or may not know the squid obtains its nourishment by sucking the goodness out of its victims, and then ..."

"That will do, thank you," said Edwards hastily.

"Anyway, this particular evening, the beast wasn't hungry," I said. "There had been a series of sacrifices the same evening—quite a holocaust."

There were gulps from our three companions.

"We've been checking on this for some time," said Commander Baron, "but we have had reports of quite a few missing persons up and down the river. Seamen and so forth."

"From what the sect members have so far revealed, the remains of victims were taken to sea by the nautical members of the sect and weighted and thrown overboard," said Neilson.

"Only they made a botch of Dobbs," I added. "He had distinctive markings and the squid wasn't hungry—hardly touched him. So Sattherwaite and his assistants had a little butchery session after hours. Parts of the unfortunate Mr. Dobbs were thrown into the Thames in weighted sacks—the police know this because they've now been recovered off the wharf. But the assistants handling Dobbs brought the whole matter to light. They were crew-members of a coastal steamer plying between London river and Bristol, among other places."

"I'm beginning to see . . ." said Edwards.

"Pray let me finish," I interrupted him. "You've been highly critical of my methods so far . . ."

I saw Baron and Neilson smile at this point and went hurriedly on. "They tossed the body overboard in a sack one night in the Bristol Channel but either they had a drop too much to drink or couldn't tie their knots, because the sack and the weight went down and the body eventually came to the surface."

"With what result we have seen," said Commander Baron drily. "This is uncommonly fine sherry, Professor. Do you mind if I have another?"

I hastened to refill his glass.

"I think the rest of the story you can fill in for yourselves," I said. "The whole case is the most beautiful example of the law of coincidence that I've ever encountered."

I turned back to Henton and Miss Daniels. "I'm only sorry that things turned out rather badly from your point of view."

Henton looked straight into Miss Daniels' eyes. "I don't think, on weighing it up, that things have turned out too badly at all," he said softly. Miss Daniels flushed but said nothing.

"That means I shall have to look out for a new secretary, I suppose?" I said somewhat sourly.

To cover up a lull in the conversation, Edwards said brightly, "I suppose the newspaper cuttings were a form of code to those in the sect?"

"A simple matter," I said somewhat smugly. "From what we've learned so far they appear to relate to procedures. 'Keels grate on the beach' for instance, would mean that the sect members would approach the chapel by boat. 'Footsteps in the mist', would mean that they should leave their cars at a distance and walk, and so forth. The sect seems to be very widespread and entries in county newspapers refer to country members in those localities."

"A thoroughly alarming state of affairs," said Baron, "that will take some time to stamp out. Though perhaps it's just as well Sattherwaite went the way he did. Without him, it's a broken backed affair."

"Well," I said, "if there are any further points perhaps we can discuss them at dinner. I am assured that my housekeeper has really excelled herself this evening."

As the others went ahead, Edwards lingered behind for a moment. His eyes twinkled mischievously.

"Apart from the abortive trip to Wales and picking the wrong man from the beginning, the mantle of Holmes doesn't fit you so badly," he said.

"Well, we're all of a pair, considering that your shot meant for Sattherwaite broke the arm of Lady Blaydon," I said testily. We stared at one another for a moment and then both burst out laughing.

"*Touché*," he said. "Are you coming in?"

"In just a moment," I said. "I've first got to phone a Fleet Street editor. And after the meal I must write a letter to America. I really feel I owe Sir Isidore Murdoch a dinner on his return."

The Academy Of Pain

1

"Welcome to the Academy of Pain," said Carstairs, squeezing in under the low, iron-studded doorway with that jarring laugh which always irritated Sanders beyond measure. Pauline Carstairs said nothing but the look in her eyes as she followed the two men in, spelt out a clear warning to Sanders: Be careful. He had been in love with Pauline for more than two years now; they were discreet, but Sanders knew that the last thing they must do was to under-estimate the square shouldered, bull-necked man in the heavy tweed suit whom he thought he hated more than anything or anyone in the world.

The man was a sadist, that was self-evident; secondly, he was Pauline's husband; and thirdly, he practised all sorts of quiet cruelties on the dark-haired beautiful girl who was his wife. All being reasons enough, in Sanders' book, for the loathing and distaste he felt for him. It was only because Pauline had insisted in one of her last letters, that he had accepted the invitation for a long weekend at all. He did not know how much Carstairs suspected—he was certainly no fool—but it was evident that such a weekend as Carstairs had suggested would be an ordeal for the pair of them; a period full of traps and pitfalls in which a second's indiscretion on the part of either could lead to some unforeseen catastrophe.

Not that Sanders was lacking in courage, and he had to admit that Carstairs would have some justification for physical violence, as he and Pauline had been lovers for almost a year; he could look after himself in a rough-house if need be but Carstairs was a giant of a man and his dark and brooding nature had been warped by years of loneliness and immolation in this rambling old house which had been occupied by his family for many generations.

Why Pauline had ever consented to become Mrs. Carstairs was beyond Sanders' knowledge; Pauline would not even tell him much about it. They had met out East, he had gathered, when Carstairs was serving in the Army and in a lonely outpost in which outlets for social activity were limited. This might have made a man like Carstairs, big, athletic and full of confidence, attractive to a shy young girl such as she would have been. Or he may then have appeared very different from what he had since become. However, he had proposed and had been accepted. It was only afterwards, when they had come to live at The Minns, near Sar Malna, in a wild and remote part of the West Country, that his character had undergone a change.

Sanders, who was the village doctor in that corner of the world, had first been consulted by Pauline about her husband and later Carstairs had come to see him; there was nothing physically wrong and Sanders thanked his destiny that Pauline was already a patient of his friendly rival at the other end of the district. He had not bargained for falling in love with Mrs. Carstairs and he had no wish to be struck off for unprofessional conduct.

Now, as he entered the donjon-room which was Carstairs' pride, he wished again that he had found some excuse to cancel the visit; only the thought of Pauline and any possible danger to her had made him come. He could have invented any one of half a hundred legitimate reasons that might have kept him away. But rather to his surprise the weekend had been perfectly ordinary until now. He had driven over on the Friday evening with his overnight things; the food had been excellent, his host uncommonly entertaining. One or two neighbours had been at dinner so the meal had not been an undue strain; he deliberately sat as far as possible from Pauline and his table companion, a red-faced gentleman farmer from up the valley had kept him too occupied with a tirade on the 'wheat price' scandal for him to do much more than catch occasional glimpses of her.

He had not so much as exchanged more than a dozen or so formal words with Pauline that evening. He slept well on retiring and indeed Carstairs had done him proud, even to leaving a bottle of whisky and an unopened box of Havanas on his bedside table. Carstairs was, in fact, treating him with exaggerated consideration and Sanders instantly became wary; he suspected a trap. All Saturday his nerves had been alert and his tension, though not obvious to an outsider, had made his reflexes instantaneous. It was a not unpleasant sensation; something like the war again, but it was Pauline and her situation which worried him most.

The Saturday morning had passed pleasantly enough; late breakfast—it was early June—with the sun streaming in mellow splendour through the French windows; a ride after breakfast in the rolling country nearby; and the morning ended with a tour of his host's magnificent garden. In the afternoon Carstairs had suggested claypigeon shooting, of which he was inordinately fond. He had rigged up butts and the release apparatus in one of his disused stockyards and the whole thing was conducted in an almost professional manner.

Sanders had at once suspected something untoward but he could not back out of the invitation without arousing Carstairs' suspicions; besides, what excuse could he give? That he was a poor shot? That would not matter in clay-pigeon shooting. And in any case Carstairs knew he was a passably fair hand with a gun; he had seen the cups himself in a glass case in his consulting room. No, that would not do and Sanders went out to the butts as though he were about to attend an execution.

But things turned out differently. Carstairs put himself out to be agreeable, Sanders shot well and after a while he forgot the man beside him and as a groom working the release mechanism began to call the shots he really enjoyed himself. His host shot slightly the better of the two, which was as it should be when one is a guest, but all in all, Sanders felt he had acquitted himself well. He returned to the house feeling quite pleased. They were met in the hall by Pauline, who looked white and strained but Sanders managed to convey, by a subtle and devious contortion of his face, that all was well.

The three of them had played billiards in a great panelled room

The Academy Of Pain

until the bell rang for dinner. They were alone for this meal which had passed cheerfully until Carstairs had got on to his favourite topic. Grown reminiscent over the brandy, he had discoursed at some length about what he called the Philosophy of Pain. All the usual claptrap about de Sade and Gilles de Rais, of course, plus the Spanish Inquisition. Sanders had listened with mounting distaste. Pauline, her eyes bright, said nothing, but watched her husband's face carefully, her cheeks pale.

Carstairs had an almost intellectual concept about pain and had evidently studied the refinements of cruelty to a stage where Sanders would have said that his reason had become unhinged. Not quite, perhaps, but it was a fine point of balance.

"I am surprised that you cannot see this, as a doctor, my dear Sanders," said Carstairs, having reached the end of a great flow of rhetoric which had begun with the Stoics of Ancient Greece, had proceeded to the flagellants of mediaeval times and had then digressed through Sawney Bean to some of the more specialized tortures of the Chinese river pirates and the refinements practised by Letang, whom Carstairs described as being one of the more enterprising Askers of the Great Question in the Tower of London during the time of Richard the Third.

"My task is the alleviation of pain, not the prolongation of it," said Sanders somewhat shortly; really, Carstairs was the most revolting brute. It was a wonder Pauline could stay in the same house with him; it was hardly surprising that she baulked at asking him for a divorce. There was no knowing what went on in that massive cranium. But Carstairs was now too far wound up on his favourite subject to let the doctor off so lightly.

"Come, now, Sanders," he said. "Members of your profession have not always thought so. Experimentation in pain has been the basis of whole philosophies in the medical profession from time immemorial. And in our own era, Dr. Pelletier in France, who made a clinical study of his victims' agonies, to say nothing of the Nazi concentration camp doctors—"

"You may say what you like, Carstairs, but you'll not convince me," interrupted Sanders, heartily sick of the conversation. His tone was a mistake. Before he had time to register the alarm on Pauline's face, his host was on his feet, eyes flashing, brows contorted.

"You will be amazed at the subtleties and lengths to which our ancestors went in their experiments to find out the width and depth and dimension of pain, doctor,' he said. 'I have my own laboratory here in this house, which is, as you know, nearly four hundred years old. Come, I will show you."

In face of this challenge Sanders did not feel like backing down, though a glance at Pauline's face confirmed his uneasiness. But Carstairs was already leading the way out of the room; in the corridor he paused to switch on lights ahead of them and then stood aside to let his wife go in front, thus effectively separating the lovers as they went along the passages. It was a remote spot to which the host was leading them, Sanders thought. The donjon-room was beneath a separate wing of the house, quite apart from the main building and the servants' apartments. In view of this, Sanders decided to be doubly on his guard the whole time they were away from outside help.

The trio passed along dim, cobwebby passages whose gloom the modern electric lighting did little to dispel. Then they were descending a rough wooden staircase of unsawn planking; far off Sanders could hear the faint tinkle of falling water. They were in a dank passage floored, walled and roofed with stone; green lichens grew here and the floor was slippery with moss. It was the most ancient part of the house. Once Carstairs paused and struck the wall with the massive key he had taken from a bureau in the hall of the main house. It rang with a curious sound that denoted immense solidity.

"Walls seven feet thick here," said Carstairs with satisfaction. And it was when he was ducking in under the low doorway that he had made the extraordinary remark, 'Welcome to the Academy of Pain,' just as though the place were still in use and not a museum. Sanders felt that he would never be able to probe human nature to its lowest depths; human beings were like a series of Chinese boxes. Discover one vice, be it ever so squalid or mean, and there were still further depths to which human vanity or lust could sink. It was perhaps a strange atti-

◊ The Academy Of Pain

tude for a doctor, Sanders thought, but it was really the way his mind worked. He supposed he was a humanist; otherwise he might have become a lawyer or a banker instead of a doctor.

He squeezed in under the low arch, past the iron-studded door, which Carstairs held open. The place was about eighty feet long, Sanders would have said; brightly lit and, surprisingly, fitted with central heating. Radiators were set at intervals in the ancient stone walls all down one side. The chamber appeared to be at some immense depth beneath the earth. Sanders looked curiously at Carstairs; from the thick, well polished linoleum underfoot and certain other fittings it almost seemed as though his host spent a great deal of time in this extraordinary place. Cataloguing, perhaps? Or writing a paper on the history of torture? Or what? He hardly dared to imagine.

Garstairs smiled a heavy and enigmatic smile as he motioned Sanders into the big room; the heavy door slammed to behind them with a sound that echoed just as sombrely on his heart. Sanders went quickly to stand beside Pauline who, white-faced and breathing heavily, kept her eyes averted from the apparatus around her.

"My wife has seen most of this before," Carstairs went on, as though taking up his previous conversation, "but this will be new to you, Sanders. Some of my collection—most of the items in fact—are originals, but a number have had to be reconstructed as the real articles were, for obvious reasons, not obtainable. I have had to consult some pretty obscure books for drawings, you can be sure."

He chuckled throatily as he looked round, a light of enthusiasm in his eyes.

"Yes, there's no denying that pain as a philosophy is as satisfying as anything in this world."

Sanders did not answer. His heart felt sick as his eye travelled over the instruments on the bench before him. There were, he saw, a set of metal pincers of varying sizes whose uses were at once too hideously clear to his medical mind; a brazier was set next to them; then sets of cuffs and chains; a metal ball and spike whose use was obscure to him; a set of metal drills for splitting bones; a curious sort of claw used for tearing out muscles.

"Genuine article that," said Carstairs with satisfaction. "Spanish Inquisition. No, the marks are not rust."

Sanders turned away, his heart heavy. They passed along the chamber. Carstairs was in a curious mood; it might be best to humour him. He saw, with some relief, that Pauline was remaining near the door. There was a small library of rare volumes in calf; she made a pretence of glancing at these. Sanders gazed around him with mounting bewilderment; really, Carstairs had accumulated a fantastic collection. He must have ransacked the archives of cruelty the world over for these specimens.

"Disembowelling knives," said Carstairs smoothly. "Finest set in existence. I had to pay the earth for them."

They passed a strange chair with clamps; a copper bowl with a singular fluted spout was suspended above it.

"Chinese water torture," said Carstairs, answering his unspoken question.

In one corner was a vast metal boot; by its side a ponderous mallet bound with bands of iron. Wedges were stacked by it; some of them were russet-coloured at their tips. Sanders did not investigate too closely.

"These are rather interesting," said Carstairs, stopping in front of a glass case. The cabinet contained a number of intricately chased pincers; next to them, in sets, were numbered human molars. Sanders recognized that without a doubt. At the end of the cabinet were long slivers of split bamboo, a small silver mallet and what appeared to be the wax model of a hand, cut off at the wrist. Several slips of bamboo had been hammered up beneath the fingernails, splitting them. The thing was hideously realistic, even down to the clotted blood.

"Chinese again," said Carstairs, the undertone of smooth satisfaction in his voice reinforced by the expression on his guest's face.

"Quite genuine. I had a job to get these out. Of course the practises are still carried out by the river pirates today, though the Communists try to keep things within bounds."

Sanders felt himself go white as he glanced at the next exhibit, which consisted of about a hundred large photographs mounted on

The Academy Of Pain

the back of a series of glass cabinets. He was inured to the results of motor accidents and all sorts of foul diseases but he felt his gorge rise as he noted some of the atrocities depicted in the pictures.

"Unusual sets," Carstairs went on. "All modern, as you will see. The Death of a Thousand Cuts here, from beginning to end. Ritual disembowelling here. And these are rather fine. From a captured Nazi collection."

Sanders passed on with head averted. He hardly knew where he was walking. He was vaguely aware of an iron couch covered with bizarre-looking knobs. Then they were in among the big exhibits. There was an immense rack with modern cable instead of chains and lead weights for stretching victims; a wheel on which the accused person was suspended head first and which passed him over a bed of spikes; he recognized with a chill of dread the Iron Virgin of Nuremburg, a monstrous effigy of a woman in which the prisoner was placed. The door was lined with spikes designed to reach the vital spots. The cover was then lowered on to the victim fraction by fraction by means of a rope and counterweights so that it would take some hours to finish the occupant off. Sanders saw with sick loathing that two blunt spikes were placed opposite the eye-sockets.

"A pity about these," said Carstairs in disappointed tones. "Copies, of course. All three. It proved simply impossible to get the originals. So I had them updated in some respects. The stainless steel cable might upset the purist but one must move with the times."

Sanders wondered dully who the fellow-enthusiasts might be who would share such a morbid interest as Carstairs; he could imagine very few. His host chatted on as though he had not noticed Sanders' sick eyes and averted face. They passed through a section devoted to death by poison; here were the various poisons in their jars; beneath each bottle ingenious wax effigies writhed in death agony while Hogarthian-style drawings in colour went into greater detail.

"I trust you are finding this absorbing?" Carstairs asked as though he were showing off a new billiard room.

"I've never had such an evening in my life," Sanders replied with grim truth. By this time the macabre tour was coming to an end, much to Sanders' relief. They were picking their way up towards

Pauline again; here were more braziers, a steel hearth and, to Sanders' consternation, piles of coke. Carstairs shot him a swift glance, pleased at the expression on his guest's face. Sanders fought to keep control of himself; he could feel the palms of his hands sweating. He glanced across at Pauline but she stood erect and avoided his gaze.

They turned a corner and Sanders bit his tongue to suppress a scream. Tortured faces, dying eyes glared at him through the thick walls of jars. In container after container along the heavy bench were preserved the bodies of large animals; here a stoat had been crucified with small pins, there a rabbit disembowelled alive; in a tableau of macabre blasphemy some perverted mind had attempted to represent the Crucifixion, using the bodies of a weasel and two hedgehogs for the purpose.

Sanders leaned against the bench, hatred for Carstairs lapping his body as though with physical pain.

"Remarkable study, this," Carstairs went on smoothly, his big body tensed, as though expecting Sanders to spring on him.

"An extraordinarily skilled model-maker in the village. Strange old man, but he has a genius in his hands. It might surprise you to know what I have to pay for these models."

Sanders knew that the things in the jars were no models but once living flesh and blood which had been shockingly tortured to give pleasure to the man beside him. All his loathing rose up until it threatened to choke him. He shook his head to clear the blurring before his eyes and was startled to hear a crash. He looked up sharply, all his medical instincts roused as he saw that Pauline had fallen to the floor. He hurried towards her, Carstairs following behind. He felt the girl's pulse.

"Only a fainting fit," he said with relief. "Rather stuffy in here."

In truth he was glad of the diversion; he had been at cracking point and Carstairs knew it. The latter looked at him with narrowed eyes.

But all he said was, "We'd better get her upstairs then."

Carstairs took his wife's head and with Sanders taking her legs and guiding his host, they somehow made their way back to the upper house. There was no one about; the servants were long in bed.

Carstairs led the way into the library, where lights still burned. They laid Pauline on a couch. Carstairs hurried over to a buffet and busied himself with glasses. He came back to Pauline and forced the rim of the glass between her teeth; Sanders caught the pungent aroma of brandy. The girl choked a little, some of the liquid ran down her chin; she coughed once or twice, shuddered and then opened her eyes.

"You look as if you'd had a fright, my dear fellow," said Carstairs. "A little brandy wouldn't do you any harm."

Sanders went to the sideboard and picked up the full glass standing there. He stood awkwardly at the edge of the little group formed by the prostrate girl and the big man who knelt in the light of the lamps, and took fierce gulps of the raw spirit. He was more shaken than he had thought; the brandy tasted no stronger than water.

Then sensation began to come back. He opened his mouth to say something to Carstairs and there came a crash; he looked down stupidly. The glass had fallen and shattered at his feet. He bent down to pick it up, an apology on his lips, when the room began to blur. He caught the edge of a chair, began to haul himself up. Realization came into his brain with fading consciousness; Carstairs' eyes were fixed on him with infinite malice as he went down into darkness and silence.

2

He came round to a sensation of intolerable pain and noise. Every muscle in his body ached for relief. There was blackness before his eyes and a surging throb in his jaws. He tried to move his hands and legs, failed. His eyes would not open. The roaring noise went on and with it a sensation of heat. Sweat ran down his body. He knew where he was; naked, pinioned on the rack in the donjon-room; the cables creaked a little as the excruciating tension was increased.

From far away a voice said, "I am sorry I had to commence without you, as it were, my dear Sanders, but these June nights are short and it would never do for the staff to become suspicious."

◈ Darkness, Mist & Shadow

Sanders opened his eyes with a great effort; lying near his head were sets of pincers, smeared and clotted with blood. Beside them were a number of ivory objects with reddened roots. The throbbing in his jaws made it only too clear what had happened. Every nerve in his naked body screaming, he turned his head to the right. In the interior of the Iron Virgin, the nude body of Pauline was pinioned and gagged; the spikes were five inches from her face and body. He looked into her eyes; eyes of permanent madness.

The brazier roaring, blew a blast of hot air into the chamber, the ashes shifted and a red glow shone angrily on the walls. Sanders heard a monstrous screaming echoing round the old donjon, stones seven feet thick he had heard, which would prevent all noise from reaching the house; indeed, would prevent all knowledge of their fate from ever reaching the outside world.

Carstairs brought the white-hot pincers up from below Sanders' thighs with a fine, flourishing gesture; acrid smoke billowed into his face and in his eyes was the infinite satisfaction of every artist who has created something perfect.

"Welcome to the Academy of Pain," said Carstairs.

Doctor Porthos

1

Nervous debility, the doctor says. And yet Angelina has never been ill in her life. Nervous debility! Something far more powerful is involved here; I am left wondering if I should not call in specialist advice. Yet we are so remote and Dr. Porthos is well spoken of by the local people. Why on earth did we ever come to this house? Angelina was perfectly well until then. It is extraordinary to think that two months can have wrought such a change in my wife.

In the town she was lively and vivacious; yet now I can hardly bear to look at her without profound emotion. Her cheeks are sunken and pale, her eyes dark and tired, her bloom quite gone at twenty-five. Could it be something in the air of the house? It seems barely possible. But in that case Dr. Porthos' ministrations should have proved effective. But so far all his skills have been powerless to produce any change for the better. If it had not been for the terms of my uncle's will we would never have come at all.

Friends may call it cupidity, the world may think what it chooses, but the plain truth is that I needed the money. My own health is far from robust and long hours in the family business—ours is an honoured and well-established counting house—had made it perfectly clear to me that I must seek some other mode of life. And yet I could not afford to retire; the terms of my uncle's will, as retailed to me by the family solicitor, afforded the perfect solution.

⚜ Darkness, Mist & Shadow

An annuity—a handsome annuity to put it bluntly—but with the proviso that my wife and I should reside in the old man's house for a period of not less than five years from the date the terms of the will became effective. I hesitated long; both my wife and I were fond of town life and my uncle's estate was in a remote area, where living for the country people was primitive and amenities few. As I had understood it from the solicitor, the house itself had not even the benefit of gas-lighting; in summer it was not so bad but the long months of winter would be melancholy indeed with only the glimmer of candles and the pale sheen of oil lamps to relieve the gloom of the lonely old place.

I debated with Angelina and then set off one weekend alone for a tour of the estate. I had cabled ahead and after a long and cold railway journey which itself occupied most of the day, I was met at my destination by a horse and chaise. The next part of my pilgrimage occupied nearly four hours and I was dismayed on seeing into what a wild and remote region my uncle had chosen to penetrate in order to select a dwelling.

The night was dark but the moon occasionally burst its veiling of cloud to reveal in feeble detail the contours of rock and hill and tree; the chaise jolted and lurched over an unmade road, which was deeply rutted by the wheels of the few vehicles which had torn up the surface in their passing over many months. My solicitor had wired to an old friend, Dr. Porthos, to whose good offices I owed my mode of transport, and he had promised to greet me on arrival at the village nearest the estate.

Sure enough, he came out from under the great porch of the timbered hostelry as our carriage grated into the inn-yard. He was a tall, spare man, with square *pince-nez* which sat firmly on his thin nose; he wore a many-pleated cape like an ostler and the green top hat, worn rakishly over one eye gave him a somewhat dissipated look. He greeted me effusively but there was something about the man which did not endear him to me.

There was nothing that one could isolate. It was just his general manner; perhaps the coldness of his hand which struck a most disconcerting way of looking over the tops of his glasses; they were a

◦ᴀ Doctor Porthos

filmy grey and their piercing glance seemed to root one to the spot. To my dismay I learned that I was not yet at my destination. The estate was still some way off, said the doctor, and we would have to stay the night at the inn. My ill-temper at his remarks was soon dispelled by the roaring fire and the good food with which he plied me; there were few travellers at this time of year and we were the only ones taking dinner in the vast oak-panelled dining room.

The doctor had been my uncle's medical attendant and though it was many years since I had seen my relative I was curious to know what sort of person he had been.

"The Baron was a great man in these parts," said Porthos. His genial manner emboldened me to ask a question to which I had long been awaiting an answer.

"Of what did my uncle die?" I asked.

Firelight flickered through the gleaming redness of Dr. Porthos' wineglass and tinged his face with amber as he replied simply, "Of a lacking of richness in the blood. A fatal quality in his immediate line, I might say."

I pondered for a moment. "Why do you think he chose me as his heir?" I added.

Dr. Porthos' answer was straight and clear and given without hesitation.

"You were a different branch of the family," he said. "New blood, my dear sir. The Baron was most particular on that account. He wanted to carry on the great tradition."

He cut off any further questions by rising abruptly. "Those were the Baron's own words as he lay dying. And now we must retire as we still have a fair journey before us in the morning."

◦ᴀ 2

Dr. Porthos' words come back to me in my present trouble. "Blood, new blood..." What if this be concerned with those dark legends the local people tell about the house? One hardly knows what to think in this atmosphere. My inspection of the house with Dr.

Porthos confirmed my worst fears; sagging lintels, mouldering cornices, worm-eaten panelling. The only servitors a middle-aged couple, husband and wife, who have been caretakers here since the Baron's death; the local people sullen and unco-operative, so Porthos says. Certainly, the small hamlet a mile or so from the mansion had every door and window shut as we clattered past and not a soul was stirring. The house has a Gothic beauty, I suppose, viewed from a distance; it is of no great age, being largely rebuilt on the remains of an older pile destroyed by fire. The restorer—whether he be my uncle or some older resident I have not bothered to discover—had the fancy of adding turrets, a drawbridge with castellated towers and a moated surround. Our footsteps echoed mournfully over this as we turned to inspect the grounds.

I was surprised to see marble statuary and worn obelisks, all tumbled and awry, as though the uneasy dead were bursting from the soil, protruding over an ancient moss-grown wall adjoining the courtyard of the house.

Dr. Porthos smiled sardonically.

"The old family burial ground," he explained. "Your uncle is interred here. He said he likes to be near the house."

3

Well, it is done; we came not two months since and then began the profound and melancholy change of which I have already spoken. Not just the atmosphere—though the very stones of the house seem steeped in evil whispers—but the surroundings, the dark, unmoving trees, even the furniture, seem to exude something inimical to life as we knew it; as it is still known to those fortunate enough to dwell in towns.

A poisonous mist rises from the moat at dusk; it seems to doubly emphasize our isolation. The presence of Angelina's own maid and a handyman who was in my father's employ before me, do little to dispel the ambiance of this place. Even their sturdy matter of factness seems affected by a miasma that wells from the pores of the building. It has become so manifest of late that I even welcome the daily visits of Dr. Porthos, despite the fact that I suspect him to be the author of our troubles.

They began a week after our arrival when Angelina failed to awake by my side as usual; I shook her to arouse her and my screams must have awakened the maid. I think I fainted then and came to myself in the great morning room; the bed had been awash with blood, which stained the sheets and pillows around my dear wife's head; Porthos' curious grey eyes had a steely look in them which I had never seen before. He administered a powerful medicine and had then turned to attend to me.

Whatever had attacked Angelina had teeth like the sharpest canine, Porthos said; he had found two distinct punctures in Angelina's throat, sufficient to account for the quantities of blood. Indeed, there had been so much of it that my own hands and linen were stained with it where I had touched her; I think it was this which had made me cry out so violently. Porthos had announced that he would sit up by the patient that night.

Angelina was still asleep, as I discovered when I tiptoed in later. Porthos had administered a sleeping draught and had advised me to take the same, to settle my nerves, but I declined. I said I would wait up with him. The doctor had some theory about rats or other nocturnal creatures and sat long in the library looking through some of the Baron's old books on natural history. The man's attitude puzzles me; what sort of creature would attack Angelina in her own bedroom? Looking at Porthos' strange eyes, my old fears are beginning to return, bringing with them new ones.

4

There have been three more attacks, extending over a fortnight. My darling grows visibly weaker, though Porthos has been to the nearest town for more powerful drugs and other remedies. I am in purgatory; I have not known such dark hours in my life until now. Yet Angelina herself insists that we should stay to see this grotesque nightmare through. The first evening of our vigil both Porthos and I slept; and in the morning the result was as the night before. Considerable emissions of blood and the bandage covering the wound had been removed to allow the creature access to the punctures. I hardly dare conjecture what manner of beast could have done this.

I was quite worn out and on the evening of the next day I agreed to Porthos' suggestion that I should take a sleeping draught. Nothing happened for several nights and Angelina began to recover; then the terror struck again. And so it will go on, my reeling senses tell me. I daren't trust Porthos and on the other hand I cannot accuse him before the members of my household. We are isolated here and any mistake I make might be fatal.

On the last occasion I almost had him. I woke at dawn and found Porthos stretched on the bed, his long, dark form quivering, his hands at Angelina's throat. I struck at him, for I did not know who it was, being half asleep, and he turned, his grey eyes glowing in the dim room. He had a hypodermic syringe half full of blood in his hand. I am afraid I dashed it to the floor and shattered it beneath my heel.

In my own heart I am convinced I have caught this creature which has been plaguing us, but how to prove it? Dr. Porthos is staying in the house now; I dare not sleep and continually refuse the potions he urgently presses upon me. How long before he destroys me as well as Angelina? Was man ever in such an appalling situation since the world began?

I sit and watch Porthos, who stares at me sideways with those curious eyes, his inexpressive face seeming to hint that he can afford to watch and wait and that his time is coming; my pale wife, in her few intervals of consciousness sits and fearfully watches both of us. Yet I cannot even confide in her for she would think me mad. I try to calm my racing brain. Sometimes I think I shall go insane altogether, the nights are so long. God help me.

5

It is over. The crisis has come and gone. I have laid the mad demon which has us in thrall. I caught him at it. Porthos writhed as I got my

Doctor Porthos

hands at his throat. I would have killed him at his foul work; the syringe glinted in his hand. Now he has slipped aside, eluded me for the moment. My cries brought in the servants who have my express instructions to hunt him down. He shall not escape me this time. I pace the corridors of this worm-eaten mansion and when I have cornered him I shall destroy him. Angelina shall live! And my hands will perform the healing work of his destruction ... But now I must rest. Already it is dawn again. I will sit in this chair by the pillar, where I can watch the hall. I sleep.

6

Later. I awake to pain and cold. I am lying on earth. Something slippery trickles over my hand. I open my eyes. I draw my hand across my mouth. It comes away scarlet. I can see more clearly now. Angelina is here too. She looks terrified but somehow sad and composed. She is holding the arm of Dr. Porthos.

He is poised above me, his face looking Satanic in the dim light of the crypt beneath the house. He whirls a mallet while shriek after shriek disturbs the silence of this place. Dear Christ, the stake is against MY BREAST!

Archives Of The Dead

1

Robert Trumble arrived at Linnet Ridge as a thin, persistent rain was beginning to fall. The house was in a remote part of Surrey and the sombre drive up through avenues of pines and fir had not prepared him for the sight of the building itself; painted white, standing four-square to the bracing winds of the uplands, it did not seem to Trumble to typify the reputation of Dr. Ramon Fabri as one of the foremost authorities on the occult.

And yet why should it? Trumble smiled wryly to himself. Surprising how one's mind still moved on conventional lines in some respects. He still found it difficult to conceal his bitterness at some facets of the world as he found it; a minor poet of some brilliance, he had somehow failed to live up to his early promise. As is the way with poets, the public had omitted to buy his works in any great numbers, the editions had passed out of print and Trumble had been reduced to tutoring and hack work over the past years in order to make a living.

This was why Dr. Fabri's Personal advertisement in *The Times* had seemed so attractive; a secretaryship, though not really the sort of thing to which a minor poet aspired, would at least see him financially stable until he should set forth again on some other literary adventure. From what he had gathered at a London interview with Dr. Fabri his duties would not be too onerous; furthermore, the salary was generous in proportion to Trumble's slender secretarial experience; he would live in and live well, judging by Dr. Fabri's reputation as a gourmet; and the post would leave him time for his literary endeavours. He had closed at once and, three days later, had driven down in his old, second-hand two-seater.

As always, the hood had leaked all the way, though the rain had held off its main attack until he was past Reigate; from then on its steady encroachment had made driving a misery and Trumble saw with relief the lodge gates of his destination compose themselves before the thin beams of his headlights in the filmy April dusk.

His tyres crunched over gravel as he drove up a well-kept drive between smooth lawns and on to the impressive Georgian façade of Dr. Fabri's residence. He carried up his two shabby suitcases between the gleaming white splendour of the pillared entrance porch and saw light shining through the circular windows that flanked the pale yellow front door. Before he could set down his cases to ring the bell, a tall, lean figure blocked out the light that spilled from the open entry.

The man was some sort of general handyman, Trumble judged by his striped waistcoat and the green baize apron he wore round his waist like a domestic servant in a faded pre-war comedy. The man had razor-sharp features with yellow skin stretched over a sharply-etched skull; his bald head echoed his face in the lamplight as he stooped to pick up Trumble's bags.

"Dr. Fabri's waiting in the study, sir," he said in correct, clipped tones. "He says he would like you to go straight through."

Trumble murmured some commonplace and then turned towards his car; he found the bald man at his elbow. A hand closed over his arm and he was held softly but immovably. The pressure lasted only a moment but the fellow must have had immense strength.

"Dr. Fabri said at once, sir," he said with slight emphasis on the last words. "I'll attend to your car if you'll give me the keys."

Trumble looked at the man's impassive features and handed them over. The grip on his arm was instantly relaxed. The man in the striped waistcoat slid swiftly behind the wheel of Trumble's old machine.

"Straight down the hall, sir, first door on the right," he called, his flat, clipped voice without echoes in the dusk and the thin, whispering rain. "I'll bring your baggage after."

Trumble went through the porch and into the hall, leaving his bags where they were, as the car trundled away round the drive towards some unseen destination in the rear. Rather an odd character for chauffeur–butler, he felt, though no doubt Dr. Fabri might have use of such a person living in the lonely spot he had chosen to make his home.

It was none of his business; and in any case the fellow had been polite enough. It was just his attitude; withdrawn strength and confidence, just this side of insolence, which rankled somewhere inside Trumble's mind. He felt he must be getting hypersensitive; rejection by the larger literary world of which he had once had such inordinate hopes might be the reason behind it. He closed the door softly behind him and blinked in the bright light of the inner hall.

He walked in over a tiled floor of extraordinary beauty. Light reflected back the smooth greens, reds and blues of the convoluted designs; Trumble recognized the pentacle and something which looked like the seal of Cagliostro. Dr. Fabri, as he knew, was deeply read in literature which dwelt on dark and hidden things and Trumble himself was intensely interested in the subject; indeed, one of his earlier volumes of poetry, On Goety, had been based on the Seven Seals, which may well have originally drawn his name to Dr. Fabri's attention.

Trumble flushed at the thought; like all failed and deeply sensitive men he was alive to every nuance and subtlety which might indicate that the wider world had not entirely overlooked his work and the notion that Dr. Fabri might actually have read and appreciated his poems gave his starved mind more pleasure than he cared to admit.

He was charmed too, to see that his future employer carried his interests to the length of including them in the decor of his house; the post promised to be one of unexpected delights. He passed several oil paintings on his way to the door of which the servant had spoken; they were undoubtedly genuine works of art, of obvious value and chosen with unfailing taste to illustrate Dr. Fabri's chosen pursuits. Trumble was astonished to notice a magnificent Bosch which he did not think had existed outside a museum in Amsterdam; though, like all of Bosch's work it had a haunting and vivid quality that one with tender nerves would find disquieting, to say the least.

Even Trumble was not sure that he cared all that much for the subject; screaming forms which fled through what appeared to be looped sections of viscera. Really, Bosch had a stunning genius, Trumble felt; he was almost a painter of the twenty-first century and the modern world still had not caught up with his terrifying fancies and extraordinary sense of colour and design. But Trumble did not have time for more than an admiring glance at the canvas; in a moment more he was at the door and, knocking on it, heard Dr. Fabri call out for him to enter.

Fabri was a man in his middle forties with a powerful frame and a tanned complexion; despite his comparative youth his hair was completely white but cut very short like a young man. His deep-set eyes were brilliant and penetrating and his square tortoiseshell spectacles gave his face a quizzical look and reinforced its strength. His jaw was square also and the glasses echoed the cubistic theme. He rose from a red-leather-topped desk to greet Trumble with obvious pleasure.

"I trust you had a good journey?"

His voice was dark-toned and deep and its timbre recalled to the new secretary that Dr. Fabri had been famous for his lecture-tours on the Continent a dozen or so years before; a celebrated series that at one time threatened to launch him into the dubious career of a television celebrity. Fortunately, Dr. Fabri had the good taste to draw back and his scholarship and erudition were henceforth confined to those comparatively small numbers of people who bought tickets of entry to the halls of learned institutions in London, Paris, Rome, Berlin and other leading capitals. Trumble had, of course, spent almost an hour in Dr. Fabri's company at his previous interview but he was now seeing the doctor in his own surroundings for the first time and he studied his employer's milieu with more than casual interest.

As the two men exchanged a few remarks, Trumble's eyes wandered about the vast study in which they sat; it was one of the most curious places he had ever seen. There was a large globe covered with zodiac signs whose use was obscure to him; tapestries decorated with cabalistic insignia writhed over the far wall while the massed shelves contained thousands of volumes of works in Greek and Latin. So far as he could make out, many of the books were rare and valuable originals. Trumble felt his spirits reviving.

At the far end of the chamber was a large platform enclosed by iron railings; a spiral staircase ascended to it from the main floor of the library. Trumble could see chemical retorts and a Bunsen-burner on one of the benches gave off a bluish-green flame in the dusk. Blue velvet curtains partitioned off part of the other end of the room and the shadowy forms of images of ancient gods ranged round those parts of the walls not given over to books.

"I see that you approve of my surroundings," said Dr. Fabri, shooting him a shrewd glance. "My collection is not so comprehensive as I should wish, but I have begun to make a start. Life is not long enough for the amassing of knowledge, my friend."

Fabri laughed as Trumble stammered out some rejoinder. But then his host rose abruptly.

"Forgive me, but I am forgetting my manners. You must be hungry. Joseph will have a meal prepared shortly."

He led the way out of the study and into an adjoining apartment, conventionally furnished as a dining-room but with panelled walls of some charm and with great glazed doors looking on to the ruin of a once considerable garden. Fabri pulled the curtains over the sombre scene outside the window and led the way over to a cabinet; whisky splashed into long crystal glasses and there came the friendly tinkle of ice. A moment later Dr. Fabri handed him the glass and they toasted one another silently by a fire of logs which spluttered contentedly to itself in a handsome stone fireplace. Trumble sank into a high-backed chair and gazed into the fire as his host excused himself; he felt that he would enjoy his stay at Linnet Ridge.

He was aroused from his thoughts by a sound at his elbow and saw the man Joseph, who had met him in the porch, busying himself at the long teak dining-table. He laid two places silently and with polished efficiency and went out through the far door. Dr. Fabri returned almost at once.

ARCHIVES OF THE DEAD

"Excuse my bad manners, my dear Trumble," he said, pressing a thin book into his new secretary's hands, "but I could not resist the opportunity. I am something of a collector, as you know, and your name was not unknown to me before we met. It would give me great pleasure if you would inscribe the work for me."

Trumble saw with surprise that the book was a rare edition of his own 'On Goety', produced on hand-woven paper in a limited edition from a private press in Paris. So far as he knew there had been only two hundred copies produced. He felt his hands tremble as he took a pen from his pocket and composed something appropriate on the fly-leaf for Dr. Fabri.

"You were surprised, eh?" said the doctor, as he examined Trumble's inscription and thanked him for it.

"There are so few copies and my work is so obscure," said Trumble, his voice quivering slightly. 'One works so hard and yet it is so difficult to become known.'

Dr. Fabri gazed at him in sympathy. "One is known to those who are of importance and that is what counts," he said simply. "It is a great honour to have you under my roof. But now let us eat. Tomorrow it will give me pleasure to show you round my house. You will not find your duties onerous and I am sure we shall find many mutual interests to share."

He led the way to the table. The meal passed in silence, the courses served impeccably by the man Joseph. There did not appear to be any other staff. Dr. Fabri made no mention of Trumble's duties and for his part the poet was content for the moment to enjoy the good food and wine with which his new employer plied him. Shortly after half-past nine Dr. Fabri excused himself.

"Joseph will show you your quarters," he said. "Until tomorrow, then."

The big man led the way up a large oak staircase that opened from the hall and along a luxuriously carpeted corridor lined with oak doors. He flung open the third and switched on the light.

"If you require anything, sir, you have only to ring," he said, indicating a brass push-button set into the wall next to a battery of light switches.

Trumble thanked him and closed the door behind him. It was a large, comfortable room to which he had been assigned; centrally heated, it was furnished with plain modern furniture and well lit from both ceiling and wall light fixtures. There were three doors opening off it; investigating, Trumble found a sitting room, bathroom and toilet. He came back to the bedroom with considerable pleasure: it might pay him to stay with Dr. Fabri for an indefinite period.

His two shabby suitcases were standing in the centre of the room where Joseph had left them; his car keys were on the dressing-table. He smiled to himself; evidently Joseph was as efficient as his master. He unpacked quickly, stowed away his few belongings in the drawers and put the empty suitcases in the wardrobe. He felt unaccountably tired, but put this down to the long and unpleasant drive. He came back from the bathroom in pyjamas and prepared for bed; the thin cry of an owl came from a thicket somewhere beyond the garden but apart from that there was no sound but the faint gurgling of water in the pipes of the central heating system.

He went idly to the window and looked down into the garden, now silvered by a moon which shone from a clear rainless sky. It was then that he saw the window was covered with bars which followed the pattern of the leaded panes. He frowned. He went back over towards the door. It was, as he had somehow expected, locked. It was curious but it proved nothing, except possibly that to Dr. Fabri he was an unknown quantity; a new employee loose in a household which contained many valuable paintings and *objets d'art*. He smiled to himself; he did not feel at all insulted. He stood irresolute for a moment, gazing at the door-lock and from there to the brass bell-push which would bring the servant Joseph to him within seconds.

Then he shrugged and turned away. He might take up the matter tomorrow, when he had thought it over further. He got into bed, his mind already embracing sleep, and switched off the light. He slept well, awakening only once as the high, sharp, piercing cry of the owl was repeated; the sound was nearer, almost in the garden. It sounded twice more. He got up then and looked into the grounds but could see nothing. He went to the door before returning to the warmth of his bed; he tried the handle gently in the gloom. It was unlocked. He got back into bed. He was soon asleep and this time slept dreamlessly and uninterruptedly until breakfast time.

2

He ate his meal alone in a small, pleasant room that opened on to the lawn, with Joseph as the sole attendant to his needs. He was astonished to find that the garden, which had appeared such a ruin from his window the previous night was, at closer acquaintance, obviously well-tended, with smooth lawns, well-kept beds and rose bushes lining trellised pathways. He was annoyed with himself, for having made such a stupid error and after breakfast walked over to the French doors for a closer inspection but was unable to open the fastenings in order to gain access to the terrace.

Just then Dr. Fabri entered with smiling apologies for his non-appearance at breakfast.

"I have much to do, you know," he said jovially. He enquired politely how Trumble had slept; the latter had decided to say nothing about the locked bedroom door and privately meant to see whether it was his employer's intention to keep him segregated from the main house during the nights. In the meantime there was much to engage his attention; while Joseph cleared the table Dr. Fabri and his new employee took a turn round the vast garden, which confirmed Trumble's estimate through the window. He resolved to have a look at his bedroom casement that evening; there might be some distorting quality in the glass.

The two men returned to the house half an hour later, chatting in a desultory way of Trumble's duties; he gathered that he would be expected to keep Dr. Fabri's appointments diary, work out his day for him, answer the telephone and do the indexing on the doctor's vast collection of books and documents. Apparently there were a great many more papers apart from the main library and it would take him a month or two to find his way around.

Trumble learned, with some pleasure, that he would have most afternoons free but, in return, was expected to put in an hour or two in the evenings, as Dr. Fabri might require from time to time; he would also have to take some dictation and he was glad that he had once learned shorthand in the days when he was contributing to magazines; the facility would obviously come in useful.

At this point in their conversation the two men had returned to the vast study, where the doctor was engaged in pointing out various aspects of his indexing system in the large green filing cabinets which lined one corner of the room.

"There is one other part of the house which will be your special domain," he said with a spark of humour in his eye, as he drew the young man down the shelving. "I think you will find it not the least interesting aspect of your new duties."

He beckoned to where the platform sprang from the floor of the main study. The two men ascended the spiral staircase, their steps echoing hollowly on the treads.

The shadowy statues leered darkly from their niches but Trumble had little time to take in their detail or any other particulars of the interesting minutiae strewn about in such profusion in this esoteric corner. Dr. Fabri took him over to the curtains which he drew aside with a silken cord. Facing the two men was a large bronze door, about six feet high, whose golden surface caught the light in dull, undulating reflections.

Trumble then saw that the bass-relief design on the door, magnificently executed, depicted a Sabbat. Nude figures writhed in a circle on some deserted heathland and the artist, with a cunning amounting to genius, had made his horrific vision stand out with startling reality, doubly emphasized, of course, by the medium he had chosen. The figures seemed to move within the frame of the door and Trumble felt a great stir of the heart as he gazed in fascination. There was a rough altar in the centre of the design, he saw, and a goat-form conducting the rites.

A naked girl formed the top of the altar; there was a bowl on her stomach and another girl lay across her knees. Assistants supported the second girl and the goat-figure appeared to be cutting her throat over the bowl. Trumble gazed on with fascinated distaste. Fabri glanced at him with obvious pleasure. "After Callot," he said with great satisfaction. "One of my little fancies."

Archives Of The Dead

He pulled back the bronze catch of the great door and led the way into a large chamber; concealed lighting clicked on as he opened the door. It was a curious room, Trumble thought; perhaps the most curious he had ever seen, though it was also strangely commonplace. Walls and floors appeared to be lined with zinc; there were grilles high up in the walls and in the ceiling, evidently to do with the air-conditioning, and racks of books, many with tattered leather bindings and faded gold inscriptions; Trumble noticed many rare works bound in vellum; among them Vermis de Mysteris by Ludvig Prinn, and De Masticatione Mortuorum by Philip Rohr; the Dissertatio de Vampyris Seruinsibus by Zopfius, Harenberg's extremely rare Von Vampyren, together with a contemporary account of the Salem Witch Trials. This section was an incongruous sight, set as it was among modern filing cabinets and a great shelf of ledgers, each numbered and indexed.

On the green-leather-topped desk which stood some yards within the chamber was an open ledger which was inscribed in green ink; and a bundle of newspaper cuttings. A faint humming filled the air.

"This room fulfills two functions," said Dr. Fabri, "and will be the scene of your main duties. My most important and rarest manuscripts are stored here. The air-conditioning keeps them at a constant temperature."

He ran his eyes over the packed shelves with satisfaction. He moved farther down the room and drew Trumble's attention to the ledgers. He chuckled softly.

"These are my records of notabilities, kept through the medium of newspaper cuttings and other material, sent me from all over the world. Obituaries, you understand, of all the celebrities and public persons whose careers interest me."

He waved his hand towards the shelf of ledgers. "I call them the 'Archives of the Dead'."

He moved back again to the desk. "You will see from this daily ledger the name of the person or persons who are to be added to the scrapbooks. Then, when the material arrives by post, it is cut out and transferred to the appropriate ledger. The information is then cross-indexed in these filing cabinets. The system is simplicity itself."

Trumble moved to the desk, his mind turning over the odd nature of the task; he saw that Fabri's records were incredibly detailed and contained much out of the way information not only from famous newspapers and magazines but obscure journals in German, French and Russian. He looked down the green-inked entries in the smaller book which stood open on the desk—like the Book of Judgement, he could not help thinking wryly to himself—and noted that the two latest names, in Fabri's impeccable hand-writing, were those of a scenic designer and a ballet dancer.

"If you have any queries, Mr. Trumble," said Dr. Fabri, waving his hand to indicate the contents of the room, "now is the time. You will be left much to yourself, I am afraid, as I have my own affairs to pursue. We are all alone here, except for Joseph, and the cleaning women come in during the mornings twice a week."

While Trumble put a few questions to Dr. Fabri, his mind continued to debate his astonishing good fortune; for he had soon grasped that his duties for the moment would be merely nominal. He could not really see why Dr. Fabri needed a secretary at all but on the other hand if he were prepared to pay so handsomely in return for such agreeably lightweight tasks, Trumble, for one, was not prepared to argue. The two men parted on the best of terms; Fabri was driving over to see some friends and would not be back until late afternoon. Joseph would prepare Trumble's lunch and he could work on at the indexing undisturbed during the afternoon, in order to get the doctor's records up to date.

If he had the time he was to go through Fabri's correspondence and prepare answers to the routine matters for the doctor's signature and would, naturally, answer the door or telephone and deal with any inquiries. Trumble sat at the desk, quietly jubilant for some minutes after the rumble of the doctor's car had died away down the drive. He glanced round at the massed volumes on the shelves and then down again to the material awaiting his attention; the air-conditioning hummed quietly to itself and the scent of the spring flowers, arranged in big jars round the main library, came to him through the bronze door of the room, which had been propped open with a large stone ornament.

ARCHIVES OF THE DEAD

He gazed at the doctor's green-ink entry once again. He picked up his pen and turned to the top of a large, blank page of the current ledger, which had been left open on the desk with the cuttings. In neat block capitals, underlined with a ruler, he wrote; FAENZA, BORIS b.1884. Then he set to work.

3

Three days passed. Three days in which Trumble gradually came to know the ascetic but not unpleasant routine of the Fabri household. In the mornings he took dictation from Dr. Fabri in answer to the incoming mail; the doctor had an astonishing correspondence from all over the world, much of it from such exotic places as Venezuela or the Gulf of Mexico. Many of these were in the languages of the country of origin and Dr. Fabri would peruse them and then rattle out his replies in English with machine-gun precision. More than once Trumble was glad that he had taken the trouble to thoroughly master shorthand during the earlier days of his career.

He thought he was doing quite a good job and Fabri evidently concurred; though he did not say so, Trumble fancied that he occasionally caught a glimpse of approval in his employer's eye, when he imagined that Trumble's head was bowed studiously over the page of his notebook to the exclusion of all other things. The two men would lunch together in a not unpleasant silence, in the room which looked on to the garden and which Trumble remembered so vividly from his first evening in the house; Joseph would wait on them without talking. The food was impeccably cooked and the wines were invariably perfectly chosen and served at the correct temperature.

Occasionally there would be time in the mornings for Trumble's work on the Archives of the Dead; he had taken up Dr. Fabri's remark, which he ascribed to his employer's somewhat grim vein of humour, and applied it in a mocking manner to the indexing upon which he was engaged. Dr. Fabri's tastes appeared to be completely catholic and it almost seemed to Trumble that he was obsessed with recording the deaths of everyone of importance who died in the world, without regard to their profession or occupation. Trumble had also taken time to study the earlier ledgers, which went back a good many years, and was astonished to see the meticulous way in which the deaths of bishops, film stars, footballers, philosophers, politicians and university professors had been noted.

Writers, musicians and those in the graphic arts were recorded in separate volumes, coded blue, and Trumble, though of course he had never questioned Dr. Fabri on the subject, concluded that the doctor had a special interest in those arts; particularly as many of the writers were also savants who had been authorities on witchcraft and the occult. In this respect the rare volumes in Latin and medieval French, which were evidently of immense value, came in useful, and already Trumble had had occasion to check a reference from an original source, when the printed information on his subject's career had been scanty.

His afternoons were mostly free and two days later Trumble motored over to Guildford, posted some letters, had tea in a cafe and then, because it was cold and raining, visited the cinema for a couple of hours. The film was good and when Trumble regained the street in the early evening the rain had stopped and the sun shone fitfully. He drove back to Linnet Ridge in high spirits and decided to spend the hour before dinner catching up on the indexing. He now worked with the great bronze door closed; there was a handle on his side and the air-conditioning made the room pleasantly fresh and conducive to uninterrupted concentration.

He filled up three pages with closely detailed cuttings and photographs on the career of an obscure South American diplomat, culled mainly from Brazilian newspapers, and blotted the gum at the edges of the cuttings with satisfaction. He wondered idly what tomorrow would bring; Dr. Fabri invariably left the names of the day's obituary subjects for him in the master ledger, in the distinctive green ink that he had already come to know so well. Trumble did not start this work until mid-morning so he imagined that his employer would make his selections from the principal daily newspapers and possibly from announcements via other media, such as radio and television. The main material for the file arrived by mail two or three days later,

⚜ Archives Of The Dead

usually from three major cuttings agencies in England and from a number of news services overseas.

The work had its own fascination, though Trumble might once have felt it to be morbid; it was certainly no more so than similar departments kept up by the major newspapers and known to their respective staffs as 'The Morgue'. In fact, Trumble felt Dr. Fabri's own system was preferable as he understood the newspapers wrote their obituaries in advance, which did rather smack of the macabre, to his way of thinking. He put down the pen, looked at the completed page and replaced the ledger on the shelf with the others. He would do the indexing on these last items tomorrow.

Trumble ate dinner on his own that evening and was sitting in the lounge engrossed in a novel at about nine o'clock when he heard Dr. Fabri's car in the drive. A few moments later the hall door slammed with hollow resonance and the measured tread of his employer passed up the staircase; shortly afterwards Dr. Fabri's bedroom door closed. Trumble picked up his half-finished drink and resumed his book.

The house was unnaturally quiet and occasionally he would put down the volume and listen briefly but the only sounds were the faint sputtering of wood from the fire, for the nights were still cold as yet and the muted sounds of Joseph from his quarters at the back of the house. The mantel clock measured a few minutes after ten and Trumble was thinking about retiring to his own room when the sharp, peremptory strokes of the front door bell, jabbed by an evidently impatient finger, startled him.

He gained the hall and was opening the door before Joseph had made his appearance. A tall, silvery-haired man of some distinction, wearing a dress suit and black tie under a dark raincoat, stood in the porch. In the background shimmered the gleaming bulk of a grey Mercedes. Trumble hesitated for a fraction and the man in the porch seemed slightly taken aback also. The older man was the first to recover himself.

"I would like to speak with Dr. Fabri if it isn't too inconvenient," he said. "He is expecting me."

Trumble introduced himself and the two men shook hands. "I

usually arrange his appointments but I am new here and the doctor may have forgotten to tell me," said Trumble. He motioned the visitor forward into the hall and closed the door behind him. Joseph had now appeared and took the tall man's coat.

"However, if you made an appointment I have no doubt Dr. Fabri is expecting you," Trumble continued. "He came in about an hour ago."

The visitor seemed pleased at this, but just then the sound of Dr. Fabri's footsteps sounded at the stairhead.

"Would you like me to announce you?" Trumble asked.

The visitor shook his head. "That won't be necessary," he said decisively. Joseph was hovering at the back of the hall but Dr. Fabri was now halfway down the staircase, and he vanished in the direction of the kitchen.

"Delighted to see you, my dear fellow," said Dr. Fabri, shaking his visitor warmly by the hand. "I was worried in case you might have been delayed."

"Not this night. You know, certainly, not this night of all nights," said his visitor sharply.

Dr. Fabri laughed shortly. "No, no, of course not," he said soothingly, laying his hand on the other's arm. "You go ahead into the study and I will join you immediately."

He turned to Trumble, his strong face impassive in the soft light of the hall lamps.

"I shan't require you any further tonight, Robert," he said. "We shall be quite late. I have told Joseph he may retire. I will show my guest out myself."

Trumble nodded. He went back into the lounge and finished his drink. There was no sound from the direction of the study, into which both men had disappeared. He dragged the heavy brass guard over the remains of the fire, recovered his book from the armchair and switched off the lights. Joseph nodded to him darkly as he crossed the hall. The big, taciturn handyman was hovering near the study door, behind which could now be made out the low murmur of voices. Trumble walked up to the landing and sought his own room.

He quickly prepared for bed, drew the covers over him and again settled down to another chapter of his book; this time, for some indefinable reason, the texture of the writing did not seem to absorb him as it had done formerly and it was still a few minutes short of eleven when he put the book aside on the table and extinguished the lamp. Thin cracks of light came through under his bedroom door from farther down the landing; Trumble was just about to shift his position so that he would be facing the darker side of the room when he saw a shadow briefly cross the light coming in under the door. A moment later he heard the faint click of the key as someone locked the door from the outside.

Trumble smiled to himself in the semi-darkness; he supposed he ought to object to this rather peculiar procedure, but he could not say the practice inconvenienced him. He had a self-contained suite and if Dr. Fabri liked to confine the occupants of his house to their own portions of the building during the dead hours of the night, he supposed that was his own business. Perhaps he would tackle the doctor about it when he had got to know him a little better. In the meantime no useful purpose would be served by kicking up a fuss; and the position was quite the best thing of its kind which was likely to come his way in the course of a lifetime.

His head occupied with these and similar thoughts Trumble soon slept. He found himself awake again in the still of the night. He lay trembling for some moments, trying to collect himself. What had awakened him, or rather what he fancied had awakened him, was a long, high scream which sounded like an animal in pain. Trumble had noted degrees of torment in animals, as in humans, and it seemed to him that the sound which had broken his sleep was of some creature in extremis. He looked at the luminous dial of his watch and saw that it was just after three am. He had therefore slept for nearly four hours.

A glance towards the door showed him that the light in the hall and on the landing had been extinguished. No sound broke the stillness but his own heavy breathing as he listened intently; the darkness of the night pressed heavily on the house and held it as though within a deep vault. Even the owl was silent from the thicket beyond the garden. Trumble felt perspiration in the roots of his hair and cold and sticky against his pyjamas. He wondered if he had caught a fever in the damp weather of the last few days. There was no footfall, not the creak of a board; his own heart was like the grumbling of a ponderous piston-engine within the confines of his chest.

Then the owl sounded, sharp and distinct, from the woods beyond the house and with this commonplace noise all the little sounds of the night crept back; Trumble felt his stiff hands relax their frenzied grip on the sheets and his body, with returning warmth, began to relax. Sleep was so subtle on this second occasion that he was not aware of it when unconsciousness finally overtook him.

4

The following day Dr. Fabri did not appear in the morning though Trumble had heard his car earlier; he took his breakfast, as usual served by the unsmiling Joseph, and just before ten began his work in the small cabinet with the bronze door; as before he had the door closed and kept it shut while he was working. The hum of the air-conditioning seemed to keep him in touch with the rest of the house and the chamber itself ensured him complete privacy as he could easily hear if anyone approached from outside.

There was a large bronze handle, mate to the one on the face, on his own side of the door and, as if that were not enough, the massive bronze key, made specially to match, was on his own side to avoid him being locked in. It was this key which he handed to Joseph in the evenings when he had finished his scholarly work among the rare books.

But already this morning Dr. Fabri must have been down, for as soon as Trumble was seated at his desk and had commenced to examine the material which awaited his attention, he saw that two new names had been added to the register ledger in the doctor's unmistakable green-ink hand. The first was that of Burnett Fairbarn, an internationally known architect. Trumble had heard his death announced on the news the night before; he had died in a mountaineering accident on a peak in the Andes the previous day. The latest name was that of Lyle Bassett, of whom Trumble had never heard; there was no information available on either man, Trumble found when he searched the doctor's heap of notes: the first details for documenting purposes would no doubt come from the evening papers that night.

Trumble continued with his usual pursuits and the day slowly assumed the pattern of those preceding. Dr. Fabri returned to the house for lunch; the two men walked in the garden; Trumble took some dictation and, a little later, drove over to Guildford for tea. He brought the two evening papers on his way back, intending to go through them after dinner.

But another session of note-taking followed and when Trumble returned to the archive room for more indexing at about half-past ten the newspapers were still on the desk unread. It was only when, his immediate task finished, Trumble turned to peruse the day's news that he saw a long story on an inside page of Fairbarn's climbing accident. There was over a column of space in both papers devoted to this, together with photographs of the architect, and some of his principal buildings. When he had finished pasting these entries into the large book and had suitably indexed them, Trumble remembered the second entry on the ledger. He turned again to verify the name and then went through the inside pages. He found what he was looking for in a short item on the front page of the Evening Standard.

It merely said that the body of Lyle Bassett, a somewhat obscure ballet choreographer and composer, had been found dead in a blazing car near the Guildford By-Pass in the early hours of the same day. Trumble entered the notice and found a smaller piece in the stop press column of the Evening News. It referred to another story on an inside page and this was an expanded version of the facts already known, but giving more details of Bassett's career. Trumble closed both books, tidied his desk and went to bed rather satisfied with his labours.

The midday post the following day contained a great deal of material for Dr. Fabri's archives, together with a number of business letters which had to be answered and Trumble was not able to return to his indexing in the room with the bronze door until nearly twenty-four hours later. He then saw that he had rather a lot of leeway to make up;

Dr. Fabri had added another four or five names in green ink in the ledger and the pile of clippings and magazine articles had reached alarming proportions.

Trumble went swiftly through the material, arranging it in piles and subject matter, preparatory to making the entries. His hand faltered when he picked up the last clipping which consisted of several inches of text and a large photograph; the room suddenly became hot and stuffy and Trumble put the cutting down on the desk with a hand which had begun to behave in an uncontrollable manner. He studied the face again; the picture was that of the man he had showed into the hall of Linnet Ridge a little over two days earlier. He checked back over the original entry; it was the man who had died in the wrecked car.

The name was Lyle Bassett.

5

Trumble did not mention this fact to Dr. Fabri. His procedure was strange, even to himself, and no application of logic could account for it. Even more unusual was the fact that Dr. Fabri himself did not bring up the subject; it was impossible that his guest's fatal accident could have escaped his attention, unless Joseph had placed the cuttings in position on the secretary's desk. In which case that would explain the matter; Trumble embraced this theory almost with relief. Joseph's taciturnity was notorious in the household and he might, in his extraordinary way, have kept his own counsel.

In the meantime Trumble avoided all conversation which might lead round to Bassett's visit to the house and hoped that the doctor himself might make the discovery while going through the record books. But in any case opportunities for conversation with the doctor were becoming more limited; as the weeks went by and the spring advanced he appeared more seldom at meals and apart from dictation and matters relating to business correspondence, Trumble had little contact with him.

He worked on in his cabinet and was left more and more to his own affairs, though he had no doubt that Joseph, who was undoubtedly in his employer's confidence, kept a discreet eye on the secretary's movements and reported back to the doctor how his time had been spent. Trumble did not resent this; after all, he reasoned to himself, the doctor was paying him well, he was living in some comfort and style and though the hours were sometimes irregular, he was not greatly inconvenienced and could not honestly say that he was overworked.

He slept more easily at nights also and he had noted during the last week that his room was no longer locked after he had gone up to bed; evidently he had proved his loyalty and the doctor had decided that he could be trusted with the run of the house. Trumble was wryly amused at the thought; Dr. Fabri might have an international reputation as an authority on the black arts, but in private life he was perfectly proper and his household disappointingly normal, so far as Trumble could see.

Not that he had expected out-of-the-way happenings, but he had hoped that his employer would unlock some of the hidden treasures of his mind to him during the long summer evenings, especially as the doctor and the poet evidently shared many tastes and common viewpoints on matters normally considered forbidden among those in what, for want of a better phrase, was termed polite society.

And yet there was an incident a few days later which illustrated vividly to Trumble the darker side of Dr. Fabri's nature. It had been unnaturally cold for an England poised on the threshold of May and fires had been lit in the principal rooms to supplement the central heating. For some reason or other the doctor and his secretary had forsaken the study and were seated at the dining-room table where Fabri had been dictating sections of one of a new series of lectures for the following autumn.

He had called this particular talk 'The Past Which is to Come', a title which had vividly impressed itself upon Trumble; in fact he wished he had thought of it himself. His pen scratched rapidly over the paper as Dr. Fabri rattled on; his employer proceeded in quick, staccato sentences as ideas came to him, though when the time arrived he would deliver the speech in a steady, leisurely flow in which paragraphs, phrases, sentences were all linked immutably like the loops of a chain. But while dictating Dr. Fabri would turn his deep, piercing eyes ruminatively on Trumble as he searched for the apposite phrase: then he would proceed to deliver it unfalteringly, so that the secretary was hard put to it to keep up. Once he had found his thought, he would polish and assemble it in his mind before giving utterance, so that he never had to correct the typed word once it was on paper.

It was an admirable method, a tribute to the skill and precision of Dr. Fabri's remarkable mind but it was a harsh discipline for a note-taker such as Trumble, whose shorthand had fallen somewhat into disuse and he was sometimes mentally panting far behind in a desperate effort to keep pace with the do'ctor's finely shaped and elaborately wrought prose. After the first session, which was in marked contrast to Fabri's methods of replying to letters, Trumble practised his note-taking alone in his room for several hours, so that he faced the second and subsequent ordeals more comprehensively equipped.

"The cancer of time eats inexorably at the fabric of human lives," said Dr. Fabri, the phrase seeming to hang on the hushed air of the dining-room.

"We drag our pasts behind us as a snail its slime."

He paused for a moment, his cigar smoke rising steadily upwards towards the panelled ceiling with hardly a tremor, the air within the room was so still.

Trumble's pen raced on over the paper until, with relief, he heard Dr. Fabri come to the end of his discourse. He flexed his hand to relieve the cramp, aware of the doctor's eyes fixed upon him with sardonic humour. Dr. Fabri stretched himself in his chair.

"Is there anything there which you feel requires amplification, Robert?" he asked.

What he really meant, Trumble understood well enough, was whether the latter had managed to take down everything accurately and wanted him to check anything again. Trumble flipped through his pages of voluminous notes, hoping that he would have no difficult transcription problems.

"There was a point here, Doctor," he said diffidently. "I believe my note is accurate but I didn't quite understand the meaning."

Archives Of The Dead

He searched for the passage while Dr. Fabri waited politely, his dark eyes a startling contrast to his white hair and tufted eyebrows.

Trumble found the place and read, "In this Key you may behold, as in a mirror, the distinct functions of the spirits, and how they are to be drawn into communication in all places, seasons and times."

"Well?" said Dr. Fabri, a little impatiently. "It is a quotation, of course."

"I understand that," Trumble replied, "and there are many such passages throughout your lecture. Am I to take it that this is intended to be taken literally?"

"Certainly," said Dr. Fabri calmly. "I could give you a number of instances. It is, of course, a power given to very few and one certainly not to be abused. You are desirous of learning more of such things—from a personal aspect, that is?"

He pronounced the last words in a very soft and curious manner and Trumble became suddenly aware that he was trespassing on very strange and dangerous ground.

"He who would learn the secrets of my Master must be prepared for long and arduous preparations. It is a hard and thorny way."

The air seemed to have grown close and sultry and Trumble's head began to swim; he was aware of Dr. Fabri's eyes which were now bright and sharp and boring into his.

"Your Master?" Trumble asked foolishly, trying to fight the nausea which threatened to overcome him.

"Of course," said Dr. Fabri.

"My Master," he added softly. "We are all the servants of One Master, Mr. Trumble."

Dr. Fabri laughed quietly and with the laughter the tension and oppression lifted from the room and Trumble felt he could breathe again; he wiped his forehead, which was wet with perspiration.

"Are you well?" the doctor asked in some concern. He went to the sideboard and came back with a full glass which he thrust into his secretary's hand. Trumble drank the whisky as though it had been water and then felt normality returning to him. He gathered up his notes with a muttered apology to the doctor. They did not again return to the subject that evening.

⁂ Darkness, Mist & Shadow

⁂ 6

Several more weeks passed and it was now mid-May. Despite the season the weather had continued cold; Trumble was by now thoroughly accustomed to his duties; he continued the odd task of indexing in the inner cabinet and felt he had thoroughly mastered the complexities of Dr. Fabri's dictation style, while his treatment of the correspondence could not have been bettered by a professional secretary, he felt. Best of all, he had commenced to write again; the sheltered atmosphere of Linnet Ridge had released something long pent-up in him and in his spare time in the afternoons and often in the evenings, he began sketching out the movements of an epic poem in praise of the Old Gods.

Curiously enough, there abruptly came a day of great heat, among those of cold, wet January-like weather; Fabri and Trumble had been seated long after breakfast was cleared that morning, going over some proofs of a projected book by Dr. Fabri on magic as practised by the older cultures of the world.

Quite casually, in the middle of their discussion on business matters, Dr. Fabri turned to his secretary and said, "By the way, I am expecting a number of people this evening. We shall be occupying the study so I would be grateful if you would arrange to vacate the ground floor of the house by nine-thirty tonight."

Dr. Fabri's tone was courteous and his words polite, but it was obvious to Trumble that his pronouncement was an order; so he did not question his employer, though he was naturally curious on the subject.

"Would you like me to wait up?" he asked. "I could go into Guilford for the evening, if you wish, and return to the house late if you require any help in entertaining your guests."

"That won't be necessary, Robert," Dr. Fabri said smoothly. "I should appreciate it, though, if you would receive the visitors between eight and nine o'clock so I should cancel any arrangements you may have made regarding Guildford. Joseph will lock up later. He is used to our activities."

When Trumble thought over the conversation later in the day he

Archives Of The Dead

felt his curiosity roused by the phrasing of Dr. Fabri's last sentence; he wondered idly what activities were meant. And if Joseph were used to them, how frequent they might be. Apart from the visit of the ill-fated Bassett there were few guests to Linnet Ridge, and those only during the afternoons. As the day wore on he found his thoughts turning more and more towards the evening and it was with something like impatience that he watched the clock during his long hours of indexing in the cabinet; or studied his wrist-watch during his turns around the garden.

Just before dinner, which was earlier than usual that night, he cleared those of his personal papers which he felt he might require, and prepared his writing-table in the sitting-room of his own suite upstairs; he felt that if he were to be denied the use of the ground floor that night he would at least be able to put his time to good use in composition before retiring. He descended to the ground floor again just in time for dinner, to find Dr. Fabri already at table.

To his surprise Trumble noted that there was a third person already seated and in conversation with his employer. The two men rose as Trumble entered and Dr. Fabri made haste to introduce his companion, though the secretary had already recognized the strong, clear-minted head of Zadek, the celebrated cellist, who was currently giving a series of concerts in the London area. Joseph, who had been standing in sullen silence, now bustled forward as Dr. Fabri snapped his fingers, and served the soup.

When he had withdrawn once more, Dr. Fabri put the two men at ease by talking smoothly and flowingly of general matters and gradually the meal was transformed into a pleasant arena of reminiscence and anecdote, of philosophical musings, all backed by a wide range of scholarship and cultured taste. Trumble had seldom heard his employer in this vein and indeed, it would have been hard to better his conversation; Trumble himself confined his own comments to brief generalities in answer to specific questions.

Zadek, Trumble thought, was either a Czech or of Eastern European extraction and though his English was good, his guttural tones and occasional hesitations of pronunciation made it sometimes difficult to follow the trend of his thoughts. But despite this, he had a wide grounding in the liberal humanities and his conversation was not confined merely to musical matters; allowing for the language difficulties, he spoke humorously and well, and the meal flowed along in a pattern composed of laughter, mellow reminiscence and good fellowship.

They had sat down to table early, a little after half-past six; and now it was nearly eight o'clock, Joseph had just come in to remind them. Trumble sipped his second liqueur with his black coffee and felt that he had more than upheld his own end of the conversation. Zadek had also heard of Trumble's efforts as a poet, to the secretary's barely-concealed astonishment and the two men had, in fact, treated him as their peer. Though nattered, Trumble did wonder, as the meal progressed, whether the cellist had not been briefed by Fabri before his arrival in the dining-room.

Even so, it was a pleasant thought of the doctor's and not for the first time the secretary felt his heart warming to him. He was a little strange, not to say eccentric in his ways, but no one could complain of their treatment under his roof. But now Joseph was standing at his elbow and communicating unmistakably by his manner that Trumble should prepare himself for the guests who were expected between eight and nine o'clock. So Trumble rose to his feet, excused himself and a few minutes later stationed himself within easy earshot of the front door.

He had not long to wait; it was just three minutes past eight when the first visitors announced themselves. These were a tall, thin woman in her mid-fifties, accompanied by a plump young man in his early thirties. Joseph, impassive as one of the wooden images in the doctor's collection, relieved them of their hats and coats while Trumble, murmuring polite conventionalities, showed them to the study. He did not enter himself but merely ushered them through and closed the door behind them.

In all, he must have passed through something like thirty people between eight and nine o'clock, when the flow finally began to slacken off. Though he recognized no one, Trumble felt there must have been more than one person of public eminence among the gathering; they were about evenly divided between men and women but the age range fell into two distinct patterns. The men were from about thirty to sixty at a rough guess, while the women's ages ranged between twenty to about fifty-five.

All were well-dressed and highly literate in their conversation and manner; without exception all seemed to have arrived by private car and none of them addressed Trumble in terms other than the polite greetings normally exchanged among total strangers. To his fumbled attempts at small talk they maintained a discreet silence until they were beyond the study door. Joseph remained in the hall throughout the entire proceedings and stationed himself directly in front of the study whenever he was not engaged in dealing with hats and coats. His manner, too, did not encourage any approach from Trumble.

Finding himself ignored in this manner, the secretary retired to a side room with a novel between his excursions to the door and back; after nine o'clock he found his services were no longer required and as the half hour chimed he found the silent-footed Joseph at his elbow.

"I think that is the last of the ladies and gentlemen, sir," he said softly, in that politely insolent manner which the secretary found so offensive. He could not have made the situation more plain if he had said, "I think it is time you followed your instructions and retired upstairs." So Trumble elaborately stretched himself, smoothed out the cushion at his elbow and took his time in closing his book.

"Thank you, Joseph, that will be all," he said by way of feeble revenge. The servant stared at him a moment longer with smouldering eyes, then abruptly turned and went silently out of the door. A moment later the main hall-light was extinguished. Trumble waited as long as he felt he dared—after all, he did not want to bring Dr. Fabri out to see what was delaying him—and five minutes later ascended the oak staircase with as good grace as he could muster.

Joseph was still standing in front of the door; Trumble saw that he was wearing some sort of dark cloak like that of a coachman. The man's head was silhouetted against the deep pinks and greys of the convoluted intestines of the Bosch painting which had so disturbed him earlier; Trumble could not help but feel that it was an appropriate background for Joseph's saturnine features. Then the secretary had passed the head of the stair and was within his own room.

Darkness, Mist & Shadow

For more than two hours he wrestled with the difficult metres of the verse-form he had chosen for his new work, but the felicitous phrase eluded him. He got up at length from the table; there was no noise in all the house. He extinguished the lights in the sitting-room and passed through into the bedroom; light shining from under the door which led on to the landing showed him that Dr. Fabri's visitors had not yet gone; otherwise the lamps in the hall on the ground floor would have been switched off. And he had heard no sound of cars departing.

It wanted but a few minutes of midnight and again Trumble felt tiredness sapping the strength of his limbs; once in his pyjamas he looked out at the garden but the night was dark and there was little to be seen. He got into bed, turned out the light and was soon asleep.

It seemed but a moment before he started awake; some unusual noise had aroused him from a deep sleep which it was usually impossible to disturb. Trumble was facing the wall, but as the room was in semi-darkness he reasoned that light was still shining in under his bedroom door. A glance over his shoulder confirmed this. His watch showed the time as being a quarter past two and its steady tick reassured him. He sat up in bed then and pushed away the sheets, his mind quite alert. A moment later he again heard the sound which had penetrated the walls of sleep; the low murmur of many voices seemingly from far away.

He got out of bed and padded over towards the door. Again he found it unlocked. Trumble hesitated for a fraction and then once more heard the low, insidious noise that mumbled like a dark sea swirling within rocky pools on some lonely coast beyond the world's fringe. His feet found the warmth of his carpet slippers instinctively; already he was shrugging on his thin silk dressing gown. He opened the door cautiously but the corridor and landing were silent and deserted.

One solitary lamp burned in the dusk of the hall he saw, as he gained the staircase; his form concealed by a thick corner post, his eyes searched the darkness below. To his relief Joseph was no longer standing sentinel. He felt no fear; curiosity had driven it out. He was impelled towards the mysterious noise which he was convinced was coming from the interior of Dr. Fabri's study. The low, mumbling sound came again as he hesitated and then he went with a rush born of desperate courage down the staircase as though the interruption had given him the confidence to move under its thick, muttered cover.

He reached the study door without incident and felt the smooth-fitting lock turn noiselessly at his pressure on the handle; he slipped inside into the comfort of almost complete darkness. He crouched behind a high-backed chair, his heart thudding uncomfortably in his throat. The darkness ahead of him was suddenly split by soft red light which blossomed beyond the windows leading on to the garden; Trumble could see little by the fantastic flicker, but he noted once again the ruinous dereliction of the grounds in the faint glare. He moved over towards the windows, careful not to bump into the furniture, but when he reached them the pale fire had burnt to a dusky umber. He was reminded irresistibly of Poe's 'red-litten windows' in *The Haunted Palace*.

While he crouched irresolute, another low moaning murmur started up within the room; Trumble felt his legs turn to water and he crouched sweating in the shadow as the red glow grew within the garden. Then he saw the explanation; the light was coming not from the grounds but from within the house.

Somewhere below him, light was flickering and shimmering from a window inside the building and staining the lawns with faint amber. With this he recovered something of his courage; his first thought was the large platform approached by the spiral staircase, but his heart failed him as he pictured the difficulty of the ascent in the dark. The sounds appeared to be coming from within the cabinet where Trumble normally worked and yet he knew that it would have been impossible to contain thirty people within its narrow limits.

Instead, he compromised; somehow, he dragged himself up the staircase and towards the blue curtains at the end of the room; lying in the comparative safety of a large settee which sheltered him, he cradled his head on his hands and listened intently. He felt he could go no farther without giving himself away, but at least he could make out what was being said by the chanting voices. And Trumble realized that it was desperately important that he should not give himself away, that he should not be discovered here in these damning circumstances at half-past two in the morning.

He felt sick and ill and his teeth began to chatter as the sense of what he heard began to penetrate his consciousness; the mumbling was repeated, a single voice then replied and the mumbling took up what the single voice was saying, amplifying it much as a congregation follows the lead of a priest. But this was like nothing Trumble had ever listened to in his life. Interested as he was in the occult and a dabbler on the fringe of things unseen, the ceremony taking place was so blasphemous and perverted that he trembled for his sanity.

All the strength went out of his limbs and he seemed to have fainted for a short while; when he came to himself again a different stage in the ceremony had been reached. Things were evidently rising to a climax; there was exultation and ecstasy in the voices and a black, savage anger, and their responses to the leader's exhortations were becoming short and staccato in their chanting phases. Trumble tried to blot out the words from his mind, but they slipped into his brain as through a sieve and burnt there like molten lead.

"Save Us, Lord Satan, we pray thee," intoned the single voice.

"Save the Ancient One, O Lord Satan," responded the congregation.

"Accept this, our Offering, with Thy blessing, Lord Satan," said the single voice.

"The Offering, Lord Satan!" almost shrieked the worshippers.

"Accept this, our sacrifice, O Lord of the Serfs," said the ringing voice.

"The sacrifice of the Ancient One, O Lord!" came the response.

"Bless us with Thy fertility, O Lord of the Flies," the calm voice intoned.

"Accept this, our sacrifice, O Lord!" the mass of voices mumbled.

Overcome with shame and loathing, Trumble remained in a trembling heap, unable to move and quite powerless to blot out the sounds of the vile things he knew were happening only a few yards from his prostrate form. There was a long silence which turned his blood to ice and kept his ears straining for the unspeakable climax.

Archives Of The Dead

"Behold, the entrails of the Lamb, O Master!" said the single voice in ringing triumph.

"The Entrails, Lord Satan, Most Holy Master!" shouted the entire congregation.

Then came a sound which Trumble sought in vain to blot from his consciousness; a great, welling cry which appeared to burst from the bowels of the earth, rising to a scream which indicated a human being at the utmost pitch of agony. It echoed and burst in Trumble's ear-drums like the last paean of souls rotting in hell and the poet, shaking uncontrollably and almost vomiting with the extremity of his terror, felt the sound to be the aural equivalent of the torn viscera in the Bosch painting in the hall. Then the shriek cut off and was followed by a loathsome slopping noise which was as quickly drowned by the roaring approval of the congregation.

Even in his piteous state of nerves Trumble felt he must make a supreme effort; by a tremendous exertion of will he dragged himself several yards back in the direction of the study door. Trembling as though with ague, tottering like an old man, he at last clawed himself upright and gained the entrance. His hand was almost on the knob when a quick footstep sounded in the hall. Trumble fell to the floor behind an armchair and crouched with thudding heart. The door was opened, letting in a long shaft of light from the hall; fortunately, whoever it was left the door open, in order to pick his way through the darkened room. As he heard the footsteps ascend the spiral staircase, Trumble slipped through the opening, praying that his shadow on the floor would not be noticed by the ascending figure, which had its back to him.

Unfortunately, as he made for the staircase, reeling as though with fatigue, Trumble knocked against a table and made a loud clattering noise; with an access of terror he heard the footsteps rapidly descending the staircase. They were coming across the study floor. There was no time for Trumble to conceal himself. Gathering the frayed ends of his shrieking nerves he forced himself to walk towards the study door without concealment. Joseph met him at the half-open door. The dark, hard face was expressionless in the dim light of the lamp. Trumble saw that he was wearing the dark black cloak, the collar of which was lined with red silk.

His legs were bare and he wore thonged sandals on his feet. He carried some sort of hood over his arm. Forcing himself to keep his voice calm, Trumble said, "I heard a noise which woke me up. I was just coming down to see if everything was all right."

"Everything is perfectly all right, sir," said Joseph, but his eyes gazed at Trumble with bleak suspicion.

"I thought I heard voices," said Trumble. He knew he had to justify his descent of the staircase and it would hardly do to let Joseph's explanation pass without some expostulation; Trumble had to steel himself to go on. He could not let the servant see that he was so easily satisfied; otherwise his suspicions might become aroused. And Trumble had much to do to prevent himself from falling when he imagined what might be the penalty if Dr. Fabri realized that he had been in the study this morning and that he had heard . . . what he had heard.

"There is a meeting, sir," said Joseph patiently, as though he were explaining a simple proposition to a child.

"That would account for the voices," said Trumble, seeming satisfied with the servant's answer.

"The Society of the Sabbat, sir," Joseph went on. "The ladies and gentlemen you met earlier tonight. They are making a tape recording of certain occult rites. It is one of Dr. Fabri's major interests. The recordings are very popular among Society members."

"I see," said Trumble, simulating relief. "As long as all is in order. I'm sorry if I disturbed you. Is there anything I can do at all?"

He made as though to move towards the study door. Joseph did not appear to shift position but his tall form was suddenly blocking the way.

"Please return to bed, sir," he said gravely.

"Well, thank you," said Trumble, retreating to the foot of the staircase. "I'd appreciate it if you didn't mention this to Dr. Fabri. I felt there might be something wrong and I don't want him to think me an over-imaginative day-dreamer."

Joseph allowed himself a faint glimmer of a smile. He had shut the study door behind him at the beginning of the conversation and Trumble could no longer hear the mumble of those hateful voices.

"I quite understand, sir," said Joseph. He stood and watched as Trumble slowly ascended the staircase. When the poet had gained the landing he heard the noise of the key of the study door being turned in the lock. The corridor started to bend and warp in front of him as he made his way to his room. He somehow groped to the bed and then his legs gave way beneath him. He lay gasping for breath until he found the strength to crawl between the sheets.

7

Trumble felt so ill next morning that he sent a message to Dr. Fabri, via Joseph. The servant brought food to his room and all day the secretary lay in a fevered stupor. He took dinner in bed and was relieved to hear from the servant that Dr. Fabri excused himself from visiting his bedside; he sent his best wishes and hoped that Trumble would be feeling better in the morning. Indeed, by ten o'clock in the evening Trumble was so far recovered that he put on his dressing-gown and sat in the other room for a little while.

When he went through into the bathroom his face in the mirror was so strange that he had difficulty in recognizing himself; apart from the stubble on his cheeks and his dishevelled hair, there was a glint in his eyes which was alien to him and his complexion was almost like chalk. Trumble had to admit that he had been badly frightened; but, looking back, realized at this distance in time that he might have been mistaken; while he had not believed Joseph's explanation regarding the recording at the time it had been made, he now felt that it could have been possible.

If there were a Society of the Sabbat they may well have been doing a taped reconstruction of a Black Mass or Sabbat, but Trumble found this difficult to reconcile with the demoniac and horrifying quality of his experience the night before. Dr. Fabri had not been to see him, neither had Joseph conveyed any message on the subject, so it was just possible that the affair had a commonplace explanation;

⁂ Darkness, Mist & Shadow

but even so, Trumble realized that he would have to go very carefully indeed during the next few days. Despite the depth of terror into which he had been plunged the previous evening, his curiosity had been aroused and he was determined to investigate further.

One thing which could not be explained away was the question posed by a simple exercise in mathematics; namely, how thirty substantial people of both sexes could have been accommodated in the small cabinet in which Trumble normally worked, crowded as it was with a desk, bookshelves and innumerable reference works. It was an insuperable problem, matched only by the equally weird spectacle of the shifting red lights in the garden. When Trumble felt equal to it he would devote some thought to the matter on the following day.

As it happened, things worked out more easily than he had supposed. Dr. Fabri had gone away for a short period, Joseph informed him when he sat down in his familiar place for breakfast next morning. He did not know when he would be back, but he had left word for the secretary to carry on as usual. Joseph pointed out a pile of opened correspondence Dr. Fabri had left by his plate and withdrew to his own enigmatic duties. Trumble sat long over his coffee and then gathered up the mail and made his way to the cabinet.

He could not repress a faint trembling in the muscles of his legs as he ascended the spiral staircase and the figures in the bronze Sabbat on the great door seemed to stare mockingly at him as he pulled it open; but once settled at his homely task of indexing the cuttings and cross-referencing his notes, Trumble's ragged nerves relaxed. The time passed, he worked steadily on and he was pleased to see by eleven o'clock that the pile of reference material in front of him was steadily diminishing. He paused in his efforts and then shuffled through the last cuttings, assessing the work remaining before lunch.

Then the clippings fluttered to the floor, his face turned pale and again there came an uncontrollable trembling in his limbs. Staring at him from the front page of a popular evening newspaper was a large photograph of a distinguished-looking man Trumble remembered only too well. The picture was captioned: 'The Late Ygor Zadek.' Over the top was a six-column headline which said: STAR CELLIST MURDERED IN ESSEX WOOD.

With mounting horror the secretary read how a farm worker had stumbled over the body of the world-famous cellist in a copse at the edge of Epping Forest. The report hinted that the corpse had been shockingly mutilated, evidently before death, according to the pathologist's report; the body had been dumped in the position it had been found after being transported there by car. The police were now concentrating on trying to trace the vehicle from the slender clues they had in their possession, including a distinctive imprint of a tyre-tread.

Sick at heart, Trumble put down the paper after examining the date-line; it was that day's early edition. The body had been found in the early hours of that morning. Trumble did not need to go into elaborate calculations to see that less than twenty-four hours had elapsed since he had last seen Zadek alive and well in Dr. Fabri's house and the discovery of his disembowelled body that same morning. Trumble remembered the cry he had heard thirty-six hours earlier and again began to tremble uncontrollably.

To calm his racing thoughts he began to rearrange his desk, the trivial, commonplace actions gradually having the effect of calming his nerves and slowing down his churning mind. He bent down to pick up the clippings he had dropped to the floor; he then saw that the grey carpeting which skirted the desk had been pushed aside in his fumbling efforts to raise the papers; a thin hair-line showed in the grey metal floor underneath the carpet. Trumble's heart gave another great jump in his throat.

He got up and went to the door; he listened intently but could hear nothing. He crossed to the study window and was reassured to see Joseph at the other end of the garden; he appeared to be trimming a rose bush. Trumble went back into the cabinet and thought long and deeply. He made up his mind. He closed the bronze door gently, isolating himself from the study and the house. The hum of the air-conditioning went reassuringly on. Then he got to his knees; unrolling the carpet, he disclosed the smooth-fitting edges of a trapdoor.

Darkness, Mist & Shadow

Raising it by a metal flange let into its edge, Trumble saw a flight of steps leading below; they were modern in design, made of cedarwood and the treads were covered with rubber. Warm air came up to him. Trumble hesitated but a moment; then, leaving the trapdoor open, he pressed the switch set on the tread at the edge of the staircase and walked down into the cellar.

As neon tubes trembled into radiance in the high panelled ceiling, Trumble saw that the mystery was solved; here was the room for thirty people, a hundred people. The place was like a theatre; there must have been over two hundred leather tip-up seats. The chamber was decorated like a church and almost sybaritic in its luxury; thick pile carpeting covered the floors. The end of the room where the stage would have been was concealed with dark blue curtains covered with cabalistic symbols. Let into the marble step in front of the curtains was the legend, in gold lettering, which the terrible Aleister Crowley had made his leitmotiv, 'Do as Thou Wilt Shall be the Whole of the Law'.

Trumble walked down, mounted the marble steps and parted the curtains; the first thing he saw were two small, half-moon windows high up in the wall, which must have been just above ground level. It was from these, evidently, that the red, flickering lights must have penetrated into the garden.

Trumble turned back to examine the area behind the curtains. There was a black marble altar with a curious dip and cavity let into it; behind the altar, in a niche towering up between the two windows, was an image which, fortunately for the secretary's sanity, was half-hidden in the shadow. The pendulous belly and the monstrous goathead made it perfectly obvious which form of worship was practised here. A copper bowl was lying on the altar, together with strange looking instruments, including a bronze knife which had a long runnel let into the blade.

The knife and bowl were sticky and the bowl contained a residue of black viscous fluid which stank in Trumble's nostrils. He was overcome with nausea; turning, he reeled against the altar and putting out his hand to steady himself, felt it come away wet and scarlet. He saw that the whole of the top of the marble was awash with unspeakable foulness. He screamed then in the gloom of that charnel-house place and found himself running up the gangway between the seats, the breath sobbing in his throat.

He found some cloth near the foot of the ladder and wiped his hands clean; he shrank when he noticed that the cloth appeared to be a white robe like a surgeon's smock and that the front of it was already stained scarlet. The nausea rose again in his throat when he realized what lay underneath the quiet cabinet which he had used all these weeks as his office. He now understood the purpose of Dr. Fabri's unholy ledgers and he knew, too, why the doctor had gone away for a few days. It was not hard to guess that one of his destinations would have been Essex. He had only taken Bassett beyond Guildford, but Trumble realized he would have to widen his area if he were to remain unsuspected.

His feet beat a nervous tattoo on the rungs of the ladder; he switched off the light, replaced the trap-door, making sure that he left no stains on the metal and smoothed down the carpet over it. He inspected it anxiously, making sure that all was as it had been originally; his breath rasped unnaturally in his throat. When he got up to the desk he saw that someone had visited the cabinet in his absence; there was a new pile of correspondence on the green leather top. Trumble turned white and bit his lip. He glanced at his watch, saw that the midday post would just have been delivered. Joseph would know. The secretary was actually turning the handle of the bronze door when he found it locked; it was quite immovable.

His hands were bleeding from beating against it, when he realized the effort was quite useless; he calmed down then, noting that the key had been removed from the inside. He would never get out that way. He turned back to the inner cabinet, searching for a means of escape but the zinc walls were smooth and blank; there was not a join anywhere that he could discern. He would have to see what could be done in the underground chapel, though he dreaded descending again. Unless he could reason with Joseph. Perhaps the servant could hear him if he called out. A microphone within the cabinet, perhaps.

Trumble sweated and he swayed a little as he turned this way and that; the rumble of the air-conditioning went reassuringly on. But

Trumble felt he could detect a faint hissing beyond this. Or was it his imagination? He licked his lips and plucked at his collar. Strangely enough, all fear was leaving him. He stared at the shelves and saw that a metal shutter had rolled back in the metal wall; there was a glass panel set into it.

On the other side stood his employer. Dr. Fabri smiled encouragingly at him.

Trumble opened his mouth as if to say something, changed his mind and closed it again; he staggered as the gas hissed remorselessly into the small chamber, smoothly expunging the life from him. He understood many things as he fell against the desk. The Satanist had not forgotten the importance of the Poet. He had just time to note, entirely without surprise, before he went down to death, that the ledger in front of him was open.

And there, in the Archives of the Dead as the latest entry, was his own name in Dr. Fabri's impeccable, green-inked writing.

⚜ Amber Print

⚜ 1

"IT REALLY IS A MOST REMARKABLE PRINT," SAID MR. BLENKINSOP, leading the way into the large cluttered room behind the shop. His friend followed him in, his sallow cheeks flushing with pleasurable anticipation at Mr. Blenkinsop's words.

"But where on earth did you get it?" Carter asked, for perhaps the thirteenth time that evening. "Deck went out in the twenties and U.F.A.'s Neubabelsberg Studios were gutted during the war, I understood..."

"Yes, yes, Henry, we know about that," said Mr. Blenkinsop, impatience corroding the edges of his usually smooth, high voice. "All in good time. But first we must have a small drink by way of celebration."

Carter sat down in a deep leather armchair while his friend busied himself at a mahogany sideboard. It was a curious room which the overspill from Mr. Blenkinsop's shop made even more bizarre. Deer's heads and antique weapons, rare glass and china, rosewood cabinets and ormolu clocks came and went in the gloom of the big sitting room, as Mr. Blenkinsop took the items to be sold in the antique shop beyond. Mr. Carter never knew what remarkable sight would meet his gaze when he next visited the private portions of his friend's premises.

The contrast was even more extraordinary when Mr. Blenkinsop's *objets d'art* were carelessly set down among cans of movie film,

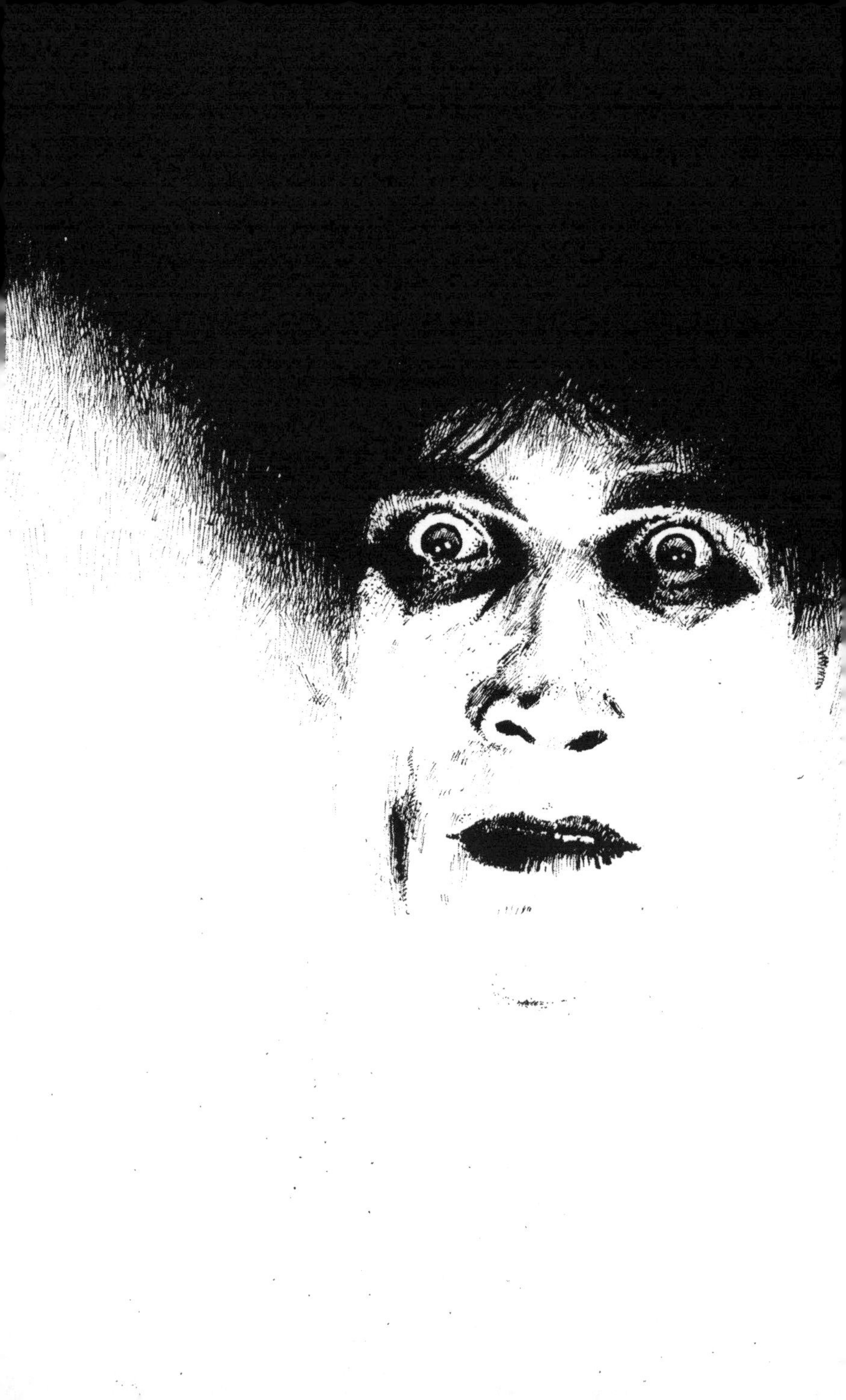

Amber Print

projectors and other equipment of a much later age. Both men were bachelors and were thus able to indulge their tastes; in the case of Mr. Blenkinsop the collection and sale of antiques and Victoriana. In that of Mr. Carter there was no such duality. He followed the profession of accountant and apart from the purchase of rare books, his principal passion, like that of his friend, was the study of the history of the cinema and, above all, the collection, listing and showing of rare films collected from many sources and from many parts of the world.

Both men spent a great deal of time and money on this esoteric and expensive pursuit; both were among the principal collectors in the world, in a field which was followed perhaps by only 500 to 1,000 people on a global scale; both were authorities in their chosen sector; in Blenkinsop's case that of the German cinema of the twenties; in that of Carter, newsreels and actuality prints of the period 1895-1920. Above all, both men had enormous collections of films on many different gauges which, encased in cans, boxes and containers, spilled over from their intended racks and shelves and invaded every corner of their respective homes.

It was against this background that Carter had expressed only the polite interest due to his old friend, when the latter had enthused over the telephone about his latest acquisition. Mr. Carter sat now, blinking amiably at Blenkinsop, as he fussed at the sideboard. He took the small cut-glass goblet filled with yellow liquid and sniffed at it appreciatively. Blenkinsop went back to the sideboard and returned with his own glass. The two old friends sat at the oval table for a few minutes, each lost in his own thoughts, sipping at the wine and glancing curiously at one another from time to time.

Carter was the first to break the silence, as Blenkinsop knew he would be.

"Well, are we going up, or aren't we?"

Mr. Blenkinsop patted his knee with a soothing gesture, as though Mr. Carter were a child who had somehow to be mollified. "Certainly, certainly," he said in his high, well-modulated voice. Then, glancing at his friend's expression, he smiled a quick smile and went on quickly, "We'll go now, then, if you really can't wait. Though I thought you said yet another print of Caligari wouldn't be of any real interest."

It was Carter's turn to smile. "Ah, but you were so damned mysterious on the telephone, George. And after all, a new print of a thing like that... and with scenes neither of us have got. Incredible, really. It's something I shall have to see."

Mr. Blenkinsop smiled again with satisfaction. "That's why I asked you over, Henry. It's worth any collector's time. I'll refill your glass and then we'll make a start."

With both their glasses recharged, the two men, outwardly quiet but each bubbling inwardly with suppressed thoughts—Carter with unformulated questions, Blenkinsop with unsolicited answers—began their long march which ended in the large attic beneath Mr. Blenkinsop's roof. The night around them was heavy with noise; the creaking protests of old beams; the subtle shift of ancient timber floorings; the minute vibration as echoes raised by the passage of their feet died away along the corridors.

Mr. Blenkinsop lived alone, except for a housekeeper who came in daily; he would allow no domestic interference above the level of the shop and the bedrooms on the first floor, so the two men's feet imprinted themselves as pallid indentations in the thick dust which coated the worn drugget of the passages. Mr. Blenkinsop seemed to prefer the atmosphere of melancholy decay which pervaded the upper storeys of his old house; fortunately, it was quite detached from its neighbours in the street, as the noise in the early morning as Mr. Blenkinsop projected an occasional sound film might have proved an intolerable intrusion on their privacy.

Mr. Carter too, though he disliked dust and muddle—his training as an accountant ensured a clinical atmosphere and an immaculate marshalling of the cans and containers on the racks of his own collection—somehow had grown to tolerate the disorder of Mr. Blenkinsop's menage; a disorder he could not have borne for one moment in his own establishment. It seemed all of a piece with the man himself and there was little or nothing Mr. Carter would have changed in his old friend. Though he liked the atmosphere of the shop he preferred the great boarded room under the roof which Blenkinsop kept as his central archive; and beyond that the immaculate viewing theatre with its large modern screen, the half-dozen tip-up chairs

Amber Print

salvaged from a bankrupt cinema; and the craftsman-built projection box with its plate glass windows and latest in sound equipment.

Here were the things Mr. Carter most believed in and which were the substance of great argument between the two friends; the racks of reference books; the filing cabinets and index cards with their carefully documented scholarship; the loose-leaf folders with the data on the films; the re-winders and viewers in three or four different gauges and, above all, the archive itself, the *raison d'etre* for all the paraphernalia that filled the two vast rooms.

On steel racks that stretched from floor to ceiling, was the accumulated treasure of more than seventy years of cinema history; from the Lumiere Programme of 1895, through Edwin S. Porter's *Great Train Robbery*, to the great films of the German silent period and beyond; from *Caligari, Vaudeville, The Last Laugh* and *The Joyless Street*; from the giant dragon of Fritz Lang's *Siegfried* to the massed legions of Abel Gance's *Napoleon*. From the cans the ghostly shades of great, long-dead artistes, picked out by the livid pencil of the projector's light, lived again for a brief while, before being temporarily banished to the gloom of the archive shelves.

Lya de Putti, Ivan Mosjoukine, Emil Jannings, Valentine, Conrad Veidt, Werner Krauss, Lars Hanson waited their turn to re-enact ancient dreams and desires that had been entrusted to celluloid thirty, forty, fifty years earlier. Blenkinsop was the instigator of a thousand adventures at the turn of a switch. And actors now past seventy were seen again—like Gosta Ekmann in *Faust*—in the full glory of youth, before time had taken its cruel toll of those once handsome limbs and unlined faces.

Though Carter did not share his friend's extreme passion for the silent drama, preferring to concentrate on the more arid but no less fascinating documentary field, he greatly enjoyed their evenings of magic under the great loft beams and appreciated the magnificent camera-work and the fine craftsmanship of the set designers and technicians of these pioneer works of the golden age of cinema. If he sometimes felt that Mr. Blenkinsop's taste inclined towards the morbid—he had a large collection of early macabre films for instance—he was too polite to show it, though he really preferred the less frequent treat afforded by the work of the master comedians of which Blenkinsop also had a definitive collection.

But tonight was to see no contortions by Lloyd high above the street; no Langdon or Laurel; Chaplin or Linder; Keaton or Keystone; tonight the comics were banished and the leering nightmare of German expressionism was to dominate the screen. And yet, as Blenkinsop courteously held the door ajar for him, and Carter stepped through into the magical atmosphere of his old friend's loft, he once more wondered just what could be so special about this print of *The Cabinet Of Doctor Caligari*.

Blenkinsop followed him in, holding his glass of wine carefully as he negotiated the step; while Carter mused among the racks, Blenkinsop went on into the theatre, throwing switches as he went so that light progressively leaped up, banishing the gloom. Carter paused by a mountain of cans labelled *Coming Through The Rye* and wished for a moment that he could again see the Hepworth, instead of the over-familiar classic Blenkinsop was intent on showing him. Yet perhaps there might be something unusual about the evening; something really special, that would justify Blenkinsop's mysterious phone call and his air of suppressed tension, beneath the easy manner.

"Come in, come in," Blenkinsop called softly, reappearing in the doorway of the projection room. As Carter lowered himself appreciatively into the comfortable padded seat his friend indicated with a wave of his slender hand, he sipped at his wine and asked mildly, "Don't I get to look at the print first?"

Mr. Blenkinsop's eyes narrowed beneath his whitening hair. "So sorry, my dear fellow, the excitement of this coup has quite made me forget myself. The print is in here."

The two men squeezed through the doorway of the large projection box; it contained no less than five machines, but Carter had no time to spare for them. He had seen them many times before. He bent over the stand on which Blenkinsop's 35 mm. machines stood and gazed at the three metal cans before him. They bore Gothic German lettering; *Das Kabinett Des Doktor Caligari* and numbers and technical details. He saw with surprise, as soon as he had the lid off,

Amber Print

that the print was on 16 mm. and not 9.5 mm., as he had expected. Blenkinsop's dry chuckle sounded behind him.

"I thought that would puzzle you."

"An original print?" stammered Carter, starting to unwind the first spool. "From Decla? This is remarkable. Where did you . . ."

"Where did I buy it?" said Blenkinsop, interrupting the question he had been going to ask and answering it at the same time. "An old chap in Highgate Village. Or at least his widow. He had died some time before and she was selling up his collection. I think I got everything worth having. But this was quite the best thing there."

"I should think so," said Carter, gingerly unwinding the reel between thumb and forefinger and squinting up at the light. He saw that the film was tinted in various colours. There were so many main titles that he didn't have time to unreel them all. He handed the print back to his friend, who started to thread it on to his big Ampro sound machine.

"Just watch," said Blenkinsop, with an unusual smile, his eyes dark and impassive, as he inched the celluloid through the chrome-plated projector gate, "You've never seen anything like it."

Carter regained his seat and sipped reflectively at his wine as Blenkinsop extinguished the lights; there was a long pause and he suddenly felt nervous waiting alone in the dark. A thin crack of light came in from the archive room next door. The only sound was the hum of a distant car from the high road nearby and the occasional creak as the roofbeams settled. For the first time Carter became uneasily aware of all the illicit nitrate film Blenkinsop had stored on the premises; this was strictly against Home Office regulations, as nitrate film was notoriously unstable and highly inflammable. He refused to think what might happen if a fire should start up in this timbered portion of the house. Yet why should it, he told himself; it was curious that he should be thinking that way this evening. It was quite alien to his normal pattern of reasoning; he had been in Blenkinsop's loft hundreds of times and the nitrate films had been there at least twenty years, so why should he begin worrying about fire hazards now? He turned the crystal goblet between his fingers, his mind only half concentrating, when he became aware of the continued silence; there was a sudden crash which jangled his nerves and a loud exclamation from Mr. Blenkinsop.

"All right?" Carter called out in a startled voice. Blenkinsop swore genteelly, which was a rarity for him.

"Sorry about that," he said cheerfully. "Knocked the tins down. Won't be a moment."

There was a click as he threw the switch, the projector whirred sweetly and a livid finger of blue light lanced out at the screen; crabbed handwriting grew before Mr. Carter's eyes, blurred, then became distinct as Mr. Blenkinsop focused up.

DECLA-BIOSCOP PRESENTS said the screen. WERNER KRAUSS, CONRAD VEIDT, LIL DAGOVER. In THE CABINET OF DR. CALIGARI the screen went on. Carter sat back as Blenkinsop eased himself into the next seat. The titles were written in sloping handwriting as the textbooks said the historic original prints of 1919 had been. The tinting was extraordinarily vivid, passing from amber to dark blue and then to greens and yellows and reds as the film progressed. Mr. Blenkinsop squinted at the screen through his wineglass as the print clicked its way out of the projector gate and cast satisfied sidelong glances at his old friend. Director of Photography WILLY HAMEISTER the screen continued. DIRECTED BY ROBERT WIENE the screen shouted.

The picture went dark and Mr. Carter almost exclaimed aloud when the first shots appeared; then followed the famous fairground sequence but as he had never seen it before. The picture glowed in its frame as though the long-dead characters could climb out and join the two men; the hues of the tinting joined and fused, dissolved and ran together again like living fire. It was diabolically clever photography and Mr. Carter could now understand fully why the film had been such a sensation on its first release: it was truly an incredible print and he could well realise why Mr. Blenkinsop should be so excited at its acquisition. But at the same time he felt vaguely uneasy as the surrealist sets glowed and wavered in the background of the scenes; it seemed to be hot in the little theatre too and a thin trickle of sweat ran down his collar. He nearly dropped his wineglass at the first appearance of Werner Krauss as Dr. Caligari; that fine actor's soot-streaked features and carefully calculated gibbering and mowing had never affected him so powerfully.

As the story continued Mr. Carter became more and more confused. As he well knew, Wiene's classic production concerned Dr. Caligari, a charlatan who ran a fairground exhibition which featured Cesare, a weird somnambulist who could predict the future. But under cover of this the doctor sent Cesare out to commit murder after nightfall; at the end of Carl Mayer's celebrated screenplay, which caused a world sensation on its release, the nightmare sets, the stylised gesticulations of the actors, were seen to be nothing more than the distorted figments of a madman's imagination, the seemingly calm and sane narrator of the story.

Cesare, as played by Conrad Veidt in his first screen role, was a fine creation, still able to inspire terror and pity after the lapse of over 50 years, but this Cesare was something more. Perhaps it was the composition of the tinting or the edition Blenkinsop had got hold of was a special release print not generally seen, but Carter had never been so affected by the film; this Cesare was not only a distinguished actor portraying a criminal monster.

The malevolent stare of Cesare, seen in a series of smouldering close-ups, had something personal in it that brought unease to Mr. Carter's soul and his discomfort was increased by a number of scenes which were completely new to him; a sequence of dwarfs re-enacting a tableau of mediaeval torture in Dr. Sonnow's clinic; a long and complex passage where Cesare, in a wild landscape full of tottering verticals and wildly dancing shadows, began obscene preparations for the disembowelling of the heroine, Jane, who was strapped to an angled upright like a Giacometti sculpture; and a disgusting shot involving the slashing impact of a meat cleaver followed by a deluge of severed fingers on to the spectator.

The close-ups of Cesare continued and there was one climax, in the second part of the film, where it almost seemed as though he intended to climb out of the frame and come at the two men; the effect of this was so menacing that Mr. Carter cracked his head against the projection box panelling behind him and cut a tooth in the process. As the writhing colours of the tinting wavered on and the sombre story mounted to the finale, Mr. Carter became aware that Blenkinsop was completely and pleasurably absorbed in his new purchase; he might have been viewing a different film, so delighted did he seem. Carter began to wonder if he were ill; perspiration drenched his collar, his fingernails dug into the padded arm of his chair, but he clenched his teeth and sat grimly on, his eyes hardly able to leave the fiery rectangle in front of him, on which such terrifying events were being depicted.

It ended at last, in the traditional manner, with Dr. Sonnow expressing hope of his demented patient's recovery but as the screen went black Carter discovered that there was an epilogue, for the picture re-appeared and with a bubbling cry of horror which he could not repress, he saw the gaunt form of Cesare follow the doctor and hack again and again at his victim's body with a long knife he produced from the folds of his dark clothing. There was a final click from the projector and the picture faded; Carter became aware that he was lying back in his seat, looking at the ceiling. Blenkinsop hovered over him solicitously.

"Are you all right, old chap? That was quite a fit of coughing. I was extremely worried for a moment."

Carter sat up. Already he felt better and quite ashamed a having given way to his feelings. He looked at the trailing end of film still lashing around on its spool, as Blenkinsop moved to switch off the motor. Of course there was nothing wrong with the film but the amber print made such a difference to the performances. And he was sure some of the scenes were different from his copy.

But all he said to Blenkinsop was, "I must apologise for my outburst. I must have swallowed the wrong way."

Blenkinsop switched on the room lights and stood rubbing his hands, his face aglow with pleasure.

"You see what I mean. It was an unusual print, wasn't it?"

Carter felt that was pitching it in rather a low key, but he said cautiously, "Quite remarkable. There were a lot of passages in that which I hadn't seen before. It's different in many respects from the version in my collection."

"I thought you'd see that," said his friend, intent on rewinding the film back on to its spools. "Let's go down for another drink and then I'll tell you something. I never get tired of this film. I've already seen it seven times since I bought it."

Carter said nothing, but drained the few drops remaining it his wineglass and presently followed his friend downstairs, his mind full of conflicting thoughts.

As the two old friends sat at the oval table sipping their wine in the big room with its antiques and gilt furniture, some of the colour was returning to Carter's drained cheeks and he was already regretting the fuss he had made over the film. Neither seemed eager to broach the subject, however, and the ormolu clock had ticked on another twenty minutes before Carter felt it safe to steer the conversation back in that general direction.

"I felt it strange," he said diffidently, holding his glass up to the light of the chandelier. The rays striking through the glass made an amber pattern of his own face as he went on. "I mean, of course, it is a strange film, anyway. But this was something special. For instance, many of those shots were completely new. And I don't believe they've ever been mentioned in any reference book. That's something the Circle would like to know. Ted Walker would be interested . . ."

"Ah, but that's not all." Blenkinsop had leaned forward, his voice a hoarse quaver. "The scenes change all the time. I've never come across anything like this."

Mr. Carter stopped examining the light through his glass and put it down slowly on the table. His head suddenly felt unsteady again.

"High?" he said bewilderedly. "Keep changing? How do you mean?"

Mr. Blenkinsop couldn't keep the excitement out of his voice. "That's exactly it. An optical illusion, of course. But every time I've seen the film it appears to me that it's never the same. There are always scenes that I haven't noticed before. Or the order changes. Though the basic plot and the progression of the key sequences remain. Or perhaps it's me." There was a long silence between the friends. "I'm not sure I understand," said Mr. Carter slowly, weighing each word as though afraid of offending his friend. "How could the scenes change? You're sure you're not ill? Perhaps you had the sort of turn that affected me. That tinting might have a curious effect on the eyes. Strobing on the retina . . ."

But once again his reply was interrupted. Mr. Blenkinsop was on his feet and pacing up and down the room in his agitation.

"No, no, it's not that," he said, his eyes shining in a curious manner. "It's something else. Something that I have to find out for myself. There's a quality about this print that I haven't found in any other film. You're sure you wouldn't like to see it again?"

Mr. Carter shook his head emphatically. He consulted his watch. It was already past ten. "Nothing would induce me to see it," he said firmly. "And I don't think you should either."

Mr. Blenkinsop seemed rather startled at his manner. He tried a laugh which failed dismally. "Oh, surely," he said. "You can't be serious. You mean you wouldn't want to see it again—ever?"

Mr. Carter looked at him quite steadily for a moment before replying.

"Never again, George," he said gently. "And you know the reason why. There's something unnatural about it. If it were my print I'd burn it, and you know what that means when a collector like myself speaks like that."

Mr. Blenkinsop laughed again but there was little gaiety in the sound, which seemed to set the shadows starting in the dim room. "You'd never do it, Henry," he said briefly. "You'll feel better tomorrow."

The two old friends didn't return to the subject again. They spoke of other things, drank their wine and ten minutes later when Mr. Carter said goodbye to Mr. Blenkinsop all was quite normal between them. Except, as Mr. Blenkinsop locked and bolted the glass-fronted door after his companion he felt, sadly, that something rare and precious had gone out of their friendship; and the cause, ridiculous as it might seem to either of them, was undoubtedly the amber print.

2

Mr. Blenkinsop sat by himself in the room behind the shop for a few minutes more and poured himself another glass of wine.

Amber Print

He glanced at the grandfather clock in the mahogany case in the corner and saw that it was still only ten-forty. There was plenty of time to see the amber print again before he sought his bed. He might not, it is true, see it all; it was perhaps overlong at 85 minutes for repeated viewing in one day and the subject was undeniably sombre. Yet it was such a beautiful copy and with so many unique features that it would repay endless study. Mr. Blenkinsop did not regret time spent in such a manner; after all time was the one thing he had plenty of and it was difficult to imagine a more absorbing way of passing it.

He picked up his glass and walked with firm and purposeful steps up the staircase to the topmost floor. The old house was full of noises at this time of night; the timbers creaked reassuringly to themselves as though confirming their presence, one to the other. Mr. Blenkinsop felt at ease as he let himself into his projection room and switched on the lights; the plush chairs welcomed him in the warm glow of the ceiling fittings. That was where he was most at home. The mundane problems of the shop and everyday dropped away and he was again in a world which he and Carter and a few other privileged souls alone really understood and appreciated. The world of art and scholarship; of amber prints and rarities; of notched titles and unique treasures that had to be pursued into remote suburbs after much advertising. Mr. Blenkinsop's eyes gleamed and he rubbed his hands briskly as he stooped to the cans containing his precious print of *Caligari*. He laced up the machine.

The sweet sound of the projector's gears fell satisfyingly on his ears. He glanced once or twice at it to see that the loops were in order and that it was maintaining correct speed and then settled back in his seat. When he finally looked at the screen he was surprised to see that the titles had already disappeared; slightly annoyed, he groped around in the throbbing light that fell on the room and checked the cans. He thought for a moment he had put on the second reel in error but then saw that this was not so. The take-up spool certainly did not contain more than about thirty feet of film, surely not enough to have absorbed the long introductory credits.

Mr. Blenkinsop then saw that an entirely different sequence was being enacted; Cesare and Dr. Caligari were engaged in conversation with the heroine, Jane. While Caligari held the girl's attention the somnambulist was fingering the flowing white draperies of the girl's costume in a way Mr. Blenkinsop didn't like at all. He frowned and found his vision suddenly blurring; he shook his head to clear his eyesight and the scene had changed once more. The sequence was the murder of the town clerk; the picture was bathed in amber light which pulsed and irradiated in a manner which filled Blenkinsop with alarm. As Cesare sidled nearer his unsuspecting victim, fondling a long butcher's knife, the very shadows painted on the walls of Reimann, Warm and Roehrig's sets seemed to pullulate like the corpuscles in a blood-cell. Mr. Blenkinsop gulped and eased a shaking finger round his collar.

Mr. Carter was right; there did appear to be something amiss with the film. Curious that he should not have noticed this before. Perhaps he was seeing it for the first time with his old friend's eyes. Mr. Blenkinsop shook himself and concentrated on the screen again; this time all appeared normal and the spectator was once again at the fairground. Then the film seemed to judder in the gate, there was a vibration in the room and Mr. Blenkinsop felt as though he were choking; his heart was like a great sponge squeezed by a giant hand.

He fought for breath as the picture went its inexorable way; he struggled towards the switch to turn off the machine. But something kept his eyes fixed with burning intensity on the screen. For the face of Francis, the hero's friend, had changed to that of his own. Mr. Blenkinsop passed his free hand over his face as if to remind himself of its familiar contours. Perspiration was cascading down his cheeks in long rivulets; but still the Francis with the mirror-face that was himself enacted out the little drama of the fairground. And Mr. Blenkinsop saw with mounting horror that it was indeed himself asking the fatal question.

HOW LONG HAVE I TO LIVE? said the screen title.

Cesare's face grimaced and gibbered with coruscating fire; the tinting ran from green to amber and then on to mauve in the frightful series of close-ups. The heavy-lidded eyes, thick with theatrical make-up, looked from the cabinet out at Mr. Blenkinsop, who sat crucified in his padded chair. Cesare seemed about to invade the

Amber Print

privacy of the room; the whole screen was running in sheets of pink fire which appeared to Mr. Blenkinsop to be already lapping at the curtains which flanked the screen. The lips mouthed but no words came. But a hot breath licked at him from the front of the auditorium.

YOU WILL BE DEAD AT DAWN! the screen said.

Mr. Blenkinsop must have shouted; how he managed it, he didn't know. He almost overturned the projector in his blundering panic. But somehow he managed to switch it off. The flickering and the frightful images died. To Blenkinsop's overheated imagination the figures of Caligari and Cesare seemed to be along the projector beam until they disappeared within the machine. He really must be ill; he operated the light switch like man suffering from palsy and was shocked to find his palm running with the sweat of naked fear.

He downed the remaining wine in the glass which he had put on the projector stand and felt better; sitting on the edge of his chair he pressed his two hands together and waited for the shuddering of his nerves to recede. Then he forced himself to rewind the film and replace it in the can. He finally picked up the cans and carried them out to the main archive, where he stacked them in their pre-ordained position in the Golden Age of German Cinema category.

He walked back down the long gallery, ostensibly to check the title of a film at the other end, but in reality to prove something to himself. He had to master his nerves or he might never again be at ease in his own domain. He put his experience down to a combination of optical illusion, nerves and a possible fainting attack. Perhaps he had had a little too much to drink that evening; he had drunk several glasses of wine with Carter and possibly the extra on top? Yes, that was it.

He reached down a print of *Koenigsmark* and ran his hand over the label lovingly; as he went to replace it on the shelf he heard the sudden clatter of metal on metal at the other end of the gallery. He turned quickly, hearing the stealthy scrapping which followed; curiously he felt no fear. The noise was that which might be made by someone who had difficulty opening the lid of one of the film cans. A light rustling passe through the gallery. Mr. Blenkinsop let the tin in his hand drop to the floor; the clatter as it hit the boards started hideous echoes from the ceiling rafters.

He trod quietly as he wormed his way into the next aisle. A long, attenuated shadow passed slowly across the white lozenge of light that spilled from the door of the projection room. Mr. Blenkinsop had seen that shadow before and knew what it portended; the shadow grew and spread until it seemed to fill all the archive weighted with its hundreds of tins containing the enshrined performances of thousands of dead artistes. A brittle scratching fretted at his nerves in the silence which followed; Mr. Blenkinsop rounded an angle in the gallery and found himself back in his original position.

His foot kicked against something; he looked down. The dim light fell on the label of a can. It said: DAS KABINETT DES DOKTOR CALIGARI. All three tins which contained the print were lying jumbled on the floor; all were, as Mr. Blenkinsop had somehow expected, empty. He raised his eyes as the shadow grew before him until it filled the whole of the loft. Something fell with a soggy thump near him and an old, dusty top hat rolled forward into the light. Mr. Blenkinsop understood everything as a soft hand closed on his arm; the fingers and sleeves were black as the night which surrounded him and the creeping shadow flowed onwards and took him to itself.

3

Mr. Carter awoke with a choking cry at midnight, frightened beyond measure at a sinister dream which persisted into his waking life. He switched on the lights and looked at the clock; he had such an oppression of spirit which was completely outside his experience. So convinced was he that something was wrong that he had hastily dressed and was already starting his car before he fully realised what he intended to do.

Ten minutes later he had drawn up in front of Mr. Blenkinsop's shop and was rapping timidly at the glass-panelled door. Lights shone from the upper storeys and there was a yellow radiance from the room behind the shop so that he knew Blenkinsop couldn't be abed. Nothing stirred. Mr. Carter was in such an agitation of spirit that he surprised himself with his actions that night. When there was no reply to his repeated knockings, he went and fetched his car jack and unceremoniously smashed in the front door. He fumbled for the catch in the gloom, caring little whether he cut himself on the jagged glass or not. His ears were abnormally attuned to the sounds of the old house as he pounded up the stairs.

In the main gallery of the archive he found three large tins in the aisle; these seemed as though they had been burned and scorched. The label identified the contents as *The Cabinet Of Doctor Caligari*. Inside them was nothing but a putrescent mass of black liquid of the consistency of mud but with such a loathsome stench that Mr. Carter was forced to clap his handkerchief over his nostrils. He noted scuffing marks in the dust of the floor. As the coroner afterwards remarked, it was with considerable courage that he went down the gallery to the crumpled remains of Mr. Blenkinsop's body.

Some time later that evening, firebells were heard coming down the night wind and a haggard Mr. Carter was banging on the door of a local police constable. Mr. Blenkinsop's shop was detached and Mr. Carter was perhaps justified in his actions, but nitrate film is impossible to stop once a fire is started and the authorities found hardly a bone left of Mr. Blenkinsop to identify. Carter himself said he had no idea how the blaze began but number of people had their own theories and it seemed odd, say the least, that Mr. Carter should have paid a second visit his old friend's premises that night.

What cleared him of any culpability in Mr. Blenkinsop's death was the testimony of several independent witnesses who stated that two tall and shadowy figures had been seen coming from Mr. Blenkinsop's shop long after the fire had started and while Mr. Carter was engaged in talking with the policemen, astonishingly, the fire did not seem to harm them and those few people who tried to follow, soon lost them as they walked at an incredible pace and vanished in a maze of alleys adjoining the shop. The coroner had inquiries made, of course, but nothing fruitful ever arose from that line of investigation. An open verdict was returned.

Mr. Carter now lives at Bexhill. Much aged, he is a changed man. He has sold his film collection and concentrates on stamps, mainly early Colonial issues. He sleeps badly and cannot bear to visit the cinema. He remembers only too well the shadows on the wall in the antique dealer's attic and the sight which prompted him to light the fire.

Not only the husk of Mr. Blenkinsop's body, all liquified as ough the essence had been drawn out of it, or even the face, which had been erased as though some deadly hand had drawn a sponge across it. All these things, bad as they were, he could have borne. It was not those alone which prompted him to light the match. Just a piece of pasteboard clutched tightly between the stumps of what remained of the dead fingers. On the card is engraved in curlicue letters:

DR. CALIGARI.

✐ Out Of The Fog

✐ Four O'Clock

THE WOMAN SAT AT A SMALL SATINWOOD DESK IN THE ROOM, which was simply equipped. She had been sitting in the same position for hours. The only sound was the occasional rumble made by the wheels of a passing carriage and the loud tick of a clock which marked the equally inevitable passage of the minutes. A single gas jet by the surgery door gave a harsh yellow light which fell upon the frosted panels. It was late summer yet the curtains had already been drawn for almost an hour. A small fire blazed in the hearth with its heavy firedogs and brass accoutrements. Outside, unseasonable yellow fog hung in acrid folds and an occasional streamer penetrated the dark green curtains.

The woman at the desk noted none of these things. She was slimly built, with strong, finely shaped hands. About thirty years of age, she would have been handsome except for her red-rimmed eyes and the deathly whiteness of her face. She had been weeping quietly to herself for some hours. Now she was quite calm to the outward eye, but a mental furnace within. Presently there came a tapping at the surgery door and the woman stirred herself and blinked about her. But she made no move to answer the knock until it was repeated, deferentially but a little louder than before.

She called out softly for the knocker to enter. He was a strong, heavy-framed man in his mid-fifties with a black beard flecked with grey. His eyes flashed mildly behind steel-framed lenses and drops of moisture glinted on the folds of the ulster he wore. He shook a broad-brimmed hat against his knee to get rid of the moisture. The woman finally rose from the desk and came towards him. She felt as though years had passed since the morning.

"It was good of you to come, Doctor Morton."

"It was the least I could do, dear lady," said the doctor, stooping to the heat of the fire. Steam came up from his heavy coat into the oppressive warmth of the room.

"You are quite sure you want to go through with this? It is not at all necessary, you know. I can deal with all the details if you wish."

He broke off as the slim woman caught him by the arm.

"I know you mean well, Doctor Morton," she said fiercely, "but this is something I have to do. Is it far?"

"Quite a long way," said the doctor, holding his hat out to the blaze. The firelight made a carmine mask of his face. "Islington Mortuary. I have made all the arrangements. There is a cab outside."

He looked curiously at the young woman whose white, handsome face showed nothing of the feelings she must be experiencing. He felt he ought to prescribe a sedative. Yet it might be presumptuous; after all, she was a doctor herself and a very distinguished one, among the first in England to qualify for the profession and still a subject of admiration to her patients. She would best know how to take care of herself; she was perfectly capable of prescribing her own remedies. He felt a flash of pity as he looked at her face in profile. The whole thing was a great tragedy; both she and Forster were at the beginning of brilliant careers. Now this had to happen. He could still hardly believe it. Even in an age of such progress it was astonishing that such inexplicable events could still happen in well-ordered Victorian society.

"Would you like a drink, doctor? It is a raw day for the time of year."

"Thank you, yes," said Morton, holding out his hand for the goblet of brandy the girl pressed on him. "It is a little early for me, but as you say, the day... If you will forgive me, Doctor Lazenby, will you not partake yourself? You might find it helpful under the circumstances."

The white-faced woman shook her head primly. "I am quite all right now."

Out Of The Fog

She led the way out of the surgery and turned down the gas jets behind them with an assurance she was far from feeling; she was glad of the solid support of the doctor's arm as they went into the raw, yellow blanket that hung over the city. A wretched horse with a nosebag stood steaming miserably in the cold air; the cab itself smelt of dampness and leather as the driver let down the steps and helped them in. Morton had already told the man their destination. There were few people about in the murk to see them as the wheels grated across the cobbles. Dr. Lazenby sank back against the cushions and watched the oil wick in the big driving lamp next to the opposite window rise, splutter and fall again in the fog.

Morton sat with his hands folded against the knob of his cane and looked down at the cab floor which was littered by the cast-off debris of many fares; he too seemed overwhelmed by the sombreness of the errand on which they were engaged. She felt a momentary stab of gratitude for his sturdy presence. Apart from the doctor who shared Gerald's rooms, she supposed this man was one of his closest colleagues. She looked again at the yellow lamp which flared and bobbed as the cab lurched on its way; it seemed to epitomise so many lives in this great city which burned up so full of brilliant promise, only to splutter out so dismally a short while afterwards.

Five O'Clock

It was a long drive and the fog seemed thicker than ever when they rattled over a tarmacadam roadway and eventually drew up in a high brick yard; they were evidently expected, for a man in a dark smock opened the big wooden gates and drew them back for the hansom to pass within. The horse steamed and stamped impatiently as though anxious to be away from this dismal place. Somewhere a clock struck the hour of five and the strokes, muffled by the fog, fell like blows on her own already overburdened heart. Morton asked the cabman to wait and bolts were already grating in front of them as they followed the man in the smock across the damp flags of the yard.

◆ Darkness, Mist & Shadow

They passed within the building which seemed, if anything, even colder than the air outside. Naked gas jets cast blue shadows on the bare stone floors of the corridors and there was a raw smell of carbolic. Presently the attendant, after leading them down a succession of long passages, tapped deferentially at a thick oak door. The Medical Director, Dr. Pruner, a stout, jovial person whose face now wore an appropriately solemn expression was not a man to waste time on ceremony. He asked Dr. Lazenby to sign a paper and to identify certain objects he took from a drawer; there was a gold hunter which she recognized, a crocodile skin notecase and an engraved ring which she had herself presented to Gerald. She signed for these too.

Pruner cleared his throat and looked fixedly at Morton.

"There is no real necessity," he began. "If Doctor Lazenby would agree..."

"The lady has already made up her mind," said Morton. "I shall accompany her myself, of course."

"As you wish," said Pruner, with an expressive gesture of hand and shoulder together, as though mentally absolving himself of all responsibility. "Come back afterwards and if I can help, let me know. Biggins will show you the way."

The attendant led them to a large green-painted door which had Mortuary painted on in black letters; a dim light burned at the entrance.

"The Registrar is waiting," he said softly to Morton as the doctor passed him.

There were six tables in the great white-washed barn of a place; sinks and marble-topped benches stood along one wall. Canvas shutters controlled by cords covered the vast skylights which lit the room by day; gas jets with conical reflectors threw brilliant plates of light down on to the sheeted shapes on the tables. The Registrar was a sandy-bearded young man with a dry cough and a wary eye. He seemed anxious to get off to his tea but he was kind enough. Introductions were awkward and brief, the tables and their burdens seeming an intrusion.

"This is Doctor Marion Lazenby," said Morton. "Doctor Forster was her fiancé."

Out Of The Fog

The Registrar coughed. "Quite so," he said, looking around him as though the sheeted forms might overhear. "I am indeed sorry that we should meet under these melancholy circumstances. Number five, over here by the window."

The two visitors were drawn inexorably to the position indicated by the Registrar, their reluctant feet seeming to take them automatically without conscious effort. The awkwardness of the moment was dissolved by the Registrar, who simply lifted the sheet from the dead face and recited a stream of technical details. Contrary to Morton's expectations the dead man exhibited none of those signs often the occasion of violent death and which are so distressing to relatives; he merely looked as though he were asleep. It was a strong, determined face; the thick moustache and black curly hair well-kept. The face of a young man of thirty-five used to making decisions and Morton wondered for the hundredth time what induced him to take such a step.

"A shotgun wound, you say?" he heard himself reciting. "The autopsy report is with Doctor Pruner. We will look at it on our way out."

It was a short, simple story, except for the motive. Dr. Forster's body had been found in thick woodland about two miles from the building where it now lay, late in the afternoon of the previous day. He had used a double-barrelled shotgun, which he had brought by canvas holdall to the spot; it was found beside his body by a sewerman who was taking a short cut across the open ground. There was no note. Dr. Forster had apparently taken a long tram ride to the remote suburb and had then walked to the point where his body was found. Morton was grateful for the Registrar's sing-song chant which gave them so much information without painful prompting by Dr. Lazenby; she had said nothing, merely stared fixedly at the table. But even the Registrar was startled when she drew down the sheet still further and examined the gaping wounds in the side, made even more ugly and monstrous by the police surgeon's rough incisions.

They were back in the Director's office before Dr. Lazenby spoke again.

"You have, I believe, Doctor Pruner, a copy of the post mortem findings?"

Dr. Pruner turned helplessly to Morton, as though seeking moral support. "We have the records here, of course, my dear Doctor Lazenby. But I could not imagine..."

"I would like to see it," the slim woman said quietly. Her voice was soft and low but there was such authority in it that the substantial form of the Medical Director seemed momentarily to melt before her. He turned again to the impassive figure of Morton and gave a hopeless shrug.

"I see no objection, doctor," said Morton stiffly.

Pruner laid his hand on the other's arm. 'One moment, if you please. These are exceptional circumstances.'

He drew the other to the end of the office; Dr. Lazenby stood looking out at the yellow bank of fog. The voices of the two men came to her like the low mumble of the sea. She did not understand what they were saying, neither did she care. She felt no impatience or anger; just a great weariness. She would have liked to have stood looking at the fog for the rest of her life; but even that soothing occupation could not erase the ugly questions that were burning at the edges of her mind. She turned at last, as she felt the soft tread of Morton on the carpet behind her. The doctor's face was white and a thin trickle of perspiration rolled slowly down his left cheek.

"I think Dr. Pruner is right, my dear lady," he said, motioning her towards the door. "I feel this has been enough for one day. Perhaps another time..."

There was rising anger in Dr. Lazenby's voice as she broke impatiently away from him.

"I have no intention of leaving until I have read the findings," she said.

Dr. Pruner looked aghast, Morton merely distressed. But all he said was, "There is a very good reason why you should not know the contents of the report, my dear. But if you wish we will call on Allardyce. He was Gerald's closest friend. He knows of the autopsy. And if he consents to tell you its findings, then I will have no objections."

He waved his hand to indicate the rigid form of the Director in the background. "And it would save Doctor Pruner unnecessary embarrassment."

⚘ Out Of The Fog

Dr. Lazenby stood hesitating for a moment. The fog seemed to roll forward and engulf the room. She shivered suddenly. Her great weariness took the decision from her.

"As you please," she said. "But it must be settled tonight."

The door closed heavily behind them as they walked in silence down the long, damp corridor.

⚘ Six O'Clock

The hooves of the cabhorse struck sparks from the cobbles as the hansom turned down Queensway; the gas lamps bloomed like glowworms in the fog. They had traversed several more streets before Morton broke the long silence.

"I feel it would be better if you saw Doctor Allardyce alone. This is a delicate matter and best settled between the two of you. But if you need help or advice you know where to reach me. Don't hesitate to call, either day or night."

Dr. Lazenby leaned forward and pressed her companion's hand in grateful silence as Morton tapped with the head of his cane on the hatch above them. The driver turned into the kerb and stopped. Morton got out and stood with his hand on the door as he gave the cabman Allardyce's address. His face was strained and serious as he said goodbye. "I wish you wouldn't go on with this, my dear. No good can come of it. Gerald would not have wished it."

"We have been all through that, Doctor Morton," the slim woman said, with a slight return of her old manner. "Please do not mention it again. My mind is quite made up."

"As you will," said Morton slowly. "I hope you will not live to regret it."

He brushed her fingers with his lips and was then gone, a blurred figure among the passers-by in the fog. Dr. Lazenby drove on, lost in her thoughts, until she was aroused by the stopping of the cab in a narrow thoroughfare of respectable, flat-chested houses, each identical to the other. The cabman ran lightly up a flight of steps in front of a door whose fanlight shone fault rays of gaslight through the mist. He rang at the bell and then ran back to help her down,

"Wait," she said. "I may need you again before the evening is over."

Allardyce was more than six feet tall and with a craggy face from which two deep-set grey eyes looked at her with a troubled gaze. His sitting room was stacked with books and papers and he had to clear a chair for her.

"I'll ring for some tea," he said and went off. While he was away she looked round curiously, conscious that this was a side of Gerald's life that she had never known. A side that she would never know. They drank the hot sweet tea and ate the little buttered scones in silence. The fog crouched at the window and muffled the passing noises of the street. Dr. Lazenby was not conscious of what she was eating; it might have been sawdust and cardboard for all the impression it made on her palate but she knew it would please her companion.

Half an hour had passed before she broached the subject of her visit; Allardyce went pale as her purpose became clear. He stammered in his explanations, grew embarrassed and red in the face and eventually fell silent before the intensity of her eyes.

"What you are asking is impossible," he said awkwardly. "Cannot you see that?"

"I can only see that my life has been ruined to no purpose," the woman burst out passionately. "There can be no rest for me until I discover why Gerald shot himself. He had everything to live for. As you know, we were to have been married quite soon."

Allardyce's face was like a mask of stone as he answered.

"Gerald was my patient as well as my friend," he said. "I had been treating him for the last two years. May God forgive me for breaking a confidence. And are you sure you are prepared to forgo your peace of mind for perhaps a lifetime?"

"My peace of mind has already gone," said the woman inflexibly. "What could be worse than not knowing?"

Allardyce got heavily to his feet. His face was enigmatic in the semi-gloom.

"I will get the report," he said. He came back with a two-page document. The lines of the printed sheets were covered in crabbed handwriting. Against the entry, Deceased, she saw the name Gerald Forster, followed by: Adult male. Allardyce went to the window and

⌘ Out Of The Fog

stared out at the fog as she read on. He was aroused by the crumpling of paper. He returned to her side. The crackling of the sheets sounded fiercely in the silent room. They floated unnoticed to the floor. Dr. Lazenby sat with livid face, her eyes fixed on the wallpaper before her.

"Syphilis..." she murmured. "Dear God, this is worse than one could have imagined. How was this possible? Could I have been so close to this man without knowing? And yet I did not know him."

Her voice had risen slightly in her agitation and she was suddenly conscious that she was clutching at Dr. Allardyce's shirt-front. She allowed him to force her back in the chair; she choked once or twice as the raw brandy burnt its way down her throat.

"Don't blame him, Marion," said Allardyce, his words coming out in an uncontrolled flood. "It happened a long time ago. He was a wild young man, like most medical students. And we thought he had been cured. He met you and all seemed set fair for his happiness. But some while ago it returned. In a more virulent form. He tried all sorts of specialist advice. We could do nothing. You understand, Marion, medical science is just at the threshold in these matters. And he could not bear to tell you or to hurt you in any way."

The woman was calm again now. She sat staring in front of her, listening quietly to Allardyce's explanations. There were many bitter things she could have said in answer to his apologia for a friend, but she knew it would be pointless. There were only one or two more facts she had to know.

"Did you guess what he was going to do?"

Allardyce hesitated for the merest fraction of a second but she knew he was speaking the truth when he replied.

"As God is my witness, I had no idea, or I would have stopped him. I found the gun missing from the rack too late. He left me a short note."

Dr. Lazenby stood up with an abrupt movement. Her voice was quite calm when she spoke.

"Did he mention me?"

"Yes, he did," said Allardyce. "It was in a postscript. He simply said, "Don't tell Marion.""

Dr. Lazenby drew on her gloves. "Why did you break that promise?" she asked.

Allardyce opened the door of the sitting room. "Because I knew you had the character to survive it. You could not have lived your life without knowing it."

Dr. Lazenby knew this was true as soon as the words were out.

"You are quite right, doctor," she said. "I am proud Gerald had you for a friend and colleague. Now I have only one last favour to ask you. Who was the woman?"

Allardyce started back against the doorpost. His lips moved but he could not seem to enunciate.

"What are you going to do?" he said huskily at last.

"Be calm," said the slim woman. "I just wanted to know."

Allardyce stood motionless for what appeared an interminable time. "I always believed it to be a woman called Mary Clarke," he said at length. "She was known as Red Meg because of her fiery hair. She was a fine figure of a girl in those days. But she's probably died of drink long ago if she hasn't come to a worse end."

Dr. Lazenby had one final question.

"Where did they meet?" she wanted to know.

Dr. Allardyce sighed. He felt tired and he knew that this implacable woman would have the information from him if they stood there all night. "It was in the East End," he said. "A place where no lady could go alone."

"I asked you where it was," said Dr. Lazenby.

Dr. Allardyce sighed again.

"A tavern called The Crippled Sailor," he said.

Eight O'Clock

The lamps of The Crippled Sailor blazed through the fog and cast a lurid glow on the smeared window panes and the damp pavements of the street. The noises of passing cabs were drowned not only in the curling tendrils which swayed in oily dance but by the raucous laughter of the raddled women half-seen through the smoky

Out Of The Fog

interior and the jangling discord of an inexpertly played piano up at the end of the long bar.

Dr. Marion Lazenby sat at a side-bench, appearing not to notice the habitues who sang or shouted at their companions as the fancy took them, but in reality her searching glances examined minutely ever human being who passed before her in the dingy room. The red velvet stage curtains were drawn and the profiles of the men could be seen through the frosted glass partitioning of the four-ale bar next door. She had sat for nearly an hour in the same position, her glass of gin, purchased of necessity, almost untasted before her. The nervous-looking waiter with handlebar moustache, slicked-back hair and wearing a dirty white apron over his black and white-striped waistcoat, had at first greeted her dubiously, as her expensive clothing and aristocratic air were obviously at odds with the atmosphere of his establishment. But the passing of some silver during a muffled conversation had mellowed his attitude amazingly and he fed her a constant stream of information as he passed to and fro with his trays of tankards.

"She mightn't be in tonight, madame," he said, shooting the words jerkily out of the corner of his mouth. "She's usually in long afore this."

He had made the same remark at least a dozen times in the past hour but, as on the previous occasion, the woman ignored him. "I'm in no hurry," she said, finishing the drink. "Bring me another. And this time put some more gin in it."

The waiter picked up the glass, pretending offence at the reflection on his honesty. He was soon back, slopping the drink on to the oak settle in front of her in his anxiety to set it down.

"Keep the change," said Dr. Lazenby, her eyes fixed over the waiter's shoulder, to where a new group of drably dressed artisans had just entered the main doors.

She did not need the almost imperceptible narrowing of the waiter's eyelids to know that the woman she sought was among the new-comers. The flaming red hair, obviously dyed and entwined with cheap ornaments, would have been enough to tell her. That and the wreckage of a once strikingly beautiful face.

But now the eyes were glazed; the face, lined and shrunken, was a mask which only animation kept alive; drink, drugs and dissipation had turned the youth and vibrancy it had once possessed into a parody of its former self and even the still magnificent teeth could not disguise the rictus of the smile. This was a woman whose age should have placed her within the full flower of maturity but the features before the watcher at the table were those of an ancient puppet sustained alone by some unknown galvanic energy.

The creature known as Red Meg must have become aware of the silent onlooker for she stopped in the middle of a laugh and turned her head. Dr. Marion Lazenby had made no sign but her stillness and the implacable hostility in her eyes seemed to draw the street-walker to her. She sidled through the crowd which pressed upon the bar and came towards the doctor's table; a feather boa vainly tried to hide the ruin of a splendid throat and the rouge on her cheeks made incongruous splashes of scarlet, so that her face resembled a wax doll.

She stopped in front of the doctor and stood swaying slightly, oblivious of the waiter's frowns.

"Seen enough, dearie?" she croaked.

There was a long silence and the menace in the seated figure began to penetrate even the sodden brain of the poor husk which was Mary Clarke.

"Enough," said Dr. Lazenby when an age had passed. "You will be dead quite soon. I know these things. I am a doctor."

The words took some time to distil their meaning; then the cheeks of Mary Clarke began to drain into a chalky hue, leaving the two crimson spots like the mark of a hideous plague on her face. She sprang forward screeching, reached out for the girl whose eyes burned with hatred into her own. But the waiter was too quick for her. Aided by two burly customers he dragged the shrieking woman away and into a side bar. He reappeared after some minutes. He looked pale and wiped a thin trickle of blood from his face.

"I'd best get out, miss, if I were you," he mumbled. "No telling what she might do when she's in that mood. Never seen her with such a bad turn. She didn't know you, did she?"

The doctor shook her head. She put some more silver into the waiter's hand. She glanced at her reflection in the gilt mirror set along the side of the bar. To her somewhat overheated imagination she looked like death at the feast. She got up, a trim figure that drew glances from all corners; a young woman quite out of place in that milieu. She passed out into the fog so quickly that her going was almost unnoticed. Two pairs of eyes only had more than a passing glance for her. The waiter's were puzzled. But Mary Clarke's, watching from behind the glass screen, held the knowledge of death.

Ten O'Clock

Dr. Marion Lazenby sat alone in the surgery. She had been there, she supposed, for more than an hour, but she was scarcely conscious of tune today. She sat as she had sat earlier that afternoon. Her hands were held tightly together in front of her and her body was quite rigid on the chair. The gas was turned low and the fire had almost burnt out; the harsh, clinical atmosphere of the consulting room was transformed into something softer. Few sounds penetrated the green curtains; only the faint scrape of a distant cab and now and then the beat of a pedestrian's footfall over the setts.

Through a chink in the curtains she could sense the fog, curled and sentient in the damp night; as though waiting for her. It had been an abominable summer and promised to be a harsh winter. She smiled a little to herself. It would have been a terrible thing if anyone had been near to see. Now, with the events of the morning, it was all one to her whether it were winter or summer. There was an intolerable pain round her heart and a dull rage that seemed to mount to her brain. She did not know why she was there and was barely conscious of what she was doing. Dr. Motion had been right; she did need looking after and she missed his comforting presence that night.

She was aware too that she had eaten little all day and with this physical need manifesting itself came a reminder that she had much to do in the time to come. One image alone danced before her; the raddled face of Mary Clarke, a woman with a thousand years of foul knowledge in her sagging features, beneath the dyed red hair of a young girl. Dr. Lazenby's raging thoughts impelled her to action at this vision; she cried aloud with pain and then realized that she had bitten her tongue. The sharp stab made her rise to her feet. Then she turned up the gas and examined her mouth in the surgery mirror. She did not expect that her experiences of the past twelve hours could have improved her looks but she was shocked at her appearance. Absently, she patted her hair into position.

Then she lifted an oil lamp which still burned on her desk and took it through into her partner's consulting room; she made up her mind and knew what she was going to do. A dull rage had replaced her previous indecision and all the events of the day crystallized and became clear to her. She put down the lamp on a table in Dr. Marsh's surgery and picked up her own medical bag; she emptied its contents out and put them in the drawer of her desk.

She went back into Marsh's surgery and unlocked the glass-fronted cupboard; instruments winked at her in the dim light of the lamp. There were scalpels, various kinds of knives, saws, clamps and wedges. She made a careful selection, her firm strong hands taking only those which she knew to be essential to her purposes. She put some bandage and gauze in last of all, together with a bottle of disinfectant.

She turned out the lamp and put it back on the desk. She paused at the mirror by the door and for the first time that day gave her reflected image a brief, genuine smile. She stood by the threshold, her hand on the doorknob and took a deep breath.

She glanced round the surgery once again, making sure she had forgotten nothing, noting the clock and the desk calendar. It was exactly 10.15 P.M. on the evening of August 6th, 1888. It was a Bank Holiday. She smiled again at the irony. Then Dr. Marion Lazenby turned out the gas. The case of instruments weighed heavily on her hand as she opened the door and stepped out into the fog and into history as Jack the Ripper.

⚜ The House By The Tarn

⚜ 1

KEMP KEPT ON WALKING. THE HIGH, SHADOWED SPINES OF the hills which reared about him emphasised and reinforced the coldness of the winter's day. Hoar-frost silvered the blades of grass which fringed the road. The road itself, its gravel coagulated and bonded by the iron-cold of the air, led up between the blunt mounds of the hills and Kemp followed it, walking easily, his hands thrust deep into the pockets of his thick overcoat, his breath smoking from his nostrils as he ascended.

There was a profound silence apart from the faint scraping of his feet in the gravel. There was no traffic on the road and no birds were in the air. The sky was overcast and unfriendly. The intense melancholy of the scene made Kemp realise why most travellers preferred to avoid the turnpike, which had long been superseded by a modern motor road which looped to the north, avoiding the clasping arms of the remote hills.

Once he stopped as if overcome by the silence and alien starkness of the terrain; on another occasion the road descended briefly, then rose again, more gently this time, between dark thickets of thorn and scrub, bare and shivering now in the keening wind. A harsh cry from the interior of the bushes startled the man and seemed to constrict his heart with momentary foreboding; he stood irresolute for a moment, peering nervously about him. Then the sound came again; Kemp's shoulders relaxed. A raven, perhaps? A crow? More fancifully still, a vulture? Kemp's lips curved in a sardonic smile; he turned away and took in the barren curve of the hills. It was not beyond the bounds of possibility with such a *mise-en-scéne*. He resumed his walk, his powerful neck hunched deeper into the warm raglan overcoat, his back turned to protect him from the full force of the wind.

It blew in insidious, fitful gusts, that had a habit of getting through his guard; the main force was directed across the bald crests of the hills and set up a low, hushed moan. The skirts of the wind, descending into the hollows, rasped unpleasantly among the dried stems of ossified undergrowth and scratched at the grass blades and the frozen masses of soil which held them undulate like a miniature sea.

Kemp consulted his watch; he had been walking for an hour. He should reach his destination in a little more than half that now. Which would leave ample time for him to retrace his steps in daylight and regain the main road. A long calvary on such a day to visit the shell of a house. Curious enough to cause Tregorran to put his car at Kemp's disposal; it was typical of Kemp to refuse the offer in a somewhat peremptory manner. That would have spoiled the game for him; cheating was perhaps too strong a word but at the very least it would have dissipated the ambiance of the occasion, have robbed it of all flavour. And flavour was the essential ingredient of such small adventures.

Kemp had left his bag at the inn; he would stay the night on his return and continue on his lecture tour the following day. His schedule would allow him two clear days before the next date on the programme. And in the meantime there was the house. His friend Tregorran had set him on to it. Tregorran was his host at the university where he had last lectured; an old friend, gruff, reliable and dedicated entirely to the higher learning, though not in any narrow way. Their talk, over pipes and punch the previous evening had turned, as conversation often will of a winter's night, on the darker things; of the legends of this gnarled and strangely fashioned countryside; of arcane secrets long handed down by the country folk; and of matters whispered by old people behind closed shutters in the small hours of the winter nights. Kemp was fascinated by the more subtle manifestations of legend and mythology; particularly when it impinged on

⊱ THE HOUSE BY THE TARN

modern life and Tregorran's halting references to the house had intrigued him from the start. The host knew that his visitor was the author of several small but best-selling volumes on such matters and he was sure of his ground when he came to broach the subject long after the clock in his study had chimed away midnight.

Hence Kemp's sudden resolve; the motor journey with Tregorran the next morning and his refusal of the use of the car. He had been right, he reflected, as he set his face upward again, into the bleaker fastnesses of the hill road. The clouds came lowering down as though to intimidate the earth; overhead, the bare branches made a heavy lattice which penned in the dark and sullen sky. Kemp was content; this was his metier, the material from which he could fashion the stuff of scholarly, fastidiously worked volumes which would sell steadily over the years. And the house had all the aspects of a classic doom which had seized upon his imagination from the beginning; the fact that it was a bare fifty miles from the direct route of his lecture tour and so easy of access during his only two-day stopover could only be regarded as providential. Poe himself could not have improved upon the circumstances.

So thought Kemp as he continued to climb, his musings blending with the steady beat of his feet, the story Tregorran had told him backgrounded by the inhuman cry of the wind which continued to rise as his measured paces brought him to the higher plateau. The hills were now harsher in outline, their flanks black, like volcanic ash and completely denuded of vegetation by the scouring gales of the uplands.

Despite his ascent towards the source of light the sky seemed, if anything, to become darker, even though it was the brightest time of day and twice Kemp paused, fearing somehow that his watch might have stopped. But the homely tick reassured him and he walked on, a diminutive and lonely figure among the austere irregularities of that lunar landscape.

He could not forget the thin form of Tregorran, his white eyebrows and tired face lit by the flickering firelight in the study the night before; and the even stranger story he had to tell. The house had been empty for some time, Tregorran said. In fact more than three decades had passed over its scarred mass; the granite walls still standing but the slate roof long since fallen; the floors rotted; the windows glassless; and the doors demolished by the constant battering of the wind.

Four Winds was its name; grimly appropriate Kemp had felt from Tregorran's description but he was only now beginning to appreciate the reality. The slamming and buffeting from these wide skies would, in time, reduce even granite to ground level, he believed.

The house had once belonged to a retired silk merchant, who had built it on a scale and in a style he felt to be commensurate with his wealth and dignity, said Tregorran. But long years in the East had inured him to more temperate climates; the winters unnerved him, he grew melancholy and introspective and his temper withered in face of the gales which howled at the house through long days and nights and months of the dark season.

His wife and three children, all girls, were equally fixed in their dislike of the place, though within all was elegance and warmth; everything that money could buy had been lavished on furnishing and interior. There was crystal and silver and pewter; fine old English furniture ransacked from antique shops the length and breadth of the land; and the collection of eighteenth century French pictures in the gallery was one of the most envied in private hands.

All this, said Tregorran, quoting Poe, was in the olden time, long ago. Yet despite the outpouring of effort and money, the family did not flourish in their new home. The fabric of the house was subject to mildew and there was much shaking of heads among the experts hurriedly summoned from long distances. A type of mould; a strange spore which left purple and scarlet lichen, infected the walls in some rooms; yet there was no perceptible trace of damp.

The drainage system was painstakingly reviewed and improved by builders but still the trouble continued, though the cellars had been filled in. The servants complained of the nauseating stench in their quarters and indeed they had just cause for comment; the owners of the house, descending on one of their rare expeditions, were forced to regain the upper floors with handkerchiefs clapped to their faces. The old kitchen quarters were thereafter boarded up and new rooms assigned for this purpose on the main floor occupied by the family.

⚜ The House By The Tarn

As if this were not inconvenience enough, there was much illness in the household, though reputable physicians affirmed that they could trace no connection between the malady complained of and the mysterious lichen which spread silently and inexorably like a plague through the lower region of the house. A more enlightened young doctor with a scientific turn of mind informally advised the owner of Four Winds to drain the lake which adjoined the main building.

But the old man was reluctant to do that; it was one of the glories of the place. For the lake was immensely old, according to ancient deeds and maps; it was its superb location on a crest of the hills which had decided the owner on the site of the house. To confess defeat on a mere point of dampness was an absurdity to one who had once held sway over hundreds of estate workers and body servants in the East.

This was the impasse which had been reached when one of the daughters died suddenly and shockingly, said Tregorran; curiously, it was not the result of the wasting fever which had attacked her father and mother. She had gone out one darkling winter afternoon on a walk round the foreshore of the lake. This had long been Estelle's practice and as she sometimes spent hours in such pursuits the family felt no unease at her continued absence.

Her father had passed the afternoon reading in a small turret chamber he had constructed out into the lake; the structure projected from the main house and was approached by a passage and the unfortunate old man often sat there in clear weather, reading and occasionally surveying the dark surface of the tarn with a telescope. And, as Tregorran proceeded with his tale, Kemp had felt as though the silk-merchant were responsible for creating a latter-day House of Usher in that remote spot.

But in reality the prosaic man had never heard of Poe and his fancy had run to the wild romanticism of Chillon, which he had once visited on a Grand Tour of Europe. Hence his penchant for the pseudo-Gothic tower in which he passed so much of his time. On this particular afternoon he had read until he was conscious that the light was beginning to fail.

Looking up from his book and training his eyes across the lake he was arrested by something moving in the water; he became aware of a slowly writhing mass of weed floating on the dank surface of the tarn. It came gradually across the field of his vision, though there was no visible current in the lake, and the merchant presently made out a broken mass of white at the centre of the weed.

The occasion was so curious as to be a cause for some comment in that placid place and the old man first called his wife before seeking his telescope from its leather case. So it fell that the wife was the first to put the glass to her eye with some pardonable wonder in the strange phenomena that floated before her.

Her horrified shriek and subsequent faint caused a minor crisis in the household; when the servants had carried their mistress from the room the old man, much agitated, had himself seized the telescope before following the small party down the corridor. What he saw was the drowned face of his daughter; the long hair of Estelle spreading out on the surface of the lake the old man's poor eyesight had mistaken for weed. The staring eyes, open mouth and mud plastering the dead features had accounted for the broken aspect of the white mass.

Kemp had remained cynically aloof as Tregorran had continued his narrative; the former's attitude resembled a mental rubbing of the hands. The blood raced through his veins at a slightly heightened rate; this was distinctly promising he told himself. But Tregorran's narrative bore all the stamps of a Gothic novella and Kemp himself suspected the tale to be half legend, half embroidery which the locals had handed down over the intervening years.

But he merely stretched himself in his corner by the fire, reached out his hand for the refilled glass of punch his host proffered and observed, "There is more to come, I take it?"

Tregorran gazed at him grimly, perhaps conscious of the slight cynicism in Kemp's eyes.

"Assuredly," he said crisply.

2

The ever-steepening road wound about in sharp, corkscrew curves; deep groves of pine and birchwood hemmed in the lane,

The House By The Tarn

the edges of which were becoming blurred with growths of moss and lichen. The ragged spears of the branches were like sentinels blocking Kemp's escape to right and left and their darkness emphasised the brooding solitude of the day.

His ear was presently caught by the thin, high tinkle of falling water and turning another shallow curve he saw the white freshet of a small waterfall, like a scar across the blackness of the landscape; falling freely beyond the trees, then torn by rocks, descending again to view and finally being engulfed by the dense thickets farther down. Curiously enough his heart was not lightened by the sight; the whiteness of the water was like the pale flabbiness of something long dead and only emphasised the surrounding desolation.

The faint roar of the water strengthened the overpowering sense of loneliness in these far hills and Kemp was glad when the final fret of the fall at last died away and his footsteps rang out clear and strong on the gritty surface of the road.

He pushed his chin down into the warm collar of his coat and set to musing on Tregorran's story of the unfortunate silk merchant and his family.

The drowned daughter had begun a long chapter of dark incidents, ranging from the sickness of the servants to the madness and eventual deaths of other members of the household. Tregorran had certain theories, which he had hinted to Kemp, but out of respect for what he called his visitor's professional ethics he had refused to clarify his suspicions. The most he would say, heavily enigmatic in the firelight, was that the two men would compare notes—after the visit.

The silk merchant had died of a wasting fever a short while after the incident described by Tregorran, and his wife had followed him within a year; a mass exodus of servants began and the household was eventually reduced to the two surviving daughters, a body servant and housekeeper. They lived a miserable existence on an upper storey and a priest who visited the family and had befriended them greatly in their troubles described the situation as being like a siége.

This old man himself died a violent and unexplainable death when he fell down an iron staircase after one of his nocturnal visits; the authorities hushed up the exact circumstances but one of the remaining servants told the sisters that spores of lichen were clustered about his mouth and eyes; his frenzied efforts to clear his throat and vision were the probable causes of his fall.

Within a very few days of this latest tragedy the survivors and their staff had decamped and the great house was left to decay on through the years, a prey to the buffeting winds of the uplands, the dark ruffled waters of the lake reflecting the sombre edifice which had been the scene of so much sorrow. So far as was known, said Tregorran, who had adopted a consciously Gothic tone when recounting the story to Kemp, only three visitors had since set foot in-side the building.

The first had been found dead at the edge of the lake; a prospective purchaser, who had walked up like Kemp, to absorb atmosphere, as Tregorran put it, his body was huddled in a curious position, with strange markings in the mud at the fringe of the lake, which suggested that someone—or something—had attempted to pull him into the water.

The second visitor, also a prospective purchaser, was a middle-aged lady. She had driven up one afternoon on a tour of inspection only to collapse an hour or so later. She had been the victim of a heart attack; or at least that was the conclusion reached by a judicial inquiry. The third intruder, for so Kemp had come to describe them in his own mind, was a surveyor sent on behalf of the family estate to assess the condition of the structure. He too had died at the foot of the iron staircase.

Since that time Four Winds had been a shunned house; legend had it that the three who died had been the only people to set foot inside the house proper though Kemp found that difficult to believe. There must have been policemen, officials, and others concerned in the investigations; but he found the stories intriguing. Nowadays, Tregorran said, local people would view the house only from a distance, across the valley from the nearest road, and then they would hurry on, leaving the broken shell to its solitary vigil.

It stood up, like a jagged tooth, against a great promontory of woodland, with the lake hidden beneath the mass of trees. A secondary road, looping round from the old turnpike, would take the visitor to its door. And so it was that at last Kemp came out from the fringe of the far woods and saw the side road below him.

He descended a spiral path that debouched from the main turnpike and found himself on a rutted, unmade road which he knew led eventually to Four Winds. The sky was strangely dark and to his surprise he had not yet seen the house; but as he set foot on the moss-strewn pathway he came suddenly to a break in the trees and there was the great mass of granite, barely distinguishable against the far slopes, its frameless, glassless windows like blank sockets in the structure. He barely paused in his pacing, the glimpse he had obtained had been so much of an anti-climax.

The boughs pressed in on him like a long tunnel and his feet in the moss made furtive, sucking noises; Kemp guessed that some freshet debouching into the lake passed underground at this point, making the ground spongy and swamplike. Sure enough, as he turned on his tracks, his solitary shoe-marks in the lichen were silently filling with water. The silvery sheen looked like metal in the dim light which filtered through the branches.

After another three or four minutes the trees dropped away and he found himself on a wild and desolate shore; it was sheltered here and only an occasional swirl of wind touched the calm and limpid water of the tarn, so that it looked to him as though subterranean disturbances were causing the surface to erupt. The place smelt bad. Kemp, with his long experience of such things, knew that he was looking at a landscape filled with infinite evil; nearer the lake-edge foul, scummy bubbles burst in the thickets of sedge which caked the shore like the poison round an abscess. The shadows of the trees wrote themselves again in the sullen waters of the lake. Yet, despite himself, Kemp was secretly exalted.

"Melancholy House of Usher," he said aloud. The words seemed to hang motionless on the freezing air before slowly dying away in tiny vibrations. Kemp looked down. In the black water at his feet weeds swirled and twined quietly where there was no current. A pale sphere broke the surface. He found himself looking at a girl's drowned face.

His smothered cry was followed by a cracking sound; as he involuntarily started back his heel had caught a dead branch, snapping it. White-faced, Kemp forced himself to look down at the water; of course, there was nothing there. What he had mistaken for hair was indeed weed; and where the pale oval of face had been was nothing but the reflection of a portion of sky, framed between entwining branches in the thicket at his back.

Kemp passed on, his ragged nerves fretting; Tregorran had done his work too well, he felt ruefully. The legends and stories with which he had kept his guest entertained the previous night had penetrated deep; even now he could not disentangle fact from embellishment. And yet he could not really imagine that his host would depart from the strict letter of the truth; he had known him far too long to be mistaken in such an important aspect.

Incredible to suppose for one moment that Tregorran had been playing an elaborate joke on him; if it were so a friendship of many years would be in the balance.

Kemp dismissed the supposition from his mind without a tremor; the atmosphere of Four Winds and particularly the lake foreshore should have been enough to satisfy him that here was no imaginative day-dreaming on the part of a fanciful savant. On the contrary, any normal person would have retraced his passage without a moment's hesitation, thought Kemp, with the suspicion of a wry smile.

His mind was alert now, its receptivity attuned to any manifestations that the place might be giving off; the professional attitude of the experienced investigator was taking over the primal fears of his unconscious. From now on and throughout the visit he would be on guard; a scientific observer merely, weighing dispassionately and putting all data on the scales of logic. Easy enough to say, thought Kemp, looking round him; hard enough to achieve under these conditions.

He skirted the lake and came closer to the house; its granite mass crouched under the dark sky and the darker trees like something waiting to engulf him. He walked towards it reluctantly, with heavy steps, as though wary of the first contact. His way took him past a great old tree with withered limbs that framed Four Winds like a

⌥ The House By The Tarn

Cranach engraving. A path wound here and passed round and beneath the massive spread of branches. The faint echo of the wind plucked at the skirts of the thicket and Kemp paused, as though a chill engendered not only of the physical conditions of the day had entered into him.

Then, he knew not why, he turned and circled the gnarled trunk of the tree, on the landward side. As he did so the wind blew again out of the freezing sky; there was a crack and an impact that shuddered the soft earth on which Kemp stood. He continued his walk around the tree and looked behind him; a branch that overhung the path, its mass larger than a man's body and its weight enough to dash the life from anything beneath had fallen; the force of the shock had shattered the immense bough to fragments, its impact burying the main shaft several inches into the ground.

Kemp stood very still; he smiled at the house, baring his teeth under the dark sky. He knew he must look foolish but it was essential to show it that he was not afraid. Backwards he could not go; the house was watching him and it was essential at all times to see what it was doing; he felt no fear now, only that he must go on. It had become a personal thing, something between him and the house; a contest that could only be resolved in one of two ways. And to bring it to a successful conclusion Kemp knew that he must not reveal, even by so much as a fraction, that he was conscious of the force of the naked fear that gibbered in that freezing air, beneath that low sky.

He studied Four Winds for a moment, under half-closed lids; the great Palladian porch, only one pillar upright now; the roof quite gone; the floors as Tregorran had said, completely fallen in. All that was left was the jagged shell, open to the wide, inhuman sky. Kemp marvelled at the stubbornness which had kept the silk merchant and his family here; perhaps kept them still.

He skirted the frontage of the house cautiously; there was not a door remaining, not a window to be seen; the wind keened uneasily through the structure, probing with expert fingers for any hidden flaws, the air ruffling the long fronds of fern and weeds that grew in dirt-grimed cracks, like the hands of a lover passing through the beloved's hair. Kemp knew he had to be careful now; he had been given two warnings. Traditionally, the third might be the last; he did not intend to be taken by surprise.

He passed the end of the building, stopped abruptly; a turret jutted out into the lake, its glassless windows showing vistas of the waters beyond. He remembered Tregorran's story of the old man's vigil and wondered again about that tragic scene of long ago. The house was challenging him; to beat it and to break the spell the dark stories had woven for the country people, he had to venture within and emerge unscathed.

He remained irresolute for a moment or two longer; then he retraced his steps and found himself again on what had once been a wide gravel forecourt facing the lake. He passed up a shallow flight of grass-grown steps and into the ruin of the porch; within the floorless walls, Four Winds stared rooflessly to the pitiless sky; the wind soughed about the shattered pediments and through the glassless window sockets. Not a bird sang, no scutter of any living creature broke the deadness of the scene.

Then Kemp saw the steps; they were a jagged ruin, little more than a thin line of slabs let into the wall at one side of the main structure but they led upwards and unmistakably towards the turret room. Kemp knew that the house was daring him; knew equally well that if he hesitated he could not face it. He pushed up the steps, his feet uncertain on the slimy paving, gained what had once been the first storey; the view downwards was like looking into an awful pit; through the gaping window-holes in front the darkness of the lake sat and watched him.

There was a curious stench as he ascended to the second floor. The steps were firm and solid; there was no danger here, but he now saw that the wall at his left hand was pitted and scarred. Looking closer he noticed minute spores; striated lichens and strangely coloured polyps which clung limpet-like to the old granite. The stench came from these; Kemp grasped involuntarily at the wall as he stumbled.

Something broke away in his hand and he nearly fell; he held a flabby object, shaped like a human finger and of pallid and unhealthy hue. The fungus seemed to pulse in his hand as he stared at it; little spores emanated from it and flew in clouds round Kemp's head. The smell was really awful; Kemp's head was reeling and his eyes smarted. He gave a muffled cry and slipped again. He hurled the fungi-thing from him with a hoarse shout of terror.

His vision cleared and he scrambled and lurched up the last remaining flights to the turret room, his heart thumping uncontrollably, his nerves screaming; there was no floor in the turret chamber, only a continuation of the rough-slabbed stone which formed the staircase. Kemp stood at an open revetment in the wall and wiped his face with his handkerchief; there was a palsied tremor in his limbs. A few grey spores flew about his head as though they had volition of their own, as he passed the handkerchief across his forehead.

He stayed crouched there for several minutes until his racing heart had steadied and his nerves were back to normal; he coughed, as though the commonplace sound confirmed his triumph. For it had been a definite victory, Kemp felt, in his confrontation with what he considered to be the evil spirit of the house. And the third sign had been overcome without anything more unpleasant happening to him than a nasty fright. He gazed down into the floorless well of the house and willed his nerves into normality.

After all, there had to be an occasion when the power of the house was confronted with the equally remorseless will of a professional occultist. Though he knew the house was not done with him, Kemp felt he was several points to the good. Four Winds squatted there and waited; it had him in its maw but the third warning had been given and overcome and still Kemp survived, like Jonah in the belly of the whale.

He put back the handkerchief in his pocket, straightened his tie and reached for his notebook. It was only then that he noticed the gap in the staircase; about ten feet farther down, over the stone across which Kemp had just advanced, there was now a space of about fifteen feet which barred him from the lower part of the house. Kemp stared for a moment; it was a nasty shock. The house's trump card, so to speak. Paradoxically, Kemp felt his spirits rising; he was equal to the challenge.

Darkness, Mist & Shadow

Kemp laughed. The sound rang round the old shell with the impact of a bell pealing in the airless confines of a vault. Let the house do its worst, the gesture seemed to say; the human spirit was unbreakable. As the last echo died away Kemp stood poised, his hands braced against the damp stone, his ears straining for a sign. Would the house accept defeat.

Aeons seemed to pass. Kemp stood by the wall, drained of all emotion; he had an unshakable conviction that he had won. At last the house had been defeated. It was growing dark but even with the gap in the staircase Kemp knew he could regain the ground floor safely.

Still he lingered, his mind filled with age-old dreams; the lake lapped below, the wind murmured coldly through the granite cage of the ruined building and his triumph soared, reflected in the smile in his eyes.

And the sign came.

Down below a door slammed where there was no door and heavy footsteps, echoing where there was no floor, advanced towards him.

✒ The Knocker At The Portico

I discovered the following papers in the form of a diary while going through some old documents. I append them here. They read as follows:

✒ 1

I WOKE AGAIN LAST NIGHT AFTER THAT HIDEOUS DREAM. I SAT up in bed in my dark chamber and listened in fearful suspense but there was no sound apart from the faint moan of the wind in the chimney piece. And yet I heard it. I am convinced of that. It was the fifth time I have heard the knocking. And it is getting worse. I intend to leave this record so that those who come after may know my fate, will realise the manner of it and may be thereby warned.

My name is Edward Rayner. I was born, the third son of a third son, in the ancient city of Salzburg, of an English father and a German mother. My father held for some years a position as Professor of Philosophy at the University there and when he accepted a similar post in London, the family followed after a few months. I was privately educated and being much younger than my two brothers grew up a solitary, introspective child, much given to walking through the little-known suburbs and odd corners of the city which still linger in such an ancient metropolis as London.

◈ Darkness, Mist & Shadow

My family does not much concern this history, apart from establishing the background and circumstances from which I sprang; indeed, my parents were long dead and my brothers and I separated before the events with which this narrative is concerned began. I had followed my father into scholarship but the generous terms of his will and judicious investments allowed me to pursue my own inclinations; I refrained from any paid employment and preferred the retiring, almost monastic life of a scholar and an aesthete to the boisterous debate and what I regarded as the distracting clamour of university life.

I was, then, settled in a large house in St. John's Wood, comfortably off, with few but loyal friends and with sufficient funds to enable me to continue the researches dear to my heart. So it came as a considerable surprise to friends and acquaintances alike when I married, at the confirmed bachelor's age of forty-five, a young and beautiful girl of twenty-four. Jane had been my secretary for several years and thus we were necessarily thrown together for long hours of conversation and study.

I had found it convenient, for the work on which I was engaged involved much tedious searching and quotation from the library of five thousand volumes I had assembled, to engage professional help and Jane had been recommended by one of my oldest friends. She settled in and my scholastic life was soon running more smoothly than I had thought possible. Gradually, she began to encroach more on my private time in the evenings. Within a year she was indispensable to my scholarly career; within three years I could not have imagined life without her.

We were married in a quiet ceremony, spent our honeymoon touring the Middle East, and on our return to London resumed a style of placid, uninterrupted happiness which lasted for more than two years. So bringing me to the heart of an affair which has introduced darkness to what was hitherto all sunshine and pleasure, albeit of a somewhat gentle and intellectual sort.

It is difficult to recollect, at this stage in time and under the present distressing circumstances, exactly when it all began. I had been sleeping badly; I was at a crucial phase in my line of investigation and long

⌐A The Knocker At The Portico

poring over the crabbed Hebraic texts had wrought me up to a high pitch of tension, which even my wife had been powerless to prevent.

Usually, I followed Jane's sensible advice in all things, but the work on which I was at present engaged, and which had occupied my attention and thoughts for more than four years, could no longer be thrust into the background; my publishers were clamouring for delivery and as the volume had been pre-advertised I had no alternative but to press ahead.

The library in which I worked was a pleasant room and one well suited to my particular vocation; I had all the latest mechanical aids, including the new type of sliding rack so that the selection of the more bulky volumes was a pleasure. But though I used glasses and occasionally a powerful magnifying disc, my eyes were troubling me.

This was no doubt due to the flickering quality of the pressure-lamps I had installed. These were not yet at a stage of perfection which they might later attain, and long hours of perusing manuscript, coupled with the minute concentration needed for the use of the glass, had made black dots spin in front of my eyes. Every half an hour I was compelled to cease my labours and a turn about the library, followed by a short rest in my chair, eyes closed, brought me once again ready for my sojourn under the lamps.

But it was gruelling, difficult labour of a kind which exacted much from a frame never robust and a constitution perpetually delicate, so that I often felt I was undermining my health on processes of research which might never come to fruition. In fact had it not been for the urgent remonstration of a publisher who had long been a friend and for whom publication augured much, I might well have put the work aside until the following year. Which would have, in my own case, meant quite a different history from the dark byways into which my life has strayed.

The urgency of my work, the irregularity of my hours and the long periods of labour in the library had at first engaged Jane as enthusiastically as myself but as month succeeded month her ardour diminished and she began to excuse herself more and more frequently from the daily sessions. I felt myself growing pale and haggard under the incessant demands of my self-imposed labours but I could not give up a task which had exacted a great deal and which promised to yield so much in distinction and satisfaction when published. So, as Jane absented herself with ever increasing frequency, I worked later and later into the small hours of the night.

After several months of this, which was the cause of some bickering between us, things reached an impasse; I cannot say I blame Jane. The situation was entirely my own fault; she had grown distant and abstracted. We met only at breakfast, apart from her occasional visits to the library and the supervision of my meals, which I now took almost entirely within its walls. In the meantime she went for long walks and cultivated such friends as we had. It was understood between us that we would, when my researches were concluded, take a long holiday on the Continent together, and in so doing recapture something of the idyllic relationship which had formerly existed between us.

This was the level to which my affairs had been reduced when the name of Dr. Spiros first began to be mentioned in the house. He was, I gathered from Jane, a brilliant physician; his surgery was no great walk from our own door. He had attended Jane when she had a minor fall from a horse in the Park; he had diagnosed a simple sprain but after that his presence never seemed to absent itself from the house for long. Summer wore away and autumn succeeded it and still I laboured on. How I sustained myself I know not at this distance in time but despite the immense labours, I managed to take an hour's walk with Jane once a day latterly—this she had at last prevailed upon me to enjoy.

It was on our return from such a walk one evening that I became aware that Dr. Spiros had assumed an important place in my own household without my becoming aware of it. He had, I think, far too great an influence on my impressionable young wife, and if my mind had not been above such base suspicions, I might have suspected darker things when I learned that he usually dined alone with Jane most evenings within my own walls. My surprise on learning this was succeeded by consternation when I found him on one occasion within the fastness of my library itself; even my servants knew this was inviolate and the doctor's lame excuse that my housekeeper had

✐ The Knocker At The Portico

showed him in there by mistake left room for the gravest suspicion on my part.

I remained courteous to Spiros but I was now on my guard. I resolved to learn more of his relationship with Jane which seemed to me to have passed beyond that of a mere physician-patient basis. Dr. Spiros was, I should have said, about five and thirty years of age; broad, black-browed and strong in feature with square white teeth which were perpetually smiling beneath his thick black moustache. He was much addicted to perfume or pomades and the aroma of these had a habit of lying subtly in odd corners about the house so that one was always conscious of his presence, even when his physical self was absent from my walls. This was then, the somewhat curious circumstance of my life, when the events I am about to relate crystallised and first assumed menacing shape on the tranquil horizon of my existence.

✐ 2

It was, I think, a cold, blustery evening in November when the first manifestation forced itself to my attention. The icy rain had been tapping with obtrusive fingers at the smeared panels all day long and I had heaped the fire in the library with small coal and turned up the brilliance of the lamps in order to keep the dreary night at bay.

The first volume of my work was about to appear from the press; the second and third were in proof form. I was now engaged upon the last, following which I looked forward to the cultivation of my wife's friendship and the resumption of that intimacy which my protracted labours had interrupted. I had just got up on to the stool before my work table when the knocking began. It seemed to emanate from the inner recesses of my brain. A great hammering thunder that commenced as a slight reverberation and then finally shook and tottered the very foundations of the house.

The noise was such that I ran from the library and to the balustrade that ran round the landings commanding the main staircase and hall of the house. The door set under the great portico of the building must have given way under the knocking, but I saw it was still secure. Moreover, to my amazement I saw one of my own staff pass it without a second glance on her way across the hall.

I stood with the massive echoes ringing through my ears before running down the stairs, three at a time. I wrestled with the bronze bolt on the oak-panelled door and flung it back. Nothing but the night wind and the tapping of the rain against my face. The entrance was empty, the brass lantern with its flickering candle, swaying uneasily in the wind.

I slammed the door to with a hollow thunder behind me and made my way back up the stairs. In the passage outside the library stood my wife; she looked at me strangely. I said nothing but returned to my place at the desk and bolted the door after me. I was not disturbed again that evening. I have a great fear over something but I know not what. I went to bed early but did not sleep. It was the beginning of many such nights.

3

Dr. Spiros is coming to assume a quite disproportionate part in my life of late. Twice more have I seen him in the last few days within my own house, on both occasions unannounced and uninvited by me. I really must speak to Jane about this some time. It was almost as if he had assumed proprietorship of my establishment; there are times when I feel like a stranger in my own household. And yet the man has a kindly face; on the last instance of our meeting I had an impulse to consult him on the subject of the knocking.

He smiled encouragingly as we passed on the stairs. But then something in his eyes hardened my heart against him and I brushed by somewhat discourteously. I do not know what to make of the man but I fear a straight encounter with Jane upon the subject. I badly need a friend and some disinterested advice, though it seems I cannot get this, even within my own family. There is a dark labyrinth in which I wander during the waking hours; I fear sleep also for that is when the knocking is certain to manifest itself.

✒ The Knocker At The Portico

But I must not run ahead. The second time I heard the knocking was an even more shattering experience than the first. It affected my nerves; I think this must inevitably be so, for curious occurrences at night, when one is hovering halfway between sleep and waking, undressed and abed, are inevitably more disturbing than when we have our wits about us during the blessed day. My dread of these long winter evenings dates definitely from this second occasion. And, like the long progression of a nightmare that has no end, I accelerate silently and inevitably into a situation which leads to the incident of the door.

The next time I heard the knocking was at night; it was so late I should rather call it morning. I had worked on in the library until well past 1:00 A.M. and it must have been nearer two when I finally sought my bed. I slept for what seemed a long time but may have been in reality but an hour or so. I was suddenly awake, it appeared, without being conscious of any transitional stage between the sleeping and the state of awareness.

It was quite dark in the chamber, the fire having died to a faint glow by which I could make out various objects in the room. I lay drenched in sweat for perhaps a minute, or longer, terror struggling with reason in my heart. The echo of some gigantic hammering was still within me, but I knew that the echo was merely the reflection of an outward tumult that had its creation in the physical world. The lurid silence was at length broken by a tremendous fusillade of blows with the knocker of the great door in the portico of the house. The tumult was again so great that it seemed as if the whole household must be thrown into uproar; I expected lights, running footsteps, startled cries.

But there was nothing; only the darkness and for the second time the echoes of the knocker's terrifying tattoo dying away against the bruised silence. I lay with my heart thumping and it was like a physical shock when that terrible summons again sounded through the corridors of the darkened house. Somehow, trembling, sick and terrified I found myself at the head of the stairs; I approached a window in an angle of a wing, which commanded a view of the porch. There was nothing but the shadows of the trees in the wild moonlight which fell across the porch door.

Fortunately, I was not called upon to undergo any further ordeal that night; I continued, with ebbing will-power to watch the empty porch, but the knocking was not renewed. It was just possible that the unknown visitor had covered the space between the door and the street corner before I had approached the window. Cold, in turmoil and half worn-out with the shadowy terrors of that sudden awakening, I was again back at my bedside. I crept between the sheets a badly frightened man and slept fitfully till the friendly light of morning allowed me the comfort of a deeper sleep.

I spent the next few days in a fever of hesitation between work and sleep until it seemed as though the night had blended into the day. I had no nocturnal disturbances until the fourth evening; Jane had been absent from the house during the earlier part of the afternoon and I had been so immersed in my researches that the tray my housekeeper brought up remained untasted on my study desk. Rain had been spitting fitfully against the opaque panes of the window glass for some hours. Towards nine o'clock I had become aware that I had not eaten for a long time and had emptied a flask of cold coffee and finished the dry toast under the cover, all that now remained fit to digest.

It must have been about ten o'clock when the knocking came. It seemed to split my head asunder. I clung to my desk, my nerves shrieking, my body wet with perspiration until that massive thunder had temporarily subsided. Once more the drama was repeated. I again rushed to the window to see nothing in the porch. But to my horror the hollow thunder recommenced, even though the evidence of my eyes told me that no knocker was within the porch. Dropping the volume I had been perusing, I ran, eyes staring and with clothing awry, to the ground floor. I flung wide the door; there was only shadow within the porch; that, a tendril of vine that tapped dismally against the wall and the ceaseless spitting of the rain.

Just then a serving woman of my household appeared, startled, in the hall behind me.

I seized her by the arm. "Did you not hear it?" I said in an agitated voice. To my anger the girl shrank away from me with a whimpering cry.

❧ The Knocker At The Portico

"Fool!" I shrieked and ran from her, leaving her to close the great door. Spiros is concerned in this in some way and I am convinced Jane is helping him. I feel so helpless and yet I am master in my own household; albeit a master without power. Even the servants are turning against me. My housekeeper has a strange face when she brings in my trays, for Jane will not now even perform that simple duty for me.

The knocking was not heard again that night, thank God, though I slept but fitfully. I hear much whispering in the house and Spiros seems to spend a great deal of time here so I am resolved to be on my guard. I cannot catch them at the knocking; they are too clever for that. But I can spy on them in other ways when they think I am in, the library; yes, that is what I will do.

What I must do if I am to solve this hideous curse which is hanging over me. How dark the house seems these winter days; even my researches, which were once so dear to me, have their savour. My eyes too, trouble me inordinately; I must consult an oculist, or blindness may ensue. Strange, how my mind is at this moment dominated by the absence of light; darkness, absolute and imbued with terror, reigns supreme.

❧ 4

Later. I have heard the knocking twice again, each time more demoniacal than the last. As before, there was nothing in the porch. I have been quite ill. I would not have Spiros near my bedside but consulted my own man, Dr. Fossey. Though I fear they have conspired together. Jane has not been to see me after the first time. She said my condition had upset her so powerfully that she could not bear to come again, at least for the time being. I suspect otherwise. She and Dr. Spiros have been drawing ever closer during these past weeks. I distrust most medical men, but he particularly, though he smiles amiably enough. But all these grimaces and airs and blandness with the patient do not for one moment deceive a person as shrewd as myself.

I feigned unconsciousness the last time Fossey called. He went away after a while. I took the opportunity of slipping from my bedchamber—Jane now sleeps apart, on the excuse of my illness—and putting on a robe descended to the lower floor of the house. I could hear muffled voices from the dining room. The door was ajar. Looking in I saw Spiros hand Fossey some strange, greenish-hued capsules. I see what he is at. What a mercy I came down.

Fossey tried to introduce Spiros' poison among my medicaments tonight. He handed me the deadly capsule together with a draught of water. On pretence of swallowing it I managed to drop it to the floor on the far side of the bed, where it rolled into a dark corner. Fossey seemed satisfied. I am better now and up and about again, working in my library. Spiros seemed puzzled the next time I encountered him in the corridor, as well he might. But for my shrewdness I should now be lying in the churchyard with its crooked headstones, which can be seen from the tallest attic of the house. If only I could talk to Jane, but she will not see me unless accompanied by a third person, usually Spiros or my housekeeper. And that will not do at all.

Thank God the knocking has not been heard for some time. I must take comfort from that. In my weakened condition it might have incalculable effects upon my general health. In the meantime I have resumed my studies, am even struggling on with the fourth volume of my sadly interrupted work. Thanks to the improved cones on the pressure lamps, which have just been delivered, my eyes are holding out. I could not bear it if eternal darkness should descend.

This was the situation which obtained for several weeks more; Jane remained aloof; the consultations with Spiros and Fossey continuing; the servants discreetly neutral; while I strove, under terrible conditions to bring my great work to a close. January of a new year came in thick with snow; I could not forbear contrasting my present straits with the happy New Year rituals Jane and I had been wont to share in earlier days. February followed with bleak winds and heavy rain. But my work was progressing well and it wanted but two or three pages more to round off the labour of more than half a life-time.

But at the same moment my health, which had been robust by my standards, began to worsen again. My eyesight too, troubled me

The Knocker At The Portico

and my peace of mind was tortured by Spiros' sly machinations. Twice had I caught him walking in the street with Jane; on another occasion I saw them one evening descending from a cab. I followed along the crooked alleys until I saw them go into the lantern-lit entrance of the Medical Institute. This situation seems to plunge me deeper into even darker subterranean passages of unfathomable depth.

5

The crisis has come. I am no longer my own master. I think that I have had more to bear than almost any wretch on earth. Tonight I finished my immense labours, wrote *fini* to the script with a triumphant flourish of my pen and flung the thing down. I even executed a little dance around the shadowy library, whose silence was broken only by the lonely hissing of the lamps. I sought the small liquor cabinet I keep in there, and poured myself a glass of port for a solitary toast.

I had no sooner lowered the glass than a splintering crash made the. whole building shudder; the amber liquid splashed in carmine rivulets across my manuscript as I staggered to my feet, my hands clasped over my ears to keep out the insane cacophony of those mighty thunder claps. I groaned aloud as the unseen knocker dispensed his mad tattoo; the crashing and pounding were enough to rend the door asunder and the echoes fled shrieking into every corner of the house.

I tottered from the library as the alarmed figure of my housekeeper crossed the hall below me. I descended the curving staircase in frenzy. We reached the door almost together. "What is it, woman?" I shouted, convinced that she knew something of this fearsome mystery which was slowly draining life itself from me. My wild and haggard eyes must have startled the woman because she fell back against the door as though she would prevent me from opening it.

"Mrs. Rayner is leaving, sir," she said.

"Leaving!" I shouted. "What means this?"

I pushed past her as a cab-wheel grated at the curb. Outside, through the porch window I could see Jane and Dr. Spiros, entering a barouche in the windy night. The glimmer of light from a nearby gas-lamp fell square upon Jane's face so that I could not be mistaken.

"Let me pass, woman," I told the housekeeper. She stood four-square against the door.

"It is better this way, sir," she said, with a white face. I was in a passion of rage by this time.

"Woman, you shall let me pass," I shrieked. There was a rack of Oriental curios inside the hall. Almost without realising it I found a Malay kris in my hand; I passed it not once but several times through her body, my hand seemingly without volition of its own. Horrified, I saw Mrs. Carfax hang there as though crucified, before sliding to the floor in bloody death. I opened the door and fled into the wild night.

I could hear the scraping of the barouche's wheels on the cobbles ahead of me. I followed, cutting through small alleys and courts. I knew this portion of the city intimately and by this method could be sure of keeping abreast of them. I still carried the knife, I know not why. Presently, I was in a deserted part of the metropolis, which was unknown to me; I could still hear the cab's progress but was obliged to keep it in sight, for fear of losing my way.

Presently it stopped in front of a fine, Georgian building with a large porch, lit by a brass lantern from above. Spiros, for I could now see clearly that it was he, paid off the cab and he and Jane entered the house. I waited until the barouche had disappeared. The street was quite empty and deserted. With a mad cry I rushed across to the house, from which light now shone brightly and seized the iron knocker.

As it crashed against the door, the same terrible thunder I had heard so many times, rushed upon me, seeming to mingle with the frenzied tattoo of which I was myself the author. I reeled in agony, clinging to the knocker. The knocking rose to a horrendous crescendo which seemed to penetrate and split my brain. A moment longer and the door was flung wide. I saw first the horrified face of a manservant, with Spiros and Jane behind him.

◈ The Knocker At The Portico

I screamed and sprang forward with the knife. "Wife-stealer!" I shouted and lunged at Spiros' throat. He was too quick and strong for me. He and the manservant attempted to pinion me. A terrible, silent struggle now began.

Jane was at my side, white and distraught. "Edward," she pleaded. "Dr. Spiros is only trying to help you as am I."

"Fools," I shrieked. "I am fully awake for the first time. It is he, THE KNOCKER, who is responsible!"

For I had looked beyond my struggling adversaries. It was indeed a dreadful sight. A tall, emaciated stranger, with parchment face, stubbled beard and the white hair of an old man. Pale yellow eyes proclaimed the madman. Then I reeled, my senses tottering, as the two men bore me down. Another servant produced a strait jacket.

As I went backwards a fearful mosaic formed before my eyes. I saw the knife in the madman's hand, still smeared with blood, and the sign in wrought iron over the porch: SPIROS ASYLUM FOR THE INSANE.

The truth was borne in upon me as my senses collapsed. For the back of the hall was a brightly illuminated mirror and this pitiful madman reflected in the glare, with writhing features and foaming jaws was beyond all mortal help. THE KNOCKER AT THE PORTICO was MYSELF!

◈ 6

The manuscript had a note attached to it in another hand. It said that the Patient 642 had spent three and thirty years in the asylum and had died there at the age of seventy-eight.

I put back the papers in the box and sat in thought. My name is also Edward Rayner. I am the third son of a third son. The writer of the narrative was my great-grandfather. I heard the knocking for the first time tonight.

ॐ The Second Passenger

ॐ 1

MR. REGINALD BRAINTREE SAT QUITE STILL IN THE CORNER of the fusty third-class compartment, with his feet up on the opposite seat and a copy of *The Times* spread-eagled on his lap. The carriage was quite empty and had been since he left Charing Cross so the liberty was pardonable. Outside, the blurred scenery of wood and stream whirled effortlessly by, the white-grey smoke from the engine fogging the windows and restricting the vision. The noise of the wheels went monotonously on and on, as though some tireless hand were rhythmically beating time in some fantastic computation.

Dusk was closing in and the carriage lights shed their yellow glare on to the wan face of Mr. Braintree, making his usually pale features look macabre. They heightened the sombre effect of his never genial eyes, distorting them into black pits, from which his pupils gleamed, greenishly and balefully. His mouth was a mere slit in the twilight, the shadow underneath making it resemble a letter box which, metaphorically speaking, it was.

He was dressed in a faded suit of salt and pepper broadcloth. His stout brown shoes were scratched and worn but they did not look old; his hat was battered, yet it did not seem antique. In short Mr. Braintree was a successful man who could afford to dress well yet did not choose to, a thing not entirely unknown among a certain class of business men.

ℐ The Second Passenger

His paper, stirred by some motion of the train, slipped unheeded to the floor, and he did not bother to pick it up. His figure slumped at the sudden motion when the carriage rounded a bend and then he automatically recovered himself as it regained the straight. In a way the railway was something like the course of Mr. Braintree's own career; it ploughed remorselessly on, unable to leave its designated route and when at length it came to a hill, instead of going round, it smashed an impetuous path through.

There were times when Mr. Braintree lapsed into compassion but they were few for he did not care to make a cult of weakness, as he called it. His first day as an office boy in a stockbroking firm in Cheapside many years before had taught him the efficacy of force, a lesson he had never forgotten; and which ever since he had used to determine the course of his life. The occasion was common enough, yet it left an everlasting impression.

It appeared that it was the duty of a certain Samuel Briggs, also a species of clerk, to fill the inkwells and run the errands, in addition to his other multifarious duties. However, being the type of person who will never do a thing if he can get someone else to do it for him, he somewhat naturally chose the moment of the newcomer's arrival to assert his authority. Unfortunately, from his point of view, the other clerks were big and determined men, not at all disposed to run his errands for him, but the entry of the diminutive Braintree altered the picture completely.

His first commissions were executed willingly enough and without suspicion, but later, one of the other employees having let something drop, young Braintree began to see the true situation, and not having a vacuum where his brain should be, sought to escape from this unwelcome and decidedly irksome yoke. The first hint of mutiny was met with black looks and a clenching of fists which, although subduing Braintree for a time, did not permanently dampen his resolution to be rid of his bondage.

The next time the dapper young gentleman told him to empty the waste paper baskets and be quick about it, this spate of rhetoric being accompanied by a well-propelled kick in the rear, the younger's temper flared. Impetuously turning, he flung the contents of the inkwell he was carrying full into the sneering, weakly handsome face of the clerk before him. The next moments were somewhat hazy for he was picked up violently, shaken like a rat and, with a vicious backhanded slap in the face, hurled unceremoniously downstairs.

As he dazedly came to rest in the hallway he heard the malicious laughter of his contemporaries floating down towards him, and the sound was like gall to his already bitter soul. Spitting curses through the mask of blood that covered his features, he swore then and there to get even with his tormentor if it took him all his life. This resolve was interrupted by the appearance of the bedraggled form of Mr. Samuel Briggs at the head of the stairway, wiping some of the ink off his mottled countenance and transferring it to a convenient towel.

But although defeated physically, Braintree had gained an enormous moral victory over his opponent, for the confidence of the bully had been shaken, and from then on his manner was less assured. The younger boy received fewer commissions and they gradually stopped. But his dark brooding spirit still rankled over the day of his degradation and the promise he had compacted with himself remained as implacable as ever.

As he grew older his feelings became more subdued and subtle, and it would have needed a very shrewd and worldly person to see that the two clerks who worked so amicably together were in reality deadly enemies, each determined to usurp the other in the estimation of their employer, should the opportunity present itself. If it were Braintree who arrived early one morning, filled the inkwells, tidied the office and waded through arrears of work, then one could be sure that it was Briggs who sat up half the night sweating over a mountain of paper.

Was it not Briggs who cycled five miles through the pouring rain to old Mr. Steyning's house with some important documents that had been overlooked? And yet had not Braintree been just as meritorious in returning from a fortnight's holiday on his first day away, in order to tell Mr. Steyning of an important business speculation which he had learned en route? Who ran for the doctor when Mrs. Steyning was ill? Briggs, of course. And who summoned the courage to risk serious injury by rescuing the old man's daughter from the wheels of a bus? Braintree, naturally.

The Second Passenger

Finally, what cloak of generosity masked the actions of two unscrupulous men who eventually jointly subscribed the money needed to put the firm on its feet again? As sure as the earth revolves round the sun it was Briggs and Braintree, but that their actions were motivated by quixotic impulse is beyond imagination. Yet later it did not seem that they had been risking anything at all. For when their employer's anxiety with regard to the future of his organisation was allayed, he naturally turned to the men who had made this reversal possible.

The result was a junior partnership for both of them, an opportunity which neither of them neglected. From that time onwards their careers were set. With the passing of the years, while increasing in prosperity, they never forgot for a single moment that they were enemies, and though no one could have divined it, the germs of hatred were breeding and multiplying within their respective brains.

Things might have gone on like this for ever except for one fact. Mr. Steyning was growing old, his business prospering and with two capable junior partners to all appearances contentedly running things, he saw no reason why he should not sit back and put the reins unreservedly into their hands. So he retired and sealed their fates by so doing.

Without the old man's restraining influence the two men immediately fell apart again, and although no one would have seen any outward difference between them, their consuming passions were more openly manifest than usual. Their morning greeting was elaborately polite, almost to the verge of irony, while now and again, the masks slipping, cutting remarks would whip about the office, to the bewilderment of those who heard them.

Everyone began to suspect that something was wrong, and the clerks, on the same stools which had accommodated their employers years before, to whisper and gossip among themselves. The business too, began to suffer. Each of the partners, in his eagerness to outdo the other, eventually deprived himself of the benefits of their transactions. With the curb of Mr. Steyning's presence acting as a restraint to their impatient spirits they were safe; without him they were lost.

Darkness, Mist & Shadow

The affair swiftly progressed to an open rift, culminating in Braintree's discovery of Briggs' misdemeanours. The whole truth of the matter was never really discovered; some said women, some said horses were the reason, but the upshot of it was that Briggs had been spending above even his considerable income. Neither had families to tie them down in any way, for both men were bachelors, and thus there were no domestic questions.

For almost a year, considerable sums of money had been taken by Briggs and only covered by dexterous and skilful handling of the books. Perhaps it was a malicious and selfish ego that enjoyed and exulted in the fact of cheating a hated partner out of the money, or a pressing and desperate need, the step being taken only after long consideration; the truth will possibly never be known.

Discovery could not be postponed indefinitely; the misdemeanour uncovered some time. The denouement occurred on a cold March morning, when the rime sparkled on pavement and railing and fog hung like a thick yellow cloak over the city. Braintree was in an unusually foul temper, even for him, and strode through the outer office, looking neither right nor left, responding with a grunt to the chorus of salutations from the staff.

Briggs, a tall, sallow man with pock-marked cheeks was already seated at his desk sipping a measure of whisky from the cap of a silver hip flask, to take 'the nip off the air', as he explained it.

"It would be more to the point if you attended more closely to the firm's affairs, instead of indulging in that debasing practice," Braintree sneered, for he was a strict teetotaller. The other, however, said nothing, which was unusual for him and the younger man commented on it.

Briggs' eyes were beginning to burn angrily and he half slewed on his seat, his right hand methodically screwing the cap of his flask; he twisted it savagely as though it were the thick head of his enemy. He opened his mouth to spit out a reply when the door was pushed back by the head clerk; he looked agitated and white.

"It's about the accounts, sir," he jerked hesitantly.

Braintree excused himself and went off irritably; if there was one thing he disliked it was any interruption to the smooth routine of the office. He was away a long time and Briggs sat staring moodily at the

ℐ The Second Passenger

swirling fog outside the window; he made no attempt to deal with the jumble of documents on the desk before him. He was still sitting there when Braintree came back. He glanced coldly at his partner before crossing to his desk. He took something from a drawer and then re-locked it.

"I shall be some time," he told Briggs in a hostile voice.

The door clicked to behind him. Briggs took another swig from the flask and re-stoppered it. He toyed idly with a bunch of keys, his hands suddenly sweaty. Perhaps he did not move into the outer office because he was already acquainted with what would be found there. The clock ticked away while he listened with straining ears. There was the confused murmur of voices, mingled with the jingling of keys and rustling of papers.

The whispered consultations were still going on when Briggs left for lunch; they went on throughout the afternoon and eventually night fell again. Instead of leaving for his home as he usually did Briggs remained behind at his desk. The fog pressed sullenly against the window. He heard the outer office door close behind the last of the clerks, waited for the heavy footfall of his partner. It was nearly seven o'clock before the door of the inner office opened again.

The stocky form of the younger partner appeared. His manner was extremely mild when he spoke, yet the curious pose of his body suggested the coiling of a steel spring. Briggs had not moved; he gazed abstractedly across the office, as though trying to discern whether the Chinaman on the commercial calendar was grimacing or smiling. He felt like doing neither. He lifted his face, his forehead slightly shiny, and coughed; a nervous, startled cough, which sounded incongruous in the pregnant stillness.

"Well?"

It was Braintree who spoke. He stood by the back of the other's chair, his thick knuckles gleaming white where he clenched the woodwork.

"You know?" the other answered dully. "You've found out?"

Braintree nodded. He kept remarkable control. His voice was dry and smooth, as though a life's ambition had been achieved. "But twenty thousand, Briggs..."

He looked curiously at the still figure of his partner.

"How did you expect to get away with it?"

Briggs turned away from Braintree with a convulsive movement. He put his head in his hands.

"I wouldn't expect you to understand," he said. "What are you going to do?"

"Do?" said Braintree. He looked at his watch. "I've already done it. I've sent Simmonds round with a note to the station. The police should be here in twenty minutes."

"A bit premature aren't you?" Briggs sneered.

Red stood out in vivid patches on his cheeks and his breathing was becoming laboured.

"I don't think so," said Braintree smoothly. "It is a criminal matter, after all. Such a huge sum of money. And your personal accounts should tally with the discrepancy."

He started back as Briggs got up with a sudden movement.

"You're enjoying this, aren't you?" said Briggs thickly.

Braintree declined to answer. He went to the window and watched the swirling fog. He toyed nervously with the heavy office ruler in his hand.

"I suppose it's no good asking you for an hour's grace?" said Briggs heavily.

Braintree shook his head. He had a sardonic smile on his lips. "None at all," he said. "You should have thought of this before. I must advise you against attempting to leave. I should be forced to prevent it."

He hefted the massive, metal-edged ruler in his hand uncertainly. Indeed, he was a somewhat incongruous figure and obviously ill-fitted for the self-appointed task. Briggs stared incredulously at him for a moment. Then he gave a short, barking laugh.

"I'm off," he said. "To blazes with you and your police."

He strode impetuously forward, thrusting Braintree aside. The partner fell against the window; he felt a sharp pain as his hand broke the glass. The sudden shock stung him into action. Briggs was at the door when Braintree reached him. The two men began a silent struggle; then Braintree was thrown aside. He fell against the desk this time and barked his shin; this second, unexpected pain sent a spurt of anger through him. Galvanised into action he struck at Briggs again and again with the heavy ruler.

Briggs gave a hoarse cry. The big man turned. Braintree saw blood on his face, the eyes filmy and horrified. He felt sick. The older man fell asprawl with a crash. His head caught the edge of the desk with a horrifying crack. He lay still. Braintree bent over him, searched for the steady pump of the heart, failed to find it. His own heart stood still.

Then another sound sent the adrenalin flooding through his own system. He started dragging the body of Briggs along the floor towards the cupboard as heavy footsteps sounded on the stair.

2

It was nearly eleven before Mr. Braintree reached the Essex marshes. It had been a long and tiring drive through East London and the little Morris was not behaving well. Braintree believed it might be the effect of the damp weather and one defective plug. He had not liked it at all when the vehicle had stalled completely at a traffic lights in Walthamstow.

But now he was clear of the more populous areas and he breathed more easily, the car positively humming along. The moon was up and its pallid light cast shadows across the humped form of Briggs on the back seat, covered by thick layers of motoring rugs. It had been a miracle that Briggs had driven his own car in from Surrey that day, Braintree reflected.

Once he had got rid of the police by telling them that Briggs had left, it had been fairly simple to bring the car to the seldom-used side alley and take the body down the back stair. Fairly simple, but how tiring, Braintree thought. Now, he had the perfect answer to the problem.

With Briggs' disappearance he had only to drive his car back to the nearest Tube and abandon it. When it was found it would merely add substance to the circumstance that Briggs had been unable to face the music and had fled. Braintree would have to stay in town tonight; that was the only flaw in his plan. By the time he got back to Central London his last train from Charing Cross would have long gone and he had no desire to wait for the early morning paper train in this weather.

He must be careful, that was all; he had no luggage. He would simply register under another name, carefully choosing a small family hotel away from the city centre and tell them the truth; that he had missed his train. There must be many businessmen who were in a similar predicament, every evening. The more Braintree thought about it on his long, foggy drive, the more he liked it. He was free of the villages at last and making for a spot he remembered from years before. Unless it had been built up since then.

He took a rutted side road, the Morris protesting at the surface, and drove carefully along it. The fog had lifted with his clearing the city and he knew where he was. When he had driven as far as he could go, he left the car; the next hour, dragging Briggs' heavy form through the undergrowth was the most tiring he had ever known. When his feet began to squelch in mud he looked down; his prints were already beginning to fill with water. It was nearly time. He got his hands under Briggs' armpits and dragged him the last few yards to the top of the bank.

He was sweating as he gave the final push. The body rocked, sagged and then started to slide down the steep slope. The moon gilded the dead face as it slid to a halt; green scum parted, viscous mud sucked at the corpse. It began to sink slowly, bubbles of marsh gas bursting in foul, scummy pustules on the surface of the swamp. Mr. Braintree waited for twenty minutes until the entire corpse had been consumed. The last thing to go was one of Briggs' hands. It seemed to wave a valediction at Braintree as the fingers slowly disappeared beneath the surface.

Braintree shivered. It was growing cold again. Or the effect of his exercise was wearing off. He waited a few minutes more and finally the bubbles stopped coming to the top. The green scum of the surface resumed its interrupted sway. Mr. Braintree made his way heavily back to the road. No one would ever find Briggs now. That swamp was bottomless, he'd heard in years gone by; what it took it kept. He looked at his watch. It was already nearly 1:00 A.M. It seemed like a long drive back towards the city.

3

The train roared on through the night and still Mr. Braintree sat comfortably sprawled with his feet up and his antique hat poised beside him. Presently there came the hiss of brakes and the carriage shuddered and was still. Came the burst of escaping steam and a nervous little pulse beat somewhere under the floorboards. Figures went by in the corridor and, after glancing at the uninviting figure of the stockbroker, their owners passed on.

Carriage doors were slamming and the hoarse, inarticulate cry of a porter drifted up wind. "Sevenoaks, Sevenoaks."

A railway employee came down the carriages, slamming the doors. He caught sight of Mr. Braintree's recumbent form and slid back the door of the compartment, annoyance on his face.

"This train doesn't go any farther, sir."

Mr. Braintree's body sagged, asprawl at an awkward angle.

The porter bent over him, hesitated. His nostrils were assailed by a loathsome stench. He saw then, in the dim radiance of the carriage lighting, a patch of damp green slime on the floor. It glimmered wetly and the stench seemed to come from this. Fighting his nerves the porter seized Mr. Braintree by the shoulder.

The dead face fell forward and the man was conscious of the slime on the features; something like moss clustered round the nostrils and a thin driblet shuddered from the corner of the mouth. A shadow fell across the carriage and the figure of a tall, burly man passed in the corridor. The porter gave a hoarse shout and stumbled away from the corpse of Braintree.

"Just a minute, sir," he called after the tall figure. "There's been an accident."

On the platform the big man marched forward under the lamps without stopping. At every footprint green slime seemed to spring up on the surface of the platform. The porter cursed as he almost sprawled on the muck. There was that disgusting smell again. The big man went on. The porter increased his pace.

"Stop him!" he bawled at a group of railwaymen who were gossiping at one end of the platform.

They looked up curiously as the form of the big man went steadily up the steps of the bridge. He did not seem to be hurrying but the porter was unable to gain on him.

He shouted again and this time the group was stirred into action. Its members ran up the stairs, searching for the tall figure. One of them turned as the porter came up.

"What was it? What was it?" he said, his eyes wide with fear. There were patches of green slime on the steps of the bridge. A putrefying stench came to them down the wind. But the tall, hurrying figure of the big man was never seen again.

◈ The Recompensing of Albano Pizar

◈ 1

AFTER LEON FREITAS HAD BEEN DEAD FOR SEVERAL MONTHS, a literary agent of notorious dubiety, determined to extract the last ounce of gold from the great author's accumulated dross, tracked down his widow, who was living in seclusion in a small resort in southern Italy. The Palazzo Tortini, though dilapidated and in disrepair, a relic of the great days of the Borgias and the Medicis, was real enough and the rent, modest in terms of today's money, meant little to Mme. Freitas who was more than well provided for from her husband's estate.

A well-preserved woman in her late forties, Mme. Freitas still retained traces of great and original beauty; her days were spent not in idle reminiscence or in vain recall of time gone by, as might have befitted a great man's widow, but in the writing of her own memoirs, the annotating of her husband's papers and in the indexing and cross-referencing of his work.

Though she might have employed an army of secretaries for this purpose—thirteen volumes of her husband's still remained to be issued posthumously—she preferred to do this herself and so found her days filled with satisfying literary labour and her nights with agreeable and diversified social life.

Her only close friend in the small community in the resort she had chosen was a Dr. Manzanares, who had once been called in to treat her for a minor ailment and had become her most intimate com-

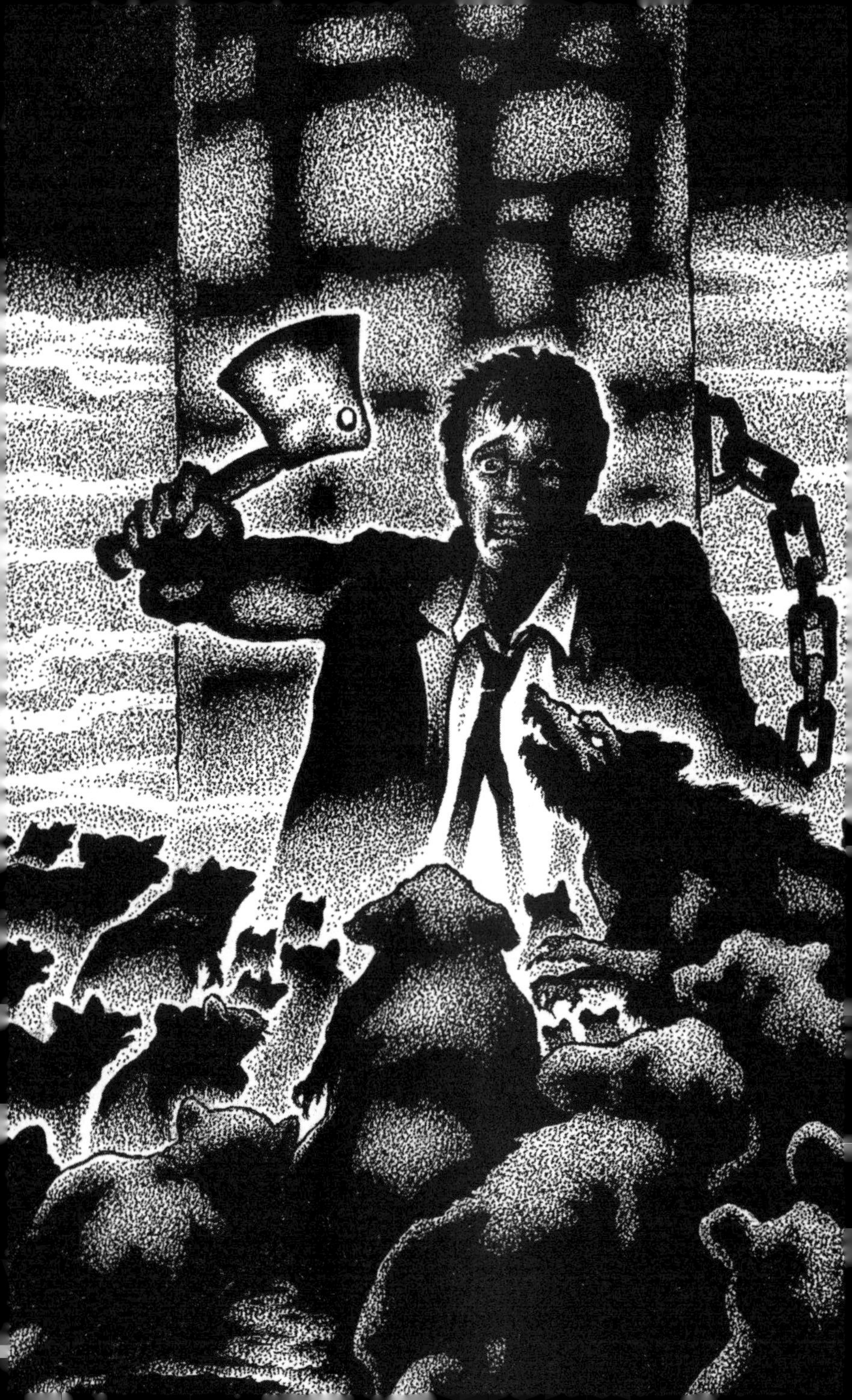

panion. Dr. Manzanares, in addition to being an admirer of the work of Leon Freitas, was also a doctor of philosophy and had himself written a number of monographs on obscure philosophers. The atmosphere of the Palazzo Tortini was agreeably outre to one of his tastes and predilections; the charm of Mme. Freitas undeniable; her cuisine excellent; and, above all, the ambiance of literary endeavour and past greatness fascinating to a man of his character.

The Palazzo Tortini stood on the banks of a canal, which gave it the atmosphere of Venice; the canal in turn drained into the sea at no great distance. It was thus necessarily tidal and indeed the canal overflowed into the great vaulted cellars of the Palace so that at the height of the two tides every twenty-four hours, all the gloomy lower portions of the mansion were filled with the melancholy echo of the sea.

Mme. Freitas recalled little of Albano Pizar and it was her infallible rule not to see persons on business connected with her late husband's estate; all his literary properties were pledged to the splendid houses in half a dozen countries who had published him during his life-time. And yet there was something about Pizar's cleverly worded prefatory letter that touched a chord of compassion somewhere in her being. As she read on, she remembered something of him, and recollected a pale, almost ethereal-looking young man who had originally been a publisher's reader in Rome.

But he had aspired to greater things and after—no one knew how—purchasing a share in a minor but greatly respected publishing house in Paris, had edited and issued finely illustrated collections of her husband's then little-known short stories. That had been in earlier days, of course, when Pizar had become a prosperous and fairly successful young man and her husband had yet to make his way; ironically, as the name of Freitas had ascended and had eventually become one of the most resplendent in European literature and belles-lettres so had Pizar's star gone into eclipse.

The publishing house had failed, he had disappeared into obscurity for a time; but then, as sometimes happens when men of little talent but keen business acumen fall on hard days, this had acted as a spur to his industry and a sharpener of his abilities so that, like a drowning man, he had once again managed to raise himself above the flood.

This time he had started a small literary agency; as is the way with many such businesses where partners come and go and authors, as they become successful, pass on to greater things, his fortunes had fluctuated. From year to year it had not been possible to foresee the swing of the pendulum, he wrote Mme. Freitas; presuming on an old friendship he hoped to visit her at a convenient date when he had a proposition to discuss.

She gathered that, recalling with some emotion the success of the early short stories which had been issued under his imprimis, Pizar was again hoping for a similar miracle. Among Freitas' old papers he trusted to find some fragments not thought worthwhile by more august houses; these, with some introductory notes and addenda by himself, he would then bring out through a publishing house in which he had some interest and so retrieve his fortunes.

All this, of course, he did not put into his letter, but that was what Mme. Freitas read into it. When she had finished she put down the closely-written pages with a sigh and clasped her hands together on the red-leather surface of the heavy desk on which she customarily worked. The brilliance of the Italian sun fell through the oriel windows of the big study and sparkled on the gilt bindings of the ancient leather volumes of the classics which her husband had gathered together during the course of a long literary career.

For more than an hour Mme. Freitas hesitated over the contents of this letter; her secretary arrived at the study at the time she usually took notes, waited for a while, and was then dismissed. At last Mme. Freitas became aware that her day, which usually ran so smoothly from dawn to its predestined end among the silver, brandy glasses and Sevres coffee cups of her dining room, was fatally disrupted. She rang for her car and was swiftly driven to the home of Dr. Manzanares.

The conversation, after passing lightly over topics which concerned them, at last turned to the literary agent Pizar; the letter was produced and the problem discussed. Normally Mme. Freitas would have dictated a gentle letter of refusal but she felt she owed something to the shadowy figure that Pizar had been in those far-off days in Rome and Paris. And he had been instrumental in launching the earlier works of Freitas to the wider world. If he came to the Palazzo there could not be much for him; Freitas' output was bound to certain publishing houses for ever. But there might be a few crumbs; the question was whether it would be worth his while to come. Mme. Freitas did not want to hold out too much hope lest he might be disappointed.

Dr. Manzanares was not enthusiastic; his only contact with literary agents had been little short of disastrous. His voice rose and he gesticulated frequently as the conversation went on. His cry of ten per cent began to sound like a knell to Mme. Freitas' deafened ears. Eventually she burst out laughing; an outburst in which the learned doctor was at last persuaded to join. She would write then, she decided; she would leave it to Pizar as to whether he came. She would promise nothing; but there might be something. The friends left it at that.

Mme. Freitas wrote a short note to the agent and then, in the general press of a busy life, forgot the matter; she had no reply and as week succeeded week Pizar's request faded to the back of her mind. But she had gone through some of her husband's papers; there was little of value that was not already committed. An early poem or two; some youthful letters; two or three essays which had appeared in obscure magazines and had never subsequently been reprinted.

Something might be made of this melange, but she doubted it. Looking at the racks of bound memoirs, correspondence and confidential documents that flowed across the great room in unbroken ranks of blue, red, green and yellow, each colour denoting a different genre of her husband's life-work, Mme. Freitas rather hoped that Pizar would not come. The little that she could spare from this vast oeuvre would seem incomparably mean; then she shrugged her shoulders. Business was business and if Pizar could make a little from the scraps flung him—in any event there was no need for her to feel guilty. And she had not asked him to come.

More than a month had gone by before she got the letter; Pizar had been away from Paris; he understood her position; he would be delighted to make the trip. He suggested a date, said he would tele-

◈ Darkness, Mist & Shadow

phone when he arrived at the station. One afternoon of torpid heat when the sun shimmered like molten metal in even the darkest recesses of the cool rooms of the Palazzo, Mme. Freitas was informed by her secretary that Pizar had telephoned to announce his arrival. She despatched the car to meet him, vaguely uneasy at something which could be only a routine matter. She went upstairs to change her dress; ordered some lemon tea, some minute sandwiches, the kind she liked most of all, and some eclairs, for an hour's time. Then she went to her study and composed herself to wait.

Mme. Freitas rose to greet her guest when the woman secretary brought him to her; her first feeling was of ludicrous disappointment, though what she expected of the interview it would be hard to say. For Albano Pizar was a pompous man of decidedly vast proportions; the remains of a handsome head rested on massive shoulders but the rest of him had run to flesh and the elegance of his well-cut grey suit could not conceal the huge pouches of his capacious stomach. The pale, interesting youth he had once been fled before Mme. Freitas and in place of this blurred memory was the hard reality of the present: a commonplace fat man with hard blue eyes and a limp black moustache.

But his manners were beautiful and she soon forgot the grossness of his exterior envelope as she rang for the tea and they chatted like old friends; for his own part Pizar was estimating the value of the documents, private papers and other débris of Leon Freitas' long and rich life which had been left behind, much as the receding tide leaves its deposits on the shore, and his shrewd glance was raking across what seemed to be acres of shelving.

In the meantime he munched delicately at the sandwiches, mentally cursing his hostess' sparse appetite—the train journey had been long and slow, as is the Italian custom, and there had been no buffet car—tinkled his silver spoon against the rim of his china cup and listened to Mme. Freitas' small-talk with feigned interest. That had always been infallible in his line of business, especially with ladies from whom there was much to be hoped; so Albano Pizar, who had a thousand dreams riding on the wings of this interview, crossed his plump ankles encased in the silver-grey silk socks, nodded wisely from time to time and continued to rake the shelves with his seemingly lethargic gaze; estimating, assessing, scheming, devouring, while all the time he kept up the polished mechanisms of polite conversation expected in the world in which he usually moved.

After the éclairs, which were more to Pizar's taste, the talk passed almost imperceptibly to business and at length, after more than, two hours, to the subject of Pizar's visit. Without raising too many hopes, said Mme. Freitas—after all, none should know better than her visitor that the whole of her husband's literary estate was committed to existing publishers—she had been able to scrape together some material; part of it previously unpublished. She did not know whether it might make a small volume, perhaps two, if he cared to take it on; she was sorry, it was all she could offer.

Though seemingly calm, Pizar was inwardly excited and hardly able to contain himself; his hopes had been rising throughout the interview. However, he remained master of his nerves, merely looked at his hostess with narrowed eyes and continued to puff with empty confidence at the cigar he had lit at Mme. Freitas' graciously extended permission. He was well aware, he said, of Madame's generosity; more than he could say. It would be impossible to know what might be made of the material without careful examination; could he borrow the documents if Madame raised no objection?

He had already engaged a room at a nearby hotel and intended to spend that evening in going through the papers to see what sort of book they would make. He would then call on Madame the following day, if she were agreeable. He thanked her for her offer of accommodation at the Palazzo but the arrangement he had already made would do nicely; he had already taken up too much of her time. If he could have the material, he would take his leave and return the following afternoon.

Mme. Freitas agreed to Pizar's proposals without raising any objection, much to the latter's surprise; she excused herself for a moment and unlocked a drawer of the desk. She took out a red leather folder containing the documents in question; the clasp was locked. She handed the folder to Pizar, together with the key, enjoining him to take great care of the contents. Scarcely able to credit his good fortune Pizar stammered his thanks. Five minutes later, in Mme. Freitas' car on his way back to the hotel, he was unlocking the folder with trembling fingers.

2

Punctually at three the following afternoon Pizar was back at the Palazzo Tortini. The interview again took place in the great study where Mme. Freitas worked. Pizar had spent long hours the previous evening on the contents of the folder, his heart sinking lower as the night progressed. A cursory examination of the original material had left him with very little hope that his visit had been successful; later and more detailed examination had confirmed it. He had returned to the Palazzo with a desperate plan half formulated in his mind.

The interview passed much as before, except that on this occasion Mme. Freitas offered him stronger refreshment. Ice clinked coolly in the glasses and as the oddly assorted couple discussed the possibilities of the book, Pizar waited for the opportunity which he knew must come if only he had the patience. So he spun out the conversation as long as he decently could; went into much pretended detail over the projected manuscript; world rights, royalties and so forth; and all the while as Mme. Freitas bent over the desk, studying the legal points he had enumerated for her approval, his eyes were searching the crowded shelves.

His chance came much sooner than he had supposed. The secretary appeared at the door of the study to say that Dr. Manzanares had called to see Madame; she hesitated a moment and then excused herself. To Pizar's delight the secretary followed her, closing the door behind her. Pizar sat very still, the drumming of his fingers on the surface of the desk the only outward sign of his nervous tension; he opened the red leather folder, left the key ready in the lock. His eyes once again raked the shelves, the red, the green, the blue and the yellow whirling into one blurred effect to his overheated gaze.

He was still sitting at the desk, the folder locked, when Mme. Freitas returned ten minutes later. She excused herself, with many apologies;

The Recompensing Of Albano Pizar

asked if he would stay to tea. Pizar declined with thanks, glancing at his watch; it had been a great pleasure. He had much to do, but he would write. A few minutes later he had left, the leather folder clutched firmly under his arm, while Mme. Freitas went back into the drawing room to attend to the needs of her second guest.

Later that night, when Dr. Manzanares telephoned the hotel, he was told that Pizar had left on the eight o'clock train. Doubtless he would be in Rome by this time. The doctor smiled grimly to himself. Doubtless. He consulted his watch, rummaged in his time-tables. Pizar would have just made the connection for Paris. He drew the telephone towards him and dialled the Palazzo Tortini.

The matter was serious enough; for, two hours after Albano Pizar had departed from the palace so hurriedly, Mme. Freitas, returning to her study, had discovered that some of the files had been disarranged. Slowly, but with mounting alarm she had gone through the documents with her secretary. A number were missing; the loss was not serious so far as record purposes were concerned. Mme. Freitas had copies of everything on file. But most of the missing documents were letters Freitas had once written to a lady with whom he had become rashly involved; they were of a sensational nature and were marked not for publication during the lifetime of Mme. Freitas.

The implications were plain; by a lucky coincidence Pizar, the type of man for whom fortune occasionally relents, had lighted on the two files which were immediately saleable for his purposes. Mme. Freitas turned white; she was a Sicilian and of a proud stock. She had a long memory and a hard, unforgiving nature. She breathed deeply when she saw the extent of the damage Pizar might be able to inflict and Dr. Manzanares was immediately recalled to the Palazzo. Then followed various phone calls culminating in the information that Pizar was presumably on the Paris express.

Little could be done at that moment but what might be managed through legal and other channels was put into immediate operation; scandal threatened the great author's reputation and Mme. Freitas spent lavishly in order to bring Pizar's plans to nothing. But he seemed to have disappeared; no information was forthcoming.

There was silence for more than two months and then the explosion occurred.

Despite the risk of libel, the copyright nature of the letters and the embargo on their publication, certain scandalous magazines, notably in London, Paris, and Rome, printed simultaneous articles on Freitas, obviously based on the contents of the letters. So carefully had the matter been dealt with that Mme. Freitas' legal advisers were powerless to act. The storm grew and the press were actually besieging the doors of the Palazzo at the height of the publicity.

Mme. Freitas, accompanied by Dr. Manzanares, fled to a retreat in the Umbrian Hills until the clamour should have died away; in the meantime Pizar was interviewed on the television and radio channels of several European countries, more stories followed and even learned and respectable journals in more than a dozen countries were running speculative articles on what had become one of the most interesting literary memoirs of the century. To all the publicity Mme. Freitas maintained a deaf ear and a stone face. But she passed many hours of quiet reflection; she had been duped and exploited by a man of mean spirit to whom she had intended to do a kindness and she could not and would not forget.

She and Dr. Manzanares, in their endless conferences, estimated that Pizar could not have made less than £25,000 to £30,000 out of the stolen letters and this fact burned with a sort of sullen inflammation in the widow's mind. Pizar's solicitors had eventually replied to her own lawyers and the ineffective exchanges of ponderously worded letters had dragged on over the months without coming to any definite conclusion. In the end Mme. Freitas had given instructions that any projected suit should be dropped and the literary furore gradually died down.

But Mme. Freitas had not forgotten and she was dumbfounded to receive for her approval some three months after this, proofs of the book Pizar had originally solicited from her. All during the long months of scandal and notoriety she and Pizar had never exchanged a letter and the receipt of the projected volume assumed an air of complete unreality in her mind. Dr. Manzanares' indignation had no end but he was completely stupefied when Mme. Freitas merely initialled the proofs and sent them back to Pizar's publishers. Surely Madame did not intend to let this unspeakable rascal exploit her further, he spluttered.

But Mme. Freitas smiled a cold, quiet smile which promised many things and Dr. Manzanares was persuaded into silence. The widow thought long on the topic. Like all Sicilians she had infinite patience and she waited with confidence for an opportunity to strike at the man who had done her family name such harm. In the event it was a whole year after the publication of the Pizar-inspired Freitas work before the widow made her move. In the meantime she had received a considerable sum in royalties from Pizar and a personal letter—the first since his flight from her house.

He mentioned nothing but business matters, hoped she was well and rendered a strict account of all sales. He was her devoted servant etc etc Mme. Freitas smiled a colder smile than ever.

A month later she replied. Dr. Manzanares was never able to discover what she had written in the letter; it must have been couched in such subtle and enticing terms that Pizar could not, as a man of business, afford to ignore it. Even so, he must have sensed a considerable amount of danger in again venturing into the Palazzo Tortini and Dr. Manzanares guessed that his deliberations had taken agonizing days and nights before cupidity won out over his natural fears.

Dr. Manzanares was astonished to hear from his old friend one sultry afternoon in July that Mme. Freitas had received a reply from Pizar; he was on his way, he would be there that afternoon.

Once again Pizar was driven out from the station in Mme. Freitas' car; he was sullen and on guard though not unprepared for scenes and arguments. His fleshy face looked more debased with the grosser pleasures of the world than ever. To his surprise Mme. Freitas made no reference to the letters. She received him in the study as before and had evidently put herself out to be charming to him. She congratulated him on the success of the Freitas volume and on the perspicacity and understanding with which he had edited and introduced it.

Pizar bowed stiffly; the inside of his collar was wet with cold sweat; he was ill at ease and something told him that the situation was very wrong. They drank tea and ate sandwiches for an hour. Then Mme. Freitas kindly thanked him for his visit and dismissed him. Pizar was stunned. He blinked, his eyes turning to her curiously, as though he had heard amiss.

"Pardon, Madame," he stammered, rising to his feet. "But I understood from your letter... There were to be other documents released... it says here..."

"I do not care what it says there," said Mme. Freitas coldly, her manner completely changed. "I have no more to say to you."

"But Madame..." Pizar began again. Sweat ran down his forehead into his eyes, momentarily blinding him.

"I have made this long and expensive journey from Paris for a specific purpose. I have hotel and other expenses. I shall have wasted a week... I demand recompense for my trouble and monetary outlay."

"Recompense!" exploded Mme. Freitas. She looked at Albano Pizar and her eyes roved over him in a cold and knowing manner which sent tremors coursing through his blood.

"You demand recompense, M. Pizar."

She stood up with a brusque movement that transfixed him where he stood.

"Very well," she said at length. "You shall be recompensed. Come with me. My husband left other bequests, which I think may interest you. Only this time you must pay the full price."

She led the way out of the study and along a corridor hung with tapestries and lit by crystal chandeliers which were now turned over to electric light. Pizar panted alongside, momentarily regretting his outburst.

"Pardon, Madame," he said. "If I inadvertently said anything—"

"Enough, M. Pizar," said Madame icily. "You have made your choice. You demanded recompense. And recompense you shall have."

The pair went down an ornate iron staircase; the contrast here to the rest of the Palazzo was marked and severe. Dusty, naked electric bulbs made harsh shadows as they descended and the silhouettes of the great author's widow and the literary agent were grotesque and

⚜ The Recompensing Of Albano Pizar

distended on the discoloured walls. She was silent until they came out on to a stone-flagged corridor at some distance below the house.

"My late husband had a little cabinet here, M. Pizar," she said. "Here he devoted himself to experiments in coarser fields of literature..."

She did not enlarge but her meaning was plain. Pizar's eye began to glisten. Pornography? Was it pornography she meant? If so... He sucked in his breath and then had to hurry to keep up. It was a curious room, Pizar saw, when she opened the door; evidently part of the great days of the Palazzo Tortini. Chandeliers with huge candles, now thick with dust; sagging bookcases, seemingly held together by the weight of the rotting leather volumes they held; red leather walls. He stared, fascinated. He had never seen anything like this. He bent to the bureau Mme. Freitas indicated. The curtains billowed behind him but his greedy eyes had time only to see the spidery handwriting before him. Then the world span and consciousness faded.

Dr. Manzanares stepped out from behind the moth-eaten curtain and looked ruefully at the sprawled form of Pizar on the carpet. He put down the heavy candlestick on the bureau and bent to feel the literary agent's heart. Reassured, he turned to Mme. Freitas. "Recompense!" he growled. "He'll have recompense enough..."

"Save your strength, my friend," said Mme. Freitas with a cold, tight smile. "We have much to do tonight. The tide will soon be on the turn."

⚜ 3

Albano Pizar awoke to confused roaring, sickness in his head and the taste of blood in his mouth. Blurred shapes flickered grotesquely in front of his eyes and the soft slurp of water came to his ears. A groaning noise translated itself into pain and the pain apparently proceeded from himself. He attempted to move and was brought up short with a clanking noise. He opened his eyes and was fully awake.

He gazed into the hard eyes of Mme. Freitas and Dr. Manzanares. He was leaning against a cold rock surface and the air smelt damp and foul. Electric bulbs gleamed high up in glass globes bolted to a dark, Romanesque ceiling. In the distance the sun burnt itself out smokily in water; dark water, which swirled among the piles and through iron gratings to lap sullenly on a shelf of stone a dozen yards away from him.

"The tide is turning," said Dr. Manzanares with satisfaction. "The flood will soon begin."

"What is the meaning of this?" said Pizar stiffly, some of his old confidence returning. "There are laws in this country which take care of assault."

He fingered his throbbing skull as he spoke and felt his left hand arrested. A stab of surprise shot through him as he saw that there was a manacle locked round his left wrist. He followed the new steel chain down with his eyes. He saw that the linked length, which was about ten feet long, was locked to an ancient ring sunk into the granite wall at his back. It was impossible to escape. He felt little fear as yet, only curiosity. He looked back to Mme. Freitas and the doctor.

The latter stood in shadow but the great author's widow seemed to be brooding over him. Pizar stepped forward to the length of his chain. The two merely retreated before him. He had his right hand free but they stood just beyond his reach.

"What is the meaning of this?" he asked again. He began to laugh as though they were having a joke with him. But the words died with a whimper in his throat.

"Let me out of here," he called, his voice echoing unpleasantly under the high vaulting of the roof. The noise seemed to stir something in the shadow. The lapping of the water was louder now and with sick numbness he saw eyes watching him down near the water's edge. He turned back to the two in front of him, their menacing immobility combining to strike into his consciousness.

"What do you intend to do?" he said. Or at least he intended to speak calmly, but his words came out in a withered shriek.

"Nothing," said Dr. Manzanares softly. The banal word struck the prisoner with more terror than any violent denunciation could have done.

He cast his eyes round desperately and then saw the meat cleaver. It lay on the cold stone floor in front of him, new, freshly sharpened and deadly. Just within the reach of his fingers. He slid his right foot out quietly, slowly, inch by inch; if only he could keep them talking. But his foot tinkled against the cleaver and the heartless couple before him burst out laughing. Pizar was more bewildered than ever when Dr. Manzanares kicked the cleaver towards him. He picked it up with his free right hand, the metal wet and chill against his sweating flesh.

"That's right," said Mme. Freitas. "Take it. It's intended for you."

"What is this, a game?" demanded Pizar quietly.

"That's right," the doctor agreed. "A game, in which your wits will give you a decision and your life is the prize."

Pizar saw that the vault in which he was chained was becoming darker; looking down at the shadowy waters of the canal he became aware that the sun was beginning its swift decline into the sea.

"You are in the vaults beneath the Palazzo, my friend," the doctor went on reminiscently. "The tide is coming in. But you have a weapon with which to defend yourself."

Pizar still did not comprehend the doctor's words; he looked back towards the iron gratings on the seaward side of the vault, then strained at the chain. It held firm. There were eyes and flapping shapes down at the water's edge. Pizar looked more closely and began to feel sick. Rats! There must have been hundreds of them, being driven in by the encroaching tide. Already the trapped man could see that the sullen wash of the water had eroded two of the ancient steps.

"You have two excellent choices," went on Dr. Manzanares, as though he were giving a lecture on philosophy. "As you will see, the construction of the vaults must drive the rats past your pillar, where they will assuredly attack you at the slightest movement. Remarkably bold, these sewer rats, I'm told. But, as you see, you may defend yourself with the cleaver. We are, it goes without saying, humanists and you have a first-rate chance."

Pizar did not reply. With a dead heart and trembling limbs he looked along the floor of the vault; it was just as Manzanares had said. It was a sheer six feet drop to the level on which he was standing; he could see that Mme. Freitas and the doctor had descended by a wooden ladder which they would no doubt pull up after them.

With a white and twitching face, he began, "If I returned the money..."

'Too late,' said Mme. Freitas, with a terrible smile. Pizar retreated to the pillar at his back; the chain rattled as he moved and the red eyes of the rats twinkled in the gloom at the water's edge. He could hear their squeaks and furtive movements, almost smell their carrion stench. They had thick black mud coated on their filthy bodies. He clutched the cleaver to his chest and blinked as the doctor spoke again.

"As I said before, my friend, you have two choices. Oh, we are being generous. You may be eaten by the rats. But we have guarded against that. You have ample defence in your hands."

But here he turned and pointed up the slope behind the pillar to which Pizar was chained.

"Though if you escape the rats, another problem faces you. They go some way farther up the slope, where they congregate to escape the tide. I am afraid you cannot, for your chain is more than twenty feet short of the high water mark. So if you elude the rats you may drown."

A scream as though he were already drowning escaped from Pizar's parched throat.

"I may drown!" he shouted. "You know I will drown."

Mme. Freitas moved then and looked Pizar quietly in the face.

"There is a third choice, you know," she said with dreadful emphasis. She moved away and climbed up the ladder. As she went Pizar could see she wore thick leather thigh boots, a protection also afforded the doctor.

Manzanares lingered. The sun was almost gone now, only a faint carmine tinting the surface of the water. The waves slapped the edges of the worn steps, leaving an oily scum, and the rats shifted uneasily at the margin, curious and afraid of the human being who barred their path. But Pizar knew, with horrible certainty, that their fear of the water would certainly outweigh their fear of man.

"If we could only come to some arrangement..." he began quickly. One look at the doctor's hard eyes counselled him to save his breath.

Dr. Manzanares looked him up and down with something like satisfaction.

"I am sure you will think of something," he said.

He moved away to follow Mme. Freitas and pulled up the ladder after him.

"I hope you can swim," he called cheerily to the man chained to the pillar.

Pizar heard the distant clang of a closing door and the sound fell on his soul like the long weight of eternity. He moved and the chain clinked; the light on the outer surface of the canal died and it was night. The tide slopped on the foul floor of the vault, damp air blew in and he caught the foetid smell of the rats. They crouched at the water's edge, moving closer now, scuttling with mincing steps as the tide menaced their feet, their red, unwinking eyes watching his face with quiet confidence. He breathed shallowly and sickly, felt he might scream and clutched the cleaver tightly in his right hand.

He braced himself against the pillar, praying that he would not trip on the chain; the tide crept in inexorably, the putrid mass of the rats shifted and changed shape before his dazed eyes. The first wavelet burst foaming on the floor of the cellar and then they were coming at him, squeaking to themselves, their red eyes murderous, their foul, slime-encrusted bodies brushing his as they leapt at his eyes and throat.

Pizar shrieked and screamed as he wielded the blade, the handle slippery with blood, slashing and hacking with the courage of a man in whom all faith is dead, hoping that he would not become entwined in the chain and fall. Froth was on his lips and madness in his heart when he paused in his blind rage; he tested the edge of the cleaver against the links of the chain but it was high-grade steel and only blunted the blade.

He awaited the next onslaught of the rats, balanced on the balls of his feet, caught his breath deeply and began hacking for his life.

4

There were inquiries, threats, police investigations and intimation of legal proceedings, of course; all the making of a first-class scandal. But to all accusations Mme. Freitas and Dr. Manzanares maintained smiling denials. Albano Pizar had never been to the Palazzo Tortini after his visit regarding the book; was his return likely after the scandalous way in which he had treated the dead author's widow?

Certainly, the authorities could visit the vaults of the house. The authorities did visit the vaults—but found nothing suspicious and retired with apologies. The servants were no better; no, they had never seen M. Pizar at the Palazzo; perhaps the authorities were confusing the occasion? The chauffeur could not recall ever having driven him to and from the station, other than in the one instance. The authorities shrugged and retired; after all, there were more important things to investigate. Mme. Freitas and Dr. Manzanares exchanged secret smiles of satisfaction and referred to the matter no more.

Albano Pizar returned to his office in Paris a year or so later, paler and thinner than before; in fact, very much more like the young man he had been in the distant past. He would never indicate to any of his friends or business associates how he came to lose his left hand, which seemed to have been hacked from the wrist, but everyone noticed how much better he treated his authors thereafter. And women clients he would not handle at all.

✦ The Gossips

✦ 1

It happened a long time ago, in Sicily—something like twenty-five years, in fact. Though many intervening events have grown dim, the extraordinary episodes which I myself witnessed and which I later pieced together through Arthur Jordan, are still present in my mind with unusual clarity.

I was on holiday and had found my way to this wild and remote corner without anything special in mind. At Messina, I had fallen in with Grisson, an Englishman who had lived in Italy for many years. He was at that time Director of the Museum of Antiquities at Naples and was currently travelling on leave in pursuit of acquisitions for his foundation.

I gladly acceded to his suggestion that we should travel together and some days later we found ourselves in a wild and savage landscape, almost lunar in aspect, that only the farthest districts of old Sicily can produce. The sun beat down with fierce intensity on stunted trees, sparse vegetation, rocks that seemed to writhe in the heat and undulate with the haze that shimmered about them, while the chirping of thousands of insects only emphasised the brooding silence of this ancient land.

It was some time after midday and an inadequate lunch in the shade of a remote village, when we set out to see something which I gathered my companion considered of special interest. We had travelling with us a guide from Messina, whom Grisson had found it necessary to engage, for, as he said, he sometimes had to deal with noble old Sicilian families who spoke no language other than their own difficult dialect. This made things tedious, for though Grisson spoke fluent Italian, even the people of the mainland often could not understand the local Sicilian tongues and these were many.

It seemed to me that the guide appeared somewhat startled, almost nervous, when he learned our destination, but he said nothing and at about one in the afternoon we had left the village far behind and were making our way in single file along a rough track through the scrubland.

It was the hottest moment of the day, the sky like beaten bronze and the heat bouncing back off the rocks so that one walked as though through an incinerator. My enthusiasm had ebbed noticeably and it was almost two o'clock when Grisson's attitude showed unmistakably that we were near our journey's end. It seemed suddenly as though we were in a garden, with formal hedges of cypress, and statues dotted about.

Then there was the glint of a lake through the trees and welcome shade. We sat thankfully upon a stone bench and though I still felt too hot and exhausted to begin a conversation, I was once again myself and began to revive my spirits. But Grisson seemed impervious to either heat or atmosphere and began to speak with enthusiasm and wide scholarship of our destination. I did not at first pay much attention but I gradually became aware of a charged tension that seemed to play around our little group among the sombre trees, and I noticed that our guide had remained standing, despite his evident fatigue, and continued to glance around him in an uneasy manner.

A few minutes passed and we continued walking. It was then, for the first time, that I became aware that we were not exactly within a garden. A fountain began to sparkle in the sunlight, there were even plots of what appeared to be dusty lawn and more statues. I do not recall at which point I realised that we had left the garden—if it had ever been a garden—and that we were within some sort of private cemetery, or perhaps public graveyard. There were great slabbed tombs with inscriptions in the ancient Sicilian language, evidently immensely old, and Grisson, who seemed to know his way about, led

◄ The Gossips

us forward with evident enthusiasm, taking photographs at intervals and silently flourishing his notebook.

We had gone on in this way for perhaps half an hour, Grisson with the dedicated purpose of the specialist, myself as a half bemused spectator, and the guide with distinct unease, when the character of the landscape changed. We were still within the cemetery, with its white and brown stone sepulchres gleaming in the harsh light—the bounds of the place must have stretched for an immense distance—and the lake was behind us now, when we entered a sort of valley.

On one side there rose a high cliff of perhaps two hundred feet, which was composed of what I should have said was a pink granite, except that there was no such stone in these parts. It may have been that the limestone had become permeated by the action of damp and lichens, as a small trickle of water made its way down the face.

Standing on an eminence as we were at the other side of the valley, we could see on to the plateau opposite. There seemed to be more hedges and formal gardens and, farther back, the white façade of a chateau or palazzo could be seen above the tops of the trees.

But what took my attention and that of my companions was a group of statuary which stood at the edge of the cliff, almost facing us. There were three figures, which appeared to be inclined inwards. At that distance it was difficult to make out detail, but they seemed to be females, clad in flowing robes. They must have been of immense weight and bulk and I judged each to be about 15 feet high to stand out in such a manner at the height we were viewing them.

Grisson saw my curiosity had been roused but said nothing. Other than a quiet smile of satisfaction he took no visible notice of the statuary, but continued his examination of the ancient, lichen-covered tombs we continued among. For some minutes he worked on and as we two walked behind him, I gradually became aware that we were not alone in the garden. I do not know at what stage this impinged itself on my consciousness.

Grisson did not seem to notice, but I sensed, though I did no look behind me, that the guide had also heard it. There was quick, sly murmuring, little chuckles and snickerings, which seemed to come and go in the light wind which had sprung up. I strained my ears but could not make out what language was being spoken, and my first thought was that some children were playing in another part of the cemetery. I mentioned as much to Grisson, whose smile only deepened. But the effect on the guide was most unfortunate. He turned deathly pale under his tan and began to tremble violently. I followed his gaze upwards and though the great statues were now partly hidden from us by the overhang, it seemed to me that the murmur of voices came from the region of their edge of the plateau.

The remark of mine, once uttered, seemed a silly one, but what other explanation could there be? Children do play in stranger places than graveyards, but the remoteness of this region from the town and its company escaped me.

Grisson explained, "There are no people here nowadays, except for the people of the Palazzo," and here he mentioned the name of a famous and celebrated duke, one of the last of a noble family.

"There was a town here once, which was served by this lower graveyard, but the people went away many years ago. All that is left now is the estate on the plateau above."

It was evidently there we were going and most probably the voices belonged to servants' gossip in the garden. As I had difficulty in restraining my curiosity any longer, I asked Grisson about the statues. I gathered they were one of the principal reasons for his expedition.

Their proper name in the Sicilian I have forgotten, but I learned they were something on the lines of the 'Three Graces' and were reputed to be over 500 years old, though the estimate, as is so often the case with folklore, was about three hundred years too early as I later came to decide.

"Some people call them 'The Gossips'," he said, referring to a savage joke, the significance of which escaped me.

We were going up a flimsy wooden staircase let into the face of the cliff as he spoke, and I shall never forget the look of fear on the guide's face, as he stumbled against me in the temporary gloom, when he caught the gist of Grisson's remarks.

Nevertheless, we continued in silence; nothing further was said and a few minutes later we emerged from the overhanging outcrops of rock into a blinding world of sunshine and greenery again. We

◢ THE GOSSIPS

were now on the plateau and leaving the staircase which ended in a sort of ornamental bridge spanning a fissure, we passed through a rustic gate and found ourselves in the extensive gardens of the palazzo.

Below us, the enormous area of the cemetery lay dazzling in the sun, with the lake piercing the middle distance and throwing back the burnished image of the sky; while the white and brown tombstones and monuments, shifting and undulating in the heat haze, crawled into the far distance and were lost among the trees.

Here, for a few minutes, I no longer heard the voices which were apparently muffled by a bluff, but as we threaded a white gravel path among well-trimmed lawns, the mumbling began again, but gradually faded as we approached the palace. This was very much larger than I had expected and was built on grand classical lines, evidently for a very ancient and wealthy family. Great stone griffons flanked an enormous marble terrace and beyond the semi-Greek façade, I could see more lawns, and peacocks preening themselves.

A major-domo appeared with silent efficiency from beyond the terrace and greeted Grisson as an old friend. Moments later, motioning the guide to follow him to the kitchen quarters in due course, he said the duke would see us at once and led the way through a maze of apartments to a very grand study, decorated chiefly in pale blue and gold.

Our host was a very tall man, in his late fifties I should have said, who exhibited nothing remarkable either in his features or demeanour which would have distinguished him as of noble lineage in Western society, other than—and this is a major differentiation—his exquisite manners, which were carried to such extremes that one eventually imagined he would rather suffer hardships and indignities himself, than that a friend or guest should be inconvenienced.

He evidently knew all about Grisson's errand and it became obvious later—despite my slight grasp of Italian—that the conversation concerned the large group of statues in the grounds. Presently, when the discussion turned to more general matters regarding the antiquities of the villa the guide was called in, and after exaggerated obeisance to the Duke—he remained standing despite the latter's injunction to seat himself—was asked to translate from the Sicilian for Grisson, as I gathered the Duke was more familiar with that tongue and the conversation could proceed with greater speed.

At some stage, my attention slackened and I amused myself with wandering up and down and perusing the exquisitely-tooled leather bound volumes that lined one of the walls of the great study. Some were undoubtedly records of the Duke's family, for they bore a great crest with armorial bearings tooled in gold on the brown bindings, and stretched away for shelf after shelf. Others, from the titles on the spines, were historical records related to Sicily, while yet others were concerned with theology and divinity.

Presently, we were served with a delightful-tasting liqueur, of a warm amber colour, the derivation of which was strange to me, and small, sweet cakes and biscuits. The coolness of the room and the abundance of our refreshment was so welcome after our long and heated trek that I had quite recovered my spirits and lolled back at my ease, when a sudden crash jerked me from my reverie.

The Duke, with customary courtesy, had asked the guide to accept a glass of wine and I was now startled to see a scarlet splash irradiating from the splintered fragments of wine glass scattered about the study carpet. The guide was full of apologies, the Duke made light of the matter; but as a servant hastened to clear up the mess, I could see that the guide was white and badly frightened.

I could surmise, from what I had heard, in both English and Italian—for Grisson had addressed me occasionally—that the later conversation had concerned the statues, which Grisson wished to photograph and include in a coming book.

The Duke had no particular objection but had warned my companion, in a semi-jocular way, that he would not advise him doing so. The guide had added his objections also, pointing out that this part of the garden had been walled off for many years and had included an unfortunate gesture of his arm—the cause of the wine glass accident—when Grisson had asked him to accompany us.

During the next few minutes the guide was banished to the kitchen, still muttering to himself, to await our return; and! Grisson and the Duke withdrew, amid many apologies on the latter's part, to

The Gossips

one corner of the room where there was a huge marble-topped desk. Here their council continued in Italian, and I soon saw that the couple had before them various volumes' bound in morocco, which Grisson was consulting and copying down portions in his notebook.

When he rejoined me he looked satisfied, as though his journey had been well worthwhile.

"Sorry about that," he remarked. "This must all have been very boring for you."

"Not at all," I answered. "I've been most interested, but somewhat puzzled by the difficulties with the guide."

Grisson laughed, quite shortly, and then added something to the Duke, sotto voce. That gentleman hurried forward to bid us goodbye temporarily, and then said, to my great surprise, that he would see us on our return from the garden—in perfect English.

I was still more intrigued at this singular turn in the situation but I could not, of course, pursue it in the Duke's presence. He evidently had no intention of accompanying us, but disappeared into another part of the palace. And I had no opportunity of speaking to Grisson alone, as another servant, middle-aged, and of dour aspect, wearing a leather apron, met us on the terrace and led the way to the garden, with a great, rusty bunch of keys.

I was again surprised at this—though by now, I suppose, I shouldn't have been—the whole atmosphere of the place was so extraordinary.

So I noticed little of the splendid grounds through which we were hurrying. Presently, we came to a huge stone wall, about 15 feet in height, and evidently quite old, which completely cut off the garden from the plateau, so far as I could make out.

It was pierced by a large, thick wooden door, reinforced with metal and I noticed that the footman, or whoever he was, scraped the lock several times in his hurry to get the door open or—as I afterwards realised—in his eagerness to be gone.

He handed Grisson a duplicate key and, another curious procedure, re-locked the door behind us. His footsteps died away up the path and we were alone in the walled-off portion of the garden.

This itself appeared to be of considerable size and the wall against which we were now standing was thickly hemmed in with vegetation;

Darkness, Mist & Shadow

indeed, we had to force our way through and could faintly make out a stone path—a continuation of the one which ended the other side of the wall—which had been over-grown by weeds, moss and vegetation a considerable time ago.

It may have been imagination, but the air seemed to have grown colder here; it was positively damp and I saw that the ground under foot inclined to lichen and gave off a nauseous odour.

At the same time that I heard the tinkling of water, the sun burst into our faces again and through a tangle of grass which had once been a lawn, we could make out the terrace and part of one of the stone figures facing towards the valley below. It was all on a much bigger scale than I had expected. And then, above the noise of the water, I once again became aware of voices.

I am not an imaginative man nor given to undue nervousness, but I must confess there was something about these sounds-reminiscent of whispered confidences, half heard in sleep—that gave me distinct unease. That, combined with the chill air, despite the evident heat of the sun which poured on us, made me consciously slacken my pace, but my companion pressed on stoutly, apparently impervious to atmosphere.

After this lapse of time, I find it difficult to recollect my impressions. The coldness in the air continued and the whispering increased, then died away and increased again, according to which direction we seemed to be facing. And how shall I describe the statues? I do not know what I had been pre-pared for when Grisson asked me to accompany him into that accursed garden. My impression was one of dampness, stench and nauseous decay.

The surface of the circular, tessellated pavement on to which we presently ventured, was covered with some slippery form of moss that gave off a most appalling odour.

And the statues themselves; great heaven, they haunt me still... The three vast figures rearing towards the bronze sky seemed to writhe and undulate in the heat haze and the veinous browny rock from which they were carved was split through with shards of scarlet.

At the same time I seemed to be mysteriously affected by the heat. I grew dizzy; hot and cold by turn; and the statues themselves seemed to change shape in some strange, unknown manner. How can I convey those faces of nightmare; carved from some weird, brown-stained basaltic material; with crooked teeth, lank-seeming hair and yellow eyes that appeared to glow as though human?

And the stench! My stomach turned at that stagnant miasma which exuded or emanated from the statues themselves, smeared with those scarlet-brown stains. Along the plinth, as I staggered and stumbled my way with Grisson impassive beside me, was carved huge lettering in an unknown character. I reeled towards the railings, away from this bestial group and attempted to focus my throbbing eyes on what would normally have been an impressive and even delightful view; I was conscious that Grisson was still carrying out his functions, translating the inscription, even photographing the group.

As I turned towards him, that obscene, unnerving whispering and tittering began again and I was sure now, with what fevered insanity I knew not, that the statues themselves were talking—discussing us in the most insidious way, and as I strained my eyes in the sun, I became convinced that they were moving. The heads seemed to change shape and expression; the eyes now glowed, now lifted, now closed; the lips writhed and the dreadful stone teeth chattered on; even the arms, the very draperies as well as the heads seemed to shift effortlessly, change position, move again, freeze, coalesce, all the while those ghastly voices seemed to be bursting my ear drums.

Now, I know the reader will say that I was the sudden victim of a fever, induced by the heat, or even that the supposed movement of rigid stone objects was an optical illusion, brought about by the combined reaction on my eyes of heat and light. There is something in that; well enough; but my senses were not so addled as to imagine the appalling suggestive power of those vile voices that echoed so unmistakably in the evil stillness of that accursed garden.

My legs were trembling as though in fever, and I pressed my nails into the palms of my hands, and attempted to look out across the valley to where the distant panorama was undulating and rippling like an agitated film developed in a dish. I was not at all conscious of my next movements. I seemed to hear a shout from Grisson; the voices boiled up and crackled in my brain, my hands were on the railings at the edge of the plateau and in another instant I should have been over and into the cool and blessed peace of the valley below.

But Grisson's iron hand was on my shoulder, his voice reassuring in my ears as he half-dragged, half-carried me through the heat and rotted vegetation into the sane quietude of the green trees and undergrowth that fringed the wall. I waited until we had regained the Duke's garden and a secluded corner of the lakeside, before I began to retch and collapse.

2

It was quite an hour before I was myself again. Grisson was all solicitude. He brushed away a servant who came to inquire too pressingly after us, bathed my forehead in icy water from a fountain and, gradually, I regained my senses. We eventually found ourselves back in the presence of an alarmed Duke. Grisson was, of course, all apologies, but he had asked me to make light of the affair to our host, who speedily produced a stiff whisky and begged us to stay to dinner.

"It will not be dark until very late, and you will be able to get well clear during daylight," he said, with an emphasis that revealed he knew all too clearly what was the matter.

As for Grisson, he soon plunged himself into further study of the massive books in the Duke's library, and that gentleman himself, though obviously concerned, did not press any inquiries regarding our experiences.

"A touch of the sun and nerves," was Grisson's own explanation to the Duke and the servants, and by sotto voce comments and gestures he asked me particularly not to say anything to the guide.

As for myself, youth and a good dinner rapidly restored my spirits and as the wine went round, I even began to wonder whether I had not, in fact, dreamed my experiences. As the after-taste of the adventure began to fade away, I became ashamed of my panic on the bluff where the statues stood, and even hoped that Grisson himself would not refer to it.

It was past ten in the evening and the light was still bright in the western sky, when Grisson and I, after many thanks and repeated

✒ THE GOSSIPS

goodbyes to the courteous Duke, made our way once again past the lake and through the valley. My last glimpse was of the statues, high on their plateau brooding over the bluff, but the sunset tinged the whole place with such beauty and melancholy that even then I said nothing and thought—fool that I was—that the group even looked beautiful against the sky, ablaze with greens and blues, reds and golds.

Grisson made only one more direct reference to the episode when he spoke shortly of the celebrated 'mirage effect' which, combined with vertigo, had brought on my attack, as he called it. I said nothing further, but later came a little incident which led me to believe that Grisson had not played fair over my ordeal. But he made handsome amends eventually, though I had to wait over three years for the explanation.

We were fairly on our way back to the village and the light was still strong enough to see clearly, when Grisson drew some papers out of his pocket to consult them. We were walking abreast and something brushed against my arm and fell on to the white dust of the path. It had evidently been carried from Grisson's pocket with the documents.

My first instinct was to draw his attention to it, but something held me back. Instead, on pretence of tying my shoe lace I dropped behind and picked up the small object. It was unidentifiable to my immediate glance, and did not appear to be of any value.

However, I said nothing and placed it carefully in my pocket, stuffing down my handkerchief on top of it. Later that night, back in a well-lit hotel room and my adventure receding into limbo, I picked up the small, round object and examined it carefully under the glare of a table lamp. It took me some while to identify it and then, afterwards, when I had thought things over, I did not sleep so well. The article Grisson had dropped appeared to be, so far as I could make out, one of a pair of rubber ear-plugs.

✒ 3

Some years later, as I indicated earlier, I met Grisson again, this time, fortunately, under less frightening circumstances. I had maintained correspondence with him, on and off, in the interim and though neither of us had made reference to our extraordinary adventure, the question marks it had raised in my mind, seemed to hang cloudily between the lines of the occasional letters we exchanged. So something in a letter he wrote me long afterwards raised my expectations, and I was not disappointed in the sequel.

I had run into Grisson one afternoon of a July when I was shopping on the Canebiere in Marseilles. I had only half an hour or so to get to St. Charles to catch my train on to Nice, but we exchanged addresses and he promised to write. I thought little more of it, until a letter, heavily stamped and addressed and re-addressed in multi-coloured inks reached me some ten days and three hotels later in Genoa.

Grisson was in Florence, attending some sort of congress of museum curators; he knew I intended to visit there, he had a friend, Arthur Jordan, he would like me to meet; would I join them for a day or two? They were sharing a villa, there was room for me, and I would not have to put up with their company for too long, as they had to attend morning and afternoon sessions of the congress, and would only be able to see me in the late afternoons.

The idea was attractive, but what decided me was a curious postscript, which Grisson had heavily underlined, not once, but three times. "Please come. Most important. Jordan has the Sicilian explanation." The last two words were again underscored.

To say that I was interested would be an understatement. Genoa was palling in the heat, despite the breeze off the sea, and I knew no-one in the city. I telegraphed the same afternoon, made an inquiry about trains and little more than two days later, was comfortably settled in at a small but delightful villa in the hills outside Florence.

I had haunted the Uffizzi, duly admired once again the incomparable cathedral and it was not until the second night of my stay, that Grisson had broached the subject which had brought me to the city. A moon like an orange was pasted to the hilly backcloth, as we passed through the square, past the massive portals then thought to be bronze, now known to be gold, and my companions selected a pavement cafe not far from the Ponte Vecchio.

There is nothing like a summer evening in Florence, with its scent

✒ THE GOSSIPS

of flowers and all the atmosphere of a Tuscan night, with a thousand years of history pressing on one, for a story; but such a story as I heard then, made me feel doubly glad that I was in such delightful surroundings, with the reassuring river sounds of the Arno only a few yards distant from my comfortable cane chair.

I had come to like Arthur Jordan immensely, in the few hours I had known him. Still young—in his late forties, I believe—with prematurely white hair crowning a boyish face, the most predominant feature being square white teeth which flashed attractively into a smile, startling in the dark brown of his face, he was a born adventurer.

He too, like Grisson, was a curator; not of a famous museum like his companion, but I gathered that his duties left him time in the summer months for a number of roving commissions, in which he not only brought himself up to date on the more important Continental collections, but from time to time had been responsible for staging unusual exhibitions of statuary, pottery and mediaeval glass of many ages and periods, in halls, galleries and museums in Paris and London.

It was on such an errand that he had gone to Sicily, and to the scene of our startling adventure, a year or two before. He was hunting this time principally for statuary and sculpture of the 17th century, mostly from gardens and parks, to be exhibited on loan, as part of a gigantic presentation of the art of that period in London.

As he spoke I gained something of his enthusiasm and remembered reading newspaper reports of that time. The exhibition had been unusual in that it represented complete rooms, looking on to 'gardens' of various palaces, each one illustrative of a particular facet of the 17th century, each complete down to the smallest detail of the art of its period.

Jordan's purpose in his Sicilian visit was to secure the loan of "The Gossips," as I continued to call them, for the show, in one of the biggest halls in London, which was to last three months. I then remembered that one of the exhibition halls had been closed after three or four days, under dramatic circumstances, and had then re-opened, but with part of it barred to the public.

Darkness, Mist & Shadow

I was trying to bring my mind to bear on the hazy details Jordan's remarks had evoked in my mind, when his narrative was interrupted by the arrival of the waiter and the renewal of drinks; and I took the opportunity to ask Grisson about the photographs he had taken for his book.

In reply, he handed me a small cardboard wallet, with a wry smile. As our drinks were placed on the table, I examined it.

I found I was holding several pieces of white, glossy paper. I could just make out hazy details of what appeared to be foliage. I was completely baffled and asked Grisson what he meant by it.

"These are the photographs I took with you," he explained, his smile widening. I did not realise the import of his remark for a moment and added stupidly, "Were they over exposed?"

"Quite impossible," Grisson retorted drily. "My books are noted for the quality of the photography. I always take my own photos and I developed and printed these myself.

"I could see the negatives were almost blank, but I wanted to make completely sure, so I printed up what I could. As you see, there is only the faintest suspicion of the foliage in the palazzo garden."

I was bewildered and turned to Jordan.

"They never have been photographed, you see," he explained, almost apologetically. "The Gossips, I mean. Nothing ever comes out."

I was still trying to get my bearings but before I could go on, Grisson asked me to be patient and said that all would be explained when Jordan had told his story. It took some little while for our companion to take up the thread of his remarks again. He said he had first to explain to me what 'The Gossips' represented in artistic terms, something of their history and why he required them for the London show.

"You might think," he said, "that it would be an enormously expensive and cumbersome job to ship all that masonry to England. I offered the Duke, of course, complete carte blanche in the matter of expenses connected with the venture. In fact, it cost the old boy nothing, as we were covered by a British Government grant, only part of the shipping costs being borne by the exhibition organisers. And

The Gossips

the inclusion of this group in the exhibition, would be a sort of coup which seldom occurs.

"The statues are masterpieces of their kind, and had never been seen outside their Sicilian setting. In fact, few people had seen them at all, which I thought at the time was a pity, in view of their antecedents.

"The exhibition as a whole, packed as it would be with so many rare and extraordinary things, would not only bring an international cachet to the museum authorities and bodies connected with it in England, but would be worth an enormous sum of money.

"This would arise, not only through entrance money to the exhibition itself, but via the many articles, broadcasts, magazine and newspaper and photographic rights in journals and other media throughout the world. A film had been planned to cover the whole field, and also coloured lantern slides, which were to form the basis of lectures by eminent men in their various spheres.

"My securing The Gossips would set the seal on all this, in view of its extraordinary history, and my hopes were high when I went on my momentous errand to the Sicilian hinterland."

Jordan said he had not warned the Duke of his intentions, only of his arrival, and though he had expected at first a flat refusal, in view of the many difficulties to be overcome in connection with transporting the statues to England, he did not at all realise that he would receive such a cordial reception as the Duke gave him.

But in fact, there was little objection on the latter's part to loaning the statues, when Jordan had explained the situation, and the Duke was enthusiastically co-operative, going into great detail on the technical problems involved. Jordan had broached his errand a full six months before the exhibition was due to begin in London, so there was plenty of time to put the scheme in train.

I must emphasise at this point, that Jordan, though he was fully conversant with the evil history of the statuary as it appeared in histories and books of various periods had himself heard little or nothing of their unsavoury reputation in the Sicilian countryside in modern times; and as he had no opportunity of discussing it with the local inhabitants, who are, in any case, reticent before strangers, it was hardly surprising.

Jordan at first confined his researches to the books in the Duke's library and, having been pressed to stay a day or two, delayed an examination of the statues in situ until the following day.

I was disappointed to hear from the man's own lips that, though he was fascinated and delighted with the group, which he thought well worth his time and long journey, nothing unusual had occurred in those early days. He had not, being a sensible man, seen anything extraordinary in the lichen, the vile stench (he had travelled too widely in South American jungles for that), or the sinister, red-streaked statues themselves. The troubles began later and in a different form from those I had experienced.

"If I may interrupt a moment," said Grisson, waving for another round of drinks. "I think I ought to put our friend more in the picture by telling him something of the history of the palazzo and of the statues in particular. Have you ever heard of Caravallo?"

I shook my head. Try as I would, the name meant nothing to me, and there was no reason why it should, for the man had been a minor Italian sculptor of the seventeenth century; his work stood really on the threshold of genius, but was marred by an evil way of life and a demoniac method of expressing his artistic impulses, that came more and more to make his work looked on askance by the patrons and nobles who commissioned the artworks of the time.

But he had apparently found a kindred soul in Leonardo, the then master of our Sicilian palazzo, Grisson told me. As he went on talking, I began to piece together a bizarre story and much that had been dark and obscure to me before began slowly to fit into place, like the well-oiled tumblers in a lock.

Leonardo was an authority on demonology and other blasphemous arts and his thoroughly dissolute way of life had made him shunned by the local people, quite early in his career.

He had succeeded to the title at the age of nineteen, on the death of his father, and within only a few years, the palazzo had become the scene of epic orgies indulged in by the local women and Leonardo and his friends.

The evil fame of the man spread far afield and beautiful women of all classes were guests for weeks at a time, from towns as far afield as Naples and Rome, as well as places on the island itself.

◢ The Gossips

Legend even had it that Leonardo's mother was made to witness and take part in unspeakable ceremonies herself—she was a beautiful woman only in her late thirties at the time of which Grisson was speaking, and when she was found dead one morning by a servant before attaining her fiftieth year, even uglier rumours began to gather.

So it was at the height of Leonardo's notoriety, that people began to leave the immediate vicinity of the palazzo; there had been a small town there originally, as I think I mentioned earlier, but bands of young bloods were out at night, abducting eligible young women from local families whenever they got the opportunity, so that the young duke and his estate were the scandal of Sicily.

It was at this stage in his wicked career that Leonardo came into contact with Caravallo. The two were greatly alike in many ways, and the duke had been delighted with the acquisition of a number of obscene but exquisitely wrought carvings, created by Caravallo as parodies in the Greek style.

And it was also then that Caravallo had the notion which crowned his blasphemous fancy. Leonardo had currently three beautiful mistresses, three young sisters, each of whom seemed to outshine the azure sea in beauty. It was Leonardo's custom to indulge with them mutually in indescribable orgies, that for lust and ingenious frenzy, far outdid the spectacles of ancient Rome; and when the moon was in certain quarters, ritual acts of sex magic took place between Leonardo and the three young girls, in an ornately equipped 'throne room' in the palace, in which other young men and women unashamedly took part—to the number of fifty or sixty persons, according to one old chronicle.

Caravallo had often painted the women and his young friend in the most erotic and abandoned of acts, and his sketch book was crammed with hundreds and hundreds of vile and shameful drawings that today, said Grisson, still exist in thirty or forty locked volumes of erotica in a sealed-off and almost permanently locked section of the present Duke's library.

It was Caravallo's idea to compose a large group of statuary to perpetuate Leonardo and his coven of three young women; the original form of this had been of a nature which had blanched even

Leonardo's shameless cheeks, but he pointed out to his erratic genius that statuary could not be hidden as could smaller *objets d'art*, and as the statue would have to be more or less public, because of its huge size, the form would have to take a semi-classical theme, and the hidden, secret and perverse meanings could be read into the public statuary by those 'in the know'.

The three young women were given, it might be added, said Grisson, almost superfluously, to endless conversations and laughter among themselves, and their disporting in a pavilion in the grounds, long since burned down in a fire, their shrill chatter, sniggerings and mutterings, had earned them the nickname—the Sicilian equivalent—of 'The Gossips' among the local people of the time.

That their intentions and discussions were malicious there can be no doubt, and it would be interesting to discover, if it were possible, just who were the personalities, public and private, that formed the subject of their scandalous talk in those far-off days.

At all events, Caravallo plunged eagerly into the new commission given him by the young duke and for a time all went well. The statues were taking shape, when suddenly, a bigger scandal than ever broke out. No records came down of it, but the story is that some incorruptible nobleman suddenly descended on the villa at the height of an orgy; at all events the coven was broken, questions were asked in government circles, and the three young women, the centre—with Leonardo—of the sensation, were hurriedly and secretly packed off to their own remote home town.

Leonardo lingered on in his villa, but his drive and energy were gone with the departure of his three 'brides', and though le was consoled by the dark genius and wit of Caravallo, the old Jays were over. Caravallo completed his group of statuary—his 'masterpiece', he ever afterwards called it—though it had been left for a time only half-finished—using other women in place of the original models. But it is believed that he fashioned the leads from original drawings of the duke's three mistresses.

The duke had by then abandoned his original idea of his own effigy appearing in the middle of the group, as the master of ceremonies, and the finished creation was as Grisson and I had seen it on that unforgettable day; as a circle of dancing women in flowing draperies, with an inscription running round the outer pedestal.

I was deeply interested in this strange story and was convinced that I had been asked to Florence for a denouement; so interested, in fact, that our glasses had long been empty and the crowds at the nearby tables were beginning to thin out, when I called for another round.

The rest of the tale grows dim and shadowy (Grisson presently continued), and his next words gripped my attention with undeniable impact, as no doubt they were meant to do. Some years after the commissioning of the statues, Leonardo was found dead at the foot of the cliffs leading to the upper garden, in the most tragic and horrifying circumstances.

His body appeared to have been reduced to a jelly, though the cliff was not high enough to have inflicted such damage by a simple fall; and the expression on what remained of his face was enough to cause a fainting fit in the first manservant on the scene.

There were uglier rumours and, amid wild stories and further scandal, the great house was closed for a time and Caravallo left the district, the death of his old friend having apparently shattered him. He eventually died in Padua a few years afterwards, and little more is known of him, other than what I have told you this evening, though minor works of his continue to come to light even today, Grisson added.

The reputation of 'The Gossips' apparently stems from the period immediately after the strange death of Leonardo and, as was said earlier, the people gradually drifted away from the area. New dukes continued to inhabit the ancient palace but parts of the library were sealed and, after a particularly bad fright, a descendant of the bad young duke had part of the garden walled off, as I had seen on the occasion of my ill-fated visit with Grisson.

The latter leaned back after completing his story, and looked moodily out over the water. Despite the warmth of the still air, and the delights of the ancient city surrounding us, I had become aware that this was not the end of the affair and that there was a great deal more to come. Grisson had been speaking for upwards of half an hour and at a sign from him, Jordan looked up with a smile; it was his turn to continue the tale.

4

He first went back to the thread of his original remarks, which had been so lengthily interrupted by our companion. Arthur Jordan smiled even more broadly as he recollected this, and Grisson stirred uneasily in his chair as if to comment obliquely that he hadn't meant to take so long.

Jordan had completed his arrangements with Duke to exhibit The Gossips in London, and all had apparently gone very well until the time came to move the statues.

Jordan was, of course, extremely anxious that no damage should come to the group while it was in his care and he had gone to considerable trouble in getting up one of the best firms in Naples to undertake the job; I did not understand the technicalities as Jordan explained them, but I gathered that the whole group of statuary and the plinth on which they stood, had first to be jacked up most carefully, and then edged on to a sort of lift which had been constructed of strong steel scaffolding up the face of the cliff.

When they had been lowered to the valley below, they were to be crated and transported by stages in a large, wheeled cradle to Palermo for shipment to England. This was the plan which Jordan explained to me, but unfortunately, things didn't work out like that. The first stages of the dismantling of the statue went smoothly and without incident; workmen from the Italian mainland had been brought in—specialists to a man—and they had laughed at the local tales and legends.

Nothing odd occurred regarding the statues, there were no voices, and nothing untoward about their appearance. In fact, Jordan regarded the whole tiling as a straightforward civil engineering operation and, apart from perfunctory supervision, his. mind was on other affairs: the shipment from Palermo, general details of the exhibition, his researches in the Duke's library, and so on.

✍ The Gossips

It seemed that the statues could be removed separately, and that the granite plinth on which they rested was also a separate entity; this would mean that the figures could be removed, one; by one, for crating and a larger crate would contain the plinth. As a start, the three figures were lifted and removed to one side; they were left for the time being, until the lifting gear would be ready to lower them down the face of the cliff.

Then the experts examined the plinth and professed themselves satisfied with what they found.

The plinth could be lifted in one section with the equipment available, and would not crack. This work occupied all of the first day and part of the following morning, and it was then that; the troubles had begun.

Perhaps Jordan had been trapped into a position of false security by the tranquil atmosphere and the deepening interest of his task. Whatever the reason, the disaster which afterwards befell, came with stunning suddenness.

During the latter part of the morning the plinth had first been lowered to the ground; this operation was not without its hazards. The plinth was the bulkiest single item of the group, though it was not the heaviest, and it called for delicate manoeuvring. Some of the workmen had anxious looks as the great mass was lowered, inch by inch almost, with much rattling of chains in the blocks, down the face of the cliff. A gantry had been erected on top of the scaffolding and a flat steel platform, with chains round it, was to be used for the operation.

But all had gone well, and by the end of the morning, the great mass had been cradled and was already out of sight along the lower road through the old cemetery. In the afternoon, though the heat was intense, Jordan was surprised to see that the workmen intended to stick to their task; unlike most Italians, they took only an hour for their siesta, though the sun was cruel, and soon after two, the sound of the winch warned him that their labours were about to begin again.

Excusing himself from his host, Jordan hurried back to the platform of rock to superintend operations, and was once again impressed with the efficiency and hard work put in, both by the principals and labourers of the firm which had been engaged. Perhaps they were being paid a bonus or special rates if they finished the job in a certain time; whatever the reason, Jordan mentally resolved to invite them as his guests to a celebration dinner, when he met them again in Palermo in a few days' time. Jordan had remarked at the Duke's lack of interest in such an unusual operation, but if he had known the real history of the statuary, he would have thought it remarkable if the Duke had felt otherwise.

Jordan was idly mulling these and other thoughts over in his mind as the winch chains rattled away, and the statues I had found so repellent, but which merely excited his keenest antiquarian interest, were lowered slowly down to the cemetery level, with infinite care and precision.

A highly-skilled contracting engineer was in charge and it was the fact that he had established close contact with him, and had been so impressed with the quality of his mind, that made Jordan refuse to accept an obvious explanation which occurred to some other people after the tragic events of the later afternoon.

Two of the statues had been lowered safely, and the third was being jacked on to the lift-like platform; the cradle crew had not yet returned from their task of conveying the plinth, and one would not have expected them to, with the weight and the distance they had to traverse. So the first two statues were simply left in the shade at the cliff bottom while the engineers and labourers concentrated on the remainder of the task.

Jordan does not yet know why he came to find himself on the lift platform; the man who performed the delicate and dangerous task of directing the operation from the platform itself during the hazardous descent, had been called to the bottom of the cliff on some errand or other, and had not yet returned. The labourers, directed by the engineer, had levered the third statue into position on the platform, and were awaiting their instructions to lower away.

And so it happened that Arthur Jordan found himself the only qualified person, and the nearest to the platform, when the signal was about to be given; the engineer in charge, looking about for his key man, saw him at the foot of the cliff.

⚜ The Gossips

He himself had to direct the winching operations, and the man on the platform transmitted his instructions to a third man it the cliff edge, who passed them on to the engineer. They were quite simple signals, and Jordan had fully understood their use during the morning's work. Rather than hold up the proceedings, he waved to the engineer, exchanged a few shouted words and, at the former's nodded assent, jumped lightly on to the platform and hooked up the securing chains.

Down below, another team of men gripped steadying cables, and as they also noted his signals, held the platform, to prevent it bumping against outjutting rocks. Jordan gave his first signal, the machinery clanked, chains ran sniftering through blocks, and the platform swung gently away from the rock face.

It descended an infinitesimal fraction and then steadied, keeping to a strictly controlled procedure. The sun baked Jordan, the rock face seemed to throw back the heat like a blast furnace, and he was suddenly afraid. He could not, to this day, ascribe any rational cause for his alarm; it was just a 'feeling'. He looked down at the brown, oval faces of the men below, and then up over the stretch of cemetery, blinding in that fierce sun. Everything began to shimmer in the haze and the platform started to vibrate in an odd manner.

I put down my wine glass as Jordan leaned forward; in my short acquaintance with the man, he had not been demonstrative, but I could swear I saw moisture exuding from the skin of his forehead and rolling down his cheek, as he came to what was obviously the most harrowing part of his story.

Jordan had gripped one of the side-chains—a simple movement which subsequently saved his life—and had braced himself to give his second series of signals; he felt better; and he platform again descended a minute distance. It was then that he became aware of the faint, insidious mumbling that I had heard in that self-same garden so long ago; an undertone of sibilant, nauseous whispering, mingled with obscene titters, that tingled the skin of his scalp in an electric fashion. The next thing that happened was a confusion of noise and motions; he heard a sharp crack, at the same time as a shout of alarm or terror—which, he couldn't tell. Similarly, he didn't know whether it came from above or below.

⌘ Darkness, Mist & Shadow

Then the platform suddenly tipped, and tilted, throwing him against the chains; there was the harsh scream of metal against rock and it was this, with the pain of contact with the chain, that convulsed him into action. Something had broken in the main bearings of the winch, or perhaps it was a cable; the platform was tipping at an impossible angle and then Jordan saw what he will never forget. The tons of statue sliding inexorably towards him to crush him down, and on the carved face a sardonic sneer.

Jordan was against the retaining chains. Instantaneously it flickered across his brain that if the statue once caught against the chains, it must inevitably tear everything with it and dash cradle and man to destruction below. As he saw the workmen scattering in panic terror at the cliff floor, Jordan, with the quickness inspired by terror, swiftly unhooked the two massive chains from their retaining cradles and hurled himself upwards into the cables above his head.

There was a noise like an avalanche, a boiling dust of stone and chippings and the flimsy platform bucked about like a cork.

But Jordan was precariously safe. The monstrous statue had gone over the platform edge as it tipped, and had fallen clear. It, and the two other statues were ground to fragments and the dust, like smoke from artillery fire, was lapping at the heels of the frantically running workmen, while boulders, perhaps weighing half a ton, bounded excitedly among them like playful terriers. Jordan clung to the cable, half dazed, the strength of his arms almost gone, borne up by the calm instructions of the engineer above him, who, with pipe securely jammed in his mouth, was testing the winch, his band of shaken colleagues only just beginning to stir themselves.

Jordan had first to be lowered, so that the gear could be freed; and then a rope had to be got out, so that the platform could be pulled back to the safety of the clifftop, for many of the fittings had been torn away. This epic would make a story in itself; as would the courage of the workman who volunteered to lower himself down from the shattered jib gear, and lash Jordan securely to the remaining cables, so that it was impossible for him to fall. Later, it was found that the chain on which this admirable man had relied for this long and complicated operation had been almost sheared through, and was hanging by a few strands.

The Gossips

When Jordan regained the safety of the ground, worse was to come; the loss of the statues was bad enough—that was his responsibility and to him would fall the heavy task of explaining to the Duke. But a small boy, an especial favourite of the workmen, had been standing beneath when the great statue fell; he had been unnoticed by many of the men who swarmed about him and though repeatedly ordered away, had insisted on returning.

The operation had some fascination for him; the statues had been conceived in blood and cruelty, and in their destruction they demanded a human sacrifice. The death of this small boy, Tonio, whose pitiful remains were eventually found beneath the biggest single intact piece of rock, had a profound effect on Jordan and all who were there that afternoon; it was a dazed and demoralised party which prepared to quit the ground on which they had started out so well in the morning.

And there was another, a final horror, of which few could ever be induced to talk again; Jordan, sipping at a new drink set before him, with a manner more like himself, now that this portion of his story was over, promised that he would allude to this again before the end.

I must confess that I had been considerably shaken at the events described by Jordan so far; compared with his experiences, my own had been trifling. Yet, though the way Jordan had described the happenings of that afternoon of recent times, it had seemed quite a normal industrial accident, I was convinced he would have some more outré explanation, in view of my own strong feelings.

And so it proved. But first, Jordan had the painful duty of informing the Duke of what had happened. To his surprise, though deeply shocked and moved at the death of the child, and Jordan's narrow escape, the loss of the statues worried him not at all. In fact, when the effect of the tragedy had worn off, he seemed relieved rather than otherwise; he hastily prevented any further discussion of details of the affair, and asked Jordan to deal with the workmen.

He himself took on the responsibility of interviewing the child's father, and though the boy should not have been where he was when the accident occurred, he insisted on paying the funeral expenses and substantial compensation to the bereaved parents.

Darkness, Mist & Shadow

While all this was going on, Jordan and the engineer made a thorough examination of the equipment used to lower the statuary down the cliff; what they found completely exonerated the company, but caused pale faces among the workmen. In fact, there was no explanation of the disaster in material terms; the only solution was of so monstrous a nature, that Jordan and his associates refused to accept this, and the cause of the accident was put down to the equivalent of an 'act of God', which Jordan felt was a tremendous irony under the circumstances.

The representative of the Milan insurance company who travelled up to the site, was at first inclined to blame some fault of the equipment used, but after he had been shown the evidence and had examined the area of the plateau, he rapidly came to the same conclusions as the others.

He departed, lips compressed and shaking his head; his last words to Jordan and the engineer were that, fortunately, such happenings occurred only once in a life-time—otherwise, nothing would be insurable.

The engineering firm, with many expressions of regret, packed up their gear and departed; Jordan and the Duke were undecided what to do about the plinth. It had already been crated and was sealed in a warehouse in Palermo, awaiting shipment to London. They left it there for a moment, while they debated more weighty matters. Jordan cabled news of the disaster to London and remained on as the Duke's guest until the insurance problems had been sorted out.

Eventually, there came a cable to say that the company would bear the full loss; this, together with the compensation which the British government had decided to pay instead of the exhibition grant, more than covered the material and artistic loss sustained by the Duke. In fact, he was most effusive over this turn of the affair and his handshake was extremely cordial when Jordan eventually left, a week later.

The inquest on the child, in a nearby village, had revealed nothing, as Jordan had anticipated, and after a perfunctory judicial inquiry by the local police, the affair died down and was written off as an unfortunate accident, though coroner and police alike were hard put to it to explain away the manner of the accident in natural terms.

⚜ THE GOSSIPS

Jordan contented himself with certain documents, drawings and other material the Duke had lent him from his library, and this would have to represent the statuary in the London exhibition. Jordan took these away with him in a locked valise and after other business had been completed on the Italian mainland, he made his way back to London just over a fortnight afterwards, a slightly different man from the one who had made the outward journey.

He duly reported to his foundation, conferred with the Chairman of the Exhibition Committee and went on with his other preparations for the opening, which was now about four months away. This work absorbed him so continuously that, combined with the trips he was obliged to make from London to other parts of England, the whole business gradually faded from his mind.

But some weeks later, it was again in the forefront. He had received an urgent message from the Chairman of the Exhibition Committee, when spending a weekend at the Kent coast; it asked him to return to London at once.

Sir Portman Ackroyd was a solid, red-faced man whose claret features seemed even more suffused, as he passed a buff message form across his desk to a confused Jordan.

The message read: *Sicilian statuary crated arrived London Docks today stop bonded warehouse for clearance stop awaiting instructions stop Ross.*

Jordan's feelings, as he read this extraordinary message can perhaps be imagined rather than felt; his first instincts, as he discussed the matter with Ackroyd, were that a mistake had been made. Then his face lightened. There had evidently been some confusion at Palermo. No doubt the plinth alone had arrived.

Sir Portman's brow cleared and he got on the telephone; Ross could not be reached, but inquiries would be made at the docks. In half an hour the phone rang again; there were definitely four crates, three of them upright and one horizontal.

To say that the room turned black, Jordan explained to his two friends, would be a slight exaggeration but the receipt of this stupefying message had something of that effect.

In fact, he looked so queer, that Sir Portman solicitously led him

◈ Darkness, Mist & Shadow

to a deep easy-chair and poured him a liberal brandy. Then the two men debated the curious mystery and Jordan decided that he would leave for the docks himself, and investigate. Sir Portman insisted that he would come also; in the meantime he left his secretary with the task of checking with the Italian shipping company who had handled the transportation of the crates. They could do little else, without appearing foolish, until they had personally inspected the contents.

At this point Jordan fell silent, and the quiet atmosphere of the Florentine cafe again came back to my ears; far away there was the thin, high note of a violin and this, mingled with the occasional clink of glasses and the splash of the river at our front, gave an agreeable touch of sanity after hearing this nightmare tale.

Grisson leaned towards me as Jordan stopped speaking. "To give Arthur a chance to catch his breath," he said. "I feel I owe you an apology. As you may have guessed, I didn't make my visit with you totally unprepared."

"I gathered that," I said. "I picked up one of your ear-plugs after we left the site. I kept it all these years."

And I handed him a small scrap of tissue paper. Grisson reddened, and then joined in the laughter of Arthur Jordan and myself; Jordan evidently knew this story, and he continued amused for some minutes, as Grisson drew out the ear-plug from the twist of paper.

"I was really sorry about that," he told me. "But I had to have a neutral observer who knew nothing of the area or of the history of 'The Gossips'. I wore these to see whether or not I would be affected, and also to ensure there would be someone on the spot who could act freely in case of emergency."

He broke off awkwardly as he finished his sentence, but was reassured by the smile I gave him. All the same, I was glad he had offered his explanation, which cleared up many things. As Jordan prepared to take up the story again, Grisson shifted his position in his chair and said something whose significance escaped me until later.

"You will not have overlooked two curious facts, I presume? One is that the statues are of women; and that, so far as is known, all the victims were males."

◈ THE GOSSIPS

I had not much time to ponder on this cryptic announcement when Arthur Jordan, who was already beginning to display impatience, recommenced his story.

He and Sir Portman had driven to the docks; there, in a vast shed, backed by cranes and all the maritime activities of a great port, were the four enormous crates, plainly labelled for their destination. Ross led the two men into the stone-floored shed, where a crowd of dockers had gathered.

As Sir Portman gave the order, several of them began to carefully pry back the stout boards on the top of one box which Jordan had indicated. In about a quarter of an hour, after boards, straw and packing had been removed, the unmistakable features of one of the hideous stone trio was revealed.

Even some of the hard-bitten dock workers were shaken at the savage expression on that vile face, and Sir Portman's rubicon features turned a shade whiter. Arthur Jordan did not shriek, neither did he faint away, but he felt the shed whirl round him and had to be helped back to the taxi.

All the way back into central London, as the mean streets of the docks fled past the windows, he said, over and over to Sir Portman, "How could such a thing be? With my own eyes I saw them smashed to fragments. With my own eyes!"

As for Sir Portman, who had never experienced the appalling atmosphere of their Sicilian setting, he no longer debated whether deviltry or science was at the bottom of the things' arrival in London. He knew he had the statues for his exhibition and that was the principal matter which concerned him. Jordan turned paler than ever, when he learned that Ackroyd intended to go ahead with the display of the statuary as planned; but all his pleading to the contrary was in vain. Sir Portman advised him to rest for several days and in the meantime he would have inquiries put in train.

Jordan turned over to him such documents as were necessary for this purpose; once arrived at his flat near the museum, where he usually worked, he went to bed for three days with a raging fever. At the end of this time, his housekeeper, who had tended his wants during his illness, admitted an excited Sir Portman and a fellow colleague from the museum. The Exhibition Committee Chairman had seldom been so enthusiastic about an exhibit.

'The Gossips' had been uncrated and re-assembled and in a month's time would be set up on their exhibition site in the hall; designers were fashioning a miniature cliff, so that they could be displayed in something of their original setting. Sir Portman thought they would be the sensation of the entire show and congratulated the unfortunate Jordan on all he had done to secure them.

As for the mystery, he confessed himself as baffled as anyone else; but what did it really matter—the great thing was that they were available for display. Sir Portman had cabled the Duke immediately, but had a reply from his steward to say he had gone abroad for a protracted tour. He had then cabled again, asking for an examination to be made at the foot of the cliff at the palazzo. This cable had gone to one of the museum's agents in Palermo, a man whom Jordan had originally contacted, and he had personally visited the site.

He had replied that the figures had disappeared, but there were boulders and crushed stone at the foot of the cliff, as though there had been a bad rock fall. Further inquiries at the Palermo docks had revealed that the crates had arrived for loading shortly after Jordan left for London.

The orders for the shipping of the consignment to London had never been cancelled; Jordan had been too upset to remember this, and no doubt the crated plinth had given the impression to the shippers that things were proceeding normally.

Records of the Italian shipping line engaged had confirmed afterwards, continued Jordan, that the crates had arrived in the normal manner; local labour had brought them to the docks on large lorries. But the greater mystery remained.

Had it been possible, asked Sir Portman, for the Duke's agents to have reconstructed the figures in time for them to have been forwarded? It would have been a colossal task, but skilled savants from one of the Italian museums could have achieved this.

Jordan had to admit that it was barely possible, but the job would have taken months. He would like to examine the group himself, he said, when he felt up to it. Sir Portman, the antiquarian in him still intensely excited by the whole affair, and far more enthusiastic than Jordan ever felt likely to be again over this particular exhibit, said the whole surface of the group was cracked and pitted, and it could well have been pieced together from fragments. He felt the effect added to the diablerie of the group.

A few days later Jordan, quite recovered, visited the warehouse in the City where the group was being prepared. Despite his fears, the figures seemed quite normal and no-one who had been concerned in their erection, had noticed anything untoward. Indeed, beneath the prosaic electric light and in the close company of other groups of figures and statues from the same period, they seemed to have lost something of their diabolical quality. To Jordan's relief, after a close examination of the stone, he felt they could have been re-assembled after fragmentation; the granite-like browny-stone from which they were carved was split and fissured from end to end—that was apparently a quality of it—but if the group had been re-assembled—and it had to be, for no other theory would account for it—then the job had been done with tremendous cunning and skill.

What dark shadows hovered round the fringes of Jordan's mind, he no longer confided in Sir Portman. With the exhibition fast coming upon them, it would have done no good; so he kept his forebodings to himself, with the mental reservation that the responsibility was no longer his. The whole affair had been discussed in camera at a full meeting of Sir Portman's committee, all distinguished men in their various fields, and they had decided to go ahead with this once-in-a-lifetime coup.

What mainly troubled Jordan still was that no-one had yet heard anything from the Duke, though they had sent him at least three cables, asking for the messages to be forwarded. Also, further diligent inquiries both in Sicily and on the mainland of Italy had failed to unearth any more information on the re-assembling of the figures, or who had given the orders for their crating and forwarding.

But as the weeks went by and with the exhibition work mounting up, he found less and less time for his more wild imaginings, and was content to leave the affair of 'The Gossips' to more stolid spirits who had not accompanied him on the Sicilian expedition and who knew nothing of their wild history.

No less than five of London's largest halls were to be utilised for this biggest exhibition of its kind ever staged in the capital, and almost a month beforehand, the three female figures and their plinth were moved to their final position in one of the most prominent positions in the Steinway Hall.

This vast auditorium had been chosen for a number of reasons; the principal one was that it featured a huge balcony, supported by enormous iron trusses of Victorian manufacture, which together provided the tremendous strength necessary for the support of such a heavy group.

Engineers had calculated the stress and had told the exhibition organisers there was a large safety margin. The balcony railings were then dismantled, slabs of stone laid down and eventually a most realistic artificial cliff was erected, to give 'The Gossips' the most impressive setting of the entire exhibition.

Skilful lighting, with sky effects at the rear, gave a day and night cycle of dawn, daylight, sunset and night, which lasted twenty minutes and was destined to be a most memorable sight for the crowds who witnessed it.

Even Jordan, who viewed the progress of the work with understandable interest, had to admit that the effect was splendid. But for the lamentable tragedy of a month or two before, which he could not erase from his mind, it would have been a triumphant climax in his career. As it was, the matter brought many congratulations from distinguished colleagues, and he was the subject of a number of articles in the press.

Curiously enough, those pressmen and photographers who were given a preview a week before the exhibition opened to the public, though delighted, like the laymen, with the group's fantastic qualities, saw nothing extraordinary in it; neither was there anything wrong with their photographs.

"But," said Jordan, looking at me with expressive eyes, across the cafe table, "within six months after the exhibition, every single photo-

The Gossips

graph or photographic block had faded and disappeared; even to the individual images in newspaper files.

"But by that time the Second World War had broken out, and people had other things to think about. The scientists had theories about the fading, too. They argued that dampness and storage conditions may have been responsible—as if that could have affected zinc and lead blocks, not to mention the countless thousands of newspaper file copies stored under dry, perfect conditions."

He was silent again for a moment, and the noise of the river a few yards away from our chairs, appeared suddenly to intrude with its compelling murmur.

Grisson seemed to awake with a start from a trance-like pose; evidently he had been deeply stirred by Jordan's fantastic story.

However, all he said, in a mild voice, was, "My round, I think," and another tray of drinks presently appeared.

The night before the exhibition was due to be opened to the public, Arthur Jordan was invited to a celebration dinner by Sir Portman and the exhibition committee; this started at seven and was attended by many distinguished guests. Later, a fleet of cars toured the five halls to view the exhibits. Everything went well and those present enjoyed a memorable evening.

Some genius had thought up a background of recordings of genuine mediaeval Sicilian folk-tunes as a background for 'The Gossips' tableau and when the day and night lighting cycle had finished, and the last quavering note died in the gallery, the large audience of invited guests broke into furious and spontaneous applause.

Arthur Jordan found himself, unwillingly, the centre of all eyes, and his introduction was sought by many of these distinguished people. Some of their questions he found embarrassing in the extreme—the music in fact was out of period, but few of the guests seemed to realise this—and it was with gratitude that he was able to excuse himself, over an hour later, and sought a side exit to make his way home.

He had to pass near the gallery in which the group of statues was exhibited and as he made his way through the now empty, echoing building, someone began to extinguish the lights, one by one. His footsteps sounded unnaturally loudly along the deserted stairs and corridors, and to Jordan's nerves, strained as they were by his recent experiences, the sounds were unpleasantly evocative.

Some light yet lingered in the galleries and he was descending a spiral staircase, whose metallic clangour gave back a sombre echo from the gallery beyond, when he heard the sharp, staccato steps of a man in the gloom below him. He clung to the staircase, as the noise came nearer, and then saw a miniature flashlight bobbing uncertainly about beneath.

"Who's there?" he called out, in unnecessarily loud tones, clamping down a rising wave of hysteria.

The light swerved in an alarming manner, and then came towards him, picking him out on the staircase like an acrobat pin-pointed in the spot lamp of a circus.

"Thank God it's you, sir."

With relief Jordan saw the uniform and peaked cap of one of the museum attendants.

"Hullo, Hoskins," he said. "Anything wrong?"

He had reached the ground floor by this time and was not prepared for the answer which came. In the dim light of the lamp Hoskins' face looked pale and strained.

"I can't help telling you, Mr. Jordan, I nearly lost my head when someone switched out the lights just now. I was up on top there, near those ugly big statues, and I heard the most horrible whispering coming from the gallery."

Jordan had started and put his hand on the other's arm.

"Let's find a light switch before you go any further," he said, with all the strength of mind he could command. As light sprang out in the nearby galleries, he reflected that his face probably looked just as pallid and un-natural as the gallery attendant's. "Right, now..." he went on.

"Well," said Hoskins, switching off his lamp, his tones mote normal as the atmosphere was restored to everyday. "I was on the Somme in the last war and I've seen some things in my time, but that whispering fair gave me the creeps. I thought someone had got in the gallery, or perhaps some of the guests were playing a joke, so I shone my torch up and went along to see what was up. Well, I didn't like it at all.

The Gossips

"To tell you the truth, I didn't dare go in among those statues. They were all in silhouette, and I know it sounds daft, but I could have sworn the faces were moving.

"I expect it was the effect of the shadow, God knows my hand was trembling enough. Anyway, I was just debating what to do when some fool put the main lights out. I couldn't face that, not in the darkness, sir, and I turned and ran."

"Quite understandable," said Jordan in a kindly manner, laying his hand on the other man's shoulder. "I don't mind telling you that I've had quite an experience with these statues myself, one way or another."

"Ah, of course, you brought 'em over, didn't you, sir, now I remember," said Hoskins, in evident relief. "So you know what I'm talking about."

"I do indeed, Hoskins," said Jordan. "I can assure you it's a mere aural trick, caused by natural draught and their clever method of construction."

He had decided to take this attitude, for the success of the exhibition meant a lot to him and the organisers, and he could not afford to let an attendant's panic—though how he sympathised with the poor devil!—prejudice the opening and spread a lot of dark rumours about.

"Let's go and have a look, shall we?" he continued to Hoskins, walking easily and naturally forward, though what this effort cost him, no-one would ever know.

The attendant, his confidence restored, went back into the main hall with him and in the full light of the floodlamps self-respect slowly oozed back.

The statues glared malevolently in the strong lighting, but the silence was absolute. For once, Jordan understood the meaning of the phrase 'not a whisper', and he was profoundly thankful for it.

"You see, all well," he said, with what he felt was nonchalance in his voice, hoping to God that nothing untoward would occur. And after this brief inspection the pair moved off, Jordan to find his car and Hoskins to continue his round. As he drove off, Jordan looked in his mirror, and saw the lights in the great Exhibition Hall dying in the night, one by one.

Darkness, Mist & Shadow

5

I had bought another round of drinks and the first infusion of late night theatre-goers and those coming out of cinemas had enlivened the terrace tables around us, before Jordan went on with the next part of his story. Though the chattering and the laughter from the nearer tables at first put him off his stride, I myself was glad to have this lively background to the sombreness of the main tapestry, and while he said nothing, I felt Grisson was of the same mind.

The next incident was very simple and very terrible, and it must have come with an appalling effect on Jordan, being in possession of all the facts as he was. He was awakened the following morning by the relentless tones of his telephone bell, to find Sir Portman on the line. Had he seen the morning paper? Something unfortunate had happened at the Steinway Hall the previous evening. Jordan said he would come round to see Sir Portman at nine o'clock and rang off.

He hadn't asked his caller what the matter was, but it must be pretty serious to warrant such an early call; it was curious, too, that Sir Portman had not volunteered any information but had merely asked him to look at the paper. If Jordan expected sensational headlines on the front page, he was mistaken; he went for his *Daily Post* on the hall mat in trepidation, but it took him almost ten minutes to find the item.

It was a small piece on page three, under a single column heading which said: GALLERY ATTENDANT DIES IN FALL. The text ran:

> Albert Hoskins, 54, gallery attendant at the Steinway Hall, S.W., was found dead on the floor by a colleague early this morning, just a few hours before London's biggest-ever 17th Century Exhibition was due to begin. Mr. Hoskins, who had been employed by the Hall authorities for about seven years, had apparently slipped from an unfenced balcony containing the group of Sicilian statuary, 'The Gossips'. The accident had happened at about 12:30 A.M., a doctor's report established, and Mr. Hoskins had fallen head-first nearly twenty feet on to a newly-laid rocky area, representing a cliff face.

The Gossips

There was a bit more, but Jordan was too sick to read it. Hoskins had died—he hardly dared say to himself, had been killed—only about twenty minutes after his conversation with Jordan. He must have been on his way back through the gallery, after letting the latter out.

It was a trembling Jordan who downed a large whisky—at breakfast of all times—and faced Sir Portman and the Exhibition committee an hour or two later. They had braced themselves, in view of opening day and though the accident was unfortunate, they had to repress any morbid thoughts, when the first members of the public would be coming in through the turnstiles at 11:00 A.M.

Eventually, Jordan saw that it would be of little use to tell them of his talk with the gallery attendant; he did stress the desirability, though, of fencing the ledge on which the group rested, to prevent any repetition of the accident. The committee saw his point, but were of the opinion that it would greatly reduce the effectiveness of the set-piece and place it on a level with something out of a public park. And in any case, no members of the public would be allowed on the ledge.

Jordan could not but agree with them, and went to his office to prepare for the opening, fervently praying that nothing further would happen to mar the long-awaited triumph. It was at this point that Grisson again entered the story. He had known Arthur Jordan for some years, and had followed the occasional newspaper stories of the Exhibition with interest. It was when he learned that The Gossips were to be exhibited that he contacted Jordan and the two men pooled their knowledge. Grisson did not at first reveal all that he knew, particularly of the unfortunate visit he and I had paid to the palazzo some years before, but he had said enough to make Jordan realise that here he had an expert and initiated ally.

So it was naturally to Grisson that he again turned in his current predicament. Fortunately, his colleague was in London for the express purpose of attending the Exhibition, though he had been unable to be present at the preview the previous evening. He hadn't seen the newspaper item when Jordan phoned his hotel, but agreed to come round to the Steinway Hall at once.

◢ Darkness, Mist & Shadow

He found Jordan in a very ragged state of nerves, which was hardly surprising; the two men spoke for an hour, and after a very full and frank comparison of notes, while realising the strange and unnatural nature of 'The Gossips', neither of them felt justified in interfering with the course of the Exhibition.

Hoskins' death could have been an accident and who would have believed such a story? Certainly not the Exhibition committee, nor any other person in his right mind. With their special knowledge, and particularly, Arthur Jordan's agonising responsibility as the person who had secured the statues for London and as a principal organiser of the Exhibition, the two men could only agree to act together and keep a keen supervisory eye on things.

In the event, it was agreed that wherever possible, one or other of the two men would be on duty in the gallery; at the first sign of any out-of-the-way manifestations, that part of the gallery would be closed. As a double precaution, Sir Portman was persuaded to have the immediate area at the foot of the simulated cliff roped off, to prevent any spectators from crowding underneath during the performances. With this much achieved, the two men felt they had done all that was humanly possible to prevent any further tragedy.

As if to reinforce this view, the Exhibition was a tremendous success—certainly, beyond anything that the organisers could have suspected; people in the thousands flocked to the five halls every day, and for every one who had heard of the death of the gallery attendant, there were at least five hundred who hadn't. Even Jordan's wan face relaxed and Sir Portman's features expanded like a sunrise in the blaze of publicity which surrounded such an unusual Exhibition.

As was to be expected, The Gossips tableau was the biggest single 'draw' at the Steinway Hall and extra performances had to be laid on every day, so many people wanted to see the dawn and sunset effects. Press and radio were no less enthusiastic, and the first week saw both record crowds and record profits for the various antiquarian funds to which the Exhibition was devoted.

But it was on the Saturday night that the incident occurred which provided the last shock for the harassed Jordan, caused a furore and

⌑ The Gossips

agitated speculation in the press, and was finally responsible for the partial closure of the Exhibition at Steinway Hall. No one could be blamed for what occurred, really. The last performance of the sky effects round the statuary was taking place at about ten P.M., prior to the Exhibition closing for the night.

A large crowd gathered, had heard an exposition on their history from a distinguished professor, and Grisson, who was on duty, had taken the opportunity to slip out for a few minutes to the buffet for a sandwich and a cup of coffee. It was as the sunset effects were at their most splendid, that a rippled murmur made itself audible among the crowd, a murmur which rapidly changed to cries of horror. A middle-aged man was seen climbing over the rocky terrain around the base of the statues; he was reeling about as though drunk, and as the helpless crowd watched, horrified, he stepped forward and plunged from the edge of the platform upon the rocks beneath.

Spectators rushed to his assistance and a doctor was soon or the scene, but the man had broken his neck, and died a few minutes afterwards. There was no rational explanation. He was; retired tailor, named Matthews, who lived at Streatham; of impeccable antecedents and habits, he most certainly had not beet drunk. No attendants had seen him approach any parts of the building closed to the general public, and the doors leading to the terrace on which the statues were situated were locked, a was the custom.

This time the morning papers took a lot of notice, and after a hurried conference of his committee the next day, Sir Portman and his colleagues decided to close down the gallery, and make arrangements to ship back the statues to their place of origin Although the committee members were far from believing that the two deaths, coming so closely, were anything more than unconnected accidents, the information Grisson and Jordan wet able to give them produced some raised eyebrows and blown cheeks in the committee room.

The fact that an inquest would also have to be held tipped the scales; reluctant as they were to lose such a fine asset as 'The Gossips' for the Exhibition, they simply could not afford an more adverse publicity. Jordan—and to a lesser extent, Grisson was relieved at the committee's decision; the malevolent group was removed from the

Steinway Hall, while that portion of the gallery remained closed for a couple of days.

The statues were then crated to await transport to the docks and a further cable was sent to the Duke. This, too, remained unanswered.

Jordan remained silent for a moment, as he reached this point in his story. He fumbled in his wallet and eventually produced an envelope which contained some scraps of faded newspaper dippings. He selected one of these, and passed it over to me. It merely said that while the S.S. Janine was loading at London Docks, Albert Williams, docker, 35, was crushed to death between a crate and the ship's side. I looked up at Arthur Jordan.

"This time the press hadn't done all their homework," he said. "The crate contained one of the statues, of course, but fortunately that didn't get out. Again, no-one could prove that it was anything other than an accident."

He had informed Sir Portman of the latest incident, as the Exhibition went on from triumph to triumph, and the Chairman had remarked succinctly that the Sicilians were welcome to the statues. The next development was almost the most curious of all. Jordan had eventually received a letter from the Duke, apologising for his absence from home during the arrival of the various cables.

He went elaborately round the ground, and without actually admitting that the statues had been broken, he did go so far as to say that the estate workers had done their best to ensure that the statuary would be in condition for presentation at the exhibition. He expressed regret at the London incidents, and acknowledged receipt of the messages regarding the shipment.

The letter covered a mere two pages of flowing handwriting, and left Jordan more puzzled and disgruntled than ever. He showed the document to Sir Portman, who was equally mystified at the contents. But the matter didn't seem worth following up and was gradually dropped.

Three weeks later, Jordan happened to pick up a newspaper dated two or three days' earlier, and his attention was arrested by a small paragraph on the front page. This he passed to me to read, also.

It was only about six lines and said that the Italian steamship Janine, of so many thousand tons, had foundered in a terrific storm in

The Gossips

the Gulf of Lions, and had been lost with all cargo. There were no casualties among the crew, who had been landed at Marseilles by a Swedish freighter, which had picked them up.

Even then, it was not quite the end of the story. Jordan smiled quizzically, as he looked back over his experiences with those cursed stones. The biggest surprise of all came at the end. Jordan was engaged in the clearing up of the Exhibition, after its closure, when he received another telegram from the Duke. This merely acknowledged receipt of the crated statues at Palermo, in good order, and thanked him for his co-operation.

This time Jordan showed the cable to no-one except Grisson; the two met in an obscure London pub and thrashed the thing out between them. Wild horses would not have dragged either of them back to that haunted bluff in Sicily, if they had the time or the money, but they just had to know what had happened to those crates.

Jordan went as far as to search the records at Lloyds. It was true that the Janine had foundered; all cargo had been lost and Lloyds made full settlement. It was not possible that four crates containing tons of stone could have been washed hundreds of miles farther south. After debating a while longer, Jordan cabled his agent in Palermo and asked him to inspect the site again. A fortnight later, he received a letter from the agent to say that the statues were once more in situ on the bluff in the Duke's palazzo gardens. So far as the man could make out with field glasses, they appeared as they were before the accident.

Even then Jordan did not quite give up. In the hope that there might be some more rational explanation, he again wrote to the Duke, asking him, as a matter of urgency, for the full details to which he felt entitled.

In reply he did get a long letter this time, and after he had read it, he wished, for his own peace of mind, that the Duke hadn't been quite so loquacious. Some of the information Grisson had already told me earlier in the evening, but much was for Jordan's ear only, and he was asked to burn the letter after he had read it.

Regarding the reappearance of 'The Gossips', the Duke had written, in what appeared to be a frantically scrawled hand, "There is no explanation; think what you will, but do not ask for one." His text had then gone into Sicilian. This, Jordan had translated by a colleague at his museum.

"It was something on the lines of the old English saw about the female of the species being more deadly," he said to me, with an apologetic smile.

The Duke did reveal that his own grandfather had been sceptical of the legend, and had actually started to have a smaller wall which then existed to separate the statues from the house, taken down. No-one knew exactly what happened, but he had such a bad fright one evening, that the young man, as he then was, had the larger wall erected as I had seen it on the occasion of my memorable visit.

Jordan stopped again, and played a little tune on the marble-topped table with the handle of his coffee spoon.

"That wasn't what frightened us in the garden," he said, with a sort of slow defiance. "I'd been pretty steady-nerved until then."

"He's saving the best till last, like all good storytellers," said Grisson, in a vain attempt to lighten the atmosphere. The cafe lights were beginning to go out along the Arno, though a few lamps still reflected back its brilliant surface.

"You see," said Jordan with a deep sigh. "The explanation was in the nature of the statues. Caravallo's masterpiece had been created from life."

From the shattered horror of the stonework in the garden after the accident to the lift, had poured the raw materials on which he had based his devilish art—mingled with the browny-red basaltic stone were the teeth, bones and hair of three young girls.

◈ A Very Pleasant Fellow

Dear Father Mapple, he wrote, the spidery writing almost illegible against the notepaper made dim by the faint, dying light of the early winter's day spilling in at the window. *Dear Father Mapple, Thank you for your kind note regarding the proposed Christmas bazaar...*

The pen scratched as the ink ran out, and scarred the paper. Mr. Philps sighed and gazed down at the street where the brown, crinkled leaves of autumn were already heaped in sheaves as the man from the council went his rounds with the small green barrow. He hated the monotony of winter which chained him to the inside of the house and his solitary vigil at the window when the cold would make it uninviting for him to spend much time outdoors.

Now that he had retired, the days began to drag and he missed the busy routine of the shop, the tins gay with their bright labels; the exotic fruits from South Africa, New Zealand, Australia; the friendly interest of his customers and the musical ring of the till which told of his mounting prosperity over the years. Already he regretted his somewhat over-hasty decision to give up. He had been away now—here he began to tot up in his head—a bare thirteen months, but it was as though it were several years. He felt quite old, though he wasn't yet sixty and not being keen on golf or such pastimes, he found it difficult to maintain an interesting routine that centred round the house.

◢ Darkness, Mist & Shadow

He had always been too busy to find much time for the pursuits that interested normal people—the shop and his work on the council and the local bench had always absorbed his time. Now it dragged and he sometimes caught himself looking forward to the evening when Mrs. Philps would bring him a hot drink and some thin toast and he could make his way heavily to bed another day—he hesitated to say 'wasted'—but at least put behind him.

It had been a mistake to continue to live opposite the shop, he now felt, where he could see so much that was going on and of which he was no longer a part. He felt somehow ashamed, as though he were slacking when, after a late morning in bed and an even later breakfast, he dragged himself to the window and looked across the High Street to where a blaze of neon lighting indicated a prosperous activity that had begun before 8:00 A.M.

In Mr. Philps' day the shop had been a place of discreet gloom, with solid mahogany Victorian fittings and plenty of ornamental gilt and scroll work, redolent of the fragrance of freshly roasted coffee; a place that stood for quality and a sense of permanent values.

Mr. Philps was happy there among his three assistants and shining machines; one for the coffee, another for slicing bacon; even the scales partook of an antique quality and his slightly awed customers would not have been surprised had a merchant prince and a turbanned retinue appeared at the door bearing spices from the East and other exotic offerings.

Mr. Philps sighed again, withdrew his gaze from the window and switched on his shaded desk lamp. Under the soft glow of this small moon suspended in the gloom he could make a fresh start. *Dear Father Mapple*, he began again, dipping his pen anew into the ink. *I regret that a clash of appointments makes it impossible for me to perform the opening ceremony.* A clash of appointments—he rather liked that phrase. It smacked of a dynamic routine ruefully at variance with the facts. He smiled wryly and went on.

When he had finished the letter he stamped and addressed an envelope and then, struck by a sudden idea, thought he would post it himself. The walk would do him good and the box was only a few hundred yards.

A Very Pleasant Fellow

The air was cold outside, far colder than he had imagined and he huddled deeper into the thick, expensive overcoat, his thin blood no match for the bitter air that merely quickened the motion of the young people who brushed heedlessly past him, their excited conversation chopped into segments by the wind. Mr. Philps crouched against the cold and set off for the postbox at a teetering stoop. Across the road the lights of the grocer's shop made a warm oasis in the general gloom and he could see the heads of the customers, so many dull blobs at that distance, clustered round the self-service counters.

A tram went by, its pole sliding icily along the cable and the thin, sharp sound seemed to accentuate the cold and Mr. Philps' isolation. He felt antique, almost prehistoric among these glowing passers-by who kept up to date with all the latest gadgets in an age of plastics. He wished now he had kept to the Eastbourne plan. The atmosphere was conducive to his own taste and a house there would have been the answer to many problems.

He could have taken up bowls—Mr. Philps always fancied himself poised on the greenest of turf against an eternally and absurdly blue sea, encountered usually only on travel posters or in the islands of Greece—but even as he formulated the thought he half realised that this dream, too, was an illusion. That even if he had retired to Eastbourne the wind would have been chilly, the sun a mirage and the bowls club would have eluded him as so many other things had slipped past his reach during the last fifty-eight years.

It had been a mistake too, his retirement from the council—this had been a side result of the abortive Eastbourne scheme and had carried with it an automatic disqualification from the bench. So with one stroke he had separated himself from a happy, useful life for one of long, heavy days, each one similar to the day before and leading... where? Mr. Philps shivered again, but it was not only the wind this time; he seemed to see a shadow even darker than the leaden sky above him. How many years might he have to face of similar inactivity?

It was a blenching thought, yet what was the alternative? That too was a question mark and a shadow. His own attitude and that of Mrs. Philps did not help; a tall, thin, anonymous woman, his wife had no ambitions other than to minister to his wants. A kind woman, not uncritical, deeply concerned for his welfare, she seemed only to accentuate the greyness with which he was surrounded.

Mr. Philps sighed heavily, as a group of leather-jacketed teenagers passed him, their brassy self assurance in striking contrast to his own timid reserve. He found the post box, slipped in the letter, wincing as his hand came into contact with the icy edge of the metal slot and turned round back into the wind, his thoughts circulating sluggishly and monotonously in his head. No, his own attitude did not help; he had seemed to shrink into himself nee his retirement and he was coming to shirk more and more public duties as time went by. He could easily have opened Father Mapple's bazaar, yet it all seemed too much bother somehow.

From where he was standing—he had paused idly for a moment to look into the window of a shoe shop—and from there, sheltered from the wind, he could see the glow of his former business, thick with customers still and then the confident, bulky from of the new owner, shouting his wares on the pavement with his usual vulgarity. Mr. Philps had never liked the man who had bought his shop; Hedgepeth was a ridiculous name to start with; Victor Hedgepeth. Not that he hadn't paid a good ice for the business; Mr. Philps had to admit that he had been generous. But he had never taken to him with his fat, red face; loud voice and sniggering laugh; his vulgarity, ignorance and bad manners; and his breezy assumption that nothing mattered in life but the making of money.

Mr. Philps, who had never envied or disliked anyone in his life, was even beginning to feel, deep down inside him, a dull hatred of Hedgepeth; it stemmed partly from living opposite: shop and partly from the new owner's unfortunate habits of vulgar whistling, his hanging about on the doorstep and loud bantering with passers-by; his flashy clothes and an atmosphere which seemed generally to flaunt the evident success of the business now that it had got into the hands of a go-ahead man.

It had begun with irritation and now the sight of Hedgepeth only fanned the smouldering resentment Mr. Philps felt. The new man had commenced by tearing down all the cherished fittings Mr. Philps had

A Very Pleasant Fellow

installed over the years after such thought and expense, though of course, he had every right to do so. And another thing which added to Mr. Philps' resentment was the evident fact that the customers preferred the methods of the brash newcomer; the shop was fuller than it had ever been in his day and the bright lights and busy air seemed to accentuate the fact that Mr. Philps himself had not done so well there—though in fact it had been a good, solid business under his management. But there was something about Hedgepeth that had begun with dislike and had developed into a definite resentment on Mr. Philps' part; in a way, he supposed, because he had been fool enough to stay on in Camford, when he should have moved away, got a nice house with a garden and made a fresh life for himself and his wife.

Every day he almost dreaded the cocky figure of his successor that would be standing across the road when he got to the window; Hedgepeth had latterly adopted the unfortunate trick of planting himself in his doorway and staring aggressively up at Mr. Philps' windows. His square face had a sinister aspect when he held it sideways; this, combined with his flat cap and squat, powerful figure gave him the aspect of a somewhat aggressive ape. An ape, moreover, who evidently felt that having given up the shop, Mr. Philps should move on and transplant himself, his goods and his household to another, more amenable atmosphere.

Of course, all this might have been in Mr. Philps' mind, he told himself, trying to appear reasonable. Hedgepeth might feel himself that his predecessor was spying on him from across the road, perhaps sneering at him behind his back, laughing at his efforts to improve trade and 'get on'. But Mr. Philps didn't think so; not after yesterday. Not after the short conversation in the new shop and the blazing row which had followed; a row which had shattered the calm and shown him what Hedgepeth really thought. It had begun over nothing; Mr. Philps, who had rarely been inside over the past year, had gone in for a can of his favourite peaches.

The impertinent young woman in the dirty, slovenly overalls had tried to fob him off with an inferior brand for which she wanted to charge threepence extra and he had asked to see Hedgepeth. He had

◌ Darkness, Mist & Shadow

started to complain in a bantering manner, assuming that Hedgepeth would immediately side with him and chide the assistant but to his surprise and horror the former had adopted a very nasty tone and told him to go somewhere else if he didn't like the service.

The two men, both white and quivering had then declared war; the row which flared between them, carried on in low tones over the counter had brought wondering and worried glances from the other customers, who edged away, and it had ended with Mr. Philps stalking out in dignified silence, his mind a mass of churning emotions and vain regrets for what he ought to have said. Since then, a bare twenty-four hours before, he had had a quiet hatred for Hedgepeth that would make it impossible to live opposite any longer. This sort of thing was going to make life difficult and retirement miserable, he told himself, still staring out blankly across the road and then, hardly knowing where he was going, he turned in a half circle and decided to walk around for a bit.

Aimlessly his feet seemed to carry him of their own volition and it was almost with a shock of surprise that he found himself a few minutes later entering the arc of Camford Crescent. He knew now he would have a chat with his old friend George Coleman—almost the only real friend he had in the town. It was a friendship which had lasted over 30 years and a rather strange one, really, considering that his interests and George's differed so widely.

But perhaps that was what had kept them together; for it was a friendship of shared silences, of reasoned sentences between puffs of pipe-smoke, and measured opinions; a friendship which demanded nothing from either, except the ability to pick up threads where they had been left, without comment, without reproach, whether the interval had been a week or a year. George Coleman was a strange individual himself. A bachelor, he kept a small antique and oddments shop in Camford Crescent; he lived above in a suite of rooms in a state of surprising luxury for one who ran a business in such an out-of-the-way back street.

But George had the most surprising things for sale at odd times, his customers came from far and wide throughout the county and in addition he had a small private income. Weekends he was often away

A Very Pleasant Fellow

seeking his curiosities but most afternoons he was to be found in his small office-sitting room behind the shop where there was always a friendly cup of tea, an erudite fund of talk and a warm welcome. Coleman's tastes were catholic and an extraordinary collection of books, totalling several thousand volumes, littered the packed shelves of his office and spilled over into row after row of bookcases in the rooms upstairs. In his study well-drilled spines of tooled leather bindings marched in columns across the spaces of his shelves, but in the shop things were more informal and modern novels were apt to be packed in with works on occultism, necromancy, surgery or bridge. Anything special which George bought in one of his 'lots' went first onto the shelves in his office and from there, once they were read and classified, into his permanent library upstairs.

But there was one shelf, just near the fireplace, where nothing seemed to change; here the volumes were larger and older looking, their bindings black with the patina of age. The subjects were again occultism, diabolism, witchcraft. Frazer's *Golden Bough* leaned against a huge volume on Cagliostro written in, as far as Mr. Philps knew, Italian. There was always something interesting to see or discuss at George's and Mr. Philps was glad he had walked that way, as he could spend a pleasant hour if his old friend wasn't busy and Mrs. Philps would never miss him or that time.

The bell rang welcomingly as he entered the shop; unlike the establishments of fiction, George's premises were nicely decorated, the wooden panelling painted white and with big windows which let in plenty of light and air. Two shaded lamps lent pleasantly dim atmosphere to the main showroom in the dusk of the late afternoon and an oil radiator gave off a pleasant warmth. Mr. Philps threaded his way through a surprising complexity of *objets d'art* as he made his way to the frosted glass door of his friend's office at the rear of the shop; no-one stirred, but George knew he was coming. Mr. Philps had noted the nail flicker in the gloom as a hatch communicating with the shop and the rear of the premises had been silently lifted and then closed as the owner surveyed him.

Twenty minutes later, seated within the area of warmth given off by the gas fire and with a steaming second cup of tea at his 'bow Mr.

⁂ Darkness, Mist & Shadow

Philps felt more at ease, as if the world were a better lace and he some worthwhile purpose in it. George sat opposite, in a comfortable armchair behind a green baize desk, checking invoices and emitting puffs of smoke from his pipe in the intervals between pouring tea and attending to the needs of the one or two customers who came to make inquiries in the dusk of the shop beyond.

His eyes were quizzical and friendly under his shaggy eye-brows and beneath his encouraging gaze Mr. Philps had been inclined to talk about his problems and especially about his feelings towards Hedgepeth. He hadn't actually mentioned him by name, but Coleman knew the history of his difficulties and had been helpful in his sympathetic silences and in his occasional terse comments. Mr. Philps' hour had expanded but still they sat on by the fire talking in low tones until George said, rather shockingly, "They had ways of dealing with people like that in the old days."

"What do you mean?" asked Mr. Philps, somewhat startled. "Oh, you know," said George with grim jocularity, nodding towards his rows of occult books. "Give him a taste of the evil eye . . . "

The words dropped with singular explosive force into the quiet room, split into segments of light and shadow by the shaded desk lamp.

"I'm not quite sure what you mean," said Mr. Philps confusedly, after a rather long silence. He moved awkwardly in his chair, throwing out his arms rather agitatedly, as he did when he was moved by thoughts beyond his comprehension.

At that moment the shop bell rang again and Coleman had to go. "It's all in there," he said, indicating two or three large volumes, opened and with pencilled notes, which stood on a corner of the desk.

He was away about twenty minutes and when he came back, Mr. Philps, with a rather white, peculiar expression on his face was standing by his chair, still studying the notes, which were a handwritten translation from one of the books. His nostrils had a strange, pinched look and he appeared to have some difficulty in breathing.

"Have another cup of tea," said George kindly, but Mr. Philps waved him away impatiently.

A Very Pleasant Fellow

"Look here, how does this work? Is it true?" he burst out excitedly. His eyes glanced from the big black volumes on the desk, up to George's face and then back round the office, as though he expected to find the answers to his questions materialising on the air before him.

He allowed George to press him back into his chair. Eyes dancing, with barely repressed emotion the antique dealer crossed over to a large oak cupboard that flanked one wall. "It's in here," he said, taking out a bulky cardboard box tied with string.

"But you don't mean to say..." expostulated Mr. Philps, who was being very excitable for such a usually mild man; "You don't mean to say that you've found it?"

Coleman laughed. "No, no," he said, stabbing the air with his pipe. "Three hundred years is a long time... No, no, I don't think it would be possible. An instrument like that couldn't have survived for so long. But it has been possible to reconstruct it."

Mr. Philips sat back and wiped his forehead with an expensive linen handkerchief. How was such a thing possible, he told himself, his mind turning to all sorts of interesting possibilities. But looking again at George Coleman he felt an inner, serene glow of self-confidence. A man like George Coleman could do anything. The dealer was speaking again. "It was a long process, by trial and error," he was saying. "I had to make the thing up in bits and pieces; some of the processes are unknown today and that cost time and money; and I had to be careful, for engineers and craftsmen are infernally suspicious. And, optically the thing had to be fantastically accurate. Then I wasn't sure whether I had the translation right and had to go to an Italian scholar. Even then I had to give him the thing piece-meal and pretend it came from different manuscripts, in order to avoid arousing unwanted curiosity."

He crossed over to the fireplace and knocked out his pipe moodily. "My biggest difficulty was in working out the calculations for I'm no mathematician. They had to be absolutely right. I was by no means sure that the original figures had come down without corruption and then the translation could have added to errors, as all the figures, for some curious reason, were given in longhand."

He studied the sheaf of papers again. "What you see here," he said, waving them and tapping the cardboard box, "Is the fruit of two years' hard labour."

And then that usually sanguine man did a curious thing. He thrust his face to within a couple of inches of the alarmed Mr. Philps and said grimly, "And, my dear old friend, it works!"

Mr. Philps goggled, bit his lip and looked into the gas fire. He hardly knew what to say.

"May I see it?" he asked at last.

It was certainly a most curious thing, when the brown paper and inner wrappings had been stripped off. Strangely beautiful, it was like an early instrument by Galileo or Newton. The heart of it was a series of crystal prisms beautifully mounted into brass and metal frameworks and these in turn were rivetted to tubes and levers and rods; there were leathery bellows like a Victorian plate camera and the heart of the whole thing appeared to be a small metal box, sealed within the centre of a ring of thin glass rods. Altogether it was a curious and a wonderful and a terrible machine.

"How does it work?" He heard himself saying in a hoarse whisper.

Coleman explained, but he hardly heard what his friend said, his mind was so full of extraordinary possibilities.

"In fact," George was saying, "this is the first instrument. It's lot quite so refined or so accurate as the large scale model I've constructed upstairs, but it will do... for your job." He added, in a curious tone, looking at Mr. Philps sideways from under his eyebrows. "I suppose you'd like a demonstration?"

Mr. Philps found himself sweating as he sat at the desk with his old friend and squinted down the arrangements of brass rods, prisms, tubes and a sort of fine-hair gunsight. By the depression of a tiny brass lever he was able to focus and refocus he prisms. As he read the figures on a milled scale and the sights of the two hairs began to slip into adjustment the machine seemed to throb within the metal box and the tubes and lenses commenced to give off a pale green light.

George Coleman's hand was on his, suddenly, preventing him com rotating the lever any further. "This is the primary stage," he said. "You

A Very Pleasant Fellow

can't go further without risk. Normally you should have the target lined up long before this. But never mind, I have something prepared."

He opened the cupboard and took out another box. From it he removed a small, squeaking, furry animal. There was a glass-fronted bookcase set against another wall and Coleman swiftly cleared a shelf and put the squeaking animal inside the glass! and closed the door. Mr. Philps didn't look very closely; he was squeamish about animals, but he knew he had to press on with the business he was engaged in. "What do I do?" he asked faintly.

"Adjust the sights against the figures, wait until the two wires intersect and then trip the lever home," said Coleman calmly, like a man who has done it all many times.

Mr. Philps bent over the instrument with an air of suppressed excitement; the animal in the bookcase, which was scratching at the glass—he supposed it was a mouse—wouldn't keep still but at last he got the blur of brown fur in the sights. As he adjusted the machine the figures spun before his eyes, the outlines of the room seemed to waver and drop away; a humming filled the taut silence and the green light cast a strange glow over his companion's face. As all phases of the instrument seemed to converge, he pressed the small lever home at Coleman's nodded command.

For a moment nothing seemed to happen, then there was a bright streak of light, like a silent thunderclap, which left a momentary impression on his eyeballs; the mouse gave a sudden squeak and fell dead. Simultaneously the lever gave a click, like a ratchet running down, and all the life seemed to die out of the machine; the green glow faded and the unwinking prisms gave back the homely light of the lamp and the gasfire. Coleman was holding out to him a limp bundle of fur. "Stone dead," he said exultantly. "Not a mark on the body. Just like all the others."

In answer to Mr. Philps' unspoken question he added, "I tried it on a cat, insects, metal plates even. It works every time. There's an infernal force in the machine which is completely untapped as yet...

"And it's undetectable," he went on. "Silent, almost invisible, odourless, untraceable... think of the possibilities."

Mr. Philps was silent, his mind full of odd doubts and of the enormity of his thoughts. George Coleman seemed to sense this and put a hand on his shoulder.

"I know what you're thinking," he said softly. "No, I have never tried it—that far. But in theory, it is quite possible. In the right hands it could be godlike . . . and in fact it can . . ." he hesitated, "destroy, without even seeing what its target is; without even the operator seeing. Through wood, stone and any known metal, and at almost any range."

He became brisk. "Would you like a more practical demonstration? One without much risk to life or limb?"

A few minutes later, Mr. Philps was sitting in his friend's shop, behind the strange instrument and feeling like a machine-gunner. In those sinister sights of winking metal and polished crystal was the homely street. He was all "focused up," his hand on the lever, waiting for George's signal. The shop door was locked—it was long gone six— and no-one was likely to disturb them.

Mr. Philps' target was a large and opulent motor car parked at a milliner's almost opposite; a young man waited in the driving seat for a woman, possibly his mother, who could be seen inside the shop talking to the manageress. Mr. Philps waited, for perhaps five minutes. This was going to be tricky. He would have to swing with the car as it started and depress the lever at maximum range, just before it disappeared from his sight down the road—he had a total distance of fifteen yards in which to make the experiment good and he had to make sure that no-one walked between him and his target.

He found himself sweating, even though the shop was by now fairly cold. There was a sharp retort from Coleman and a stout woman was walking to the car. A door slammed, there were several seconds of suspense and then the sound of the motor starting, harsh, loud and raucous in the quiet street.

Mr. Philps' hands were now steady on the strange machine, the lever moved obedient to his will. He followed the slowly moving car with uncanny precision, and his hand was already pressing the lever home when Coleman's final shout came. There was a flash of light in the dusk, the noise of metal shattering, followed by smoke and flames and the shocking sound of a loud explosion—all immediately

A Very Pleasant Fellow

smothered by the alarmed shouts and running feet in the street outside.

Mr. Philps felt ill and sat back weakly against a Chippendale cabinet at his elbow. A moment later Coleman appeared at the door, flushed with excitement. "All well," he called. He clasped Mr. Philps' hand, "A bulls-eye..." He hastily put the machine into a cupboard drawer, drenched the shop in light at a touch of a switch and led the way into the street.

The great car lay beautifully wrecked, its bonnet against a lamp post; the engine or what was left of it, had flown from its seating and was half buried in a front garden, a shattered fence attesting its passage. Half of the front of the car was gone and the youth and the stout woman, both arguing fiercely, were being assisted from their seats. It was all most satisfying, thought Mr. Philps, surveying the drifting smoke with a workmanlike pride.

"Are you convinced?" said Coleman at his elbow.

He forced his way back through the crowd, hearing phrases like "crankshaft went," "these modern cars." He felt like an author on the first night of a successful play. His mind was made up. His eyes were shining when he said goodnight to Coleman half an hour later. The cardboard box was under his arm and he felt a giant power. He grasped George's hand more effusively than usual. "Thank you, George," he exclaimed. "You won't regret it. I shall take every care of it."

George looked at him anxiously; he was a man who was obviously having second thoughts about his rashness.

"Don't overdo it," he said in parting. "And if you do get into trouble don't hesitate to throw it away. I've got another. But above all be sure to see it's destroyed rather than let it get into the wrong hands."

The streets of Camford rang beneath Mr. Philps' heels; no Prussian ever strutted into a conquered city with greater pride. Even Mrs. Philps' scolding over his spoiled tea didn't upset him for long. When his wife had gone to bed—rather surprised to find him up so late—he unwrapped the paper and looked at the machine again. It seemed to wink oddly in the moonlight as he sighted it on the grocery shop across the street. Exultant, he replaced it in his desk, locked the drawer and went to bed. For once, he was looking forward to a new day.

The following morning Mr. Philps rose early, which had long been foreign to his habit. Mrs. Philps looked surprised, but said nothing, and her husband felt constrained to explain that he had a bad headache and couldn't stay in bed. Early as he was, Hedgepeth was earlier still; through the window bleared with rain, Mr. Philps could see the pompous figure of his successor, standing underneath the lowered sunblind of the shop, shouting his wares with all his accustomed vulgarity. Mr. Philps gave an excited glance towards his desk, decided reluctantly that the weather conditions were not propitious for his first experiment and promised himself a trial as early in the day as circumstances would allow.

He shaved, dressed, ate a surprisingly hearty breakfast and by nine o'clock had to physically suppress himself from rubbing his hands in an almost gloating manner, an action which would have caused his wife the gravest concern. The truth was that he was as excited as a schoolboy with his first train set and he longed for Mrs. Philps to set off on her usual shopping expedition, which would leave him a clear field of action. But she seemed to find one interminable task after another and Mr. Philps, sitting at his desk and kneading a copy of the daily newspaper with hands grown unexpectedly moist with the sweat of excitement, almost savagely willed her out of the house.

But, aggravatingly, Mrs. Philps found still more tasks to occupy her and by the time she was ready for her shopping, it was too late to go out that morning. So she put off the trip until the afternoon and set about lunch, humming primly to herself. Mr. Philps, putting on as pleasant an air as the circumstances allowed, bided his time with commendable outward calmness, though inwardly he was simmering. He got through his lunch somehow and sat with a glassy smile as Mrs. Philps found first one excuse, then another, to put off the forthcoming trip.

For one horrible moment he felt that she might not go until the next day, after all, but fortunately she found there were certain provisions

A Very Pleasant Fellow

she had to have for the meal that evening. Mr. Philps' pipe had gone out and he was biting with agonising self-control on the clenched stem, when at long last Mrs. Philps announced that she was ready to "pop round the corner."

"Take your time, dear; I'm quite happy with the paper," Mr. Philps announced insincerely, quite oblivious of the fact that he had been sitting on it for the past half-hour.

"I shan't be long," said Mrs. Philps, giving him a shy wave as she went out the door. "Beth said she might look in later."

Mr. Philps made an inward gesture of distaste. Mrs. Macklewood was a near neighbour and an old friend of theirs—or rather his wife's—but how she would go on! He glanced swiftly at the clock at the slam of the outer door. It was nearly a quarter past three which would give him at the outside, about an hour or slightly under—rather less time than he would have chosen, but he had to take the opportunity as he found it. He wished their bedroom overlooked the main street; he could have retired to bed with a cold, which would have given him all the time in the world.

However, there it was, and he was already wasting precious minutes with such musings. Blinking with excitement Mr. Philps rose, unlocked his desk with a somewhat unsteady hand and took out the wonderful machine.

His thoughts were confused as he set it out before him, lined up on the window and the street below. Soon Mr. Clever Hedgepeth would be in his sights and one would see what his smart vulgarity would make of that. For some reason Mr. Philps did not want to look across the street for a while and he concentrated on setting up the machine. It was surprisingly complicated; he seemed to have lost all the expertise he had learned at Coleman's yesterday. He glanced at the clock in alarm; what a time had passed! It was already five and twenty to four and he was nowhere near ready. He found himself sweating. Must get hold of yourself, old man, he told himself and was surprised to find he was talking aloud.

Fortunately the weather had lifted and it was now dry, with good vision; otherwise it would have upset things a bit. Mr. Philps found himself sweating again and loosened his collar, which had suddenly become unbearably tight, with a hand which alarmed him with its uncontrollability. At last he was ready, but it was already a quarter to four. He wiped his glasses with a clean handkerchief and glanced over the road to Hedgepeth's; a stroke of luck—his first that day. The hated grocer was standing in front of the door again, bowing in his unctuous way while he exchanged pleasantries with a customer passing out of the shop. This was too good to miss.

Mr. Philps gulped, but he had gone too far to back out now. Once again there was the faint pulsation, the glow of green light; he had got the top of Hedgepeth's head lined up. He just wanted to give him a shock, show him what was what. As the green light winked and glowed and the machine seemed to throb as though it would explode, Mr. Philps tripped the lever, just as there came a strident ring at the doorbell. The instrument trembled in his hand, the streak of light disappeared and Mr. Philps, in his confusion, realised that something was badly wrong. He had a momentary glimpse of Hedgepeth, quite unharmed, finishing off his conversation with a flowery flourish and there was just time to wrap up the machine and lock his desk before the determined jab at the doorbell sounded again.

"Blast the woman!" said Philps as he hurried down to let Mrs. Macklewood in. She would choose this moment, of all times. As he regained the room with a florid, matronly woman in her early fifties, Mr. Philps was vaguely aware that there was something wrong in the street after all. He had already forgotten the streak of light the machine had emitted; he had thought, in his momentary panic, that the thing had misfired, but it must have struck home after all. But for a second or two his brain refused to believe what his eyes were seeing.

There was the strident ringing of bells and a fire engine stopped opposite with a squeaking of brakes. Still refusing to believe the evidence before him, Mr. Philps saw that the sunblind and part of the front of Hedgepeth's shop was aflame and blazing rosily.

With Mrs. Macklewood gawping beside him Mr. Philps felt a glow not entirely emanating from the fire; a crowd surged to and fro in front of the grocer's and he could see Hedgepeth, all his bluster gone, dancing ineffectually about as the firemen tried to connect up their hoses to an adjacent water cock. Mr. Philps had something of the

A Very Pleasant Fellow

vision of an Attila or an Alexander the Great as he surveyed the scene of destruction he had created, though he was somewhat disappointed to see the rapidity with which the firemen reduced the blaze to a thick smoke and the smoke in turn to a sodden effusion of occasional vapours.

It had taken three minutes to get the outbreak under and the total result was a charred sunblind and a small area of blistered paintwork above and to one side of the shop. Still, Mr. Philps decided, it had been a worthwhile experiment and a worthy opening to his campaign. The deflated Hedgepeth had gone indoors amid the commiseration of his customers—otherwise his victory would have been complete. When Mrs. Philps came home an hour later, the whole town was talking about the fire at Hedgepeth's. Mr. Philps kept a discreet silence. "Funny thing is," Mrs. Philps was saying, "the fire brigade couldn't find any reason for it, although they did say a cigarette-end might have dropped from a window above."

Mr. Philps smiled in a superior manner when he heard this, but had the good sense to say nothing; surprising how difficult it was to avoid blurting out that he was responsible. Somewhat different feelings prevented him from seeking the company of George Coleman. He guessed that his old friend would add things up correctly when he heard the news, and sure enough there was a paragraph in the late edition of the evening paper that night which made an eight-line mystery for local people to puzzle over.

Mr. Philps read it with a prim, almost smug smile and cut out the short piece of print, which he later placed in the cardboard box in the locked drawer of his desk. This was better than anything he had ever previously been engaged in and now provided him with some purpose in life. He waited a week before making the next move. This time the consequences were more severe.

The shop front of Hedgepeth's premises had been repainted and a new sun-blind fitted. The weather continued cold and rainy but at last came a day of strong winds and fitful sunshine which would suit his purpose. Mr. Philps had long pondered his position. His intention was merely to give Hedgepeth a bad headache on this first occasion and by increasing the dose he intended eventually to drive the man off, so that he might sell up and move away. At least, this was how Mr. Philps reasoned, but the affair soon became more complicated and out of hand.

While he put these arguments to himself, Mr. Philps felt reasonably secure in his motives. He had taken to frequenting one of the little local street-corner public houses for an occasional solitary glass of beer—life was full of minor surprises for Mrs. Philps these days—and, frowning fiercely at the assembled rows of bottles on the shelves before him, unconscious of the landlord's restrained loquacity as he tried to catch his customer's eye, Mr. Philps battled the matter out in his mind.

But however persuasive his own arguments against himself, he still could not justify to his conscience the dreadful, irrevocable steps he felt himself to be taking. For, despite all George Coleman's claims, the thing was still at a definitely experimental stage; anything might happen when it was used, and in the hands of a tyro like Mr. Philps one could argue that things were bound to go wrong as they had in the case of the sunblind—though no-one could have foreseen Mrs. Macklewood ringing at such an untimely moment.

Finally, Mr. Philps had sighed and decided to let providence take its course. He had to wait nearly a fortnight this time for the right combination of circumstances, though owing to his coarseness of touch on the control lever, he had almost done it again. The results were highly spectacular, Mr. Philps had to admit. The circumstances were approximately the same; the machine pulsed and emitted its green light. There had been a bright, lightning-like flash as before but this time there had been no interruption and Mr. Philps was calmly sure that he had interpreted the situation correctly.

Nothing had happened for a moment; Hedgepeth had continued to shout his wares for perhaps two seconds and then suddenly he seemed to turn a somersault and fell backwards into a box of oranges, as though pole-axed. A knot of startled spectators soon crowded around and Mr. Philps could not help shrinking back behind the curtains in terror as the authoritative figure of a policeman elbowed his way through the crowd. Hedgepeth was tenderly carried inside and the crowd eventually dispersed.

A Very Pleasant Fellow

Sweat from Mr. Philps' brow dripped down on to his shaking hands as he locked his desk drawer once more and he cast fearful glances about him, as though he expected retribution at any moment. He paced the room in an agony of torment, his perambulations broken only by the decanting of a local doctor from a taxi opposite his window. Hedgepeth's sudden collapse, combined with the recent fire at the shop, both unexplained mysteries, fanned a storm of gossip in the street and some of the stories circulating within the hour easily outdid the truth.

The doctor's diagnosis was the most baffling of all and he himself found a pretext to rush back to his surgery and consult some of his more obscure text books. Hedgepeth was not badly hurt, would live, had suffered no permanent damage but, in the face of all the evidence—the cold winter weather, a chill wind and the absence of sun—was suffering all the symptoms of heat stroke. What the patient had experienced was in fact what he might have suffered had he been exposed to the fiercest Indian sun in the main streets of Calcutta at noon for a couple of hours.

Some people laughed openly at the doctor but his opinion, even more bafflingly, was backed up by the word of an unimpeachable specialist in tropical disorders and the affair became a nine-day wonder. And even before that had time to die down, the people of Camford were plunged into horrified speculation over the finale of the affair, which became a cause celebre even in the national press. But before that storm broke and shortly after he had used the strange and terrible machine for the last time, Mr. Philps came face to face with his own soul and what he saw there sent him into the blindest panic of his life.

Hedgepeth had decided on a few days convalescence after the extraordinary business of the heat stroke, but instead of taking a short holiday at the coast he decided to stay on at the shop. He moved into a bed-sitting room over the business where he could keep an eye on things and be available if any queries came up. Unfortunately, this meant that his window was almost directly in line with that of Mr. Philps, which gave the latter his most interesting idea.

Though Hedgepeth was still feeling weak and debilitated after his unfortunate experience, he took to sitting at his window for hours on end; ostensibly reading magazines, in which his taste was deplorably lurid, but more in order to view the passing crowds. Mr. Philps thought that he gazed many hundreds of times down in the direction of the shop blind and more than once he caught a worried frown on the grocer's fleshy face, as though he expected to see the answer to the two riddles that preyed on his mind somewhere on the façade of the premises.

It occurred to Mr. Philps, who had now purchased a powerful pair of binoculars in order to study his prey in more detail, that Hedgepeth was more likely to be seeking a rational and reassuring explanation of the two most baffling incidents of his life. If that were so Mr. Philps did not let it deflect him from the course he had marked out for himself; even Mrs. Philps had noted an unexpected firmness of manner in his attitude of late, but she put this down to her husband's final coming to terms with his retirement. She thought he would settle down in time and was pleased to note his old brisk attitude to everyday events.

On that terrible final night of what the national press later came to call the Camford Horror, passers-by in the main streets on a wet, dark evening were surprised to see the spectacle of a hatless, dishevelled middle-aged man with a cardboard box clutched under one arm, who blundered in blind panic in and out of the traffic at a speed which belied his mellow years. Mr. Philps cannoned off a rotund woman, stammered his apologies, went to raise a hat that wasn't there, and then dashed off in headlong flight. It was after ten o'clock before he reached a more deserted part of the town and his pace had then slackened to a more sober level.

His elliptical flight had taken him in a curving arc across the town and it was the Great Ourse which now flowed beneath the ornate Victorian iron bridge on which he had paused. A quick glance to right and left and Mr. Philps hoisted his parcel on to the parapet. Weighted with iron as it was and bulky in many brown paper wrappings and convolutions of string, it was as much as he could do to heft it out from the bridge into the centre of the river. It fell in a short arc and the splash was almost inaudible amid the hissing of the rain; brief bubbles burst in the feeble radiance of a lamp from a timber yard

A Very Pleasant Fellow

across the river and George Coleman's wonderful machine had gone for ever in the dank brown waters of the swiftly-flowing Ourse.

It was a shocked and bewildered Coleman who answered ring at his door at eleven o'clock and who fetched whisky for the untidy and rain-sodden figure before him which blurted out its terrible story.

Three days had gone by and Mr. Philps felt decidedly better. He sat at his desk and thought over the events of the past week with a more sober and confident air. What was done was done and there was nothing further to be achieved in the matter of profitless speculation. The police had come and gone but had been just as baffled as the doctors; the press had a field day but by that night international events had begun to overshadow eve such an incredible business.

There was only one relief in the whole affair, or two, rather—if you counted Mr. Philps' anonymity; thank God he could rely on George Coleman here—George, who was already in process of dismantling the great machine which stood in his upstairs attic. The salving mercy was that Hedgepeth could have felt hardly anything; death must have been absolutely instantaneous—it was so quick, in fact, that Mr. Philps did not even see him fall. And in his reeling back from his front window, his executioner had been spared the final horror.

For the particularly hideous details which had so fascinated the press and puzzled the police were that the corpse of Hedgepeth had been completely incinerated and charred almost to the bone; in an instant of time, on an icy cold day and without even breaking the window in front of which he stood. On top of this the fire in his grate was not even lit.

Where Mr. Philps had gone wrong or why the machine had acted as it did, he could not hazard a guess; it was something he did not like to dwell upon.

The papers had head-lines; BLAZING CORPSE MYSTERY; and many were the ingenious theories both press and public put forward to explain the unexplainable. Heartless wags, of whom Camford had its share, had not been slow in commenting that the manner of Hedgepeth's passing would save cremation expenses, but this was not a felicity which commended itself to Mr. Philps, who liked a proper feeling about such things. No, it was not a joke he relished.

ⒶDarkness, Mist & Shadow

Mr. Philps got up from his desk, his face working, as he thought back over the hideous nightmare of the past few days. This afternoon would see the finish of it; then he and Mrs. Philps would get away for that long-delayed holiday at Eastbourne they had both so often talked about.

For once he was glad that Mrs. Macklewood was coming; it would prevent him from thinking and would help to get through a very difficult afternoon. But even as he heard the ring at the door and half-heartedly acknowledged the greeting of his wife's old friend, his mind was already off at another tangent. Though it would have been atrociously bad taste at a time like this, if done publicly, he had already made tentative inquiries of an old business colleague, Charles Elkins, who was the principal of the largest firm of estate agents in the town; he had been assured informally that when the time came he would have no difficulties in securing the first refusal of his old business once again.

Mr. Philps got up heavily from his chair at an unusual stir in the street. He went to stand at the window overlooking the road; he was so erect one would have imagined him to be at a military parade.

The front door of the grocer's shop opened and the small party came down; the coffin looked small for such a large man and the undertaker's assistants had difficulty in negotiating the step in front of the forecourt. Some sentences of Mrs. Macklewood's finally penetrated his consciousness. The two women had drawn closer to him at the window and he derived comfort from their presence.

"How silly of me," said Mrs. Macklewood in hushed tones. "Of course you knew him, didn't you; he bought your business. A very nice man, wasn't he?"

"Yes, yes," said Mr. Philps, blinking rapidly, hardly conscious of what he was saying.

He suddenly found his eyes filling with tears as he replied, quite sincerely, "Yes, I knew him. A very pleasant fellow..."

A Message From The stars

1

It was early January when Anstruther first began to receive what he considered to be messages from the stars. He had been up all night in the observatory at the top of the house, either making notes or with the eyepiece of the great telescope clamped to his face and his eyes were still filled with star-dazzle as dawn began to break. The sun climbed heavily and reluctantly into the winter sky, as though tired by the weight of the long night.

Anstruther got down from the padded seat which followed the telescope's tracking of the heavenly bodies on its vast circular rails, took off his dark goggles and wiped his eyes which were aching from hours of overstrain. He went back over his notes of the night and checked his more recent figures; at this late stage in the experiment he did not think it possible that he could be wrong. Over six years of preparatory work and reasoning had gone into his observations and he had calculated that it would be at least two more before the considered opinions formed after exhaustive cross-checking would allow him to publish a long-projected paper on the subject.

But the night's work had been promising, extremely promising and even Anstruther's cautious nature was a little aflame with romantic curiosity as he left his work table and poured out a cup of coffee from the thermos that stood always ready on the small table by his camp bed and electric fire in a corner of the great-domed chamber. As he drank the coffee, cupping the beaker with both hands, chill from the night's work of adjusting the brass control wheels and focusing devices, he ran over the results again in his mind; it was impossible that the positive reactions he was now getting could be anything other than emissions from animate beings out there in space.

He put down the beaker, unrolled the thick blinds from the lower windows and looked out over the acres of crumbling brickwork and the bleak vistas of the North London suburb in which he had chosen to make his home. It was on high ground and free from the haze and fogs which obscured the sky at night in other parts of the metropolis. His friend and neighbour Mr. Starkey, while tolerant of his passion for astronomy, did not always quite understand the drift of his remarks on the subject of the messages and though Anstruther was a member of the Royal Society he himself refrained from unveiling his theories at this early stage to any more learned gaze.

Anstruther was a bachelor and while Miss Johnson was an excellent housekeeper not even the kindest of friends would have said she had the sparkle to enliven the duller moments of a man of Anstruther's intellect. Miss Johnson, a woman of mature years and, one would have said, beyond the wilder stirrings of romantic inclination, occupied a self-contained wing of Anstruther's house and to avoid scandal he had had the communicating doors blocked up and a low hedge grown between the two wings to demarc her domain; in effect they occupied two separate buildings.

Punctually after dinner every evening and in any event well before ten, Miss Johnson withdrew to her own wing and as Anstruther was a creature of the night, he would have been thrown much on his own resources had it not been for his neighbour, Mr. Starkey. For Mr. Starkey was also a bachelor and being a man of independent means, of an intellectual turn of mind and of an inquiring nature, he and Anstruther found themselves much together. Mr. Starkey had an indoor staff of two male servants in his big Georgian house next door, in addition to gardeners and odd-job men and, as he kept an excellent table and an even more remarkable cellar, Anstruther, on those nights when he was not in the observatory, found himself dining out more and more.

A Message From The Stars

As time went by the friends began to frequent one another's houses almost as though they were extensions of their own; Anstruther benefitted by Mr. Starkey's superb library of rare and esoteric books; while Mr. Starkey spent many an exhilarating evening in the wild and lonely sweeps of the sky under the guidance of his friend within the arc of Anstruther's greatest extravagance, the vast shadowy observatory dome.

The two men had been friends and neighbours for several years before Anstruther began to confide in Mr. Starkey regarding his researches among the stars. He found him a kindly and sympathetic listener, though, as has been remarked before, a layman in this particular field. Anstruther had felt it best at first to touch on such matters lightly, and his friend responded in a joking manner. They sat in Mr. Starkey's comfortable study after a substantial dinner; a coal fire burned in the big brick hearth and threw shining bars of light across the sheen of pewter and the gilt backs of the books in their glass cabinets that occupied the whole sweep of the room.

Mr. Starkey himself was a man of remarkable aspect; broad and powerful in the shoulders, he was above middle height. Anstruther would have put his age at something nearer sixty but his friend's prodigious strength and occasional feats of athletic prowess—he had once swung a heavy sack of brass-bound ledgers from floor level up into his loft with almost contemptuous one-handed ease—made it obvious he must be much younger. Anstruther decided Mr. Starkey's appearance gave an erroneous impression of age.

For example he was almost bald and wore an embarrassingly obvious toupee of a dark red hue, completely unsuitable; his eyes were deep-recessed and covered in mauve-tinted glasses; and his voice was oddly high-pitched and squeaky for so powerful a man. Nevertheless, he was a kind and loyal friend who had made open house for a lonely neighbour and Anstruther counted himself fortunate in his choice of companion.

This particular evening the topic had again run upon astronomy and Anstruther's fanaticism on the subject had become a joke between the pair. With a glass of whisky at his elbow and the ice-bowl within easy reach, Anstruther was conscious that he had run on rather; but his host did not seem to mind. He shifted comfortably in his chair and there was a smile on his broad, powerful face as he tried to follow the drift of Anstruther's argument.

"I am a complete layman," he said, "but would not the vast distances involved preclude the transmission and reception of any such messages as you suggest? For instance, as I understand it, the farthest stars which can be seen with the most powerful telescopes are many millions of light years away. This being so, what would be the point of sending messages? The transmitters, allowing that there are sentient beings out there in space, would be dead thousands of years before the messages reached earth and the stars involved themselves may have ceased to exist."

"Well argued, my dear Starkey," Anstruther interrupted, conscious of the flush of pleasure which showed on his friend's face.

"All you say—and more—is perfectly true, but you have not quite followed the drift of my argument."

He waved his hand protestingly as Mr. Starkey advanced the whisky decanter, but allowed himself to be overborne.

"Light is the fastest thing we know," continued Anstruther, "and some of the nearer stars preclude such vast time-lapses as those you have quoted. Supposing, for argument's sake, that sentient beings who wished to communicate with earth established some sort of satellite far out in space, near enough to our system, to obviate such a time-lag. By means of relay stations, say, supposing they could pass a light source to the satellite which in turn would relay a visual message to the earth? What would you say then?"

Mr. Starkey laughed his high-pitched laugh. "It sounds plausible enough," he said. "But is it feasible?"

Anstruther was silent for a moment, playing with his crystal goblet and looking into the fire.

"With our present knowledge and the advanced state of interplanetary travel, can you doubt it?" he asked. "I am not, of course, talking about the optical illusion of light pulsation obtained by looking at the heavens with the naked eye. I am envisaging something much more sophisticated than these crude fancies."

"Something of the order of infra-red?" said Mr. Starkey.

A Message From The Stars

"Good," said Anstruther. "I see you begin to follow my meaning. But I am imagining something far more subtle still than your analogy. The forward transmitter then, is passing messages on to earth, which would be unseen by our present instruments. Imagine something like 'black light' if that were possible. Something that would be invisible to the most powerful telescopes, but which could be recorded and deciphered by someone in possession of the knowledge."

Mr. Starkey smiled a curious smile as he re-stocked his glass with ice.

"And you have developed some new kind of telescope which will pick up these messages?" he asked.

Anstruther's face was alight with excitement and enthusiasm.

"Exactly, my dear fellow!" he burst out. "Crude, primitive perhaps, just as Newton's telescope seems to us today, but a practical means of screening the ray-emissions and recording them in the form of pulsations."

"Capital," said Mr. Starkey. "I really must congratulate you on one of the major discoveries of this century, if all you say is true. But what of the messages themselves? You speak of them as though a regular postal service had been established. How send and receive messages when presumably a still considerable time-lapse might render them unintelligible or nonsensical?"

Anstruther's eyes sparkled as he put his glass to his mouth. He wiped his lips with an immaculate handkerchief.

"This is one of the curious things," he said. "I have not, of course, at this early stage broken the 'code' or indeed anything like it. But I can say that the pulsations and regularities of the emissions are too complex and repetitive in their nature to be anything other than code or intelligible messages. I have succeeded in breaking them down into fairly definitive symbols. And the extraordinary thing is that the same messages seem to be repeated—with intervals—over and over again."

Mr. Starkey put his glass down on the table with a sudden clatter in the thick silence.

"Dear me," he said softly. "Curious indeed."

"And that is not all," Anstruther went on after a short pause. "If these messages are beamed at the earth, as I sincerely believe them to be,

Darkness, Mist & Shadow

then for whom are they intended? Because in our present state of knowledge no one is equipped to read them or would in fact know of their existence."

Mr. Starkey's eyes were very round in the lamplight as he took in the implications. Anstruther leaned back in his chair, finishing the whisky, enjoying the effect he had created.

"Very curious," he said, echoing Mr. Starkey's words.

And he would say no more on the subject that evening.

2

For some time after this strange conversation Anstruther kept his own counsel, though he continued to keep Mr. Starkey company. Sometimes the two men played a game of billiards at a nearby club and on exceptional occasions attended a cinema or theatre after a dinner in town. But the favourite venues on most evenings when both were in London were Mr. Starkey's library and the observatory and finely equipped optical laboratory of Anstruther's home.

The astronomer had hit on an excellent method for his research. With his powerful, specially adapted telescope, eyes protected by smoked glasses, he would focus up visually on a promising pulsation and when he had it on track an automatic recorder would electronically preserve the transmission. Anstruther was planning to install a computer to evaluate the results and to break down the pulsations into an intelligible form but the cost was too heavy for his pocket at the present time; the most he could do was to prepare a programme which could be fed into a computer at a Northern university of which a friend was in charge.

Here, he would have to buy computer time and while this was also a considerable outlay, was well within his means. The difficulty was the time taken to programme the machine; the actual period required for solving the problem was incredibly short. Meantime Anstruther continued to accumulate his data and transcribe his notes. He was already in correspondence with his friend and had been given permission for the experiment about a month ahead. He was

A Message From The Stars

now working systematically, night after night, to prepare his material. It was all high excitement and hard achievement, and Mr. Starkey rather tended to drop into the background as the weeks went by.

But his friend quite understood and when they met for an occasional lunch—the nightly dinners were temporarily suspended while Anstruther got on with this urgent work—things were as convivial as ever. Mr. Starkey would occasionally tease him about the messages from space and jokingly ask whether Anstruther were not more concerned in establishing a profitable postal service with the planets. Anstruther took this in good part but his pale face and his dark eyes belied the quiet good humour with which he received his friend's shafts of ponderous wit.

Presently the visits ceased altogether and a few days afterwards Mr. Starkey received a hastily pencilled postcard from Manchester. Anstruther merely said that he was well, the weather was abominable and that he hoped to be with Mr. Starkey within a fortnight. Of the purpose of his visit he said nothing, even in the veiled language which one might use on a postcard. In the event it was ten days before Mr. Starkey saw him again. His demeanour was much changed; he was smiling, in high spirits, and it was evident that his trip had been a success.

The occasion was one for a small celebration and Mr. Starkey rose to the challenge; after an excellent dinner which had included an unforgettable Brie, the two friends gathered in Mr. Starkey's library. When the brandy and the big balloon glasses had been brought it and left on the table, Mr. Starkey poked the fire into a blaze and drew the curtains even closer. The friends were on their second glass before Mr. Starkey broke the silence.

"You have been successful, then?"

"I have made a great deal of progress," said Anstruther eagerly. "The machine was quite fascinating. But we had the devil of a job in the programming. It took quite three days longer than intended. I am not sure what my banker is likely to say next month when the statements are presented."

He was silent for a moment; the fire crackled in the warmth of the room. That and the faint drumming of Anstruther's fingers on the table were the only sounds in the study.

Anstruther got up abruptly and looked around. "Will you excuse me one moment?"

He went out in the hall and came back with a leather briefcase, closing the study door carefully behind him. He drew from the case, which he unlocked with a key he took from a leather wallet in his hip pocket, some spools of perforated paper and a black notebook.

"For your interest, Starkey, these are some of the machine's conclusions. The notebook contains my detailed observations."

Mr. Starkey pondered over the punched symbols on the paper spools, his brandy untouched at his side.

"This machine has saved me a whole year," Anstruther was enthusing. "Quite a year's work."

He took one of the spools from his companion and held it towards the light. "One great thing the machine has done is to break the messages up into component parts or groups. These would correspond to words in earth language."

Mr. Starkey looked bewildered.

"But where does this get you?" he asked. "All this looks absolute gibberish."

He tapped with his finger impatiently at an unrelated jumble of symbols on the paper.

Anstruther was pleased at his friend's obvious puzzlement.

"Ah, but we ran a great many more tests, with millions of possible combinations," he went on. "But we always came back to the same basic symbols. I have taken them a great deal further forward in this notebook. Working on a lot more data than you have on these spools here, you understand."

He held out the book towards Mr. Starkey. The latter squinted through his glasses as though the lines of letters were tiring him. What he saw were similar groups to those he had seen in the punched symbols of the spools. Here and there Anstruther had underlined a group. Working down several pages Mr. Starkey at last began to catch the drift of his friend's argument. In each case the group of letters underlined was the same and in each case also they were the same words or symbols. And what they spelled out was: ZHRO AHNT CHEDZOY

A Message From The Stars

There was a long silence. Mr. Starkey poured out two more glasses with an unsteady hand. The two men sat looking into the fire, each busy with his own thoughts. Then Anstruther went on.

"I shall take this matter on by a simple process of elimination. The symbols can be broken down into a language understandable on earth if one has the time and patience. I may have to use the computer again. But naturally I shall start with English. The group you have just read, ZHRO AHNT CHEDZOY seems to be a key phrase or symbol but the extraordinary thing is that it is repeated in varying degrees of frequency over the last six years—in other words since I began the present series of experiments with black light. As you know, a and e are the most common letters in the English language; once I can establish a relationship between the most common letters or symbols in the messages from space then I shall have a basis from which to start deciphering."

Mr. Starkey turned towards his friend and raised his glass.

"Incredible as it all sounds, I must salute your ingenuity and perseverance. You will keep me informed?"

"At all stages," said Anstruther.

The two men drank again.

3

From this time onwards began a change in Anstruther. Some called it a gradual decline. He had hardly any friends so there were few to notice. It was apparent to Mr. Starkey who was in close contact throughout: once or twice Anstruther's housekeeper, Miss Johnson, attempted to remonstrate with him, advising shorter hours, more leisure activities. But her advances were met with what seemed brusqueness in Anstruther, who was usually punctiliously correct with Miss Johnson and she retired, puzzled, to her own quarters, not to mention the matter again.

But whether or not his health or his nerves began to suffer, Anstruther was certainly making progress. He had occasion to use the computer again and after this he gained ground more swiftly insofar as he revealed details to Mr. Starkey. Though the two now met more rarely—Anstruther tended to spend a great deal of time in the observatory—Mr. Starkey gathered that Anstruther was beginning to master the language. The breakthrough came on the night in early January when Anstruther received what he ever after considered to be the first true message received on earth from beings in outer space.

Certainly he went into copious detail in his notebooks and he again sent to his friend in Manchester, who ran a further series of tests for him. It was from this point in time that a general deterioration in Anstruther's health began to be observable to people outside his intimate social circle. He became furtive and secretive in his looks, though he was as forthcoming as ever to Mr. Starkey.

But to his housekeeper and those in his employ there was a great change; he started to lock even the most trivial data away and there were one or two rows because quite innocuous things had been moved when his workshop was dusted. Eventually he began to shut out people from the observatory area altogether; it was his custom, when eating alone, to read at the table. Usually abstruse mathematical or philosophical works, sometimes his own notebooks and sets of data. These latter would be quite unintelligible to the layman and yet Anstruther would cover even his printed textbooks with sheets of newspaper whenever anyone in his service came in to change the dishes on the table.

This went on for some time until a dark, wet evening in late March. Conditions had been bad for star-gazing and Anstruther had dropped in to Mr. Starkey's for one of his increasingly rare chats. Mr. Starkey, although he had seen his old friend only a week before, was somewhat shocked at the change in his appearance. There was a sense of strain hanging over him and he had a curious way of looking over his shoulder when speaking, as though he feared someone approaching from behind.

He told Mr. Starkey he had made great progress in deciphering the star-messages; there was something in his voice which implied to his listener that for the first time he regretted embarking on his long and dark pilgrimage.

A Message From The Stars

"They are signalling," he said to Mr. Starkey with a strange thrill in his tones. "I have deciphered several complete messages. I have them safe among my papers."

His talk became increasingly rambling and Mr. Starkey had difficulty in getting a coherent sentence out of him. He mumbled something about The Old Ones and someone called Chedzoy who was mentioned in several messages.

"The messages originate with the People of Vhrar," he told Mr. Starkey. "They are a dying race among the stars. They have sent spies and messengers to the earth. They live in secret among us and for more than a thousand years they have been awaiting a signal to take over the earth."

Despite himself a weird shock ran through Mr. Starkey as he heard these last words. It was in vain that he attempted to reassure his friend that there could be little in such talk. But at any mention of overwork or strain on his part, Anstruther became almost unbearable and began to speak in a high, loud voice so that Mr. Starkey became quite alarmed for his friend. He did arrange for Anstruther to sleep at his house that night and the next morning, at breakfast, he was relieved to see that his guest had slept well and that he seemed greatly improved both in his general health and his manner.

Anstruther took Mr. Starkey aside after breakfast, before returning to his own house and thanked him most kindly and sincerely for his help and for what his friendship had meant.

"Had you not better seek outside assistance with this business?" said Mr. Starkey, accompanying his friend to the gate of his own house. "Your doctor, for instance. Or your spiritual adviser, if you have one."

In all the years he had known him, Mr. Starkey had never inquired about Anstruther's personal affairs; it was a measure of the seriousness of the occasion. Anstruther shook his head and his face was pale and resolute.

"This is something I must see out, my friend," he said, taking Mr. Starkey's hand. "Only I hold the key to this horrible business. When the right time comes I shall consult the highest civil and military authority."

He walked away round to his own gateway and Mr. Starkey stood and watched him go.

4

The end came on a clear, mild evening in mid-April, a superb night for watching the heavens, though the wind had been gusting around the house since early afternoon. Messages had started coming through unusually quickly after Anstruther had switched on his great machines. A wild humming filled the dome of the observatory, mingling with the rushing of the wind about the top of the high building. The draught made the electric light cords waver to and fro and the light rocked across the dome, casting dark shadows and crazy patterns on the rushing walls.

Anstruther sat at his tall desk and worked at the decoding notebooks, sweat beading his face. His pencil raced over the paper as he compared the groups of letters with the English equivalents he had so painfully worked out over the years.

ZHRO AHNT CHEDZOY said the last message. He still had not learned what that meant. WE HAVE WHAT YOU KNOW OF. WE COME AT THE NEXT MOON. PREPARE ALL, ZHRO AHNT CHEDZOY.

Anstruther felt sick. He knew all along. This was what the people of Vhrar had been planning for the last thousand years. And then the Old Ones would take over the earth again. He sat pale and silent with the wind roaring round the house, amid the whining of the generators and felt small and lost and helpless. He looked up at the pale stars which burned and writhed with subdued fire in the limitless blackness of the sky and raised a puny fist at them through the thick glass of the dome. He mouthed a prayer as he jumped up from the desk, all indecision gone. He knew what he must do. The highest military and civil authority.

His throat burned dryly as he got to the phone. He jiggled the receiver rest for more than two minutes before he realized that the instrument was out of order. He put down the phone and went out on to the metal balcony, down the railed staircase to the observatory door. The handle revolved uselessly in his hand. Either someone had locked the door or it had jammed. He beat helplessly at the thick glass, his breath coming in sick gasps at his throat.

He rushed back to the desk, put two of his notebooks in an inner recess that was hidden by an ingenious spring device and put the rest of his evidence in his breast pocket. He went back again to the door with a heavy metal bar. The glass starred and splintered at the first impact and then he saw Mr. Starkey's face, grotesquely distorted through the shattered panel. Relief flooded through his body, draining it of any other emotion. He felt the door-knob turn under his hand and Mr. Starkey quickly glided through.

"We must get help," babbled Ansthruther, knowing he was being hysterical, but unable to conceal his state of emotion and his ragged nerves from his old friend.

"These creatures are planning to invade the earth. We have only a few weeks. Their spies have been here for hundreds of years."

"Yes," said Mr. Starkey sadly. "And there are thousands of us."

And Mr. Starkey seemed to collapse and dissolve as Anstruther stood powerless to move.

The red toupee fell away and disclosed what Mr. Starkey and his previous entities had so cunningly hidden for half a thousand years. In its place was a deep pit and from the pit cylindrical, triangular and elliptical eyes all the colours of the rainbow stared out at Anstruther in all the intelligences of the universe. The mauve spectacles tilted and shattered to fragments on the observatory floor. From the dark shafts which showed in place of human eye-sockets, long antennae thoughtfully probed the air, receiving delicately, as they had done over all the ages, the messages from the stars.

"ZHRO AHNT CHEDZOY," chanted the thing that had been Mr. Starkey triumphantly, in a high, insect-like voice and in its own language at last.

Trying to scream but unable to, Anstruther felt the antennae seize him each side of his face with a grip like steel and then he knew no more.

A Darkness, Mist & Shadow

5

The dreadful death of Mr. James Anstruther in his observatory on that April evening was never properly explained. The papers made much of it, of course; of how the whole of one side of Anstruther's head had been—it is an unpleasant word but it must be used—sucked off, leaving part of the brain exposed. Certain notebooks and papers had been hastily burnt in the observatory but later discovery of two other documents in a secret drawer in the dead man's desk had made it clear that his mind was unhinged by the nature of his interest and by long, lonely years spent in solitary contemplation of the heavens.

The notebooks spoke of some people called Vhrar and a projected invasion of the earth by beings from outer space who were apparently to be helped by some of their number who had been sent on to earth for that purpose ages before. The police inquiry and the coroner himself quite rightly put that in its true perspective. The whole thing was a mystery; Anstruther's closest friend, Mr. Starkey, was unable to add anything to it. He went briefly into the box at the coroner's hearing but could not shed any further light on the business.

But as he had been such an intimate friend of the deceased, the coroner felt able to direct that the dead man's notebooks and effects should be turned over to him. These Mr. Starkey felt quite disposed to accept. It was evident that his nerves had deteriorated at the terrible incident which had taken place next door and within weeks he had arranged to sell his house and had moved; to a place no one was able to discover. The coroner said the proper verdict to return was one of murder by a person or persons unknown and there the matter was allowed to remain.

The only individual who seemed to suffer lasting effects from this tragedy was Miss Johnson, Anstruther's housekeeper. From her evidence at the inquest those present would not have been surprised to learn that when Miss Johnson found her employer's body, he was clutching a splinter of moonbeam in his hand. The housekeeper must have been a brave woman. For, advancing over the dark floor, an hour later, she found that the bright luminescence in the shadow was the shimmer of starlight on what remained of the dead face.

⁂ CRY WOLF

⁂ 1

THE VILLAGE IS VERY QUIET. BUT THEN THAT IS TO BE expected AT this time of year. It stands in a notch of the frowning mountains far from the nearest town. And after all, it is the main reason we bought the house. In summer the meadows are carpeted with red and yellow flowers while in the winter the majesty of the snow and the unearthly beauty of the mountains against those changing skies more than compensates for the cold and the lack of modern amenities.

The wolf came early in November. That in itself was curious because the weather had been mild until then. It was first reported by Jaeckel, the frontier guard. He had seen the trace of its paws down by the stream in the moonlight, he said. Even an outsider like myself could not resist chaffing him. Wolves had not been known in these mountains for generations said the older heads of the village. Now if it had been much higher up or on the Italian side and January as well, and one of the hardest winters on record. But a mild November! They flung up their hands with laughter and continued smoking their long pipes.

Jaeckel just smiled and said he knew what he knew and he trusted the evidence of his own eyes. A big dog, perhaps, said Jean Piotr, who owns the largest general store in the village. Jaeckel derided the suggestion. Quite impossible, he said firmly. It was a wolf's print, coming down a path from the village to the stream. In fact he'd seen the animal, or at least its shadow passing over the snow, a few seconds before. Even allowing for the moonlight and the elongation of the shadow it had been too big for a dog. And the pads were enormous.

Jaeckel said that, to settle it, why didn't we all come down to have a look at the prints ourselves. We were gathered in the auberge at the time and it was warm and friendly and the vintage was uncommonly good that year. So only a few of the less comfort-addicted spirits said they would go along. I went too, together with my son Andrew, who was eager to see the tack of this fabulous beast.

We had a disappointing afternoon. The village children were using the path as a toboggan slide after the new snowfall and nothing remained by then.

"Let us try by the stream," said Jean LeCoutre, who apart from owning a logging company, was also maire of the village. So aside from his natural authority, coupled with that of his office, it was also his duty to look into the matter. We drew a blank there too. Jaeckel was puzzled and humiliated. He looked at the turned-up snow in disgust and scratched his head. He spat thoughtfully.

LeCoutre remained on his knees for a moment, staring at the ground.

"You are certain this is the place?" he asked the frontier guard.

The latter turned and surveyed the length of the stream. "As you can see, the remainder of the banks are covered in virgin snow," he said simply.

The maire got to his feet and brushed down his trousers. "It seems as though someone has obliterated the tracks with a rough broom," he said in a puzzled voice.

There was a general laugh among the men who had accompanied us but I noticed we all went back to the village in a thoughtful frame of mind. That was the simple beginning and nothing else happened for more than two weeks.

Then a frightened child came running into the hamlet one evening to say he'd been chased by a big dog. The child was obviously terrified and his clothes had been torn by something sharp and jagged so his family were forced to take the story seriously. They sent for the maire and the doctor and within half an hour a search party was organized. I joined it, naturally and though Andrew was anxious to go, I told him to stay behind. He was only fifteen and I knew that he might do something foolish in his excitement.

We all got lanterns and big electric torches and thoroughly searched the track along which the boy had been coming. Sure enough, there were large paw marks right behind the half-impressions of the boy's running feet. There was no joking that night and a noticeable tremulousness in the voices of some of those who made suggestions.

LeCoutre sent back to the village for his rifle and a message summoning the best shots in the community. We left two men to guide them down. After the attack on the boy, the paw marks circled aimlessly and then started to go downhill. They followed the path the village children used as a slide and then went into the stream and disappeared. This was strange in itself, as wolves avoid water, except for drinking purposes.

We were circling up and down when there was the crack of a rifle.

"The opposite bank," shouted Jaeckel, his eyes bright with excitement. Smoke curled thinly from the barrel of his rifle. He pointed into the thicket on the opposite bank. We all distinctly heard a crackling noise following the shot.

"Now perhaps you'll believe me," said Jaeckel with quiet triumph.

"If it satisfies you, this is serious enough," the maire agreed.

By now the riflemen from the village had arrived, alarmed by the shot and disappointed at being cheated of a chance at getting the animal.

The maire led the way back in, having decided that it was too dark and dangerous to attempt to ford the stream and seek the beast out that night. He consulted with the doctor over the boy, who was found to have only minor scratches and then telephoned the civil authorities to put them on their guard.

The auberge was packed that evening, while we all debated the events of the day.

When we got back to the house I found the door locked. Andrew's voice, shaken and hushed, sounded from inside. He opened up when I called to him.

"I was frightened, father," he said. "I think the wolf was here about half an hour ago. I heard something padding round the house and a snarl like a dog so I locked the door quickly."

"You were very wise, son," I comforted him.

"Shall we go and look for it?" said Andrew.

I got angry then. After all, Andrew was the only thing I had left in the world, now that his mother had gone.

"That is what we won't do," I said. "If you've had your supper, get off to bed. The authorities will handle this."

I telephoned the maire and presently another party arrived. We went over the ground minutely. We found the wolf tracks outside the main balcony windows of the house. LeCoutre looked grave.

"We'll have to keep the young people indoors after dark until this is over,' he said. 'Til see if we can get some extra rifles up from the militia until the beast is shot."

We followed the tracks half-heartedly for a few hundred yards. We saw they went in the general direction of the village path before we turned back.

A party sat up at my house drinking cognac into the small hours discussing the affair.

2

Nothing happened for a week. Then there were further scares. Two little girls had looked from their window one night and had seen the wolf—as big as a cow, they said, though everyone allowed for their childish imagination—running across the meadow near their house. When their mother had come, alarmed by their screams, all she could see was a thin man running across the field, probably in pursuit of the wolf.

Then two goats, which were kept under cover at Papa Gremillon's, one of the last farms at the edge of the village, were found half-eaten and with their throats torn out. A minor wave of panic swept the district. One of the most alarming aspects of the business was that the outhouse in which the goats were kept had been padlocked and the key left in the lock.

Whoever had killed the goats—and the prints and evidence of the fierce struggle among the beasts pointed unmistakably to a wolf—had first unlocked the padlock and then turned the key again on leaving. When these facts became generally known the unease became tinged with terror. LeCoutre and I and some of the more undaunted members of the community talked the affair over for long hours in the auberge. It was while we were there one bitter afternoon shortly after Christmas, that the rumour of 'le loup-garou' first came to be mentioned.

"A lot of superstitious nonsense among the hill people," snapped LeCoutre. "The legend of a man-wolf is as old as these mountains," he added, turning to me.

"There may be something in it," said someone farther down the table. "The story of a man who can change into a wolf to kill his prey and then turn back into a man again, has come down from classical times."

"So have many things," said LeCoutre, his face purple with outraged indignation. "But that doesn't mean we have to believe minotaurs are still running about."

"But how do you account for this beast's cleverness?" said Jaeckel disarmingly. "And what about that padlock at Papa Gremillon's?"

The maire stroked his chin before downing his glass of water spirit. "I don't doubt we've got something serious here and something fiendishly clever," he said. "But I exclude the supernatural. We've enough to think about at the moment."

There was not one of us who disagreed with him on dispersing. But after that things gradually got worse. Some soldiers on winter manoeuvres in the mountains came for a bit, boosted the custom in the cafes and escorted the children to and from their various errands. Nothing happened of note. Some of the younger national servicemen fired off their rifles at shadows, alarming the countryside. And when the weather closed in, blocking the pass, the militia were, of course, withdrawn. We were left to our own resources.

3

The first deaths occurred in March, with the warmer weather. There was little Rene Fosse, a 12-year-old schoolboy who was found with his throat torn out one night only a few yards from his back door. He had been on his way to the barn to see that the stock were all right. With the deaths of two small sisters later the same week then truly began the reign of terror. Paw-prints of the wolf were found on each occasion but the creature was fiendishly cunning, as the maire had hinted. Despite the combing of the foothills by massive search-parties, aided by militia, the prints always ceased at the stream.

And searches up and down the banks always failed to find the place where the beast had once again regained the ground. During all this time hardly anyone had spotted the animal which fed the legend of the werewolf; a legend which was seized on first by the regional and then the national press. Hordes of journalists came with their cameramen, everyone was interviewed, old griefs disinterred and any clues there might have been of the beast's whereabouts were soon obliterated by the boots of hundreds of sightseers.

Then, at the end of March or early April, just before the snow was due to disperse, we had a report that an adult this time had been attacked. He was a man named Charles Badoit, a mechanic at the village's only garage, who lived in one of the smaller houses at the end of the settlement. The beast had jumped on his back from an embankment as he was returning on foot from work and had torn a piece out of his neck. With great courage Badoit had fought it off; fortunately for him he was still carrying a box of tools and as he was a big man and made such a threatening sight as he whirled the box around his head with the strength of despair, the wolf had given up the attack and slunk off.

Swathed in bandages and fortified by cognac, Badoit reclined on a sofa at the doctor's house and told his story. LeCoutre swiftly organized one of his biggest search parties and this time I allowed Andrew to join it on condition that he kept close to me and didn't handle any firearms. Two burly gendarmes from the police de la route had been left in the village and they added a useful stiffening to our party. The wolf had torn away a piece of flesh from the neck of Badoit and had apparently stopped to eat this no more than a few yards away from the scene of the attack for we found bloodstains and an area of disturbed snow in a nearby thicket.

"This is an audacious brute, all right," gritted LeCoutre grimly as we pressed on, following the clear trail in the snow. But after going in the familiar direction, the paw marks diverted from the track and started up a nearby hill. The wolf may have had its appetite whetted and might be trying for another victim the other side of the village, I said. LeCoutre nodded assent.

We plunged uphill for twenty minutes, through quite thick snow, following the clearly defined trail. We all heard the crackling branch at the same time. Andrew gave an excited cry and the wolf bounded out from behind a clump of fir trees about fifty metres ahead. Several rifles cracked out in a ragged volley and puffs of disturbed snow made plumes in the air around the big grey animal. One of the shots had apparently connected for the brute gave a whimpering cry and limped off back into the trees.

Encouraged, we plunged after it. I told LeCoutre and the gendarmes I thought one of us had hit it on the front offside paw and they were inclined to agree. But half an hour later, with the bloodstains growing fainter and dying out before the trail ended at the stream, we had to give up once more.

4

Next morning Andrew was pale with shock. I had been out for a talk in the village and on my return found him lying on his bed, immobile with pain. There was a bandage on his right hand.

"Don't be angry, father," he said. "I cut my fingers chopping wood. It's not serious."

"Have you been to see Dr. Lemaire?" I said, alarmed.

"Yes," Andrew assured me. "And he says it's nothing to be concerned about. More painful than anything else."

"I'm glad to hear it, my boy," I said. "But you really must be more careful."

Truth to tell, I was more worried than I cared to admit, but at suppertime the colour had come back into Andrew's cheeks and he was eating with all his old appetite. The matter slipped my mind as

Cry Wolf

the jangled state of nerves of the villagers gradually came to crisis point. Not that I blamed them, because I was by now almost as nervous at night-time as anyone, despite the heavy Mauser pistol I kept by my bedside. The maire had issued a ration of ammunition to every responsible male adult. Like him I had no patience with the werewolf theories which many of the villagers were quite openly advocating, but I had to admit that there were many terrible and unexplainable things about this horrifying series of events.

Poor Badoit's neck was taking a long time to heal and he had to be removed to hospital in a major town fifty kilometres away. But for a miracle we would have been following his cortege to the local cemetery as the latest in that series of pathetic funerals of earlier victims. We were hoping that the wolf had had the fight knocked out of it by the flesh wound inflicted by our shots and had retired to the higher mountains. But it was not to be.

It was only two nights later when the beast struck. In some way known only to itself it had secreted itself in a locked woodshed almost in the heart of the village. Its audacity was such that it had apparently stayed there all day. In the early evening the unfortunate old woman who owned the nearby house had run short of fuel for her stove. Opening the door in the semi-darkness of the courtyard she had her throat torn out in the first onrush of the wolf and had died immediately. The beast, not at all incommoded by its wound of three nights earlier, had dragged her off to another backyard nearby and had commenced its meal. This delay had enabled the hurriedly summoned shooting party to come up while the beast was still in the vicinity. LeCoutre was arguing with some of the more superstitious villagers as Andrew and I got there.

"I tell you could an animal have done this?" said a stolid, elderly villager with a walrus moustache, after the problems of the locked shed had been explained. "C'est le loup-garou!"

"Werewolf be damned!" said LeCoutre, choking with rage. "Bullets will put paid to it, the same as any other wolf."

I had just pointed out that the missing woman might still be alive and that we ought to be following up the trail when the most dreadful growl came from the shadows. This was followed by a worrying noise mixed with the sound of snapping bone which made several members of the party feel sick. We all set off through the maze of courtyards. Someone wheeled a motor cycle with a bright headlamp on to the scene.

A grey shadow leaped over a wall as a gun flamed, leaving a scene of Goyaesque horror behind it. While some of the party remained to take charge and to cover the mangled remains with a tarpaulin a dozen of us rushed forward to take revenge on this devilish animal. LeCoutre and I pressed ahead of the two gendarmes. I had brought Andrew with me, to spare him the scenes behind us, and he was well up with the maire and myself. We heard a snarl from the thicket in front and Andrew dashed ahead with a torch and a thick stick, despite my shouts. I called to him to come back but the party was now widely spread out. My main fear was flying bullets from excitable trigger fingers as I didn't imagine that the wolf would stop.

It suddenly appeared, eyes blazing, and several shots rang out but the animal ran off. When we got to the spot there were no blood marks. Then Jaeckel appeared behind me, his eyes inflamed with excitement. His chest heaved with his exertions. "There," he said excitedly. "There!"

I followed his pointing finger, saw the branches of the thicket moving and undulating.

"There he is," Jaeckel screamed. "The wolf-man!"

He raised his rifle before I could stop him. The explosion fell like a heavy wound on my heart. A large body lurched from the thicket and rolled almost to our feet. I ran forward in horror. Andrew sprawled on the ground, darkness running from his mouth, soaking the snow.

I lifted his head, hardly knowing what I was doing. His bandaged hand fell forward over his chest. There was a gasp from the search party behind us.

Andrew opened his eyes.

"I cut my hand chopping wood, father," he said very deliberately in English. "That is the truth."

Then he died.

"I believe you, my boy," I said.

A Cry Wolf

The group around us made way for Dr. Lemaire. Powerful electric torches illuminated the scene.

Jaeckel, the frontier guard, was stammering in my ears. "Pardon, monsieur, a terrible tragedy, but I was right. Le loup-garou! The bandage on his hand."

I hardly heard him. There was a strange look of triumph in Jaeckel's eyes and I understood many things.

As he turned away I saw he too had a bandage on his right hand.

☙ The Trodes

☙ 1

THERE IT WAS. AUGUSTA BASSETT SNIFFED TO HERSELF AS SHE gazed out of the conservatory window at the bleak autumn sunset which hung over the misty valley beyond. Gas lamps bloomed along the steep road leading down the far side of the hill and the trees were already bare and skeletal in the evening light. The child was standing toward the end of the ornamental path, scuffing his feet in the dried leaves. She could hear the scraping of his boots through the chill autumn air.

There it was, she added, as though repetition of the phrase would solve the problem. Cynthia's boy was a constant source of complication and difficulty. Augusta Bassett hardly liked to mention it to herself but Cynthia's death was almost an abdication of responsibility. She hesitated, her lean, spare form bowed toward the window embrasure, one slim white hand resting against the thick pane of glass, her troubled eyes fixed on the sullen figure of the boy in the garden beyond.

Her lips curved into less severe lines as she again thought of her sister; Cynthia had been too young for marriage altogether and the circumstances had not been propitious. Her death had been a shocking blow and had taken place in an equally shocking manner. Augusta hardly liked to recall the details even now.

For the sake of her sister's memory she had to make Guy happy; but there was no doubt the boy was ill adapted for life in a quiet

✣ The Trodes

country town. He had a subtle way of showing displeasure and his manner of standing on one foot while his pale green eyes surveyed his aunt, sometimes for minutes on end, quite put her nerves on edge at times.

This afternoon he had been particularly trying. He was extraordinarily mature and self-possessed, even for a thirteen-year-old, and his obsession with science-fiction to the exclusion of almost all other pursuits could not be healthy for a child of his age. He had now taken over the woodshed on the south side of the garden and Augusta had heard dark hints from the gardener that he had turned it into a laboratory.

She had had to smile to herself when Kendall had told her; the old man had been quivering with indignation and she remembered that the shed had formerly been sacred to his own pursuits. They were innocent enough; he liked to smoke and read the paper there on wet afternoons, out of sight of the house, and the boy's taking over would have driven him to the toolshed, a bleak metal building, cold and cheerless; or the greenhouse, where he would be in full view of the drawing room windows.

But Augusta herself had passed the woodshed a little later that afternoon and though Guy was not in possession a glance through the dusty windows had tended to strengthen her impression of the gardener's forebodings. From what she could see through the dark panes, the benches were covered with bottles, tubes and apparatus. It all looked rather elaborate for a child of Guy's age and she wondered idly where it could all have come from.

Packed in the trunks, she supposed; Guy had rather a lot of luggage when he had arrived after his mother's death and many of his books were scientific tracts and textbooks in addition to the fiction. Augusta was annoyed to find the door of the shed secured with a strong chain and padlock, or she would have investigated further. Indeed, she was rather put out at the whole thing and intended to speak to the boy about it at teatime but, as so often happened of late, the conversation took another direction and she forgot all about it.

That Guy was engaged in annoying chemical experiments was certain; there had been flashes of light and smoke from the shed only yesterday. She was inordinately obsessed by the dangers of fire—indeed, her teacher friends said they had never yet seen a private house which had fire extinguishers on the walls of the kitchen—and Guy's activities in the woodshed might be dangerous and of an inflammable nature. And she had a duty to her dead sister as well as to the boy to prevent him coming to harm.

The matter might still have rested there, for Augusta feared an open clash; Guy was a particularly stubborn little boy and like all people of a gentle and studious nature, she wished to avoid an open confrontation. But this afternoon's events could not be overlooked. They involved Mrs. Randall, an expert cook, who came in three days a week and whom Augusta regarded highly.

At about three o'clock there had been a smell of burning. Augusta herself was in the drawing room writing letters and her first impression was that there was a fire in the kitchen. As she hurried into the hall there was a metallic clang, a brilliant flash and a terrified scream from Mrs. Randall. Wrenching open the kitchen door in alarm Augusta found nothing but a lot of smoke hanging near the ceiling and an indignant Mrs. Randall with a hand pressed to her ample bosom.

"It's that wretched boy," she told Augusta Bassett accusingly. "He had another of his chemical gadgets."

She turned a grim face towards the glass-topped kitchen door around which smoke was still wreathing.

"Are you hurt?" Augusta asked anxiously.

"Shock, rather," said Mrs. Randall, opening the window over the sink to let out the residue of smoke. "That boy wants a good beating."

"I'll speak to him, Mrs. Randall," Augusta Bassett said firmly. "We can't have this."

"I shan't stay if it goes on," said Mrs. Randall determinedly, clattering vigorously among the pans in the bowl with her big, capable hands. Her attitude spoke more plainly than words. To Augusta's alarmed and somewhat exaggerated thoughts was added the mental image of Mrs. Randall's hands round the boy's throat.

"He said the Trodes were coming," Mrs. Randall continued with pursed lips.

The Trodes

Augusta looked at the large figure of the cook with astonishment.

"What on earth did he mean?"

Mrs. Randall shrugged.

"Don't ask me," she said. "Something out of one of those awful science-fiction books he's been reading. That boy needs firm treatment. You're too gentle with him."

Augusta was uneasily aware that Mrs. Randall was right but she did not wish to enter into a debate on the affair at that moment. She found Guy standing near the apple tree outside the back door. He had his hands in his pockets and was whistling nonchalantly. He looked at her with deceptive innocence, his rosy cheeks glowing with health, his green eyes dancing with mischief.

"You shouldn't torment Mrs. Randall so," Augusta said mildly. "If she left we would never get another cook like her."

Guy burrowed his hands even deeper in his pockets and regarded his aunt with radiant self-confidence.

"I shouldn't worry, aunt," he said airily. "I was only trying to warn Mrs. Randall of the Coming. Like most adults she wouldn't take any notice."

"That's all very well, Guy," Augusta Bassett said worriedly.

She put up a nervous hand and pushed back a wisp of greying hair that threatened to disturb the smartness of her coiffure.

"But you really should be more careful with those gadgets of yours."

The boy laughed as though she had said something extremely amusing.

"You don't understand, aunt," he said. "Those gadgets, as you call them, aren't mine at all. Kendall made the same mistake. I expect he has been Summoned Away."

He gave her a curious look from his green eyes as he stood with his head sideways so that his aunt felt quite unnerved for a moment. Really, he was the most extraordinary boy.

"That's another thing, Guy," she said. "It could be dangerous with all those chemicals in the woodshed. And you ought to have asked Kendall's permission before taking it over like that."

Guy shuffled his feet but there was no annoyance in his voice as he replied.

"Oh, Kendall won't mind," he said enigmatically.

Now, Augusta Bassett, holding on to the conservatory window and straining her eyes through the dusk at the figure of the boy scraping his feet on the path, growing ever fainter in the evening light, was aware that she should have been firmer with him. But he had a maddeningly vague way of turning the conversation so that she often quite forgot what she had intended to ask him.

And strangely enough, Kendall was nowhere to be found this afternoon. She had looked high and low for him, the whole length of the garden. Though perhaps Guy had taken her words to heart after all. She had glanced in at the woodshed before returning to the house and had seen the old man's folded newspaper and his pipe lying on the bench near the window.

The sun flared and sank lower, staining the far tree-tops carmine but still the boy stood at the end of the path, aimlessly scraping his feet until it grew too dark to see him. Augusta sighed and pulled the blinds.

2

The next day was a Saturday and Augusta Bassett was too busy to check the boy's movements. She had asked Mrs. Randall to keep an eye on him in the morning and had told her she had spoken strongly to him the evening before. Mrs. Randall, who left on Saturdays in the early afternoon had merely sniffed but Augusta was too preoccupied to notice the irony in the little mannerism.

She had a library committee that morning, immediately following her little coffee club and then she would have to dash back from town to supervise the boy's lunch. She always liked to be present at meals; she felt it a duty to her dead sister. And with Guy so troublesome lately she felt that the two of them would give greater emphasis to dealing with any problems which arose.

She felt a tightening of the heart as she thought of the current difficulties. She was standing in the hall and turned to look at her white, set face in the mirror. She was taking everything far too seriously as usual and yet there were strange undertones. She pinched her cheeks with well manicured hands, bringing the blood back and freshening her complexion.

There was another annoyance too. Kendall had not turned up this morning and she had planned to start work on the coppice at the end of the afternoon. He would be needed for the heavy digging. She wondered if she ought to look by his cottage. He might be ill. Here Augusta consulted her watch and made some rapid calculations. She would not have time today. He was not on the telephone but if he did not turn up on Monday she would get the boy to call at his home with a note.

The thought of Guy recalled something else to her mind. She had just heard him hurry up to his room. On impulse she went through into the library. The room was the domain of her late brother and Guy had taken to sitting there of late, reading his cheap paperback books when not engaged in his chemical dabblings. She went straight to the heavy leather swivel chair that had been Joseph's favourite place.

Sure enough, there was a pile of dog-eared paperback novels on the seat of the chair and stacked on the table. Augusta turned them over with a nervous forefinger. They were lurid, science-fiction things, with revolting covers showing vague, amorphous beings menacing the population of the world. Augusta flicked through them with mounting annoyance. Really, Guy should occupy his time with more worthwhile and rewarding pursuits.

She wondered if she ought to get his teacher to call for a chat. She found a mauve-covered volume, more restrained and less strident in its cover illustrations, at the bottom of the pile. She smiled as she glanced at its title. So this was what the boy had meant. She would let Mrs. Randall know. She picked up the book. It was called: The Return of the Trodes. She looked at the author's name but it meant nothing to her.

Surprisingly, its category seemed to be non-fiction. There was a disquietingly line-drawing on the cover, showing menacing, three-pronged creatures standing on a gaunt skyline limned against a purple sunset. The heads were squat and shapeless and partially obscured because of the helmets of some reflective material which completely encased their skulls.

Augusta Bassett's shallow breathing quickened as she read the synopsis on the cover. Something about alien creatures waiting in Outer Space to take over the world again. Then she relaxed and smiled as she read that the manifestations were accompanied by bright flashes in the sky. So this was where he got his ideas. She carried the book through into the kitchen, her heart quite light.

Guy was still upstairs, as she could hear the water swirling from the wash-basin in the bathroom. The kitchen door was ajar, kneaded dough and pastry-covers ready for filling on the big plastic table top. Augusta Bassett went over toward the door, the mauve-jacketed book clutched against her breast. She could faintly smell burning in the air.

She thought Kendall had come back and started a bonfire but the garden was empty and peaceful through the big kitchen window. No wisp of smoke rose in the chill autumn air. Augusta Bassett walked with firm measured steps across to where the cook's hat, coat and handbag hung from the pegs behind the kitchen door. Quickly, her mind a blank, she searched the ground floor rooms. Mrs. Randall was not there.

3

On Sunday, in church, Augusta watched the well-scrubbed back of Guy's neck bent piously in the pew beside her. The boy had been behaving himself this morning. Like many youngsters of his age he alternated wild fits of outrageous behaviour with periods of comparative calm. Augusta breathed more easily. Evidently Sunday was to be one of the latter. She needed a respite, however brief.

And she was still worried about Mrs. Randall. Though she had been somewhat relieved at the explanation. She had met the boy on the stairs went about to search the first-floor rooms. His green eyes were wide and guileless as he faced her.

"I'm sorry, I forgot to tell you, aunt. Mrs. Randall had bad news. Her sister has been taken ill."

⚜ THE TRODES

"Thank you, Guy," Augusta stammered. "I was worried about her, to tell the truth. She went off and left her things, you see."

The boy nodded, moving down the stairs.

"She was rather upset," he said. "Still, I expect you'll hear something by Monday."

And he moved in his sauntering way out into the garden. Now, as she automatically murmured the responses, Augusta Bassett could not repress the darker thoughts that hovered round the fringes of her mind. This morning she still had heard nothing from Mrs. Randall and she had not sent anyone to collect her things.

This afternoon, on impulse, she had driven round before church, to the house where Mrs. Randall lived with her maiden sister. But the house was shut and empty and she had to come away without the answers to her questions. She automatically took Guy's arm and steered him toward the back of the church as the service ended. She was but dimly conscious of the Vicar's murmured banalities at the porch door.

Then she and Guy were driving away down the lane and back through the town to her own house. They had an early tea and, as so often happened of late, Guy wandered out into the garden. She saw him pass the drawing room windows and knew he was on his way to the woodshed. She washed and stacked the tea-things on the draining board herself tonight.

It was already turning toward dusk. How she was beginning to hate these autumnal evenings, harbinger of winters which seemed to get harsher each year. But she supposed that was only another symptom of advancing age. She went back into the drawing room and sought her favourite chair. She noticed that the mauve paperback was on the corner of the table. Where she supposed she had left it the previous day. Or was it Friday? She could not remember now.

She picked up the book and turned over the pages. She sat reading for perhaps a quarter of an hour. Then she threw the book down as though it were venomous. She rose to her feet, her face white, her breathing fast and shallow. She understood now. She had to speak to Guy. A bright flash lit the darkening garden. Her feet beat a staccato tattoo on the concrete path as she ran toward the woodshed.

⚘ Darkness, Mist & Shadow

The place was full of smoke. The door was ajar and she pushed it open and stepped inside. It was bigger than she remembered and the shadows seemed to stretch away toward infinity. The smoke was sweet-scented and quite pleasant. Here were the retorts and apparatus but she could not see Guy. Light was growing somewhere at the end of the shed and she went to stand by the bench, the blood beating heavily in her head.

The flashing came again, brighter now, and a vast humming seemed to fill the structure. She saw Guy then. He was standing outside the window. He waved cheerily to her. She heard the door grate back and the rattle of the chain and padlock. She beat against the panels but knew she could not get out that way. The brightness grew about her. She turned, her breath a faint whimpering in her throat.

The three-pronged things stood and looked at her gravely. The shining helmets made an iridescent shimmer in the semi-gloom of the smoky interior and she could not see their faces. Her screams went unnoticed. The shed was, after all, a long way from the house.

⚘ 4

Matron Garside yawned heavily and pushed back her chair from her desk. She frowned out from her glass-cubicle office at the small figure of the boy in the waiting room. She felt a momentary twinge of pity. Guy really was a special case. He bore such a load of tragedy for his tender years. First the horror of his mother's death; then the disappearance of his aunt and her servants.

She sighed. It would be difficult to settle such a boy in the home. Though his interest in science would make him particularly fitted for that side of his schooling. The new laboratory wing was admirably suited for one of his gifts. And Mr. Tisdale had only this morning commented on the boy's enthusiasm.

Already, only a week after entry, he had commenced experiments there; experiments which, said Mr. Tisdale, indicated exceptional brilliance. The only drawback was his addiction to rather garish books.

The Trodes

He was reading one now, she noticed; a particularly violent mauve disfigured the cover as he raised his head from the paperback. He approached at her welcoming smile.

His green eyes looked at her trustingly as he poked his head in at the door. Really, he could be quite enchanting at times. But first she must question him about the inexplicable disappearance of Mr. Tisdale.

"Hullo, Matron," said Guy cheerily, coming."The Trodes are coming.

⚜ Dust To Dust

Mr. Appleton bought the house almost at first glance. It was within the confines of the village, but just far back enough in its own trim orchard grounds to be unobtrusive. The building was well maintained and really, there was a wealth of accommodation for the money. The price was not cheap and yet certainly well below the market value for a property of such character. Not that there was anything historic about Dotterells, Mr. Appleton judged.

The house was Edwardian, he would have said. Tile-hung and well converted to modern standards it had an air of old-maidish smugness, as though it sat like a contented cat, back from the bustle of the street, its two clipped ornamental trees each side the path almost like paws reaching out to embrace the village.

The simile was fanciful, Mr. Appleton felt, and he was not normally a fanciful man. As the last rays of spring sunshine stained the upper windows of the house carmine it seemed to smile at him. He smiled to himself at the notion and was inevitably reminded of Carroll's crocodile welcoming the fishes in 'with gently smiling jaws'. He stood back in the road, leaning on his stick, and glanced at the house again. It was benevolent. A heartening omen, he felt, and nothing in the subsequent negotiations led him to believe otherwise.

The surveyor's estimate was good; there were no hidden snags in the property. To Mr. Appleton's surprise—and he was usually a most

Dust To Dust

cautious man—not more than eight weeks had gone by before he was ensconced in Dotterells, had arranged his vast array of books and papers, and had engaged a housekeeper. A most sensible woman, Mrs. Grice seemed a very superior and intelligent person for one of that station. In the necessarily brief conversation he had with her before he moved into the house, he had gathered that the previous occupant, an elderly retired gentleman, had died rather suddenly; the relatives lived abroad, and as they wanted a quick sale had asked a price well below the market value.

Mr. Appleton was satisfied. He was incurious about the everyday affairs of life and he had more than enough to occupy him; he was on volume three of his monumental work on primitive superstition, and he had promised his publisher the book would be ready in time to figure on his Christmas list. He had all summer before him, he was settling into Dotterells nicely, and if he could bring the book in by the autumn he would have a pleasant year.

Mr. Appleton sat back in his study and blinked about him, warming at the prospect. He really was more satisfied with his new home than he cared to admit. He had not, it is true, been overeffusive with the agent for the vendor, on the principle that the prospective purchaser should never appear too eager. And he was not naturally an affectionate man; his austere, bookish life had left him little time or opportunity to make lasting friendships.

But there was no doubt that the atmosphere of Dotterells was conducive to the contented spirit. His study for instance, a large, L-shaped room on the ground floor, with a huge bay window overlooking the orchard and road beyond, could not have been more convenient for his purposes. Just now it lay bathed in late May sunshine and with its cream-painted walls and rows of varicoloured books that faced him along the far corner, soothed all the instincts of a book-lover or collector.

Mr. Appleton shifted his weight in his leather armchair and swivelled back to the window. He glanced again at the neat typescript in front of him and the tumbled heaps of reference works on the surface of the great rosewood desk and sighed. He should, he supposed, be a little more sociable, and make himself known to his neighbours on either side. But his work pressed and there would be time for the social niceties later. In the meantime he would set the house in order and press on as fast as he could. There were still eight chapters to be laid out and completed; more than enough work for his autumn deadline, for he was a writer who could not be hurried.

Mr. Appleton thought ruefully of the turmoil in his affairs over the past year; the demolition of the block of London flats in which he had spent more than half a lifetime had upset all his working habits. It was responsible too for the long delay on the work which was to crown more than three decades of achievement in scholarly literature. He had been lucky, he supposed, in making such a drastic break with town life, to find such a haven as Dotterells and the village in which it was situated. Only thirty minutes from Charing Cross and the wider world of publishing, yet it might well have been in the farthest depths of the West Country.

Mr. Appleton frowned. He was daydreaming again. He glanced at his watch. Already an hour had passed and it would soon be time for lunch. He could hear the clink of utensils as Mrs. Grice laid the table in the dining-room. He shook his head and bent over the typescript again. It was true, he had noticed, after more than a week in the house, that he was not producing as much as in the past. He attributed it to the upsets of the past months and the newness of his unfamiliar routine in the country, but it was a fact also that the house was relaxing in the most delightful way. It was almost too comfortable in its assurance and cheerfulness and Mr. Appleton realized that this new malaise of inertia would have to be energetically fought against.

He pressed on with his corrections for another ten minutes and then found Mrs. Grice at his elbow.

"Lunch, sir, in a quarter of an hour, if you please."

"Thank you, Mrs. Grice."

He looked up, grateful for the woman's quiet efficiency, the well-bred gentility of her manner. With her neat clothes and the touch of white at throat and wrist she would have passed muster in almost any company. He wondered idly what her past history had been; but Mrs. Grice never volunteered any information and he had always been too polite to ask.

A Dust To Dust

"I shall be in directly," he added, as she continued to hover in the background. He waited until the door had clicked to behind her before he made the last one or two corrections in his neat, precise hand and then capped his pen. As he rose to leave the room he was suddenly conscious of something offensive to his neat sense of order. Glancing back towards the window, through which the sun poured in benevolent serenity, he realized what it was.

The inner window sill which was of some old, dark wood, possibly oak he supposed, was made of a single beam six inches thick. It was obviously much older than the house of which it formed a part. But it was not this which was responsible for Mr. Appleton's temporary irritation. The whole sill, he now found on closer inspection, was coated with a thick film of dust.

The sight was so at variance with the neatness of the rest of the room that Mr. Appleton felt it might possibly be an optical illusion; but no, as he tested it tentatively with the tip of one finger, he felt its gritty texture on his skin and there was the pallid imprint of his touch on the sill's surface. He clicked his teeth in positive annoyance. This was unlike Mrs. Grice and he would have to speak to her about it; Mr. Appleton was pathologically obsessed with the cleanliness and order of his surroundings and the state of the sill was an obvious breach in the otherwise carefully ordered household arrangements.

But Mrs. Grice was such a pleasant and normally efficient woman that he would have to be tactful in the way he mentioned it. He resolved to tackle the matter after lunch. It was such a trivial thing, really, but it would be as well to make his views known.

In the event Mr. Appleton waited until after dessert had been served, and he was appreciatively stirring the depths of his first cup of coffee before he mentioned the matter. Mr. Appleton's eyesight was not what it was, but he thought he detected a slight paling of Mrs. Grice's face. But she only drummed softly with her fingers on the back of one of the dining-room chairs.

"I wouldn't have mentioned it normally, Mrs. Grice, apart from the fact that it isn't like your way of going about things. I have no objection to a little dust here and there, from time to time, but the study must be kept in impeccable order. And the sun strikes across that sill so strongly that it makes it worse."

Mrs. Grice bit her lip and Mr. Appleton felt that perhaps he had been a little too harsh. And he hadn't meant to upset such a conscientious and pleasant worker.

So he added swiftly, before she could reply, "If you think I'm being unfair..."

"It's not that, Mr. Appleton," said Mrs. Grice. "I'm annoyed with myself, really. I could have sworn that I attended to the sill when I dusted the room yesterday."

"Well, it's no great matter," said Mr. Appleton cheerfully, glad at having won his point without a scene. How he hated scenes...

"Perhaps you could give it your attention when it's convenient. I thought it best to make my views known straight away."

"Certainly, Mr. Appleton," said Mrs. Grice in a subdued voice. "You are entitled to have the house as you want it and I'm only sorry you had cause to complain."

All the same there was a strange look on her face as she hurried out and once again Mr. Appleton regretted having spoken so sharply. After all, he could have cleared the sill himself with a few strokes of a duster; though in that case, why employ a housekeeper? He drank his coffee, poured a second cup from the silver pot, and banished the petty annoyance from his mind.

Back in his study that afternoon Mr. Appleton rapidly forgot the incident and found he was able to concentrate much more firmly on the work in hand. He was barely conscious of Mrs. Grice leaving his tea and biscuits at his elbow and it was almost dusk before he had finished typing and had gathered up the mass of completed sheets with suddenly aching hands. When he had stapled the chapters together and placed them ready for checking, he stood at the window for a while, conscious of the beauty of the dusk, the faint outlines of trees and bushes visible against the light from the road beyond.

Moved by a shadowy impulse he stepped to the casement and opened the window wide. He stood for almost a quarter of an hour lapped in the peace which came with the cool, damp air.

Dust To Dust

The following day was an unusual one in the familiar context of Mr. Appleton's life. He had a visit from the people who owned the manor house, whose boundaries abutted his back hedge, and who were in fact his next-door neighbours but one; the large timbered house flanked the road about a hundred yards from Mr. Appleton's own property. The visitors were a youngish couple, the man in his mid-forties, the woman about a decade junior, and they brought with them two children in their early teens.

Mrs. Grice was kept running to and fro with tea and cakes and while Mr. Appleton made polite talk with their elders, the youngsters could be heard exclaiming with pleasure as they wandered from room to room and discovered their host's treasures. Mr. Appleton had tea served in the study and he and his guests sat round a table abutting a circular window at the end of the big room. Despite Mr. Appleton's fears, the children were well behaved and an agreeable hour passed before the visitors departed, urging him to visit them the following week.

The host went with them to the gate and when he had returned to his own garden, musing agreeably on the small details of the not unwelcome interruption, his feet took him, somewhat of their own volition, down the flagged path at the side of the house. The sun shone fiercely, though it was long past five in the afternoon, and Mr. Appleton could hear the rasp of a saw from the orchard beyond. He noted, as he paused near the hedge, that a party of workmen were engaged in lopping or felling a group of trees about a hundred yards away from his own boundary. He stood watching for a few minutes, lulled by the soft country voices, and then presently, as the dull bite of an axe began to reverberate through the garden, went back indoors.

Mrs. Grice had already cleared the tea-things and he bent to resume his seat at the desk when he let fall an exclamation that was normally foreign to his lips. The sun shone brightly through the casement and there once again was the sill thickly coated with dust. Mr. Appleton felt rage beginning to choke his throat; he was thinking mainly of what his visitors must have thought of his standards of tidiness but the emotion was so unlike him that he resumed his seat, shocked at his own reaction. When he looked at the window again he saw that someone or perhaps some blunt object had scribed a pattern in the dust.

He stooped to look closer and found, albeit its crooked formation, an unmistakable word. TREE the sill said, in wavering writing. Mr. Appleton's annoyance was increased twofold. He guessed that his visitors' children had seen the dust and were making their own pert, juvenile comments. Another gust of irritation swept him. He turned on his heel and quit the study. As he got near the kitchen he heard Mrs. Grice give a stifled scream. There were muffled exclamations from the garden beyond and a single loud report, like an explosion. Mr. Appleton ran into the garden to find Mrs. Grice before him; the two of them hurried towards the hedge.

The cause of the explosion was soon obvious. A large branch of a tree which the men in the orchard were lopping, had fallen. A ladder lay tumbled in the long grass and a figure was pinned beneath a tangle of branches. Mr. Appleton forced his way through the hedge with an energy that surprised himself. He saw that the tree was an elm and that the branch was a big one. A groaning noise came from out the boughs and the small knot of men had their shoulders beneath and were lifting and pulling in a kind of compassionate chaos that Mr. Appleton found touching. He panted his way up to the group, conscious that he could really do little to help. A rope dangled uselessly from the tree. Easy to see how the little tragedy had happened.

A thickset man turned a white face to him as Mr. Appleton touched his shoulder.

"Can I help?" he said. And added, before the other could reply, "Is it bad?"

"Bad enough," said the thickset man shortly. He turned again to get his beefy shoulder under the branch. Mr. Appleton stood back and found Mrs. Grice behind him. She twisted her thin hands nervously but her eyes were bright and steady. Mr. Appleton was surprised to hear her say, "Let me have a look. I was a nurse . . ."

The thickset man gave way readily to her and she had wriggled in beneath the mass of boughs to make her inspection. She came out and brushed some leaves off her skirt.

"It looks like a broken shoulder," she said, speaking to nobody and looking fixedly between Mr. Appleton and the thickset man.

"I'll telephone for an ambulance," said Mr. Appleton, glad of something to do.

It was an hour or more before the injured man was removed, and the ambulance was no sooner gone and he and Mrs. Grice enjoying a welcome cup of tea together in the kitchen than a shy young constable knocked at the side door with some questions. It was dark before Mrs. Grice left and Mr. Appleton made a makeshift dinner of cold meat and pickles in the kitchen nook, pondering on the events of what had been for him an extremely momentous day.

Mr. Appleton was actually reaching for his book, on the verge of stepping into bed, before he remembered the inscription on the window sill. The single cryptic word took on an undue significance in his brain. On a sudden impulse he flung on his dressing-gown. The house was silent except for the tick of a clock as he opened the study door. The soft lamplight shone on the calm appointments of the room. Shone too on a window sill that was gleaming and bare of dust.

A month passed away and the summer continued in a blaze of blue and gold. One afternoon Mr. Appleton had been down to the lower orchard; the season was reaching its full height and even the long grasses of the paddock appeared to be wilting with the heat. Their stems looked flaxen and of the consistency of metal in the baking air, which made the far distance of the hills which surrounded the village vibrate and dance in the haze. It was cool and fresh, in the house after the almost tropical brilliance of the garden and Mr. Appleton paused momentarily on the tiled surface of the hall. When he had taken a glass of iced mineral water from the kitchen refrigerator he went through into the study; Mrs. Grice was out shopping and he had the place to himself.

He sat not at the desk today but in one of the large brown leather armchairs which flanked the hearth and sipped gratefully, conscious of the sensuous coolness of the glass's chill lip against his mouth and tongue. It was dark after the garden, but as Mr. Appleton's eyes grad-

⚔ Darkness, Mist & Shadow

ually adjusted themselves to the change of light he was again conscious of the feeling of irritation which he was beginning to experience in this room. He glanced over towards the window and saw with a sense of familiarity that the sill was blurred with a fine coating of dust.

He pulled himself out of his chair, uncomfortably aware of the sweat trickling down inside his shirt. He leaned forward, half expecting what he found. It was just the one word, scraped into the dust, with the same crooked finger. This time it spelled out: WELL.

Mr. Appleton sat down abruptly in his chair again, aware that the perspiration which started from every pore was not entirely engendered by the heat of the day. He stared fixedly in front of him at the familiar contours of the stone fireplace, thinking deeply for perhaps twenty minutes. Then he got up heavily and sought a duster. He grimly wiped the sill clean of its enigmatic message and went back into the garden again. His steps took him towards the front gate this time and he became aware of a blue light which was flashing in the distance.

He turned out of the gate and walked aimlessly towards it. He then saw that the light came from the top of a grey-painted ambulance belonging to the County Council. There was a knot of people in the garden beyond and then in a moment or two a small group detached itself; men in dark uniforms carrying something on a sheeted stretcher. A child's limp arm dangled below the sheet like a broken doll. The face was covered.

The ambulance door slammed and the engine murmured into life. Still Mr. Appleton lingered, listening to broken fragments of conversation. His eyes went beyond the garden wall to a stone parapet, half-hidden among roses and honeysuckle. Mr. Appleton recognized the Vicar, his arm about a woman's shoulder. He felt faint suddenly and looked wildly about him. He pushed into the throng of people, glancing this way and that. A pink-faced constable was listening to three conversations at once, his sympathetic face knotted in concentration over his notebook.

"The child was playing and fell in the well," said an elderly man in front of Mr. Appleton. "You can see where the cover gave way."

⚜ Dust To Dust

The voices began to recede in Mr. Appleton's ears in a most peculiar manner; he became aware that he had stumbled. Someone helped him up. Consciousness faded and he knew nothing more until he came around in his own kitchen to find Mrs. Grice's solicitous face before him. The constable was hovering by the table and Mr. Appleton's own doctor, a thickset, middle-aged character was saying, "Nothing serious. Just the effect of the heat, I think."

Mr. Appleton was relieved to hear the doctor's verdict but he was seriously shaken nevertheless. He refused Mrs. Grice's kind offer to stay the night. She lingered curiously when her usual time came for departure. Mr. Appleton sipped gratefully at his second small brandy and kept his gaze lowered at the floor of the dining-room. He was in pyjamas and dressing-gown but the heat still seemed to rise in tangible waves from the floor. Mr. Appleton felt words come awkwardly to his lips. He continued to keep his eyes lowered.

Then he said, "How did the previous owner of the house die?"

The words came out in a stumbling rush and Mrs. Grice looked startled, as well she might.

She stood shifting from one foot to the other and Mr. Appleton thought again how graceful and cool she looked. Her answer came at last.

"Heart, I believe, Mr. Appleton."

And then, when he had long given up any thought of further enlightenment, she added gently, standing in the dining-room doorway against the soft lamplight, "He was very old, you know."

It was a comforting thought and Mr. Appleton was oddly touched. He felt grateful and he rose to express his thanks. When he had bolted the door behind Mrs. Grice he crossed to the study and locked it for the first time since he had come to Dotterells. He lay awake thinking for a long time that night.

It was nearly three days before Mr. Appleton used the study again. He had been to London in the interim and had made some enquiries about the village, but as he was never able to speak clearly of the matters which so deeply troubled him, his researches achieved

Darkness, Mist & Shadow

little. He walked round the house in the early afternoon before entering the study; he glanced through the window, conscious of the absurd figure he must have cut to any watcher, and nervously examined the sill on the inside. So far as he could make out it was completely free of dust.

He went in and sat down at his desk and started to write; there was silence for a long time, broken only by the brittle scratching of his nib. Presently Mr. Appleton paused, put down his pen, and rested a moment, one hand on his head. He was conscious of a subtle change in the room and at first was at some difficulty in placing it. Then he became aware, absurdly it seemed, that the scratching of his pen had continued after he had laid it down. And as soon as he became outwardly conscious of it, the sound ceased.

There was a fearful silence, worse than the minute interruption. Mr. Appleton moved his head ever so slowly towards the window. He saw quite without surprise that the sill was thickly coated with dust. Saw too the scraggly outline of something scratched into the gritty surface. He went over heavily and read what it said. The same distorted writing spelled out APPLE, followed by part of another letter. Mr. Appleton at first thought in terms of the orchard but then, on reflection, saw that the upright of the next letter was an obvious continuation; the addition of a crosspiece would make it a T. It was the first part of his own name.

Mr. Appleton was conscious of a great weight on his heart; even breathing was an effort. The silence of the room was like a black cloud which made respiration difficult. Then a passing motor vehicle vibrated the windows and he moved again.

He went over and sat in one of the fireside chairs; he remained motionless for more than an hour, straining his ears for the slightest sound from the windows. Towards tea-time he heard the scratching again. He put off the moment as long as possible and then went over. The silent writer had completed the inscription of his own name.

Mr. Appleton went quickly out; his shirt was wringing wet and clung stickily to his back. He turned the key in the door behind him and went into the dining-room with an unnecessary speed and noise. Mrs. Grice looked surprised but said nothing. Somehow Mr. Appleton forced some tea and biscuits into his mouth, though he was unconscious of what he was eating. He had neither taste nor feeling at the moment. He sat with his spoon poised, his head on one side, as though he could hear the minutest sound from the study, now separated from him by two walls and the width of the corridor. Then Mrs. Grice came in and the spoon clattered loudly against the side of the cup.

The housekeeper's face looked white in the cool dimness of the dining-room, with its heavy oak furniture.

"I'm off now, Mr. Appleton," she said. "If there's anything else you want..."

He made a perfunctory remark and waited until he heard her go into the kitchen. Then he was in the study, hardly noticing the door was ajar, making for the window. He stared incredulously at the sill, his mind suddenly stirred to furious activity. He made a gasping noise in his throat; his heart started to pump heavily. He stared again at the window sill, unable to take in the implications of what he saw; then he looked out through the window. He began to run towards the door like a madman.

Mrs. Grice, on the opposite pavement, turned at his call. She saw her employer gesticulating wildly at the gate of the house. Mr. Appleton was not aware of the surprised faces about him in the street; he strode rapidly towards Mrs. Grice, one question only hanging tremulously on his tongue. He saw Mrs. Grice throw up her hands; there was a great noise in the sky and an intolerable pain in his body. The fading daylight changed to all the colours of the rainbow and he had time to note the horror on Mrs. Grice's face before all consciousness faded.

The jury returned a verdict of accidental death and the matter was closed, though the Coroner, a patient and prosaic sort of man, could not help observing that it was difficult to see why a gentleman of Mr. Appleton's ordered and temperate habits should rush headlong into the path of a heavy lorry which he had apparently neither seen nor heard. Indeed, other witnesses had testified that he had looked neither right nor left as he hurried into the road.

It was a minor mystery as mysteries go and though it remained for long a matter for speculation in the village, the jury preferred to deal with the available facts. Mr. Appleton's book appeared in the autumn and Mrs. Grice, though not addicted to what she felt was an essentially morbid type of literature, read it with great interest. If Mrs. Grice sometimes thinks of Mr. Appleton today it is perhaps merely to reflect what could have upset him. For of course she had no way of knowing that her thoughtful action in dusting off the study window sill had erased the warning of his own death.

Basil Copper and Stephen Jones at the launch of *Basil Copper: A Life in Books*, London, February 23, 2008. Photograph © Peter Coleborn.

BASIL COPPER (1924-2013) became a full-time writer in 1970. His first story in the horror field, 'The Spider', was published in 1964 in *The Fifth Pan Book of Horror Stories*, since when his short fiction appeared in numerous collections and anthologies, and was extensively adapted for radio and television. Along with two non-fiction studies of the vampire and werewolf legends, his other books include the novels *The Great White Space*, *The Curse of the Fleers*, *Necropolis*, *The Black Death* and *The House of the Wolf*. Copper also wrote more than fifty hardboiled thrillers about Los Angeles private detective Mike Faraday, and he continued the adventures of August Derleth's Sherlock Holmes-like consulting detective Solar Pons in several volumes of short stories and the novel *Solar Pons versus The Devil's Claw*.

STEPHEN JONES lives in London, England. He is the winner of three World Fantasy Awards, four Horror Writers Association Bram Stoker Awards and three International Horror Guild Awards as well as being a multiple recipient of the

British Fantasy Award and a Hugo Award nominee. A former television producer/director and genre movie publicist and consultant, he is one of Britain's most acclaimed anthologists of horror and dark fantasy with more than 120 books to his credit. You can visit his web site at:

www.stephenjoneseditor.com